Jessica Peterson writes romance with heat, humor, and heart. Heroes with hot accents are her specialty. When she's not writing, she can be found bellying up to a bar in the South's best restaurants with her husband, Ben, reading books with her adorable daughters, Gracie and Madeline, or snuggling up with her seventy-pound lapdog, Martha.

A Carolina girl at heart, she fantasizes about splitting her time between Charleston and Asheville, but currently lives in Charlotte, North Carolina.

Also in the *Lucky River Ranch* series
by Jessica Peterson

Cash
Wyatt
Sawyer
Duke

JESSICA PETERSON

**ЯENE
GADE**

First published in the United States in 2026 by Bloom Books
an imprint of Sourcebooks
First published in Great Britain in 2026 by Renegade Books
an imprint of Quercus
Part of John Murray Group

1

Copyright © 2026 Peterson Paperbacks, LLC

The moral right of JESSICA PETERSON to be identified
as the author of this work has been asserted in accordance
with the Copyright, Designs and Patents Act 1988.

Cover illustration by Jenny Richardson.

All rights reserved. No part of this publication may be reproduced or
transmitted in any form or by any means, electronic or mechanical,
including photocopy, recording, or any information storage and
retrieval system, without permission in writing from the publisher.

This book is a work of fiction. Names, characters, businesses,
organizations, places and events are either the product of the author's
imagination or used fictitiously. Any resemblance to actual persons,
living or dead, events or locales is entirely coincidental.

A CIP catalogue record for this book is available from the British Library

MMPB ISBN 978-1-40875-048-3
EBOOK ISBN 978-1-40875-049-0

Printed and bound in Great Britain by Clays Ltd, Elcograf S.p.A.

Papers used by Quercus are from well-managed
forests and other responsible sources.

Quercus
Carmelite House
50 Victoria Embankment
London EC4Y 0DZ

John Murray Group
Part of Hodder & Stoughton Limited
An Hachette UK company

The authorised representative in the EEA is Hachette Ireland, 8 Castlecourt
Centre, Dublin 15, D15 XTP3, Ireland (email: info@hbgi.ie)

PROLOGUE
Love Story
Billie (Age 10)

FOURTEEN YEARS AGO

Air.

I wake up gasping for it, lungs burning, heart pounding.

I had the nightmare *again*. That's the third freaking time this week.

Bolting upright, I put a hand on my chest and take a heaving inhale. The oxygen hits my lungs, making me lightheaded. The faint outline of the contents of my tiny bedroom tilts queasily to the left before righting itself. I suck in a breath, let it out.

The panic gripping my insides slowly dissipates.

My body prickles at the sudden influx of cool, crisp air. Mom finally agreed to set the thermostat lower than usual at night after I woke up sweating for the hundredth time last week.

Apparently she, too, had bad dreams as a kid. Mine started a few months ago, right after I turned ten. It's always the same nightmare: I'm sitting on a chair in an empty room, trying very hard to stay still. I can't, though, because the urge to fidget, to wiggle my hips, radiates from my center outward.

It's like my heart is a rising sun, glowing and moving and warming me from the inside out. It almost feels like being tickled. In the dream, I bite back laughter. Squirm against a rising tide of something that feels cozy and good, something that makes me want to move and be silly but that I know I should tamp down.

Sit still. Be sweet. Your dress looks so pretty, don't wrinkle it.

The thing is, the more I struggle to sit still, the smaller the room gets. The walls creep in, bit by bit, until they're pressed up against my shoulders and back and knees.

That's when the air gets thin. Or disappears, really, because all of a sudden, I can't breathe even though I try to inhale. It's like being stuck underwater.

I want to bang on the walls, but I also don't want to wrinkle my dress or startle anyone. That's not what nice girls do.

I feel myself suffocating, the lack of air sending a burst of white-hot agony through me.

Just when I'm about to pass out or die, I wake up feeling like this: scared, sweaty, sure I've done something wrong.

A couple times I've even woken up with the word *sorry* stuck in my brain.

Sorry for what, though?

I *did* cuss at the mean mailman the other day when he kicked one of the dogs. Mom said I needed to watch my mouth and stop causing trouble, but I wasn't about to let poor Petey get treated that way.

Throwing off the covers, I rub my eyes. It's still

really, really dark out, which means it's probably close to midnight. Every time I sneak into the kitchen after having a nightmare, the clock on the microwave almost always says 12:07. Weird.

I'm too shaky to go back to bed. I also don't want to wake up Mom or Dad. They get up so early and work so hard. None of my five brothers will be able to give me the comfort I need. They always make fun of me, calling me a baby for still having nightmares. Well, everyone except Tate because he's too little.

So I go to the one place I can find comfort. Our house is all one story, so I'm able to put on my barn boots and slip out my window easily. I can hear Colt, my oldest brother, snoring through the window next to mine as I tiptoe through the grass.

I roll my eyes. He and his best friend, Ryder Rivers, were probably sneaking sips of Dad's whiskey after he went to bed. Colt is a couple years older than Ryder—they got close because they love to hunt—and while my brother is definitely the ringleader, Ryder's happy to be along for the ride.

Dumbasses.

It may be the middle of the night, but the air is hot and sticky. That's summertime in Texas Hill Country for you. The stars make up for it, though. For a second, I stop and tilt back my head to admire them. We live in the middle of nowhere, so you can really see everything in the night sky: a billion stars, the bright half-moon, even other planets if you know what you're looking for.

I love it here. I was born on my family's ranch, and I hope to live here for the rest of my life. I just wish…

I don't know. That I could do what I want, same as my brothers. As the only girl in the family, I feel like I have to follow all these stupid rules that no one else does. *Girls don't talk like that. Girls shouldn't ride like that. Girls shouldn't get so dirty.*

The horse barn is down one hill and up another. Our foreman, who we call Grumpy Bud even though he's actually pretty nice, always leaves a light on. Sometimes I wonder if he knows I sneak out here at night.

Whatever the case, I'm grateful. Stepping inside the barn, I'm hit by the familiar smells of hay and warm animals. Closing my eyes, I take a deep, steadying breath.

I already feel better.

I head for a stall toward the middle of the aisle that splits the barn in half. A chestnut-colored horse with a white star on her forehead peeks out, her huge, dark eyes shining in the light overhead.

Everything inside me lifts.

"Hey, you." I tuck my hand underneath her velvet chin and give her a rub. "Don't tell the others, but you're my favorite."

Meredith nuzzles my hand in reply, licking the pad of my thumb.

Yeah, I named my horse after Taylor Swift's cat. So what? She looked like a Meredith to me.

I just hope my parents keep letting me ride her out with the cowboys. Dad's always pushing me to help him in the office, where I put stamps on the bills and letters he sends out, and where I pretend to be interested in his lectures about how much everything costs and why. I don't know who hates sitting at a desk more, me or him. He says he wants me to "learn the business side of things" because I'm "the smart one who's good at math."

But really, I think he wants to keep me away from cowboying or working with the horses. There aren't any other women who work on the ranch, other than Mom, Aunt Lee, and the lady who comes to help the farrier sometimes. There are definitely no women who work cattle or break horses. It's only the boys who train fillies or ride out in the mornings with our small herd of cattle or do fun stuff like rinse off in the creek after a hot day in the saddle.

Girls, meanwhile, have to do *indoor* things, like lick stamps and fold laundry.

Meredith's breath is warm on my hand. I lean into her, my heart rate finally back to normal.

Of course I'm your favorite, I imagine her saying back to me. *I'm wild and I'm full of heart. Just like you. We can be both things at once, wild and warmhearted, no matter what other people think.*

"They're always saying I'm wild." I stroke Meredith's silky neck. "Why is that a bad thing all of a sudden?"

"Because boys are scared of wild girls. We'll never admit it, but we scare a lot easier than y'all."

I jump at the sound of the voice behind me. Whipping around, I see Ryder, my brother Colt's friend, standing a few feet away. He's in a rumpled T-shirt and shorts, and he's holding a guitar in his hand.

Why is he always *carrying that thing?* The dude's obsessed.

"Well, you just scared the shit out of me, and I'm a girl!" My heart thumps. But instead of putting my hand on my chest, I put it on my stomach.

It keeps doing this funny somersaulting thing whenever I see Ryder. It only started happening recently. Maybe because he's gotten a little bit cute since he turned thirteen?

I like his smile. And the way he doesn't make me feel like I'm any different from the boys. Like he can talk to me and hang out with me the same way he does with my brothers. I'm not some porcelain doll he ignores or mocks or handles with such care that he can't be himself around me.

I also *really* like his thick mop of dark blond hair, the way it curls out at the ends.

Speaking of his hair: It falls into his eyes as he shakes his head. "You and the cussin'."

Growing up surrounded by cowboys who curse like sailors and brothers who talk smack like nobody's business, I learned the art of cuss words early.

"You gonna tell me to watch my mouth like everybody else?"

"Hell no." Aw, Lordy, now he's smiling, and he's brushing back his hair, and my stomach's flipping again. "Cussin' don't bother me one bit."

"Even if a girl does it?"

"Especially if a girl does it. To be honest, I don't care who's doing it. I think it keeps things nice and relaxed."

I grin. "Mom and Dad aren't relaxed when I cuss."

"Well maybe I'm able to relax when you cuss because I don't gotta watch myself around you. I like that."

Dang, now my heart's doing somersaults too.

I don't have many friends that are girls. None, really. Mom homeschools my brothers and me, so the only time I see other girls my age is at church on Sunday downtown. I used to be able to play with other girls in the "kid room" where our parents would drop us off before service. One of the older girls would babysit us while everyone else went into the chapel.

But now that I'm older, I'm expected to *sit still* and *look pretty* in the pews beside our parents. That means I don't get to run around with the other kids anymore even though I've begged to be one of the babysitters in the kid room.

Back when I was five, maybe six, I distinctly remember the older girls giggling over how "cute" they thought the Rivers boys were. Something about their blue eyes and the little cowboy hats they'd wear to church.

I nod at Ryder's guitar. "Why did you bring that?" Putting my hands on my hips, I tilt my head. "No, wait. Why are you even here?"

He shrugs. "Couldn't sleep. Colt snores like a goddamn bear when he drinks. I heard someone creepin' around and wasn't sure what to expect. So I grabbed the nearest weapon, which just so happened to be my guitar—"

"So y'all *did* get into Daddy's Jim Beam."

"I'm allowed to be wild too, you know."

I roll my eyes. "Boys are always allowed to be wild."

"We live on a ranch in the middle of nowhere, Billie. There ain't nothing else for us to do around here."

"Yeah, well, some of us still gotta act right, Ryder."

His smile broadens. "You actin' right creepin' around like this?"

"I couldn't sleep either."

His smile fades. "Another nightmare?"

"So Colt told you I've been having them. A lot." Looking down, I kick at the dusty floorboards.

"He's worried about you is all." A pause. "Truth be told, I am too. What d'you think they're about? The nightmares."

A surge of something strong and awful moves through me. Before I can think, I spit out, "Why do you care?"

Another pause. It strikes me how different Ryder is from my brothers.

Heck, he's different from *his* brothers too. If I asked them that question, I feel like they'd just tell me to shut up and walk away.

But Ryder stays. He *thinks*.

He really does care, and that makes my chest cramp.

"You're a lot like Cash," he says at last, referring to his oldest—and least friendly—brother. "Always got your dukes up. But it's when you're throwing the most punches that you're the most scared. So tell me why you're scared so I can play some Taylor Swift for you already." Ryder shifts the guitar so he's holding it across his middle. "I wanna show off all the shit I learned in my guitar lessons this summer."

I'm laughing, and I don't want to be.

Scratch that. I really like laughing, especially when Ryder laughs *with* me, not *at* me the way my brothers always do. As their kid sister—I'm number three in the birth order, smack dab in the middle—I've always had to hustle to keep up with them. They find it hilarious when I inevitably fall on my face.

"You're really gonna play for me?"

"If it will make you feel better, yeah."

"And you know Taylor Swift?"

"I've heard you listening to her. I can learn."

Turning back to Meredith, I tuck my cheek against the star on her head. She feels warm. Safe.

Maybe that's why I'm able to say, "I'm just noticing things now. Like how people treat me differently, and not in a good way."

"What do you mean?"

"So after dinner, Mom always makes me stay to help her do the dishes even though Colt and the rest of them get to 'go do their homework,' when really everybody knows they're just going to play their stupid video games. And Dad—he's trying to teach me all this budgeting nonsense that's boring as all get-out. Meanwhile, my brothers get to ride out with the cowboys all day. I miss that, but Dad doesn't seem to care." I sigh. Damn, it feels good to get that out.

Ryder's eyes are serious when he replies, "I hadn't thought about it like that. Sounds like it's harder for girls—doing what you want."

I lift a shoulder. "Maybe. I think that might have something to do with these weird dreams I keep having. I feel…sometimes, in real life and in these dreams, it's like I can't breathe. I wanna move, but I can't. It really pisses me off."

"I can tell." He grins, strumming his guitar. The pretty sound is calming. "I can promise you two things. One, I'll try my very best not to treat you any different."

My face splits into a smile, the kind I can feel in my cheeks. "Okay."

"And two, I don't know the lyrics or the notes to any Taylor Swift song, but I'm gonna learn. Here." He tips his chin toward my horse, then reaches out to give her chin a tickle. "Maybe Meredith can help us out. You know how to sing, right, pretty girl?"

Meredith eats his pretend sugar up, tucking her lips into his palm. She likes Ryder.

He's grown up on his family's ranch about twenty miles from here on the other side of Hart County, so he's been on horseback and around animals all his life. It shows. He's tender with Meredith, but confident too. I like that.

Ew, but I don't like Ryder. He's Colt's friend, not mine. And I think Colt would punch us both if we—

Nope. Not even gonna think that disgusting thought.

I should probably get back to my room. I don't think anyone would like it if they found Ryder and I alone out here together.

More than that, though, all these things I'm feeling have me *super* freaking confused. I'm hot, but I'm also kind of happy? But also nervous, which makes no sense because I've known Ryder forever. He's like the sixth brother I never wanted but now I'm glad to have.

Only, I don't want him to be my brother. I want him to be my friend. And something about that is scary for reasons I don't understand.

Yup, need to get the hell out of here.

"Hey, Ryder—"

"Yeah?" He sits down after giving Meredith one last tickle, settling his back against her stall. "Chocolate Chip likes it when I play for him. You think she'll like it too?"

I let out a burst of laughter. "I still can't believe you named your horse Chocolate Chip."

"Hey." Ryder strums the guitar again, reaching up to tune a string. "I was seven. And anything with chocolate chips in it still happens to be my favorite food. Also—I don't know if you know this—but I did this thing called animal therapy when I was little. I had a speech delay, and being around horses apparently helped me work through some of that. When Mom and Dad gave me my own horse, I think they knew how big that moment was. So they let me name him all by myself."

I blink, startled—warmed—by Ryder's vulnerable admission. "I didn't know you were in therapy."

"From what I remember, it was pretty cool. I'd recommend it."

"I'll keep that in mind." I scoff, glancing at Meredith. "Maybe I need to spend more time around horses, then. To, you know, work through this nightmare stuff."

"Can't hurt. So what's your favorite Taylor song right now?"

I'm sitting beside him and folding my legs into a pretzel before I know what I'm doing.

"You're gonna make fun of me." The door of the stall bites into my shoulder blades, but I don't care.

"Probably. Lemme guess, it's a love song."

My face burns. "Maybe."

"That's okay. I'll still play it." A pause. "You know I'm joking, right? I don't mind love songs."

I elbow him. "Duh. Of course I know that." *But I'm really glad you said it anyway.*

"Some of the best songs ever written are love songs. At least that's what my mom says."

"I like your mom."

"I do too. You know I'm her favorite."

I grin. "Everybody knows that. Babies are always the favorite. Tate is my mom's favorite."

"He is." Ryder's grinning too. "Can you hum the song?"

I clear my throat. "Uh. Yeah. I can, um, do that. Sure." I clear my throat again, feeling like an idiot.

But the way Ryder looks at me, his eyebrows curved gently upward, makes me feel…like I can actually do this.

I start to hum the song, closing my eyes as the lyrics pass through my brain. I don't know why this one is my favorite. It's just cute. And fun. And sometimes I secretly wish what happens in the song might happen to me one day.

Your father's such a romantic, Mom always says. They kiss a lot, which is kind of gross. But they look happy together. Everyone points to them having six kids as proof of how in love they are, although I don't understand why.

Whatever the case, ending up like Mom and Dad wouldn't be so bad. I don't want to be in the kitchen as much as Mom is. But she and Dad smile a lot when they're together, and smiling is kind of the best.

I'd know because I start to smile all over again as I hum. My eyes fly open when Ryder starts to play along on his guitar, picking out the notes without missing a beat.

I stop humming. "Do you know this song?"

"No," he says with a chuckle. "Keep humming."

"Then how can you play it on the first try?"

"I'm a prodigy. Keep humming, Billie."

The song sounds so pretty on the guitar, and I don't want him to stop playing, so I sit up a little straighter and hum another verse, then another chorus.

This time, Ryder doesn't notice when I stop humming. He just keeps playing, his fingers delicately working the strings of his guitar like he's been doing this all his life.

He hasn't. When you get to middle school in these parts, they make you play an instrument. Ryder picked the guitar when he entered sixth grade. He's only been playing for a couple years now.

Still, he's really, really good.

I like watching the way his hand moves up and down the neck of the guitar. Steady. Gentle. Behind us, I hear Meredith shuffling in approval, ducking her head to sniff Ryder's hair.

He chuckles again. "Is that her version of throwing her bra at me?"

I blush at the word *bra*. I know girls start wearing them at some point, but my chest is still as flat as a pancake. "I don't know what that means."

"Girls at concerts throw their bras at lead singers they like."

"Aren't I the one singing, though? I don't want any bras thrown at me."

"You can sing if you like."

I clear my throat for what feels like the hundredth time. "Do you think I have a good enough voice?"

"If you think I'm good enough at playing guitar, then sure, I think you have a good enough voice." His eyes sparkle.

I look away. I'll probably sound stupid if I sing. But my humming was okay, right? And the way Ryder is playing my favorite song—the notes soft and pretty—it's hard *not* to sing along.

Taking a deep breath, I do.

I sing.

Judging by the way Ryder's smile grows and grows, I'm doing an all right job of it too. Maybe I suck. Maybe I don't. But I keep singing, closing my eyes. I hear Meredith let out a snort, which means she's happy. I am too.

Ryder pauses, not sure where the song goes next. I open my eyes and meet his. I continue to sing, my voice echoing down the long hallway. Ryder starts to play again, picking up what I'm laying down. It takes all of one verse for us to get back in sync.

We sit like that, me singing, him strumming, smiling at each other like he's not my older brother's best friend and I'm not some stupid kid sister who's a pain in the ass.

The more I sing, the better Ryder plays. The notes get louder. Bigger. My heart feels bigger too. So big that I worry it's going to burst clear out of my chest.

I'm sad when the song ends. Ryder's hand drops from the strings, and I hunch forward a little, suddenly shy. The quiet in the barn is so loud I wonder if it's alive too, just like I am, and Ryder too, and the horses and all the cowboys sleeping in the bunkhouse next door.

Ryder's eyes are *blue*. Not regular blue, but *blue* blue. What I imagine the color of a tropical sea would look like.

"I like that song." He shifts, rotating the guitar out of his lap. "What's the name?"

Disappointment settles over me like a wet blanket. *Do we really have to be done?* But I didn't want to be out here with Ryder in the first place. Why do I feel short of breath at the idea of him leaving?

"It's called 'Love Story.'"

Standing, he grins. "Of course it is. Want me to walk you back? I'm pretty tired, and I know you need your rest too."

"Um. Sure. Yeah."

He holds out his hand, and I take it. Helping me up, he tucks the guitar underneath his arm. Then we walk together in silence back to the house.

I don't sleep a wink. Instead, I stay up thinking about Ryder. How happy he looked playing his guitar. How much better I feel after spending time with him.

You should've told him that.

Ryder was wrong. Girls scare just as easy as boys.

We're just better at hiding it.

CHAPTER 1
First Rodeo
Ryder

PRESENT DAY
SEPTEMBER

Cowgirls.

They're everywhere I look. In the stands. On horseback in the arena.

A particularly cute one with dark hair approaches down the wide walkway that wraps around the stadium. My body perks up, warm with interest.

I always enjoy the rodeo, mostly because it's the perfect place to pick up cute girls I don't know for hookups I may or may not remember.

I like brunettes. Especially ones in cowboy hats and chaps.

There's a pervy little saying that cowboys ride harder and stay on longer. I've found the same is true about cowgirls too.

But when I see that this cowgirl is Billie Wallace, I immediately hit the brakes on whatever, er, *interest* I was feeling. Before I can duck into a nearby restroom, however, she spots me. She throws up her arms, her face lighting up.

"Ry! Hey!" She jogs toward me, the tassels on her fancy rodeo chaps flying. "You came!"

She barrels into me and wraps me in a fierce hug. She's...Christ, soft in all the right places. She also smells real fucking good. More sultry than sweet, like juicy, just-picked peaches.

I close my eyes and take a silent, steadying breath. It's like she's trying even harder than usual to push my fucking buttons tonight, and I am not here for it.

I'm not dead. Of course I know how gorgeous my best friend's baby sister is. She may be the girl next door, but she's also pretty in a movie star kind of way, with a wide, white smile, dark hair, and hazel eyes that are the color of the Colorado River at sunset. More green than brown, except when she's pissed. Then her irises are straight whiskey—they burn right through you.

Duke was just warning me to keep my distance when we drove over to the Wallace's to pick up a horse we bought from them recently. And I do. Usually, anyway. But she and I are both flirts, and in the past, I've let myself slip up a few times. What can I say? I like the attention.

Tonight, though, I'm not in the mood. I also promised myself I wasn't gonna give anyone mixed signals. I'm good at keeping people at arm's length. Billie Wallace is no exception.

I give her a quick pat on the back before untangling myself from her grasp. "I always come to the rodeo."

Billie's eyes shine with a mischievous glint. "But this time you came to see *me*, right? Because you wanna watch me dominate my very first race, and then you'll take me out afterward for celebratory drinks and dancing and se—"

"Billie." I roll my eyes.

I *also* know Billie's had a crush on me for about as long as I can remember. Girl makes no secret of it, clearly. But I try not to rise to the occasion for obvious reasons.

More than that, though, I know Billie well enough to recognize that she'd be interested in a hell of a lot more than a one-night stand. Her free-spiritedness doesn't fool me; behind all her bravado, Billie is a romantic at heart.

I'm a one-night stand kinda guy. Always have been. I like to keep things simple. Safe.

"*Seven-card stud*." Billie's lips twitch. "That's what I was going to say. Wyatt's always down for a round of poker. Bet I could convince you to play."

My older brother Wyatt runs a not-exactly-legal poker ring out of the basement of our local honky-tonk, the Rattler. Billie's not wrong about him putting together a game of seven-card stud.

She is wrong to think I'd ever play it with her. Or dance with her, for that matter, even *if* she wins her very first official barrel race.

But we both know that. She's just busting my chops, as usual.

I slip my hands in my front pockets, running the fingers of my right hand over the familiar shape of my dad's pocketknife. Every pair of jeans I own bears a visible outline of the knife on the right front pocket—I never leave home without it.

I always feel a little better—more centered—whenever I reach for it.

I glance inside the stadium and see most of my family has already taken their seats.

"You should probably get going, yeah?" I glance at Billie. "Good luck out there."

She rocks her hips. "You could be my good luck charm, you know."

It's all I can do not to groan. This woman is a piece of fucking work.

"You don't need a good luck charm."

"But what if I want one?"

"You're gonna do great."

"You sound so excited about my prospects." She's wearing a shit-eating grin now.

I take another deep breath and look away. "You really should get going."

"Fine." I can picture her pouting, sticking out her bottom lip the same way she did when she was a kid. "But if I lose, it's because you refused to sprinkle me with your special sauce—"

"Bye, Billie." I manage a tight smile as I turn and head for the concession stand.

"Bye, Ryder. Love you!"

Like a brother. Same as I love *her* like a sister.

I grab a beer and some popcorn, and then I head down several flights of stairs toward our seats, which are so close to the arena they're practically on the dirt.

I take my seat beside two miniature cowgirls, their pink and purple boots and matching hats catching my eye.

There's lots to see at the rodeo tonight, but these two stand out.

The cowgirl closest to me turns her head and smiles.

My heart squeezes. She's a fucking cutie, no two ways about it.

"Whatcha lookin' at, Uncle Ry?" Junie swings her little legs. She's the daughter of my older brother Sawyer's girlfriend, Ava. "Is it my beautiful cowgirl boots? I'm sorry, but you can't have them. Also, can I have some of that popcorn?"

Now I'm the one smiling as I set the bucket in her lap. "I got my own boots."

I drop my beer in a nearby cupholder. Lifting my leg, I pull back my jeans just enough to show off the pair of Bellamy Brooks boots I've been wearing nonstop since Duke gave them to me for our birthday back in July. "Not as sparkly as yours, granted—"

"Because ours are better." That's Ella, my four-year-old niece, who sits next to Junie. "It's just a fact."

Sawyer, Ella's dad, holds up his hands. "Whoa whoa whoa. Them's fightin' words, you know. Auntie Mollie and Auntie Wheeler made Uncle Ry's boots."

Mollie, the wife of my older brother Cash, and her college roommate Wheeler—my twin brother Duke's girlfriend and soon-to-be mother of their twins, whom they'll welcome over the holidays—started a fashion boot company, Bellamy Brooks, in their college dorm room years ago.

Now their boots are featured in big-time magazines. They've made so much money they even hired Duke to help them design and manufacture a men's collection.

"Hey." Duke narrows his eyes at Sawyer. "You're forgetting one very important member of the Bellamy Brooks operation."

Cash rolls his eyes. He's got his infant daughter, Daisy,

strapped to his chest in a carrier. She's conked out, a pair of baby headphones in pink covering her little ears.

He absently moves the knuckle of his first finger across her chubby cheek. "Dude, the entire population of Texas knows you got the job. You've told everyone and their mother about it."

"Nothing wrong with that." Wheeler brushes Duke's hair out of his face as she peers into his eyes. "Shout it from the rooftops, baby. I'm proud of you."

He puts a hand on her pregnant belly. "Blue, I'm proud of us."

There's a tiny spasm inside my breastbone. An electric shock. Digging my first two fingers into the spot, I rub it until the unpleasant feeling is gone.

I'm happy for Duke. Honestly. Even if he and Wheeler are the kind of cute together that borders on sickening. He's always had a serious case of wanderlust, and it was pure kismet that he fell for a girl who dreams as big as he does.

He and Wheeler have been together for all of six months, but they've already visited a dozen new places. Maybe more. All this while she's been pregnant too. They had a little too much fun on their very first road trip back in the spring, and three weeks later, Wheeler got a positive result on a pregnancy test.

If the past year has taught me anything, it's that my brothers move fast. All four of them have paired off with excellent women over the span of a little more than twelve months. We've had lots to celebrate: engagements, new jobs, new opportunities, weddings, babies.

But time in Hartsville moves slowly, which is more my speed. I'm not jealous of my brothers. I've made my choices, same as Cash and Wyatt and Sawyer and Duke made theirs. I'm okay with how the chips have fallen.

Yeah, I may have shut off parts of myself when my parents died. I was only fourteen, and I had to figure out a way to keep going somehow without falling apart.

Out here in cattle country, you do what you have to in order to survive.

Case in point: I was able to survive another big blow when our mentor, Garrett Luck—Mollie's dad—passed suddenly last year. It was a shitty time, but my brothers and I were able to make some lemonade out of those lemons by working our fingers to the bone.

Work is what keeps me sane. I consider it an offshoot of the therapy I had when I was little. Being around animals helped me then. Definitely helps now.

Ava, Sawyer's girlfriend and Junie's mom, gently nudges me with her elbow as she nods at the arena. "Billie is gonna be so thrilled you came, Ryder. She's been working hard. I think she has a real shot to win this thing."

Dipping my hand into the popcorn perched on Junie's lap, I wink at her. She winks back.

"I actually just saw Billie."

Ava chuckles. "She asked you to be her good luck charm, didn't she?"

I turn to her, leaning in so I can hear her above the growing noise of the crowd. "She sure did. Didn't she just pick it up? Racing? I'm kinda surprised she'd want to be back in the saddle like this after working in her daddy's office for so long."

Billie is the Wallace Ranch's in-house accountant. Her old man began her education in the ranch's finances early, so it was no surprise that she ended up with a degree in accounting after she graduated high school.

As a former pro barrel racer, Ava's been running the cloverleaf since she was a kid. It's a rodeo sport where a rider on horseback runs a cloverleaf pattern around three barrels as quickly as possible. When Ava became head of the Wallace Ranch's barrel racing training program last fall, Billie Wallace signed up for some lessons.

I'm not sure why Billie wants to race. She's still young—twenty-four—but most barrel racers start when they're really young, like Ava.

Here we are, though, about to watch Billie run her first official race at the Hart County Rodeo.

"Billie's a newbie, yeah," Ava says. "But every spare second she's had, she's been in the arena working her butt off. To be honest, I'm not sure I've seen anyone more dedicated. She loves it."

Don't doubt that one bit. Billie's been hell on wheels for as long as I can remember. Of course she'd love a sport where she gets to ride like the devil.

And I remember plenty, considering her older brother Colt is my best friend outside of my brothers.

"Testament to your coaching skills." I nudge Ava back. "Sawyer told me y'all recruited some promising gals to join the program."

Ava turns her head to glance at Sally, who's tapping her tallboy can of local beer against Wyatt's before taking a long, thirsty sip in the row in front of ours. "Helps that we have the best of the best working at the Wallaces'. Sally really brought our program to a whole new level."

Sally is a veterinary surgeon who trained at one of the top programs in the country. I think she surprised us all when, over the holidays last year, she passed up a big fancy job to stay in Hartsville and help the Wallaces build their horse breeding and racing programs.

Wyatt puts a hand on Sally's thigh, the thin gold band on his left hand winking in the arena lights.

Am I surprised my wildest brother settled down and got married? Not one bit. As a matter of fact, Sally and Wy's engagement was long overdue. They've been in love with each other for, well, ever.

Theirs has been a very happy ending. Everyone's has.

I tell myself I'm happy enough too. Sometimes I think I got all the happiness I needed when I was little and lived on Mom's hip. I got no shame in admitting I was a mama's boy. In fact, I'm proud of the bond Mom and I shared.

I miss her. A lot. But Duke and I have a special bond too as identical twins. I try to remind myself of that fact when I'm feeling down. Lonely.

Thing is, I'm *not* alone. My life is full of people who love me and who I love right back. Life is good.

"Sometimes I wonder how we all got so lucky to get a second act as solid as this one." I say, wiping my hand on my jeans. We recently joined forces with Mollie, combining her family's ranch with ours to create Lucky River Ranch. It's made us very busy—and very wealthy—ranchers.

Ava chuckles. "The universe isn't stingy, Ryder. And karma is real. We're living right."

"Maybe. Yeah."

I feel her looking at me. "You know it's your turn anytime you want it to be, yeah?"

My hand tightens into a fist. "My turn for what?"

But before she can reply, a shout interrupts us.

"Aw, y'all really beat us here? If that don't make me feel like the world's worst brother…"

Looking over my shoulder, I smile when I see Colt Wallace moving down the arena steps, the entire Wallace clan, save Billie, of course, hot on his heels. There's her five brothers—Colt, along with Beck, Nash, Mack, and Tate—all dressed up in their cowboy finest. I bite back a laugh when I see that Nash is even wearing a massive silver belt buckle that matches his bolo.

He's definitely looking for some action tonight. Glad I'm not the only one.

Standing, I reach across the row behind us to shake Colt's hand. "These cowgirls refused to be tamed." I nod at Ella and June, who are now busy trying to toss pieces of popcorn into each other's mouths. "They were chomping at the bit to get to their first rodeo."

"It's not my first rodeo, Uncle Ry!" Ella rolls her eyes. "It's like my one hundred thousand billionth rodeo, okay?"

"Mine too!" Junie squeals. "My mommy used to be *in* the rodeo."

"Your mama is just the coolest, isn't she?" Sawyer reaches across to thumb away a stray bit of popcorn from the corner of Junie's mouth. "We've got lots of talent in our family."

Ava bites her lip. "You're making me blush, cowboy."

"You're making us all blush, and that's a beautiful thing." Mrs. Wallace, the matriarch of their family, smiles down at us as she takes a seat on the row behind ours. She's moving slow on account of the surgery she recently had. "Thank y'all for coming, truly. Billie is blessed to have such wonderful friends."

Dean, Colt's six-year-old son, comes over to give me a high five. "What's up, Uncle Ry?"

Not gonna lie, out of all the literal and proverbial hats I wear—brother, rancher, businessman, cowboy, (sometimes) degenerate—"uncle" is by far my favorite.

"You learn to read yet or what?" I ask. "You been goin' to kindergarten every day, right?"

Dean grins. "I have perfect attendance so far. *And* I was one of the first ones to read a sentence this week. Ms. Loo was so proud she gave me a sticker!"

"A sticker! That's awesome. Proud of you."

"I'm proud of me too." His grin is shy, but I know he really is proud of himself.

Colt's smile touches his eyes. Guy's been through hell and back over the past couple years, but he's doing a damn fine job of raising his son. He has every reason to smile today.

Bull riding is up first. Then we watch several racers compete before Billie's name is announced over the loudspeaker. Ella and Junie squeal. Ava throws up her arms.

A buzz of excitement darts up my spine when I see a brunette in a white cowboy hat dart into sight.

Smiling, I resist the urge to clap my hands and shout, *Get it, girl*. Watching these races always gets me psyched up, and seeing someone I know out there—even if it is the woman who lays it on a little too thick with me sometimes—has me feeling doubly excited.

Billie dashes through the arena, her dark hair flying, pretty face split into a smile. She's going so fast I catch the glint of tears trailing horizontally across her temples. Her body moves rhythmically, expertly, as she guides her horse around the first barrel. I'm transfixed by the easy roll of her hips in the saddle.

She lets out a holler of utter delight, drawing cheers of approval from the crowd, because *of course* she does.

I'm Billie fucking Wallace, I imagine her saying. *And I'm about to knock your goddamn socks off.*

She's fully immersed in the excitement of the moment.

Fully, completely, vibrantly alive. No holding back.

My stomach bottoms out like I'm on a roller coaster. Billie looks fierce and wild and so fucking joyful out there it…shit, it kinda hurts to watch her.

Literally. My chest is squeezing so hard I feel like I'm having a heart attack.

That, my pulse shouts. *I need that.*

What about *that*, though, is making me feel like I can't breathe? Maybe I just haven't seen Billie let totally loose like this in a while. A long while. Really, since she started working with her daddy in the Wallace Ranch offices years ago.

It's like she's in her natural state running that cloverleaf. Uninhibited. Zero fucks given.

She's plugged in. Connected to some higher force. Or maybe just to her true self, unafraid of what might happen next.

For a split second, my torso fills with that same wide-open feeling. I can breathe again. It feels nice to set down the need to be in control and just…feel. Excitement. Anticipation. Hope.

Makes me realize how numb I've felt in comparison all day. All week.

All the time.

"Go, Billie, go!" Ava leaps to her feet. Sticking her fingers into her mouth, she lets out a shockingly loud whistle. "That's right, sister, you make that barrel your—"

"Friend!" Sawyer finishes for her, grinning.

Junie and Ella are on their feet now, so I hop up too. I pat my right front pocket, making sure the pocketknife is still there.

All good.

Mom gave Dad this pocketknife as a wedding gift. Like me, he carried it every damn day. He saved the lives of more cattle and horses and kids with this thing than I could count. Figure it's good luck to keep it close.

What would he think if he could see my brothers and me now? Bet he'd love being at the rodeo with his sons, their better halves, and all these beautiful babies.

Mom would lose her mind over how much Ella looks like Sawyer. And she'd eat up Cash's chunky baby with a spoon.

Emotion clogs my windpipe. *See? This is what happens when I let myself feel shit. Everyone is hooting and hollering and having a grand old time celebrating a friend's achievement, and here I am, making a goddamn fool of myself.*

Get. It. The fuck together.

Blinking, I try to bottle up all those feelings inside my ribcage and swallow away the moon lodged in my throat.

Gotta keep the focus on Billie.

Billie, who looks fucking *good* in a pair of jeans and the tightest white button-up I think I've ever seen. A big old silver-and-turquoise belt buckle completes the ensemble.

Another sensation moves through me, this one a hot heaviness that settles between my legs.

Yep, can't feel that either.

Even *if* her perfect tits strain against that shirt in the sexiest way imaginable.

Even *if* I got a thing for cowgirls.

Ordinarily I'd keep trying to ignore all this goddamn excitement. Billie is my best friend's sister for Christ's sake. I gotta show some decorum. I have years of practice keeping steady, staying in control. Numbing shit so I don't drown.

But all of a sudden, that feels wrong.

It's impossible.

So instead, I let myself be overwhelmed by the thrill of being here, now, and I holler like an idiot as Billie rounds the second barrel. Just as I imagined *her* hollering as she bolted through the gate to start her race.

"Ava. Jesus. She's a rock star," I marvel over the clamor that fills the arena. "You'd best get ready to win some money, honey, cause y'all got something special here."

Ava is smiling from ear to ear, pride written all over her features. "Don't jinx us!"

Too late.

Just as Billie is rounding the third barrel, she guides her horse a smidge too close to the inside. As they straighten out to take it all the way home, the horse stumbles, losing her footing in the dirt. Billie does her darndest to stay in the saddle, but the centripetal force of their movements pulls her right off the horse.

A horrified gasp moves through the crowd as Billie launches ass over teakettle through the air. She throws out her arms, letting out another holler as she slams into the ground hard, her left arm bent beside her body at an unnatural angle. This holler is a sound of agonized shock.

Then she goes still.

The image hits me like a freight train: my parents flying through the air the same way after they were hit by a car going thirty-plus miles per hour. They were walking across Main Street just as it was getting dark, and an elderly man didn't see them until it was too late.

No. Fuck. Not again.

I can't stay in control. Pretend not to care. Not when someone's life is on the line.

Before I know what's happening, I'm pushing my way through the crowd. Somewhere it registers that Colt is behind me, and so are Cash and Ava and Duke, who calls my name.

I don't stop. I have to get to Billie.

I don't remember hopping the railing, but all of a sudden, my boots are in the dirt and I'm making a beeline for the lifeless figure thirty feet away.

A guy wearing chaps and a paper number pinned to his shirt approaches from the right. One of the bull riders? What the hell is he doing out here?

I'm the first to get to Billie. Falling to my knees, I see that her eyes are closed. Her chest isn't moving.

I manage to keep my voice steady as I tap my shaking hand to her face. "Billie? Billie, can you hear me? Are you all right?"

Nothing.

Leaning down, I listen for her breath. It's not there. Did the impact cause her heart to stop? Did a rib puncture her lung, or worse?

No no no.

I should probably wait for the medics, but fuck that. I got CPR certified after Dean was born, and then I brushed up with another class when Ella was on the way. I wanted to make sure Colt and Sawyer would let me babysit their kids.

I know every second counts right now, and I'll never forgive myself if—

Not gonna think that. Instead, I start CPR—the three letters, *C, A, B*. Start with chest compressions, then open the airway, then start giving her breaths.

C, A, B. *Simple as that.*

"Dude, what the hell are you doing?" It's the bull rider. The wad of dip stuck in his lower lip makes it sound like he's chewing on the words. "She don't need that. Let's wait for the medics."

What do you know? Get the fuck away from her, I want to growl.

"I got it," I say instead. No time to explain myself.

I start the compressions. Nothing.

"If you hurt her—"

"*I got it.*"

I'm a man possessed. I just—I can't lose someone again to a tragedy like this.

I won't survive it.

My whole being is shaking as I open her airway. Then I start mouth-to-mouth.

Billie's lips are warm. She tastes like—dang it, is that tequila? She must've taken a shot before her race to calm her nerves.

I push air into her lungs, silently begging her to come back to me.

Back to us, I mean.

Back to *us*.

CHAPTER 2
Mouth-to-Mouth
Billie

I wake up on a throbbing wave of pain.

My left elbow has its own heartbeat. Hell, the whole left side of my *body* is lit up with a screaming burn I can only describe as, well, hell on earth. I'm vaguely aware of the sounds of the crowd around me, but inside my head, it's eerily silent.

Also, someone is kissing me.

The warmth of his lips—their softness, the gentle way they're pressed against mine—is unfamiliar and really fucking lovely. I can tell it's a *him* because of the way his scruff brushes against my skin. Is that popcorn I taste?

Also, why is he holding my nose shut?

Whoever's kissing me, it's not Xander. The bull rider is a good enough kisser, but his lips are always weirdly lukewarm.

He's also never, *ever* gentle. Which I usually like. But this…

It's new, and I don't hate it. Maybe because I'm in so much freaking pain? The kiss makes the throb in my body fade away a bit. Just enough so that I can breathe without being in total and complete agony.

Wait, someone else is breathing for me.

The way the air is being pushed into my lungs—it's different. I don't have to work for it. Oxygen floods my body, the relief so intense I could cry.

This is exactly what I needed.

Air. Simple as that.

I flutter my eyes open, my heart lurching when I see the slant of a cowboy hat over the shell of a familiar ear.

"Ryder?" I blurt, my mouth moving against his in a way that sends a bolt of heat through my middle despite the very real terror that grips me. "What the—"

"Billie." He says the word on a pained exhale. His cobalt eyes meet mine, and I can suddenly breathe through my nose again. "Oh. Oh my God. Thank God."

My stomach takes a tumble at the naked emotion in his eyes. He's the guy who *never* shows his cards—never lets his feelings show. Sure, he's always ready with a smile or a smart-ass comment, but I know it's all an act. A deflection. Because behind that mask lies a deep, *deep* well of pain. I glimpsed it for the first time at his parents' funeral thirteen years ago, and every so often he'll let his control slip and I'll see it again.

The grief. The hurt. The longing.

Ryder turns his head, lifting it a little so that he's no longer kissing me. Touching me. Doing whatever he was doing.

I'm hit by a crushing sense of disappointment.

"Ryder?" I repeat, and my voice shakes. "What—how am I—why are you—"

"You took a nasty spill, Billie. I just—" He puts a hand on his chest. "I'm so relieved you're conscious. Tell me what hurts."

Ryder gets right to the heart of the matter. No preamble. No niceties.

I like that.

"Everything hurts when you fall from heaven," I deadpan. It's my way of dealing with the wash of embarrassment that moves through me. My first race and I fall off the damn horse? I'm better than that.

Apparently, though, I'm not.

He lets out a bark of laughter, and my chest lifts. "Aw, Billie Wallace, you're many things, but an angel ain't one of 'em. Now tell me what hurts."

Is it wrong that I like it when he says my full name? When we were younger, he'd always make me feel like a whole person. A real human being, and not the perfect, well-behaved Barbie doll my parents wanted me to be.

He's making me feel that way now.

He's making me wish he would put his mouth on me again even though I can see my family hovering just a few feet away.

Never in a million years would Ryder ever date me. But that didn't stop me from falling in love with him that night in the barn fourteen years ago, when he learned how to play my favorite song. My nightmares were so bad back then.

They still are, if I'm being honest.

Sometimes I wondered if ten-year-olds can even fall in love. But over the years, I've come to realize with deep certainty that you're never too young to notice a kindred spirit.

Even if Colt wouldn't murder us both if we ever got together, though, Ryder's definitely not interested in me. He's always so…aloof when I'm around. Polite, yes. But not at all the open-minded, curious boy I sat next to that night in the barn. He changed after his parents died. Which I understand—who *wouldn't* be traumatized by losing their parents so suddenly, so young?—but I still miss who he was before the accident.

We're friends now. But really, we're more like acquaintances, which sucks. I see him around, but we never really hang out.

He runs with a…different crowd. Like his brothers, Ryder can get any girl he wants. And he does. No surprise there; he's six-two, hot as fuck, smart, and super charming when he wants to be.

He's a lady-killer, no two ways about it. I'm just one of his many victims.

I often fantasize about breaking through his carefully guarded walls, the ones he put up after his parents died. Walls that got even taller when Garrett Luck passed too.

When we were kids, he was more of a free spirit like me. But as we got older, that side of him went the way of his guitar: gone for good.

It's not my place, though, to bring that side of him back, right? Ryder seems content enough. He has fun. He loves his family.

Yeah, it kills me to think he'll never play another song again. Hard to forget how *happy* he looked with a guitar in his hands. Sometimes I worry he's sleepwalking through life, surviving but not really enjoying much.

But we're not kids anymore. And Ryder was never meant to be mine.

Two medics, a man and a woman, arrive. Ryder leans back just the tiniest bit to give them room, but he stays close enough that I can smell the aftershave on his skin. Ironic, considering the guy definitely doesn't shave. But he always smells delicious, a combo of citrus and pine that's somehow sexy and soothing at the same time.

"My elbow." I bite back a howl when I try to lift my arm. "And my ribs. Mostly my pride, though. I was fast, right?"

The female medic is opening a package. "We're going to perform a quick exam, so we can assess your injuries."

Ryder's eyes crinkle at the edges when he smiles. "Like a bat out of hell."

Oh my God, oh my God, he's being playful. Cute, even.

"More my speed. Pun intended." I bite my lip when the medic touches my elbow.

"You're funny," Ryder says.

"You're here."

He blinks. "Well, yeah, I'm here. We all are." He turns his head, and I see my brothers, plus Cash and Ava, standing nearby with tense expressions. "I couldn't wait to watch you fall on your ass in front of five thousand people."

I laugh, wincing when my ribcage lights up with pain. The man is making me hurt in every sense of the word tonight.

"That ain't very gentlemanly of you." Xander is standing over us, hands on his hips. There's not a speck of dirt on his pristine chaps, and his expression…It's blank.

Then again, his expression is always kind of blank. He's not the most, ahem, *charismatic* guy. It's why Xander's not great boyfriend material.

He is, however, a sexy-ass bull riding star. He's also really good in bed. Of course I'd love to meet "the one" and fall in love. But a girl has needs, and I figure there's no harm in enjoying some hot sex while I wait for Prince Charming to show up.

Ryder's brows snap together as he looks up at Xander. "Who are you?"

"A...friend."

Ryder's face is still inches from mine, like he's worried I'll pass out again and wants to be close enough to administer CPR a second time.

Not gonna lie, I wouldn't hate it if that happened. Asphyxiation, even death, seems worth the risk if it means getting to kinda-sorta kiss Ryder again.

I'd die happy at the very least.

But seriously, I hope I don't die. It hurts so much to breathe right now. I hear the faint sound of a siren that gets louder and louder with each passing heartbeat.

An ambulance.

Shit, this really is serious. As if being knocked unconscious from the force of a fall didn't hammer that point home already.

Xander looms over us, but Ryder is down in the dirt with me. Not a care in the world for his clothes, and I know he's wearing his *nice* clothes. All the cowboys wear their Sunday best when they come to the rodeo. It's one of the few places they can meet new people.

By people, I mean girls.

The medic asks me if I can move my arm. I

shout when I make the attempt, pain radiating up my forearm and into my fingers. They listen to my lungs with a stethoscope, and I watch the medics exchange a meaningful glance.

An icy wash of panic moves through me. *Is* something really wrong? What if I need surgery? Surgery requires needles, and I don't like those.

A searing burn presses on the backs of my eyes.

Aw, shit, I'm gonna cry, aren't I? Because I haven't embarrassed myself enough tonight.

"I'm terrified of needles, y'all," I manage. "Last time I got a flu shot, I legit passed out. Makes me a wimp, I know—"

"Not a wimp." One of the medics, the man, smiles at me as a stretcher appears. "It's much more common than you think."

Despite the medics' attempts to carefully load me onto the stretcher, I still whimper at the punch of pain I feel when my elbow meets with the hard plastic.

A warm, calloused hand slips around mine just as the first tear trails down my temple. My heart—my stomach—*everything* inside me flips when I see that it's Ryder's hand.

The panic I felt dissipates in the wake of a comforting warmth that floods my limbs despite the way my body jolts when the medics begin to push me toward the approaching ambulance.

"She's gonna be okay," Ryder says to the medics. It's not a question. Not a guess. He says the words like he means them, like he's just as sure they're true as he is of the sun rising tomorrow morning and the morning after that.

The woman nods. "Yessir, she'll be just fine. Ma'am,

did you hear that? We're going to do our best to make sure you're comfortable, okay? The ambulance is here."

"Okay." I *am* okay as long as Ryder keeps holding my hand. I look at him. "Please stay. Can he come with me in the ambulance?" I ask the medics.

"You should have family with you," Colt says. How am I just realizing that he's jogging beside us? "I'll go—"

"You need to stay with Dean," I tell him. "Ryder is more charming, anyway. He'll sweet-talk me into getting the best of the best, right?"

Ryder's lips twitch. "Best of the best what? Hate to break it to you, my little hellion, but the ambulance isn't exactly a Rolls-Royce."

Did he just use an endearment that's cute as fuck when referring to me?

Is he actually playing ball after years of ignoring my jokes, my jabs, my attempts to get a rise out of him?

"Ain't that the truth," Xander says with a scoff.

Part of me is hurt he hasn't offered to come with me to the hospital. Xander and I may not be officially dating, but we have been hooking up for a while. I'd certainly offer to go with him if he were in my position.

Another part, though, is relieved. Ryder is proving to be *much* better company than Xander tonight.

More comforting. And yeah, better looking too.

"You should let your brother go with you, Billie." Ryder arcs his thumb over the back of my hand. If I wasn't laid up on a stretcher with a bum elbow, I'd be swooning right now.

Is this what it took to finally get my lifelong crush to notice me? Fall off my horse and break my arm in front of everyone I've ever known?

I bat my eyelashes. "Don't make me beg."

"You? Beg? I'd like to see the day."

"I really am scared, Ryder."

"Your mama is here, you know. She's gonna be worried sick."

"She and Dad will follow us to the hospital. And you know Mom can't move that quick."

Mom has a bit of a limp after getting a knee replacement six months ago. The woman hasn't sat down in almost forty years, so it's been an adjustment for us all.

"They're gonna give you good drugs."

"You're the best drug there is. And I'm gonna need a lot of drugs if I have surgery."

He searches my face, the corners of his eyes crinkling in the most adorable way imaginable as he shakes his head. "Your flirting ain't gonna work on me. And no one said surgery, Billie."

The female medic sucks a breath through her teeth. "From what I can tell, this is a bad break, y'all. I don't want to scare you, but surgery could very well be on the table. We may have some broken ribs and a punctured lung too."

My stomach dips. I squeeze Ryder's hand. "Please."

Ryder blinks, rolling his tongue along the inside of his cheek. I *love* that he's growing out his scruff. It looks almost copper in the lights of the arena.

"Why you gotta be so damn convincing?" His voice sounds different. Deeper. A little gravelly.

"Dad always said I could've been a lawyer if the accounting thing didn't work out."

"A lawyer?" It's Ryder's turn to scoff. "Nah. That'd be too easy for you. Too boring. You'd win every case, and then what? I see you as more of a…"

My heart pings around my chest cavity. "What?"

"Washed-up barrel racer."

I'm laughing again, and it still hurts like hell, and the medics are asking me to tone it down so I don't mess myself up even more as they load me into the ambulance. But I don't care because Ryder climbs into the vehicle beside me.

He's actually coming.

He's actually *staying*.

I may be in a hell of a lot of pain, but part of me still wonders if I'm actually in heaven, because this…this is everything.

"You sure you're okay to go?" Colt pokes his head inside the ambulance.

Xander steps up beside him. "I don't like this."

Ryder cuts him a nasty look that makes my skin feel two sizes too tight. "No one asked you. Colt, we'll meet you at the hospital?"

"Sounds like a plan."

I'm in pain. A lot of it. Even now, I feel nauseous at just the *idea* of being poked with needles in the ambulance or in the hospital. I also worry that I'm never going to be able to race again because this could very well be a career-ending injury. Even if that's not the case, there's a good chance my parents won't let me race after seeing tonight's shitshow.

Let this be your last hurrah, they said when I told them I wanted to give barrel racing a try. *Then it's time to settle down and focus on your future.*

Thing is, I love this sport. Everything about it speaks to me: the mix of speed and skill, the delicate balance you need to strike between being fearless and being in control. I also *love* the excuse to hang out with Ava and Sally. I feel like I've been starving for girlfriends for my entire life, and two really great ones fell into my lap when my parents hired them to work on the ranch. Racing makes me feel like I'm firing on all cylinders. That's so different from how I feel at my day job on the ranch.

I'm a good accountant. I work hard. I'm just slowly dying of boredom and frustration, and no one seems to give a shit.

Maybe that's why I don't want to let Ryder go tonight. He seems to legitimately *care* about, well, me. He was the first one to reach me after I fell, wasn't he?

Usually I'd tell myself not to read too much into how quickly he must've had to move to be at my side like that. That's just what people do in our little corner of the world—we take care of each other.

But fuck that. Right now, I'm reading into it.

I read into the fact that Ryder keeps his hand wrapped around mine as the ambulance begins to move. The pain and the fear and the uncertainty I felt seconds ago fade bit by bit until I feel almost…relaxed. Calm.

I like you, Ry. What I wouldn't give to have you like me back.

My parents are always telling me to keep my feet on the ground. But for tonight, I let my head live in the clouds, if only so I don't literally die from anxiety or a broken body.

I let myself believe that tonight is the start of something I've dreamt about for a long, long time.

Cowboy, I'm gonna make you mine.

CHAPTER 3
Brass in Pocket
Ryder

***"So you're not family."** The nurse glances up at me from* her tablet.

"No, ma'am." I run a hand over the back of my neck and look toward the door. *Where the hell is everyone?* We got to the hospital twenty minutes ago. Granted, we were able to run some red lights.

Still, shouldn't Mr. and Mrs. Wallace have arrived by now? I imagine they weren't driving the speed limit either.

"And you're not her boyfriend." The keyboard clacks as the nurse takes notes.

"I'm not, no."

Billie cracks open an eye and smirks, her full lips curving upward in a way that makes my pulse skip. "Ryder doesn't do the boyfriend thing."

How is it that she's laid up in a hospital bed but still looks so fucking pretty? Ain't fair.

"*You* sure know how to pick 'em." I fall into a chair and stretch out my legs. "Boyfriends, I mean."

She chuckles. "Xander not your type, huh?"

"That rodeo clown? Hell no."

"Good thing he's not my boyfriend, then."

I close my eyes and grit my teeth. Billie is always trying to get a rise out of me. I typically don't respond, but tonight, I figure a little levity will go a long way in helping Billie cope. Poor thing is scared. And hurting.

Luckily, the X-rays we just took ruled out a spinal or head injury. But Billie's arm is in a bad way, and she has some bruised ribs.

"You can do better than him," I manage carefully.

She rolls her eyes. "I don't know if you've noticed, but it's slim pickings around here. A girl's gotta do what a girl's gotta do."

The nurse is chuckling now too as she looks back up. "All the good ones are taken, right?"

"Yes! Pairing off like it's their job." Billie gives me a meaningful look. "Everyone except you, Ry."

There's that stab of electric pain in my center again. What the hell do I say to that?

Not my style to lead anyone on.

I like to have fun.

I had to numb myself when my parents died, and no one can fall in love with a person who's only half alive.

The nurse saves me by speaking up. "So if this cowboy here isn't family, and he's not your boyfriend, then was he just the first person on the scene, or—"

"He was." Billie's smirk broadens into a smile. "He's also hot, and all y'all nurses and doctors like him, which I hope means you'll like me and be extra gentle and let me have dessert after you fix my bum arm?"

My turn to roll my eyes. I also bite back a smile.

Billie is a firecracker wherever she goes. Gotta respect the consistency—there's not a fake bone in this girl's body.

This time the nurse flat out laughs, looking me up and down before returning to her computer screen. "Solid strategy. I'll just say he's a close friend, then."

"Wish I had more of those." Billie sighs. "Girlfriends especially."

I blink. "That's random."

"No it's not. Y'all take for granted that it's practically all dudes, all the time on a ranch. When Ava and Sally came to work for us, I almost cried I was so happy. They're part of the reason I was so hellbent on learning how to race—I wanted the excuse to hang out with them more."

The nurse nods. "My girlfriends are a lifeline. Couldn't do life without them."

"Do you think I'm gonna need surgery?" Billie's voice sounds thin all of a sudden, making my heart cramp.

The nurse continues to type on the keyboard. "The doctor will be in to examine you shortly. Whatever happens, just know you're in good hands, honey, all right?"

Billie looks at me, her big hazel eyes earnest. "You gonna put those healing hands of yours on me too? If I need 'em?"

This time, the nurse and I both laugh. Feels good to let myself enjoy Billie's admittedly great sense of humor for once instead of responding with my usual grunts or deflections.

"Pretty sure your brothers wouldn't love that," I manage.

"They wouldn't like it if I died either."

"You're not gonna die."

"From my arm? No. But from a broken heart?" She bats her eyelashes. "Those have killed more people than falls from horses ever did."

The nurse cuts me an amused look. "Is she always like this?"

"No. She's worse."

Billie just grins. "I love being bad."

The nurse shakes her head. "Can I trust y'all to behave while I go get the doc?"

"No," Billie replies.

At the same time, I say, "Yes."

Grinning, the nurse heads for the door. "Just clean up after yourselves."

"Oh, this cowboy cleans up real nice, doesn't he?" Billie asks.

I hang my head, smiling so hard my face hurts.

Danger danger danger.

But I choose to ignore the alarm bells going off in my head. I'm dealing with a legit emergency, for crying out loud. It's a sin to put effort into keeping my guard up instead of keeping Billie's spirits up.

"Since when do you know CPR?" Billie asks after the nurse leaves, closing the door behind her.

"Since your brother needed my help with Dean after Abby got sick. I was on babysitting duty a lot for a while there, and I wanted to be prepared in case, you know. Anything happened."

Colt's wife Abby died of cancer a few years back. Their son, Dean, was really young when she was diagnosed, so it was all hands on deck to provide childcare while Abby underwent treatment.

Billie sticks out that fucking bottom lip. "Aw, Ry. That's adorable."

Look. Away. From. Her mouth.

"Not so adorable when you have to perform CPR because you think someone's in trouble. You gave us a real scare, Billie."

"I leaned into the turn too much. I could feel myself coming out of the saddle, and next thing I know, I'm flying through the air, and then, *bam*." She blinks, her throat working on a swallow. "Thanks, by the way. For the mouth-to-mouth."

I scoff. This time, I have the peace of mind not to respond.

Instead, I lean forward to rest my elbows on my knees. I feel weirdly sore in my back and legs, like I was the one who fell off a horse. Who knew performing CPR for real was such a workout?

Or maybe it's just my body coming down from the horrible adrenaline rush of thinking Billie Wallace might be paralyzed, or worse. To be stuck in a wheelchair after the ride of a lifetime—I can't imagine. She looked so... fierce riding that cloverleaf. So free.

So *alive*.

As cowboys, my brothers and I like to claim we're free. Free from the tedium of desk jobs. Free from the pressures of the rat race.

Sometimes, though, when it's late and I can't sleep, I wonder why, if I'm so "free," I feel like I'm slowly suffocating. Duke would talk about feeling suffocated too, before he met Wheeler. But that was because he was bored with life on the ranch and wanted to travel the world.

Me? I don't mind life on the ranch one bit. In fact, I love being a cowboy. Working outdoors with animals, being part of a team of great people, the strength and stamina the job's given me—I enjoy the hell out of it all.

No, this sense of being stifled comes from something else. Some*place* else.

Someplace inside me. Maybe it's the numbness I keep thinking about. Sure, not feeling much keeps me safe. But maybe it's also cutting off my air supply. Because watching Billie ride was like having oxygen pumped back into my lungs. Now that I'm thinking about it, it feels...almost like waking up.

This girl's gonna ride again. She has to.

"I really enjoyed making you squirm in front of the nurse," Billie continues. "She's cute, by the way."

"I didn't notice."

Billie rolls her eyes. "Sure you didn't."

It's the truth, though. The nurse could've been Shrek, and I don't think I would've batted an eye. Billie has my attention, and despite her sly little remarks, she knows it.

I start to feel hot underneath my collar. This focus on her, this possessiveness, the flirting. It's inappropriate. I should leave, even if everything inside me yells at just the *thought* of walking out of this little room.

"I hope everyone is okay." Glancing at the door, I run my hand over my nape for what feels like the hundredth time. "Where is your family?"

Billie lifts a shoulder. "They're coming." A pause. "You were the first on the scene."

"What?" I blink, turning my head to meet her eyes.

Hers are soft. Vulnerable. So is her voice when she

says, "There were medics in the arena, but you beat them to it."

My face flushes. "I don't know if you remember, but I was All-State in the 100-meter dash."

"I remember." She cracks a smile. "You were the only one who ran track."

The rest of them—my brothers and hers—played baseball and football. But I liked the way my body felt when I was hurtling around the curves of the track. It felt like meditation. The thump of my heart, the steady beat of my sneakers on the asphalt.

I'm not a runner anymore—don't have the time or the energy for anything other than cowboying and hunting—but back in the day, I loved it.

"Everyone leapt out of their seats when you fell." I straighten, sighing when my spine meets with the back of the chair. "I just so happened to be the fastest."

That's mostly true, anyway.

Billie's eyes glimmer. My heart tips over. The hazel in her irises looks amber right now. Pretty and soft.

"Thank you." Billie says the words with heartfelt sincerity. "For being there. And for—"

"Knock knock!" A jovial woman in blue scrubs and matching skullcap steps into the room. "I hear we have a rodeo queen in our midst!"

Billie grins. "Are you going to help me straighten my crown *and* the bones in my arm?"

Goddamn it, this girl won't stop making me laugh. Go figure, when I allow myself to actually engage with Billie on a real level, she's fun to be around. There's this sense of lightness to her that somehow complements her sharpness.

"I'll do my best. I'm Dr. Mansfield, and I'll be operating on you today."

Billie's grin fades. "So I do need surgery."

"I'm afraid you do, yes. But don't worry, we'll have you right as rain in no time at all. We have an OR opening up in just a bit here." The doctor pulls up Billie's X-rays on a TV screen and proceeds to walk us through where the fracture is and what the fix will look like.

In short: eight screws, two plates, and three hours of surgery.

Billie's face is as white as a sheet. When I grab her hand, it feels cold and clammy. My stomach churns.

She swallows audibly as she turns her head toward Dr. Mansfield. "Is it going to hurt?"

"We're very good at keeping you comfortable, but if you experience any breakthrough pain, please let us know."

"Okay."

Only, Billie doesn't look okay after the doctor leaves and a team of nurses comes in to prep her for surgery. Her eyes nearly bulge out of her head when a nurse wheels in a tray bearing multiple needles.

I strain my neck to look out the door. "I can ask if your parents are here—"

"No." Billie squeezes my hand. "I want you. I mean, I'm sure they'll come in when they arrive, but—"

"There's a traffic jam on Highway 21," a nurse says. "Some stray cows in the road. Just waiting on the cowboys to round 'em up."

I groan. "Of course." *Of course.* If there's ever traffic in Hartsville, chances are livestock is involved. You just hope it's not *your* livestock that's causing the trouble.

Although the idea of leaving Billie right now, even if her parents were here, doesn't sit right. She's clinging to my hand like her life depends on it.

Also, I can't stop thinking about the way her voice sounded when she said, "I want you."

Raw. Real. A little wild. She's in her feelings, but she's not trying to run away from them.

Danger.

A nurse wheels the tray over. "I'm going to get an IV started, all right, honey?"

Billie is shaking now. "If I pass out, will you please let this gentleman here administer CPR? He's very good at it."

"If you want me to kiss you again, Billie, you just gotta ask."

Before tonight, I would've never made that joke. But when Billie cracks a smile, I know it's the right call. It's my turn to make her laugh.

At the very least, it's my turn to keep her conscious so these nurses can do their job.

The nurse smiles too as she preps the IV. "Y'all make a cute couple."

"Don't we?" Billie manages thinly. "All right, lover boy, your services might be required sooner rather than later. I'm feeling woozy."

My chest lurches when I look down and see Billie's eyes well with tears before she quickly squeezes them shut.

I think I've seen her cry all of three times in the fifteen years I've known her. Woman is tough as nails.

But I know what it's like to be scared shitless over something that, rationally, shouldn't be a big deal. I was on a super bumpy flight years ago, and I've hated flying ever since. I get full-on heart palpitations just *thinking* about getting on a plane again.

Duke is horrified by my reluctance to travel. He lives for it. But me? I'd rather you pull out my fingernails than get on another flight. I'm a homebody through and through, and I like being on the ranch more than anywhere else on earth.

Bet Billie here would probably prefer to have a limb sawed off without anesthesia than get this IV inserted.

"Keep breathing, honey." The nurse pats Billie's free hand. "You're only going to feel a quick pinch."

Billie nods, keeping her eyes closed. But her brow is all scrunched up, and I notice sweat beading along her top lip. She's trying very hard not to fall apart.

Now I'm the one who needs the reminder to breathe. I fucking *hate* seeing her like this.

You can fall apart with me, I want to tell her.

"Let's play a game," I say instead, the idea hitting me out of nowhere.

Billie opens an eye. "A game?"

"Remember when you hummed that song for me? The Taylor Swift one about Romeo and Juliet and her dad or whatever? And I played the guitar while you sang?"

Now both her eyes are open. "You remember that?"

"Well, yeah." I squeeze her hand again. "Your voice was prettier than I thought it would be."

"Shut up."

"So I'll hum a song for you, and you try to guess what it is."

The look of terror on her face fades. "If you're trying

to distract me, taking off your shirt will do the trick a heck of a lot faster."

"I'd prefer not to get arrested tonight, thanks. Pretty sure it's a crime to strip down in an emergency room."

"I'd let it slide," the nurse says with a grin. "Just this once."

Billie heaves out an exaggerated, long-suffering sigh. "Fine. I'll play your stupid game."

"Eyes on mine." I use my first two fingers to direct her line of vision away from the nurse. "All right, song number one." Clearing my throat, I start to hum. I feel ridiculous, a little embarrassed even, but I do my best to keep my voice steady and strong.

Billie gasps, and my stomach drops. But then she smiles, and I realize she made the sound not because she's in pain, but because she's delighted.

"Shut up!" she says.

"You keep saying that."

"Since when do you know another Taylor Swift song?"

Now I'm really blushing. "Since you introduced me. Her stuff was fun to play on the guitar, so..."

"And 'I Knew You Were Trouble' is your favorite because it clearly makes you think of—ouch!"

The nurse smiles. "IV is in."

Billie's eyelashes flutter. "Seriously?"

"Yep. All done for now."

Billie turns her head to stare at me. "Keep humming."

"Right. On it. Song number two."

She bursts out laughing after I hum for all of three seconds. "'Chattahoochee' by Alan Jackson. I hope you know that *you're* the one who's hotter than a—"

"Don't finish that thought. Okay, song number three."

This one takes her a little longer, but she finally gets it when I hit the chorus. "Nirvana. 'Come As You Are,' I think?"

I let out a chuckle. "Since when do you know your nineties grunge?"

"Since you and Colt played it nonstop growing up. You forget his room was right next to mine. I swear I heard Eddie Vedder singing in my sleep."

"I'm impressed." *And if you weren't my best friend's kid sister, I'd be a little turned on by the fact you know your Pearl Jam.*

Billie kicks her feet. "I like this game. Your voice is better than I thought."

"Ha."

We keep playing as we wait for Billie to be wheeled into surgery. By the time we leave the room, she looks… not relaxed, but not like she's about to pass out either.

Is it wrong that my chest swells a little knowing I have that kind of power?

Only when the nurses tell me that I have to let her go do I realize I'm still holding Billie's hand. It's not cold or clammy anymore, but she does hold my palm in a grip I can only describe as fierce.

A little afraid.

Without thinking, I lift our joined hands and brush my lips over her knuckles. "You're gonna be just fine, Billie."

"How do you know that?" The words are threadbare. I can hear my heart pounding in my ears. I don't know who's more nervous about Billie's surgery, her or me.

"You said it yourself. I put this healing hand on you."

She scoffs. "Will you put it on me again if I need it? And the other hand too? All over?"

"Put what all over you?"

I nearly jump out of my skin when I look up and see Colt jogging toward us, his parents on his heels.

No sign of the rodeo dickhead. Good.

"Nothing." I drop Billie's hand and shove my own inside my back pocket. "The Lord's blessing."

Billie outright laughs. "That's exactly what I want put all over me. I need some Jesus in my life. Thank you, Ryder."

Colt draws to a stop beside Billie's bed in the hallway. He's out of breath as he leans in to kiss her cheek. "I'm sorry we're so late."

"You helped clear the cattle from the road, didn't you?" Billie wrinkles her nose. She looks really fucking cute when she does that. "You stink."

"You're welcome for busting my ass to get here!" He laughs. "And yeah, we all lent a hand. Still took an age. Are you feeling okay? They told us you were being brought into surgery."

"I'm…okay, actually." Billie glances at me. "Ryder kept me distracted while they did the needle stuff."

Colt sends an appreciative look my way. "Thank you, brother."

"Welcome." The word comes out more gruffly than I intended. Maybe because I'm suddenly gripped by an awful sense of guilt even though I know that, logically, I didn't do anything wrong.

I still can't kick the sense that I crossed a line tonight. Many lines. I've done a good job of keeping Billie at arm's length, but tonight I let her in—I let myself get close to her—and now I feel funky. Or maybe I'm in a funk thinking about how I'll have to put up my guard again in the morning.

Before I lost my parents, I wasn't afraid to open up to Billie. I even played my guitar for her, both of us getting deep in our feels as I strummed her favorite Taylor Swift song.

But after my parents died, I stopped playing guitar, and I stopped opening up too. And maybe it's hitting me that I've missed out on some really excellent things by keeping my distance.

Shit like Billie's wry sense of humor and her bravery and the way she lights up a room. I want to witness it all again, because…well, because it made me feel fully and completely alive for the first time in ages.

What am I supposed to do, though? If I keep letting her get close, I might do something stupid. Like cross even more lines, blow up my friendship with Colt, and risk complete and total annihilation.

Not to be dramatic. But I've already been through so much loss. Losing people you love—it wrecks you, and I'm not sure I can survive that kind of loss again.

Mr. Wallace claps my shoulder. "Thanks for taking care of our little girl."

"I'm not little anymore, Dad." But Billie's eyes still well when he kisses her cheek. "Love you. I'll be okay."

I step back, giving Billie's family space to get closer to her.

"You hurting?" There's a deep groove between Mrs. Wallace's brows. I know that groove well; as the mother of six children whom she raised on the ranch,

Mrs. Wallace has experienced dozens of injuries over the years. I've been there to witness the appearance of that groove more times than I can count.

"Mostly my pride, Mom."

Mrs. Wallace grins. "You did so great tonight, Billie. We're proud of you."

"We also hope you'll be hanging up your spurs soon." Mr. Wallace puts a hand on his chest. "My nerves can't take this kind of scare anymore."

The life in Billie's eyes dissolves almost immediately. She looks down at her hands, which are now clasped in her lap. "You've been saying that forever, Daddy."

"I mean it this time, sweetheart."

"But it was my first real race—"

"All right, y'all, the OR is ready." A nurse releases the brake on Billie's bed. "We'll see you in a few hours."

Mrs. Wallace grabs her daughter's hand. Colt kisses Billie's cheek again, and Mr. Wallace kisses the top of her head. For a full heartbeat they stay in this pose, a slightly awkward but entirely heartfelt group hug.

Sister, brother.

Mom and Dad.

Seeing the four of them together, a hand grips my windpipe and squeezes. I learned a long time ago that feeling sorry for myself is a useless exercise. I miss my parents. I miss Garrett. I'll always love them. But I can't dwell on the fact that I lost them, or the grief will swallow me whole. I can't walk along the edge of that complete and utter destruction I was talking about.

Goddamn it, though. I'd give anything to be able to hug them one more time.

I'd give anything to be held by them one last time.

The Wallaces step back. Billie turns her head on the pillow, looking up toward me. For a split second, our gazes lock.

A palpable, heavy beat of…something passes between us. Understanding? Shared grief? Delayed shock at the things we said and did tonight? Whatever it is that moves in the small space between her body and mine, it arrows right through my heart.

It hurts.

"Thanks again, Ry," Billie says.

I blink, struggling for breath. Instinctively my hand goes to my front pocket, my fingertips tracing the outline of Dad's knife. "Good luck."

Looking away, I turn and stalk out of the emergency room.

CHAPTER 4
Meet the Wallaces
Billie

I stare at the box of toothpicks on my desk, wondering if I really could use them to hold my eyes open. Lord knows I need the help.

I'm beyond wiped. Really, bored out of my goddamn mind. Surely it's almost quitting time?

Glancing at my laptop screen, I see that it's 10:02 a.m.

"You gotta be kidding me. What the *fuck*?"

I remember how fast the time would go when I was in the arena training with Ava. Really, how fast the time would go anytime I was on horseback.

But in the office? I swear to God, time moves backward.

Probably a bad sign, considering it's my first day back at work since my accident three weeks ago.

I've also had some of the worst nightmares the past few nights than I've had in a long time. I'll wake up covered in sweat and gasping for air, just like I used to do when I was little. In one dream, I was being held underwater. I struggled against the hand that held me down, realizing right before I woke up that it was *my* hand that kept me submerged.

It was weird. And more than a little terrifying, if I'm being honest.

"What's that?" Dad spins around in his swivel chair. His desk is directly behind mine, and his legs are so long that he can almost brush the bottom of my own chair with the toes of his boots. "Your arm botherin' you again?"

The surgery went well, and while I had a fair amount of soreness right afterward, the pain has gotten much more manageable. Still, it's a struggle to find a comfortable position to sleep in. Every once in a while, I'll forget I'm injured and push myself a little too hard, and then I'm back to popping my ibuprofen every four or so hours.

Right now, though, my arm feels fine. Surprisingly I never needed a cast; my doctor just had me wear a heavy-duty brace for two weeks post-op and gave me instructions for exercises that will help improve mobility, so I can eventually get back in the literal and proverbial saddle. Now I just wear a sling whenever I leave the house.

What's really chapping my ass, though, is being back at my day job. I couldn't really type after my surgery, so it didn't make sense for me to work until today, when my doc gave me the all clear. While dealing with a broken elbow is not a walk in the park, I enjoyed the hell out of being away from the office.

Sitting at my desk has been depressing in a way I

wasn't prepared for. I hadn't realized what a lifeline barrel racing was until I couldn't do it anymore.

"I think…" I roll back my shoulders. "I'm all right. Just tired."

"You're bored. I know you better than you think, sweetheart. Coming back to work after an extended break is never easy. I keep saying this, but you really do get used to it."

It's all I can do not to groan. I've been the ranch's full-time bookkeeper for over three years now, but if anything, the days feel longer than ever.

"You even start to take pride in it because you know you're doing work that's just as important as the work the ranch hands do," Dad continues. "Because the bookkeeping is important, Billie. You can't run an operation like ours without money and someone to manage it. We need you here. And this stuff"—he motions to the laptop computer behind him—"you can do it anytime, anywhere, as long as you have a calculator and an internet connection. That kind of flexibility might come in handy one day."

Really, he's saying flexibility is important for women. In my parents' world, women are the ones who take care of the kids, do the cooking, and clean the house so the men can go do their "Important Cowboy Things."

Or maybe I'm just reading way too much into his comment because I'm feeling salty today.

Whatever the case, I don't want to get into an argument this early. Dad means well. And it's ultimately on me to figure out a way to be happy in the world I was born into.

I survived a nasty fall, didn't I? And my older

brother's very hot best friend gave me the next best thing to an actual kiss. Not gonna lie, I've thought about that mouth-to-mouth moment every damn day—and night—since it happened.

Life isn't all bad, right?

Right.

I spin my own chair around to face Dad and manage a smile. "I know. Gotta think practically." Mom is always telling me that too.

"Practical ain't a bad thing when so many lives and livelihoods are at stake."

I don't need to tell Dad the respect I have for that fact because he already knows. He raised us with a deep understanding of our responsibility to care for our land and our animals. This is life-and-death stuff we're talking about.

I get it.

I just wish I felt more enthusiasm for my role in all of it. Or maybe I just wish I was able to *choose* my role. I think that's part of the reason why I was so gung ho on learning how to barrel race. I felt like I had some control—like I was choosing my destiny, as cheesy as that sounds. And that destiny felt exciting.

Now that those dreams are pretty much dead—I'm not sure I'll have the ability to ever race again, and even if I did, I doubt I'd have my parents' support—*I* feel dead inside. It's not like I expected to be any kind of real rodeo star. I guess I just was secretly hoping that racing would point me in a new direction. One that's more exciting—that's a better fit—than bookkeeping.

"No, sir, it's not a bad thing." I turn back to my computer.

Dad is quiet for a beat. I wait for him to return to his laptop, but instead, he clears his throat. "I know I'm not, uh, the best at this. Talking. But if you ever need to get something off your chest, I'm always willing to listen. You're at an age…"

I put my fingertips on the keyboard. "Yeah?"

"Your twenties…It can be a difficult time. I didn't get much guidance, which is why I try to give it to you."

My shoulders slump. "I know. And I appreciate that, Dad."

He's a *good* man. I know he's just trying to do the right thing by making sure I have a solid start on a solid career path. But sometimes I wonder if he really gets me, really knows what's best for me, or if he just wants to keep me safe and away from the bunkhouse, where "boys will be boys."

Or the "cowboys will be cowboys," I guess. I understand why Dad thinks that way. When he and Mom were my age, they were already married with a couple of kids underfoot. Grandpa Mack was still around, so Dad was foreman before Grumpy Bud came into the picture a few years later. Dad spent his days running the ranch, while Mom stayed home with us. The roles they took on were—are—very traditional. I think that's why they both keep bringing up how important "practicality" and "flexibility" are in my career.

I wish practicality felt like freedom. The kind of freedom I felt racing at the rodeo or humming along with Ryder to Nirvana at the hospital.

Instead, flexibility feels like a cage.

I close my eyes and try to take a deep breath, but I still feel like I'm suffocating. The idea of being stuck inside this office for another interminably long day makes me feel like crying.

I am not a crier.

God, what is wrong with me? Why can't I just go along with the great little plan my parents set up for me? Most people would kill for a plum job like this to land in their lap, one with benefits and, yes, flexibility. I feel like a brat for wanting something else.

For wanting more.

I also feel like I'd be letting down my parents—my whole family—if I bowed out of the position. Sure, we could hire someone else to do it. But our focus, and our resources, have been building out our training facilities and staff here on the ranch. No one wants to take the time to find a replacement for me and train him or her.

More than that, no one wants to help me figure out what *my* new job would be. We don't need any more ranch or stable hands, and my brothers have filled any other positions that might interest me.

I've thought about working with Ava, but I'm more interested in racing itself than teaching people how to do it. I'm also no expert, not like Ava, and I'm pretty sure she doesn't need an extra trainer on her roster at the moment.

Blinking, I will myself to finish the invoices that need to be sent out by the end of the day. The minutes creep by. I pay some bills. Chat with a hugely unhelpful rep from the accounting software we use about an issue I'm having reconciling our accounts. I skip lunch with my family and eat a sad turkey sandwich at my desk.

After a long day, I'd ordinarily tack up my horse and go for a ride before supper. There's nothing like being in the saddle to help you blow off some steam and wear out your body. I miss how tired I'd be after a good ride. I would grab a quick, satisfying rinse in the shower, and then I'd collapse into bed where I'd sleep like a baby for eight hours straight.

But Dr. Mansfield gave me strict orders not to ride for another three weeks. Maybe more, depending on how my arm continues to heal.

I miss the smell of the barn and the feel of sun on my skin. I feel like I'm turning into a fucking vampire being stuck inside all day.

I also miss Ryder. He's texted me a couple times to check in. My heart always skips a beat when his name pops up on my phone screen. We don't text all that often, so it's always a thrill to hear from him. Even if his texts were more friendly than flirty.

Would he play that humming game again with me? The game itself was simple, but there was something almost…magical about the way Ryder opened up when we played. I saw a side of him I haven't witnessed since we were kids. He was silly and sweet and vulnerable.

He also looked really happy. Or maybe carefree is a better word. Of course he wasn't happy we'd ended up in the ER, but he didn't seem to mind goofing around with me for a bit.

Is it wrong that I wanna see that side of him again? Being with him when he was like that—relaxed, real— was comforting.

I wonder if I could convince him to dust off his guitar.

It's a breath of fresh air I could really use after a hellish day. Truth be told, I've felt lonely at night. Xander's been bugging me to get together, since I haven't seen him since my fall. I know he only wants to have sex—it's what he always wants—and I wasn't up for it then.

I'm definitely not up for it now. Which is kinda strange considering how I was always the one initiating sex with him prior to my accident.

Yeah, I'd definitely rather go hang with Ryder. First, though, I gotta get through my first family supper since the accident. We don't eat together every night anymore, but Mom always invites everyone over when she's cooking.

Walking into my parents' kitchen, I'm hit by familiar smells: Ivory dish soap, baking bread, a hint of Mom's jasmine-scented hand lotion. My chest cramps.

I may hate work, but I love my family, and I've missed being around them. Even if I have loved the excuse to rot on my couch every night for the past three weeks.

"There she is!" Beck flashes me a shit-eating grin from his perch beside Mom at the stove. "Glad you're joining us for dinner again, sis."

Taking a deep breath through my nose, I paste on a smile. "My freezer is stocked for the next hundred years, thanks to all that takeout you dropped off. Sorry not sorry I've been pigging out on that."

That's why this is one of the first times I'm joining my family for supper since the accident. They've brought over so much food that I haven't had to come to Mom and Dad's for meals.

"Just out here doing the Lord's work." Beck taps the metal tongs he's holding to his forehead in a salute. "The food's good, right?"

I set down my phone on the kitchen island. "Delicious. You should be proud."

Usually I'd roll up my sleeves and help set the table or wash whatever dishes are already dirty. But that's physically impossible at the moment, so I stand there, not quite sure what to do with myself.

"Sit, honey." Mom reads my mind. "You're still healing, and I imagine you're pretty dang tired. How'd the first day back at the office go?"

It was even more awful than I thought it'd be.

"It was fine."

"Just fine?" Beck raises a brow. "Try not to sound so excited."

"Not all of us are lucky enough to have cool jobs like you."

He grins. "I do have some pretty cool jobs."

Beck, who's a major foodie, recently invested in the Homestead Hen, Hartsville's very first farm-to-table restaurant. He had the chef make me a ton of food after my accident, which Beck delivered to my house when I got home from the hospital.

My parents wanted me to live with them after I graduated high school and began taking online accounting courses. I did that until I convinced them to let me move into the teeny-tiny apartment above an old equipment barn on our property. I've been happily living there for close to three years now.

In terms of the food Beck brought over, we're talking a whole tray of butternut squash lasagna, two roasted chickens with the most delicious jus ever, and quarts of autumn kale salad dotted with goat cheese and the gala apples a local farmer grows in her orchard.

Truth be told, the Homestead Hen is Hartsville's *only* restaurant. When a fancy chef from Austin decided to relocate to the country and open her dream restaurant that served up American classics with a casual, elegant twist, Beck jumped at the chance to be involved.

Now he's a ranch hand by day, restaurateur by night. Since we eat supper so early here on the ranch—we're usually at the table by five—he's able to head to the restaurant afterward. I have no idea where he gets the energy, but my older brother loves his new gig.

"I am mighty proud of *you*." He turns back to the stove, where he gives a cast iron skillet a quick shake. "Haven't told you in person how great you looked out there in the arena."

"You were riding *so fast*, Auntie Billie."

Glancing over my shoulder, I smile when I see Dean and Colt enter the kitchen from the side door.

"Faster even than your dad?" I lean down to give my nephew a hug, planting a kiss on his mop of dirty blond hair.

Dean grins up at Colt. "I think so. Bet I could ride that fast."

"We gotta get Miss Ava to teach you how to stay sat in the saddle first." Colt leans in to kiss my cheek. "How ya feeling, Billie? First day back go okay?"

My heart squeezes. *This* is why I've stayed in a job I hate for so long.

It's because my family is great.

Really, really great. And sometimes I think that I just need to suck it up and do what's best for *us* instead of what's best for *me*.

There's six of us Wallace kids. Beck is the second

oldest, after Colt. I'm number three in the birth order, and after me there's Nash, Mack, and Tate.

Mom only had one sibling, my Aunt Lee, and Dad had none. They both wanted a big family of their own—I think they were both lonely growing up—and only after six babies did they give up on tying to have another girl. Because girls are the best (obviously), and Mom also loves having a sister, so she always wanted one for me.

Don't get me wrong, I loved growing up with my brothers. But I really do wish I had more girlfriends. Especially now that I'm getting older and everyone is starting to pair off.

I wasn't especially close with Colt's wife, Abby. I was only sixteen when they got married, and then there was all the shit that went down before she got sick. I had a hard time liking her after she did my brother dirty like that.

"I feel better. A little sore. Pretty tired. But otherwise, I'm all right." I give Dean one last squeeze. "I appreciate y'all coming to visit me so much. Believe it or not, Dean, the flowers you picked for me are still alive. I love them."

"Dad says girls love flowers."

"Everyone loves flowers. They smell good."

Dean wrinkles his nose. "Sometimes I don't smell very good."

"Stinky feet?"

"And armpits." Colt wags his eyebrows.

Dean laughs. "And butt cheeks!"

Colt rolls his eyes as he saunters in and hangs his Stetson on the rack beside the pantry. "Why does *everything* have to be about butts?"

"Hey." Tate is hot on Colt's heels. "What's wrong with butts? They're awesome."

Dean high-fives him. "They smell bad, though."

"Not if you keep your cheeks clean. Hey, Billie." Tate loops an arm around my neck and gives me a hug. "Happy you're back."

"Are *your* cheeks clean?" I ask.

Tate grins. "Always. Mind's not, though."

Mack slaps him on the back as he moves past us. "Filthiest out of us all for sure. Hey, Billie. You recovered yet?"

"Getting there." I carefully raise my arm to show off the six-inch scar on the back of my elbow.

"I mean, have you recovered from embarrassing yourself in front of everyone you know in Texas?"

Nash appears at the side door now, along with Dad. They both wipe their boots on the mat before coming inside and hanging up their hats too. They smell like fresh air and sunscreen, scents that have my chest cramping for a different reason.

I wish I could be out there with y'all.

"My timing is perfect as always," Nash says. "I feel a fistfight brewing."

"It's not a fair fight when she's only got one good arm." Mack motions to my sling.

I roll my eyes. "Please. We all know I could take out any of y'all with one arm, no problem."

Mack grins, his dimples popping. "You win. Still sore?"

"It's not so bad anymore."

"Good. Hasn't been the same around here without you."

"Yeah, it's been much more peaceful." Dad's eyes twinkle. "But a lot more boring too." He moves toward the stove. "Hello, Wife. Whatcha makin'? Smells good."

"Hello, Husband." Mom puts her hand on Dad's face, and he leans in for a kiss. "I'm making your favorite—smoked pork chops with 'shrooms and potatoes."

"Kissing is gross." Dean makes a face. "That's how you get germs."

Nash ruffles his hair. "I believe the scientific term is 'cooties.'"

"Coo-*ties*!" Beck singsongs, and I immediately think of Ryder singing because apparently *everything* makes me think of Ryder right now.

I must have the worst case of lady blue balls *ever* from that kiss-slash-lifesaving-CPR-moment. How the hell do I come back from that?

Was it the most romantic—erotic—thing to ever happen to me even though Ryder got nowhere near my pants?

"I'll take Mama's cooties anyway," Dad says.

Colt gives them a look. "I still think it's weird that you call her Mama. And Wife. And Love Dove."

"I don't care what you think," Mom replies. "I like it, and that's what matters."

Dad gives Mom's backside a playful tap. "That's right, Love Dove."

CHAPTER 5
A Brunette and Some Blondies
Billie

Even though my parents have done very well for themselves over the years, they still live in the single-story ranch house they built when they outgrew the old foreman's cabin after I was born.

It's fifteen hundred square feet. Four bedrooms, two baths, with a kitchen that's big enough to hang out in. But we always, always have eaten in the formal dining room.

"Formal" is a bit of a misnomer for the cozy but less-than-fancy spot where we eat all our meals. It's dominated by a huge oak table and the antler chandelier that hangs above it.

We've ribbed Mom more times than I can count about that light fixture.

"How many innocent bucks had to die so you could pretend that you're John Dutton?" Tate asked her once.

Mom just smiled, ignoring him as she drank her longneck of Miller High Life. Her style of decorating can best be described as "shabby chic meets hunting lodge," and while it's not my personal favorite, she's made it work over the years. Our house is comfortable, lived-in, and full of memories. A true family home, and I wouldn't have it any other way.

We all have our places around the table. Mom and Dad sit at either end, while I grab my usual spot to Dad's right. I claimed it as soon as I was old enough, thinking it would keep me closest to Dad so that I could therefore become his favorite, and *therefore* do whatever I wanted, just like my brothers.

Alas, that idea obviously hasn't come to fruition. But I still sit to his right, and he still grabs my hand and gives it a squeeze as he says, "All right, y'all, time for roses and thorns. Dean's up first."

"Because I'm the cutest," Dean says with a grin.

"Or the youngest," Dad replies. "But you're also the cutest, so that works."

Roses and thorns is a family tradition going back as far as I can remember. Growing up, we ate dinner together at this table every night. And every night, Dad would go around the table and ask us what our favorite part of the day was (our rose) and our least favorite (the thorn).

Cheesy? Sure. But I've realized it's his way of staying connected to us—of knowing what's going on in our lives.

Dean clears his throat. "The best part of my day was reading a whole book by myself."

I gasp. "You read a whole book by yourself?"

"Yup." He smiles proudly as he shoves a scoop of Mom's famous roasted smashed potatoes in his mouth. "Guess what I read?"

"Hm." Mack chews thoughtfully for a minute. "*Curious George?*"

"Yes! How did you know?"

Mack chuckles. "I've only read those books to you a thousand times. Is that who you're going to be for Halloween?"

"No," Dean replies like it's the most obvious thing in the world. "I'm going to be a zombie football player. Duh."

I hide my laugh with my napkin. "Sounds spooky."

"I'm not scared of zombies." Dean shovels a forkful of food into his mouth and chews thoughtfully. "Although Curious George is definitely more friendly than that."

I reach over the table to give Dean a fist bump. "Proud of you for reading, bud. Will you read some *Curious George* to me after dinner?"

"Maybe. If I'm not too tired."

I can't help but smile. He is *cute*. I've wondered in a vague sort of way if any kids I have will look like him. He's a Wallace through and through, with his thick blond hair and big brown eyes. Like his daddy, he's obsessed with horses and Texas football. He also loves it when I paint his nails funky colors—neon blue is his current favorite—and he shares my obsession with all the *Hotel Transylvania* movies.

"And your thorn?" Dad asks.

Dean tilts his head back and forth. "The way I write my name isn't perfect. My teacher keeps asking me to write lowercase letters, but that's really hard."

Colt is already reaching for seconds from the plate of pork chops. "Aw, bud, it doesn't have to be perfect to be good. You're learning, so cut yourself some slack."

I probably could take that advice myself. I know in the grand scheme of things I'm young, and it's okay if I'm not where I want to be yet. I just wish I had the ability to figure out things for myself instead of my parents figuring them out for me.

Thing is, as much as I admire my parents and the life they've built, I want something different. I *am* different, at least from the women in my family. I want kids, but I also want a successful, fulfilling career. I want to honor my family's legacy, but I also want some semblance of personal happiness.

I know who I am. I just don't know where the true, authentic version of myself fits in.

I'm up next for roses and thorns.

"My rose?" I wipe my mouth on my napkin, fighting a grin. "It has to be Ryder saving my life at the rodeo, right? It was weeks ago, but it was so epic that it's still gotta count."

Dad chuckles. "Your rose isn't actually racing in that rodeo?"

"Well, that too." I glance at Colt across the table, but he's busy shoving more pork in his face. "Racing was just as exhilarating as I thought it'd be. The crowd, the energy, how fast it all went—"

"It's the kind of thing you live for." Tate gives me a knowing look. "So are you gonna do it again?"

"Lord, I hope not," Mom says with an exhausted sigh.

I know Mom is only looking out for me, but her comment feels like a poke nonetheless. "I hope to race again, yeah."

Dad skewers a pair of brussels sprouts with his fork. "I wish you coulda seen the way Ryder leapt over all those seats into the arena. It was like something out of a movie."

Nash nods. "Dude is fast."

No shit.

"You would've thought he had the hots for Billie by how quickly he ran." Tate gives me a playful look as he gulps his wine. "That's what I thought, anyway."

"Not funny." Colt stares down Tate.

Tate holds up his hands. "Or maybe it was just a *friendly* burst of energy that got him into that arena."

"We'll leave it at that." Dad, ever the peacemaker, is good at smoothing ruffled feathers. "And your thorn, Billie?"

Wanting Ryder but not being able to have him.

Despising my job but being too chickenshit to quit.

"The surgery." I'm gulping my wine now too. "All those needles."

Dad pats my hand. "You were so brave, sweetheart."

I'm not brave, though. I haven't been honest with my parents about how much I hate my job. I haven't been honest with *myself* about what that means for my future. I need to make some really big changes if I'm ever going to be happy, but I've been too scared of letting other people down to even *think* about what my next move might be.

I'm not sure what bothers me more: the fact that my family views me in a totally different way than I view myself, or that I *let* them think of me as this brave, steady, wholesome girl, when really, I'm something else entirely.

I wonder what Ryder would have to say about that.

I wonder if I'd feel any better if he hummed for me again.

———

Tate, Mom, and I are the last ones left in the kitchen after dinner. Tate loads the dishwasher while I wipe down the counters and Mom finds a spot for leftovers in the fridge.

"Hey, Mom?" I set down the countertop spray beside the dish soap at the sink and drop a handful of dirty paper towels in the trash. "Could I possibly bribe you for the rest of those blondies?"

Mom loves to bake, and she makes us dessert from scratch almost every time she cooks dinner. Today, she whipped up some blondies. They're basically a chocolate chip cookie in brownie form, with a decadently thick, chewy center that oozes with melted semisweet chocolate chips.

They are to die for. Especially when you're a literal cookie monster like Ryder, who loves a chocolate chip moment. Everyone thought he'd puke his guts out after eating an entire package of Chips Ahoy! on a dare from Colt. But the smug bastard just smiled when he was done and asked for more.

Ryder's got a sweet tooth, a fact I haven't taken advantage of until...well, right now.

Mom grins. "You don't need to bribe me, honey. Take all you want."

"Where are you off to?" Tate doesn't look up from the dishes he's rinsing in the sink.

My stomach dips. Leave it to him to sniff out my not-so-secret plan to visit my not-so-secret crush. "Nowhere."

"Tell Ryder I said hello," Mom replies.

I scoff. Am I really that transparent? True, I've pushed Ryder's buttons plenty around my family. But for Tate *and* Mom to automatically know where I'm headed, my crush on Ryder must be even more obvious than I thought.

I consider denying the fact that I'm going twenty miles out of my way to ask Ryder Rivers to *hum* with me.

Sounds kinda kinky, actually.

If only.

But they'd know I was full of shit if I made up some story about needing this much comfort food in my house. I mean, there's almost a whole tray of blondies left.

So I manage a sheepish smile and say, "I haven't properly thanked him. For, you know, saving my life. So I thought I'd go over and, yeah." I clear my throat. "Do that. Thank him."

Tate rolls his eyes so hard I can practically *hear* it. "You were gonna be just fine with or without Ryder Rivers."

"That's not true," I reply, a little hurt. Embarrassed, more like it. "He kept me calm in the hospital. Distracted me—"

"I'm just teasin'." Tate turns off the faucet and grabs a towel, wiping his hands while he leans a hip into the apron of the sink. "Tell him I said thanks for taking such excellent care of my sister."

My eyes sting. I blink. "Will do."

"And y'all be good." Tate's eyes bore into mine. "By 'y'all,' I mean 'you.'"

Wanting Ryder is like banging my head against the wall, I know. But I can't seem to quit. Especially after seeing the swell of emotion in his eyes when I woke up in the arena. Made me think…I don't know, something is different between us now.

I wanna know more.

I wanna see more.

Mom clucks her tongue as she tucks a sheet of tinfoil

over the paper plate of leftover blondies. "Have some faith in your sister, Tate. She's just going over for a quick visit. Right, Elizabeth May?"

I'm named after my grandmother, who passed away before I was born. They called her Eliza, but Mom liked the nickname Billie for me. When she's mad, though, or she wants me to know she means business, she calls me by my given name: Elizabeth May.

I paste on a smile. "Right."

I don't wanna keep it *quick*. But I'll take what I can get.

On the drive over to Lucky River Ranch, I roll down my windows and wonder if this is a selfish move I'm making in the guise of altruism. My boredom and existential angst are not Ryder's problem. But I can't stay home another night. Alone. Bored.

And, yeah, horny.

I just…can't.

Even driving makes me feel better. More like myself. This is my first day behind the wheel of my old silver 4Runner since my accident, and I suck in lungful after lungful of crisp autumn air, the sun slanting through the windows and warming my skin as I sing along to the radio.

Mom wasn't restless like this at my age. I can't imagine her ever being even the least bit angsty. She's so…steady. Sure of her place in the world.

Why can't I be content with what I have too? Do I *want* to be content? Or do I like this part of myself, the inner child that yearns for more?

Taking the turn onto Ryder's ranch, I slide my sunglasses onto my head. I don't come to Lucky River

Ranch that often these days, but I've lived all my life in Hart County, so I've visited this part plenty over the years. I'm always struck by how lush and pretty the Luck's property is.

Ancient-looking oaks create a dappled canopy overhead. A rainbow of leaves, mostly red and yellow and orange, float lazily through the air and catch on my windshield. The brush is still verdant, and it covers the ground in a carpet of varying shades of green.

I slow as the road rises onto the edge of a limestone canyon. The view up here—my *God*, it's pretty. The Hill Country stretches for miles and miles to my right, an undulating landscape of gentle slopes and stretches of pasture. The Colorado River is a shimmering ribbon of blue that winds its way through ridges and valleys, its surface glinting beneath a wide-open sky.

Hitting the brake, I take a second. Take a deep lungful of fresh air that's scented with the sweetness of falling leaves and woodsmoke.

The way it fills my chest and clears out my head makes me almost dizzy with delight. I've been exhausted all day, but suddenly I'm wide awake, the heaviness in my eyelids and legs disappearing without a trace.

I feel alive.

For the first time today, I feel like I might not die of boredom or frustration. This is the opposite of feeling suffocated. I'm free to do what I want, be who I want, with the wind in my hair and the sun on my face.

I need more of this. Is it ridiculous to allow myself to believe I need the outdoors to feel alive? Not everyone gets to spend their days working in the sunshine. It's not always clear skies out here anyway.

But damn, I sure do feel a hell of a lot better than I did this morning back in the office.

I blame my buoyant mood for the thoughts that flicker through my head the way the sunlight flickers through the thinning trees. *What would life be like on Lucky River Ranch?* It's just far enough from home to feel like a fresh start, but close enough to Mom and Dad and my brothers and our horses to visit whenever I wanted.

Aaaaannd I need to quit daydreaming while I'm ahead. That thought alone, the one about shacking up with Ryder on his family's property, lets me know I need to pump the proverbial brakes here. Crushing on Ryder has been fun for the most part. I don't think anyone takes it seriously.

I don't think anyone takes *me* seriously either. That's beside the point, though.

But this crush could get real serious, real fast if I'm not careful.

Glancing at the foil-covered plate on my passenger seat, I contemplate turning back around. But it's silly, right, to be afraid of spending time with a dear family friend? One I've known forever?

Or is it silly to scramble for an excuse—any excuse—to spend time with a guy who will never, ever want me back?

I look up, and my eyes catch on a smudge of something in the distance. Peering through my windshield, I watch as a tractor comes into view, kicking up a cloud of dust in a large field that appears to be planted with hay.

The tractor is enormous, a shade of John Deere green I'd recognize anywhere. It's dragging a mower that makes quick work of cutting the hay.

Watching the tractor make a perfect, hundred-and-eighty degree turn at the end of a neatly cut row of hay, I'm gripped by the sudden certainty that Ryder is driving that machine.

Only he would still be working at—I glance at the clock on the dash—quarter past six. Cowboys start their days so early that it's practically bedtime for them at this hour.

Not for Ryder. As the last remaining single dude out of all his siblings, he doesn't have anyone to go home to. He's always been a hard worker. Although sometimes I worry that he puts in such long hours because he's avoiding something. His past, maybe? His feelings?

Whatever the case, the man loves driving a tractor. As luck would have it, I make a pretty damn great passenger princess.

I grin like an idiot and hit the gas. My heart pops around my ribcage as I approach the field on a dirt road that slowly becomes hardly more than a pair of shallow grooves in the pale earth.

Putting my car in park, I kill the engine. The low rumble of the tractor greets me as I grab the plate, push open my door, and hop out.

The green, grassy smell of freshly cut hay fills my head. Hint of diesel too.

I can't stop smiling.

The tractor turns again, giving me a perfect view of the driver. My stomach takes a tumble when I see the familiar profile of Ryder's face: square jaw, straight nose, full mouth. His overgrown hair curls out from underneath a backward baseball hat.

Christ, what is it about a backward hat that gets me every damn time?

The light catches on the gold chain he's wearing around his neck, making it glint through the tractor's windows. I can just make out the white tee he's wearing. It hugs his shoulders and biceps in a way that makes my middle feel hollowed out.

The only possible thing that could make him hotter is if he were singing. Smiling. *Sparkling*, the way he did at the hospital.

I'm on it.

Throwing up my arm in greeting, I head his way.

CHAPTER 6
"She Thinks My Tractor's Sexy"
Ryder

I blink.

Blink again.

Then I lean forward, squinting through the windshield to get a better look. My heart launches into my throat.

Is that—

Is she—but why—it has to be her—the dark hair, and the ridiculously enthusiastic, and ridiculously cute, way she's waving—

Wait a second.

Wait.

Is the girl in the teeny-tiny shorts and tall boots a mirage, or is she actually waving me down? She's too damn adorable to possibly exist in real life.

She's also wearing a sling, her other arm tucked against her chest.

I'm tired as shit, so it's entirely possible I've started imagining things. Probably time to quit for the day.

But judging by the way my dick perks up, the girl is very real, and I very much want to say hello.

Which is a problem.

"Jesus fucking Christ, Billie," I murmur as I cut the engine. "What the hell are you doing here?"

But watching her head toward me, I still throw open the door. I still smile and say, "You know the rules, little lady. No one rides for free."

"Of course I know the rules." She holds up the plate she's carrying. "Why do you think I brought treats?"

The motion of her straightening her arm over her head really pushes her tits out. Are *those* the treats?

My immediate reaction is to try to erase that thought from my head. Usually I can tamp shit like this down no problem. Now, though, my effort to think *friendly, safe* thoughts hits a snag.

The idea that these feelings are 'friendly' is a lie, and you know it.

I could politely but firmly suggest Billie head back home. That's what I would've done before that night at the rodeo. But now…

I don't wanna numb this shit that I'm feeling. Maybe because that accident has me thinking a lot about how short—precious—life can be, and I wonder if I'm wasting it by just surviving my days. Because that's what I've been doing by holding everyone and everything at arm's length.

If I'm being honest, part of me has been waiting three long weeks for Billie to show up. I contemplated driving over to the Wallace Ranch to check on her, but that felt a step too far.

I'd started to think she wasn't gonna come see me

at all. Now that she's here, I'm not about to spend another night working alone, trying *not* to think about her or the things she made me feel that night at the rodeo.

A little flirting never hurt anyone, right?

Shifting in my seat, I lean an elbow on my knee and clear my throat. "What kinda treats we talkin' about?"

"The kind you're gonna like."

Kill me now.

She stands beside the tractor's front left wheel, looking tiny next to the seven-foot-tall behemoth.

Squinting, she looks up at me. "So you gonna ask me to come up there or what?"

"Billie Wallace, we both know you're coming whether I ask you to or not."

Her lips twitch. "That's awful cocky of you, thinking you could make me—"

"What?" Fuck, I'm still smiling.

Worst of all, I *like* that I'm smiling at her like a big, dumb goofball.

I can't flirt with Billie like this anymore. Have our interactions always been so…inappropriate, or is this something new?

How do I not know the answer to that question?

"You're cocky thinking that you could make me do anything I didn't want to." She holds my gaze with the confidence of someone who knows she's won.

Oh, darlin', you'd best believe you'd want me to make you come.

Hell, give me a minute, less than that, and I'd have you begging for it.

Damn it, this was *not* a good idea.

I don't even know what "this" is, but in my gut, I know I gotta cut this shit off at the pass, or—

Or what? What's worse than sleepwalking through your life?

Getting crushed by grief, dipshit.

"I had a bad day." Her mirth fades. "And my arm still makes it tough to sleep. I could really use a pick-me-up."

I frown. Next thing I know, I'm climbing out of the cab and I'm standing beside her. The scent of something girly fills my head. Shampoo, maybe, or perfume. It smells like peaches, and my heart contracts wondering if Billie has a hard time washing her hair with her broken elbow.

"You in pain? What can I do? Do you think we should go back to the ER, or—"

"I'm fine." Her eyes flick over my arms and chest before returning to my face. "Honestly, the doc said my elbow is healing beautifully."

Gotta be a good sign, right, that she's only wearing a sling and not a cast?

"Should you be driving, though?"

Her smirk is back. "I'd like it better if you drove."

"You really wanna go for a tractor ride?"

"Ry, I spent the day chained to a desk. Next to my *Dad*. With a *broken arm*. I'd love to go for a ride, yes."

I'm smiling again too. "That desk stuff don't sound like much fun." I nod at the plate. "Talk to me about this situation."

"Mom's blondies." She offers me the plate, and I take it and remove the tinfoil. The rich smells of butter and chocolate flood my senses. "She made 'em just how you like—extra chocolate chips, no nuts."

"Yeah, because nuts are gross."

"*You're* gross."

"You're smiling, ain't you?"

Her eyes are soft when they meet mine. "I am. Yeah. Thank you." Then she glances at the field. "You planning to finish cutting this bit, or…?"

I sigh. "I was, yeah."

"Working late." She cuts me a questioning glance, and my pulse hiccups.

Yeah, Billie, I've been working fourteen-, fifteen-, sixteen-hour days. Because ever since I saw you at the rodeo, I can't sleep.

Can't stop thinking about you or the loneliness that is pressing in on me from all sides all of a sudden. Three weeks of this torture, and I'm losing my damn mind.

I look away. "Lots to do. Lots goin' on right now on the ranch."

"It looks great. You should be proud."

Nodding, I grab a blondie and take a big bite. Its buttery sweetness is absolutely delicious. Paired with the bite of the semisweet chocolate, the whole thing is a mouth orgasm.

Why is that the metaphor I come up with while Billie is at my elbow? Her gaze is steady, curious too, as she watches me eat.

"That's good," I manage. "Real good."

"You're welcome." She grabs a blondie too, and I have to look away when she gets this look of pure bliss on her face as she eats. Only, I can't help sneaking another glance her way, because I'm a masochist like that.

Closing her eyes, she chews thoughtfully for a minute. "Do you ever get this feeling—like, you don't know how you're gonna survive the rest of your life?"

I let out a bark of laughter. I don't know what the hell else to do with myself when she asks a question like that.

I know all about surviving. Beyond that, I got nothing.

"I'm gonna need you to explain that one," I say, if only to buy myself some time. I like this side of Billie—the one that takes the deep dive into ideas and life—a little too much. Probably why I never let myself experience it before now. I always stopped her before our conversations could get too…real.

Now I'm feeling seen, I'm curious, and I'm turned on, and I like this shit just a little too much.

Billie sucks a bit of melted chocolate off her thumb. I nearly choke.

Or I really do choke, because Billie's expression contracts. "You okay?"

"Yep." I pound my fist against my chest. "Went down the wrong pipe."

"I *do* owe you an accompaniment to the ER, so just say the word and we'll be on our way."

I laugh. "You don't owe me anything. Explain."

"You sure you're okay?"

"I'm sure."

"Okay." She takes a deep breath. "You know my dad has me doing the ranch's bookkeeping."

"Yep."

"I did well in those online classes I took after I graduated high school because, well, I like to learn new stuff, and it gave me a sense of purpose, which was helpful."

"You always did well in school. No surprise you crushed those classes."

"Well, when I was younger, I thought I might like

doing it as a career. The accounting stuff. Or, at the very least, I wouldn't hate it. Dad was so convinced that I was the perfect person to take over that job. He'd outsourced it until then to an accountant in Austin, but he'd wanted to bring the role in-house for a while."

I tuck the tinfoil back over the blondies so the flies don't get at them. "Makes sense. Especially with y'all expanding your operation."

"Right. So anyway, I agreed to do it. But I began to figure out pretty quickly that I didn't love accounting. Mom and Dad were so proud, though, and I'm decent with numbers, so"—she shrugs—"I did it. Now I'm realizing that I was kind of sleepwalking through the past few years. That's why I decided I wanted to learn barrel racing when we hired Ava and started our training program. Seemed like a random idea at the time—most girls, you know they start that shit young, training as soon as they can stay upright in the saddle. Thinking back on it, though...I knew I needed an outlet. Something to wake me up. Being in the arena, having an excuse to work with Ava and her team, being on horseback again—it was what kept me from losing my mind sitting at a desk all day. Having that to look forward to."

"And now that you don't have that outlet..." I glance at the arm she cradles carefully against her chest. "It's really hitting home how unhappy you are sitting at a desk."

A look of almost pained relief washes over her face. "Yes. Wow, Ry, for someone so good-looking, you're awfully intuitive."

"Deadly combination."

"Makes sense why you had to resuscitate me that one time."

I roll my eyes. My face hurts from smiling so much. "So now you want to cut some hay with me because you can't get on a horse, and you also can't stand the idea of going back to work and entering expenses into a spreadsheet for eight hours straight because it makes you feel like you're asleep at the wheel again."

Now the look on her face is one of utter delight. "You really are deadly."

"The hay thinks so too." I offer her my hand, setting the plate of blondies on top of the tractor's rear wheel well. "All right then, little lady, you paid the fee. Now let's get to work."

She grins. "This is the kind of work I like."

"Figuring out a way to survive your life? Fuck that. Billie, we're gonna get you *thriving*."

That's rich, coming from you.

Then again, aren't I the expert in what being in survival mode costs you? I don't want Billie to have to numb herself like I do. I want more for her.

What if you wanted more for yourself too?

A buzz of awareness zips up my arm when she takes my hand and meets my eyes. It happens again, the charged exchange of understanding between us as we hold eye contact for a beat too long.

I wish I'd known you were feeling this way sooner.

I wish I could tell you I've felt the same, and I know I need to make some changes, but I'm scared out of my fucking mind. The concept of "thriving" is foreign to me too. Maybe we learn how to do it together?

That's just dumb, though. I'm fine. Everything is fine.

Bullshit.

One thing I am certain of is that I don't want this conversation to end. Rare for me to be able to talk to people honestly this way.

Even rarer for them to be honest with me too.

"Are you?" Her throat bobs on a swallow. "Thriving?"

Not by a long shot.

"Tonight ain't about me." I lift our joined hands, guiding her onto the tractor's step. "Go slow, yeah? I'm not wiping your ass if you break the other arm too."

She throws back her head and cackles. "That would not be thriving, no."

I try very hard not to look at said ass and her legs as she carefully climbs into the cab of the tractor and stands against the far window, her head ducked beneath the ceiling. Billie usually wears jeans—as ranchers, we all do—so to see this much skin is…a lot. I notice a birthmark high up on her left thigh. It's light, barely visible, and it's shaped like a spoon of all things.

Makes me think of how it'd feel to spoon her. Which is fucking weird, but whatever. Billie is tough as nails. In bed, though, I bet she'd be all softness.

Soft skin. Soft moans. Soft little cuddler who'd tuck in nice and tight as the small spoon to my big one.

Even though the late September evening is mild, I'm sweating by the time I climb into the cab while she continues to wait, standing. I set the plate on top of the little cooler behind my seat.

The only seat in this tractor.

Fuck me for life.

We have newer machines on Lucky River Ranch, ones that have multiple seats and are a more comfortable ride. But this particular tractor is my favorite. It's the same model that was Dad's favorite. I remember feeling like the king of the world when I would sit on his lap way high up in the cab. It felt like we were flying.

Billie Wallace is gonna have to sit on *my* lap now. And I'm gonna have to try with all my might not to get hard with that perfect peach of an ass pressed against me while we bounce around this godforsaken field.

Why does sitting suddenly feel more dangerous than spooning?

Too late to turn back now, though. I sit and try to make light of my terrible predicament.

I pat my knee. "You're right here."

"I prefer here"—she bends down and settles her ass smack dab in the center of my lap—"thank you very much."

"You don't listen to a damn thing I say, do you?"

She turns her head to give me a hot little look. "You'd be bored if I did."

Then she leans back a little, resting her shoulder blades against my chest, and I close my eyes and take a deep, steadying breath through my nose. She's so warm.

She smells so good.

Her body feels so fucking good tucked against mine. She is temptation personified. Not just bodily temptation. But she also tempts me to let down my guard. Feel my feelings. Be fully present in the moment.

An ominous heaviness gathers low in my belly. Gritting my teeth, I start the ignition. The tractor rumbles to life.

Dear Lord and Savior, please help me keep my shit together tonight.

Then I wrap my arms around Billie so I can take the wheel.

We sway together as we start to move, and I nearly bite off my tongue when the side of her breast brushes my arm.

Billie shifts a little, turning her head to look out the window. My chest cramps thinking she must really be unhappy if she's this quiet.

"What do you think you're missing?" I start to make the turn at the end of a row, careful not to jostle her bad arm. "Being a bookkeeper?"

She turns her head the other way, giving me a view of her profile. Her mouth looks especially lush from this angle, and I tamp down the urge to remember how soft her lips were.

How they tasted.

"You know what's funny? I've been wondering that myself. And then when you and I played that game at the hospital—"

I groan. "God, that was cheesy. The humming? So embarrassing. Sorry."

"It wasn't cheesy at all." She puts a hand on my knee. "It was great. You were totally lit up, and it made me realize that the only place I'm lit up that way is when I'm…outside. Moving my body. It's when I'm working with people and I'm around animals and just, like, real *life*, you know? Remember that time you found me in the barn in the middle of the night and I was cuddling with Meredith?"

I let out a soft chuckle, my pulse skipping a beat at the memory. "We talked about that at the hospital. You were having those bad dreams then, right?"

"I was. And you made me feel better by playing your guitar. I hummed the song, and you picked it right up."

RYDER

I groan again, despite the weird flutter that happens inside my chest. I loved that guitar. But I stopped playing after Mom and Dad died, and I haven't so much as touched the damn thing since.

Last I saw it, the guitar was in the old storage shed on the Rivers' side of the ranch. No clue if it's still there.

Not like I'd wanna play if it *were* still around. But if I did—

"Do you ever think about picking up the guitar again? You were really good, and I had fun playing that game with you."

I swallow. Why is my throat tight? Is it the way Billie can read my mind?

Or is it the memory of how happy I felt—how alive—whenever I played music? No one's ever pushed me to take it back up. I think my brothers and my friends know it's a sore subject.

I don't know *why* it's a sore subject. Music, singing, playing…maybe I associate all that with my parents? Our time as a whole, happy family?

I wonder if I stopped playing because music made me feel, period. And feeling got dangerous after I lost my parents.

My guitar had the power to make me feel happy or sad or lonely or excited or turned on. Which meant I *didn't* have power over my emotions—the music did. And once my parents died, I was afraid that playing music would make me feel things I couldn't handle. I've always known that grief is lurking in the corners of my consciousness, and if I played music, I worried it would flood my body and I'd drown in it.

So I set down my guitar and never picked it back up again.

My chest spasms, a vast, empty feeling opening up inside me.

That seemed like the right choice at the time. Now? I'm not so sure. I remember feeling proud that I didn't cry at my parents' funeral. Come to think of it, I haven't cried since.

But closing off my feelings might be more of a problem than a cure. Am I ready to face that fact, though? What if I let myself experience that grief and it absolutely destroys me?

"Nah." I sniff. "Don't got the time."

"That's a lie. You should do it."

"You should mind your own damn business."

One side of that pretty little mouth kicks up. "I know. So anyway, the other night I did it again—I had a nightmare, so I snuck into the barn and I was cuddling the horses and I was feeling real sorry for myself that I only got to be around them on my own time. Dad runs a tight ship, and he wants me in the office seven to four every day, five days a week."

"Brutal."

"No shit." She puts her hands on the wheel inside mine. "Can I drive?"

"Do you know how?" I can't help but notice how different our hands look next to each other. Hers are paler than mine, and about half the size.

"No." Her pinkie darts out to brush my thumb knuckle. "But you could teach me."

It's all I can do not to hang my head. This girl ain't afraid to *push* my goddamn *buttons*.

Problem is, I like it.

"Should you be driving with that hand?" I motion to her broken arm.

"My elbow's busted, not my hand. I'll be fine. But maybe you should keep your hands close to mine on the wheel, just in case."

I chuckle, a low, gravelly sound I don't recognize. "Billie."

"I know."

"*Billie*."

"I *know*. Now show me how to drive this tractor, damn it!"

"Fine!"

"Fine!" She's giggling now, and so am I.

I carefully glide my hands over hers, ignoring the way my core pulses at the smoothness of her skin, and move them to the correct position on the wheel. "Ten and two. Nice and easy."

"Just like me," she deadpans.

"Hey. You're not nice."

"But you are easy."

"Easy to please, yeah."

"I bet you are."

My dick twitches. "That tool been buggin' you? The bull rider." I only ask the question because I need to change the subject, quick.

Only this is not a subject we should really be talking about either.

"Xander..." She sighs, and together we make the turn around another row. "I don't know. I think he might be history."

Relief swoops through me. *Thank Christ*.

"Good. He sure as hell isn't gonna help you thrive."

"What should I do, Ryder?" She pauses. "What would *you* do?"

"Not date bull riders. That's just life 101."

Somehow she manages to elbow me. "Talk about someone needing to mind their own business. I'm talking about my *life*, not who I'm sleeping with."

"I think..." *I actually can't think when I have you in my arms.* "I think you try to follow that feeling."

"What feeling?"

"The one you get when you're doing the stuff you mentioned. Like, how did you feel during that race before you fell?"

That makes her smile. "I felt free. And scared, but also...alive? Like fully, completely, totally alive. Connected to the universe, as dumb as that sounds. I was *happy*. So freaking happy, Ry, I can't even tell you. But I think you get it, though, because it looked like that's the way you felt when you and I were playing your cute little humming game."

The tightness in my throat returns with a vengeance. "It wasn't cute."

"Can we play it again right now? Pretty please?"

Part of me really, really wants to say yes. I loved revisiting my favorite old songs with her.

Right now, though, my feelings are a flashing neon sign that says *Danger, danger. Uncharted territory.*

"Another time," I manage. "I understand your daddy's thought process—why he wants an in-house bookkeeper. I just can't figure out why he thought *you'd* be right for the job. Clearly you're not meant for an office gig."

Billie turns to look at me for a second. I get why she's confused. I had fun playing that singing game too. But we're not kids anymore, and I need to keep some boundaries in place here. Hence the reroute back to the original thread of our conversation.

"I'm gonna find out, you know," Billie says.

"What's that?"

"Why you're afraid to play." She turns back to the windshield. "So anyway, I think my parents don't believe it's 'proper' for a girl to do the kind of things I like doing." Her smile fades. "Dad keeps saying I'll get used to working at a desk. I want to make him proud and do right by my family. I just…"

She's not able to finish the thought because we have to turn again. That's when I realize my hands are still on hers even though she's clearly gotten the hang of driving. This definitely isn't the first time Billie's driven a tractor.

It is, however, the first time she's confided in me. Questioned me.

Called me out.

I like her brazenness just a little too much.

CHAPTER 7
Where There's Smoke
Ryder

"Hey, dickhead. Thanks for the invite."

Looking up from packing the ATV, I nearly have a heart attack when I see Colt standing inside the barn.

Not because I'm surprised he's here. But because I may or may not have tugged one out the other day while thinking about coming on his sister's tits.

I'm going straight to hell.

"Hey." I straighten, groaning inwardly when I see that, like me, Colt is also dressed head to toe in camo. Hell, even his blind case and hat are printed in the green and brown pattern. I'd hoped to go hunting alone today—clear my head some—but obviously that's not going to happen now. "What're you doing here? Doesn't Dean have soccer?"

"I'm keeping you company. Mom and Dad have Dean today." He strides across the barn and sets his gun case in the back of the ATV next to mine. Then he squints at me. "Why're you sneaking around like this?

Going hunting all by your lonesome? Makes me think you're hiding something."

My pulse picks up pace. "Uh—"

"I'm just kidding, dude." His face splits into a smile. "Wyatt said you ditched the herd to hunt, so figured I'd keep you company. How the hell are you? I know today's a tough one for y'all. I brought some cigars. Tequila too"—he pats his chest pocket—"so we could pour one out for Robbie and Anne."

It's been thirteen years to the day since my parents passed. But hearing their names said out loud *still* makes my chest hurt.

Add that to the fact that my friend came to be with me on a shit day, and my eyes are misting over. I blink hard. Try to breathe around the lump in my throat.

I woke up after a shitty night's sleep feeling like I got run over. I expected to toss and turn; it's the same rigamarole on this day every year.

What's not the same? How staying busy hasn't eased the ache deep in my center. Usually I can spend a few hours working cattle or mowing hay, and I'll feel better.

Less flattened, at least.

Today, though? Today I feel like I'm coming out of my skin. Like my grief threatens to burn me alive from the inside out.

Which is why I decided to give hunting a try. It's dove season in this part of Texas, and Lucky River Ranch is a hunter's wet dream this time of year.

Going out to sit in a blind is also a last ditch attempt to quiet the screaming pain inside me. You gotta be fully alert when you have a rifle in your hands. And sometimes being out in nature, surrounded by nothing but bird calls and the sound of the wind through the trees, is the best way to clear your mind.

The best way to get a grip on your emotions.

Numb them, really.

I can't help but think that this tidal wave of grief has something to do with my conversation with Billie last week. There was a rawness to her words, and the way she felt, that has me feeling raw too.

Probably because she's being honest with herself in a way you haven't, and you know it's time to make some changes, or you're going to end up working yourself to death with nothing real to show for it.

Work is easy.

Grief, connection, honesty—those things aren't.

I wince at the electric shock that ricochets through my breastbone. My body knows the truth. My mind, though, doesn't want any part of it. Apparently neither does my heart.

Which sucks. I feel like I was able to let my guard down with Billie. I was moving in the right direction. But now I have my walls back up, and it's that one step forward, two steps back bullshit that makes me wanna scream with frustration.

I know I gotta go easy on myself. Still feels all kinds of wrong to keep this conversation with my best friend surface-level.

To keep the grief at arm's length. I know better, but turns out it's really hard to *do* better.

Colt rounds the ATV and puts a hand on my shoulder. "You all right there, bud?"

I nod. "Yeah. Glad you're here."

"Heard you been workin' over-overtime. Which is a lot, even for you."

"Word travels way too fast around here."

Colt smiles. "That's just us lookin' out for you. Speaking of, thanks for bein' so good to Billie. My family and I appreciate it, brother. She's been smiling from ear to ear the past week, so whatever wisdom you imparted during her visit, it helped."

So Colt heard about the tractor ride. *Of course he did.*

A white-hot wave of misery moves through me, even as my pulse picks up at the memory of Billie's face after she let her thoughts air out.

Relief.

Confusion.

Hope.

She's hurting, but she's still showing up. Still trying. And her courage—

Yeah, it's fucking sexy. And scary.

Colt is a crucial part of my support system. Especially now that my brothers are all paired off and they're focused on growing their own families. Him showing up today is a case in point. I can't risk losing him by starting some weird hookup situation with his sister.

Let's not forget, Colt's wife betrayed him in a way that still affects him. Deeply. Loyalty matters more than anything to my friend—to all of us, really—and I'd rather die than sneak around on Colt the way Abby did. There's only so much betrayal one man can withstand before he breaks.

I'm not gonna be the one to break Colt Wallace.

Clearing my throat, I say, "Billie was sweet to come all this way just to bring me dessert."

Colt chuckles. "My sister is many things, Ryder, but sweet sure as hell ain't one of 'em."

We climb into the ATV and head out into the ardent autumn sunshine. It's a beautiful day, the breeze cool, not a cloud in the sky. October blew in this week with a major storm, but in its wake, we've been enjoying cold mornings, crisp air, and all-around gorgeous weather.

"Why do you think your old man is so hellbent on her being in the office?" I ease off the gas as we cross a small creek. "Billie."

Colt digs a cigar out of his pocket. "I think it's his way of trying to get her to settle down."

"Why the rush? She's still young."

"I hear you. She's a free spirit, no doubt about that. I'm all for letting her do what she wants. But my parents—you know they're traditional. Mom and Dad are old souls. Always have been."

"Mine were too. I think it might've been a generational thing?"

"Maybe. I don't think they understand her. Or maybe they don't understand why she hasn't figured out her life yet. Why she hasn't gotten married, or at least why she doesn't have a steady guy in her life."

I nod. "At her age, you were married."

"Yup. I wouldn't say I regret marrying Abby so young." He rolls the cigar between his fingers. "But maybe…I don't know, shit could've gone down a little differently if we'd had more time to grow up and have some fun before settling down."

"Maybe. Although you did get Dean out of the deal."

He smiles. "Best thing I ever did. But…"

He takes a long enough pause to make me turn my head. "Should I be asking if *you're* okay?"

Colt lifts a shoulder. "Just wish he had a dad *and* a mom around. He misses Abby. You know the grief. Comes and goes. It's complicated."

"Right. Yeah." It's a lame response, but I'm swimming in…something that doesn't feel great. Sorrow, I guess?

"Anyway." He shifts in his seat. "My parents' intentions are good when it comes to Billie. I think they believe that if they help her get on the right path, her life will fall into place. Yes, she's a free spirit, but she's also a romantic. She wants to be in love. Pretty sure she wants a family someday. Mom and Dad know that, and this is their way of helping her support that dream."

I chew on my lip. "What if it's the right path but the wrong way of getting her there, though?"

"That's up to Billie." Colt shrugs. "What is it that Cash is always saying to Mollie?"

I smile. "Cowgirls can't be tamed."

"Right. We gotta trust Billie to figure out what's right and to advocate for herself too. I've nudged Dad a bit. Told him he needed to give Billie some space. I know she doesn't love the bookkeeping gig, but she also hasn't really said much about doing something else, so…"

I swerve to avoid hitting an armadillo that darts onto the path, and the ATV groans. "Critters are out today."

"They're always out," Colt says with another chuckle. "Billie will get her life together. We all do eventually."

"Do you have your life together? Because I sure as hell don't."

He chuckles. "Fuck no."

"Good. Not 'good,' I don't mean that. But I'm glad I'm not the only one struggling to figure it out."

I feel Colt's eyes on me. "Nothing wrong with being a work in progress."

"Yup. I just…" Running a hand over my face, I sigh. Usually I'd shut the hell up at this point. But today, I can't seem to quit running my mouth. "I dunno. I'm feeling frustrated with myself right now."

"Why?"

I'm all mixed up, and it's hard to tell up from down. "Fuck if I know."

Colt nods. "Give yourself a little grace, yeah? You been through it, and today is not the day to beat yourself up."

"Thanks." My eyes prick. Is the fact that I'm about to cry good? Bad? Both? "You're a good friend."

I'm not. How could I be, thinking about your sister like this? Letting her flirt with me even though I know it can't go anywhere? Am I leading her on? Or am I just trying to be a good friend to her too?

Do I need her honesty—her bravery—as much as I need your friendship?

"I'm the best fuckin' friend ever. You're welcome." Colt's accent is thicker. He's in his feels too. "Maybe… you gotta release the pressure somehow."

I lift my fingers on the wheel. "That's why we're out here."

He clamps the cigar between his teeth. "Let's do it, then."

Only, sitting in a blind all day, enjoying the fresh air, nips of good tequila, and my friend's company somehow leaves me feeling *more* agitated.

RYDER

I have half a mind to skip supper at the New House altogether. Maybe I really do need some solitude. Or do I need a square meal and the company of my family to soften the edges of a horrendous day?

It's a bad day for them too. I gotta remember that. They need me as much as I need them. So I grab a shower and head to the New House.

We sit around the big oak table in the kitchen, just like we always do. But tonight, everyone is quiet. Subdued, even. Pretty standard for the anniversary of Mom and Dad's death.

Cash will shed a tear or two. Wyatt and Sawyer will give everyone bear hugs. Duke always cries.

But me? I can usually power my way through. All of a sudden, though, it's a struggle to stay in control. To keep it all in, the sadness and the regret and the gut punch of grief.

Again, is it a good thing that I can't keep these feelings at bay? Or am I finally going to lose my goddamn mind feeling my feelings tonight? Billie's made me want to turn on the spigot of my emotions and experiences. But now I'm realizing I had no plan of action beyond that.

What do I *do* with this grief?

How do I sit with it and not let it pull me under?

Patsy gives each of a big old hug while we clean up from dinner. One by one, my brothers and their partners head home.

For Sally and Wyatt, home is the old farmhouse Garrett lived in after his divorce from Mollie's mom.

For Ava and Sawyer and the girls, it's the house we grew up in, which we recently renovated so Sawyer could have a family home of his own.

Wheeler and Duke are splitting their time between his cottage on the Rivers' side of the ranch and her townhome in Dallas. Along with Mollie and Cash, they're the last couples left in the kitchen. I busy myself at the sink, pretending to wash dishes that are already clean.

"Hey." Duke leans his side against the nearby countertop.

"Y'all don't have to wait on me." I tilt a plate underneath the faucet. "Have a good night."

Wheeler comes up behind Duke and rests her cheek on his shoulder. "You were awful quiet tonight, Ryder."

"Tired. That's all."

"Is it?"

"Yeah."

A pause. That's when Duke reaches over and shuts off the water. "Can we talk for a minute?"

CHAPTER 8
Breaking and Entering
Ryder

Resting my wrists on the lip of the sink, I sigh. "Sure."

"I'm worried about you." Duke's eyes burn a hole through my head. "You wanna come hang at the cottage with me and Wheeler for a bit?"

Wheeler reaches out to squeeze my arm. "You're always welcome. Duke's s'mores game has gotten pretty excellent."

"I'm an expert." Duke pats his chest proudly. "Wheeler has me makin' 'em every damn night, so I'd better be."

"You're the best." She grins up at him.

Grabbing a towel, I use it to wipe my hands. "Y'all clearly need to get a room."

"We *have* been making something *else* every night too." Wheeler's lips twitch.

Mollie nods sagely from her perch at the table where she's nursing her daughter. "It's so good when you're pregnant."

"What is?" Cash says with a smile.

So many babies.

So many *people* and families and new beginnings.

I'm thrilled for my brothers. Genuinely. When they're happy, I'm happy.

Can you be happy, though, when you're kinda-sorta lying to yourself? When you haven't faced shit in years, and now all of a sudden, it's coming back to haunt you for reasons you don't entirely understand?

All I know is that I can barely breathe around the moon in my throat. Excusing myself, I make a quick exit.

Next thing I know, I'm in my truck and driving through the deepening darkness. My hands shake as I guide the truck to the Rivers' side of the ranch.

When the green clapboard siding of the storage shed comes into view, a rush of heat hits the backs of my eyes.

The house I grew up in was barely a thousand square feet, with very little storage or attic space. So my dad built this little shed beside the equipment barn to serve as a storage space.

The shed is where we kept all our shit when we were growing up. Hopefully no one's messed with it since I was here last. Why would they? Last I checked years ago, there wasn't anything of value in the shed. Just a bunch of photograph albums, bins of our artwork from school, and other random stuff like bikes and baby walkers.

My legs feel like Jell-O as I walk across the gravel road, which has been taken over by weeds. The shed's never had a lock, so I'm able to walk right through the door.

I'm hit by the smells of hay and must. Underneath all

that, though, I can detect the faintest trace of a familiar scent.

Home. Fresh laundry and rose-scented lotion.

Yeah, this obviously isn't the physical structure I grew up in. But this is the stuff I grew up *with*. I guess that particular scent's clung to our things the same way it clung to the house itself.

My chest cramps as memories unfurl inside my head. Mom rubbing lotion into her hands after doing the dishes. The way my stomach would growl when the smell of whatever she was cooking filled the house at the end of the day. Waking up to the smells of coffee and fried bacon. How Mom would let us sleep with her on the rare occasions Dad was out of town. I remember how his pillow smelled like the Listerine mouthwash he used.

Tears leak out of my eyes. I don't try to fight them. Surely that's a step in the right direction?

Instead, I reach overhead to pull on a string. I pull it again, and again. Nothing happens.

Welp, the light doesn't work anymore.

I turn on my phone's flashlight and wade forward. The shed is still, warm, and quiet.

It's also a mess, which is a relief. No one's touched it.

I don't spend much time browsing. Hurts too much to see the old crib Mom kept for God knows what reason, or the tarnished gold figurines of trophies that poke over the top of a nearby box. Cash was always the overachiever of the family, so my guess is those trophies belong to him.

I guide the beam of my flashlight over the undulating landscape of stuff.

So. Much. Stuff.

Then again, Mom and Dad did have five kids. They were so proud of us, and I get why they didn't want to throw away anything they didn't have to.

The light catches on something reflective, and I blink at the sudden flash. My stomach seizes as the familiar curves of a guitar come into focus. Reaching over a pile of old *National Geographic* magazines, I carefully curl my fingers around the guitar's neck and lift it up.

It's an acoustic guitar, the one Mom and Dad gave me for Christmas when I was in seventh grade. Up until then, I'd rented one from school. But I loved playing so much that my parents bought me my own.

It was a big deal considering we really had no money growing up. Hell, my brothers and I only recently paid off the mountain of debt my parents left when they died.

My throat closes in all over again when I think about all the sacrifices they made to give us the best childhood ever.

I wish they were still around.

The force of that desire, the weight of it, knocks the wind out of me.

This is why I don't revisit the past.

This is why I don't play the damn guitar anymore.

Before the accident, I never went anywhere without this guitar. That's why I had it with me the night I played Taylor Swift for Billie. I loved showing off, playing songs by ear. She was so freaking *delighted* that I'd even try to learn what she liked.

The skin on my face feels tight from tears that have already dried. A voice in my head repeats over and over again that I should put the guitar back down. What business do I have playing music? I'm a grown-ass adult. I got things to do. Sleep to catch up on. Feelings to avoid.

Only I'm not trying to avoid them anymore. I'm trying to feel them, sit with them without dying, and I think this guitar might help me do that.

Ain't gonna be any sleep for me tonight anyway.

Maybe…hell, maybe playing will also help me capture some of that joy, that exhilaration, I saw on Billie's face when she was racing. I can't stop thinking about it. The good's gotta come with the bad, right? Right now, all I'm feeling is shitty stuff. Grief and sorrow and regret. But there's two sides to every coin.

What if joy's waiting for me on the other side of this valley of awfulness?

So before I can talk myself out of it, I tuck the guitar under my arm and head outside. There's a full moon tonight, and the gravel drive is lit up enough for me to see across the yard.

My knees crack as I sit on the step by the door and settle the guitar on my lap. Gliding my fingers along the dusty strings—by some miracle, all six are still there—emotion clogs my throat. I realize I've already curled my body around the guitar the way I did when I would play, left hand on the neck, right arm draped over the front of the instrument. I'm leaning forward a little, just enough so I can see the strings.

Muscle memory is a weird fucking thing.

The knife in my pocket digs into my thigh. I suddenly remember that time Mom lost her wedding ring. Dad used his knife to cut a length of kitchen twine and tied it in a little circle before slipping it onto her finger.

Touching my fingertips to the strings, I hesitate. What if this just makes the grief worse by unleashing…I don't know, memories that will kill me to revisit?

Today, I faced down a five-hundred-pound bull, had several near misses with a huge rattler that followed me around everywhere, and dodged a literal bullet when Colt's rifle misfired.

And yet *playing a guitar* is the thing that scares the living daylight out of me.

Which means I gotta play, right? Otherwise this will haunt me too—the knowledge that I was too chickenshit to pick out a single song.

I brush my fingers over the strings, and I'm shocked when I let out a bark of laughter. The guitar is horribly out of tune.

I take a minute to tune the strings as best as I can. Years of heat and humidity have clearly done a number on my instrument.

I'm taken aback by the knowledgeable way my fingers turn the knobs that tighten the strings. It's like I've been possessed by the ghost of my middle school music teacher, Mr. Martinez, who taught me how to tune my guitar. The experience of not knowing how to do something, but still doing it, is a mind fuck.

I strum the strings. They need to be replaced, but I get them to a good enough place to play.

My fingers slow. I adjust my leg, straightening my knee a little.

Next thing I know, I'm playing a song.

My whole body rises on a tide of *feeling* that has goose bumps breaking out on my arms when I realize—

Hell, it's a Brooks & Dunn song. A *love* song—"Ain't Nothing 'Bout You."

Brooks & Dunn was Garrett Luck's favorite band. Mom played their music a lot, too, on the little portable speaker she kept on the windowsill in the kitchen. She was always shimmying to one country song or another, with regular appearances by Fleetwood Mac, Carole King, and Bonnie Raitt interspersed between Tim McGraw and Trisha Yearwood.

I don't sing the lyrics, but I do hum along as I pick out the notes. I only stop when a tear lands on the top of my thumb.

I can't breathe.

I can only hang my head, my fingertips falling off the strings, and try not to die from feeling, well, all these fucking feelings.

Mom, I wish I could call you.

I wish I could hear your voice and see your eyes light up when you smile.

I wish we could be together again, all seven of us, and talk about everything and nothing over the King Ranch casserole you'd make. The one with the corn tortillas and chicken and cheese? God, that was good. We all loved it so much there'd never be any leftovers even though you'd double the recipe.

Remember that, Mom? Because I do.

My heart feels bruised, like it's been run over and left for dead.

It's too much.

This is all too fucking much.

This is what I was worried about. I'm sitting with my grief, and it is absolutely kicking my ass.

I start to play again, only because I don't know what

else to do. The stuff inside me is too big and too heavy to keep inside, so I let it out note by note with my fingertips.

Now I'm playing a sad Brooks & Dunn song—"You're Gonna Miss Me When I'm Gone." And while I feel sad playing it—and angry and lonely and drained—when I'm done, I feel…

No better. But lighter, maybe? Like I can breathe a little easier.

Shit, I just survived something, didn't I?

I just connected with feelings—a side of myself—I've had closed off, and I didn't die.

I just took a swan dive into the grief I haven't let myself feel in more than a decade, and playing my guitar from middle school, of all things, is what kept me from drowning in pain.

What in the world? Can simply acknowledging your feelings make them less terrifying?

Cash always says the universe is one sick motherfucker. I believe him now.

Billie, this is all your fault. She's the one who put the idea of *connection* in my head. She's the one who had me humming songs and being playful and wanting…I don't know, wanting to feel *more* than mostly numb.

I do not feel numb right now.

Flattened? Yes.

Exhausted and terrified and lost? Yes, yes, and *yes*.

But I gotta give credit where credit is due. Billie was onto something here. What if I kept playing?

What if I leaned into this instead of running scared?

You risk even more pain. More loss. No big deal.

My life—it's good enough, right? I don't gotta open

myself up to all this shit to do my job and keep my family's legacy alive.

But you do need to open up if you wanna be free, truly and deeply free. The way Billie was in the arena.

And the thought of living the rest of my life holed up in this weird little fortress I've built, safe but never free, distanced from everyone, distanced from *myself*—

My center spasms.

Fuck me.

Really, fuck Billie Wallace. I was *fine* before. I'm fine now.

But suddenly, fine ain't good enough.

Whatever Billie gave me, I want more of it.

I wanna thank her for getting my ass out here tonight. Yeah, playing music again hurts like hell. It's also the first time in forever I had the courage and the patience to *feel* something.

And turns out, you have to *feel* to, well, feel better.

Finishing the song, I rise to my feet. Dust off my jeans.

I head home, my guitar riding shotgun beside me in the passenger seat. I have some ideas. And a favor or two to ask.

CHAPTER 9
Booty Call
Billie

RYDER: U up?
BILLIE: It's seven a.m. Of course I'm up. But I'm not coming over for a booty call. You gotta buy me dinner first
RYDER: Ha
RYDER: Long shot, but any chance you have time to swing by the ranch again today? Not for a booty call but for something better
BILLIE: My God YES but also, what's better than a booty call?
BILLIE: Name the time and I'll be there
BILLIE: Also, why?
RYDER: Cuz I got a surprise for you lol
BILLIE: I don't know if I like it when guys use lol in texts
RYDER: That's it, invitation rescinded
BILLIE: lol
RYDER: Every year Cash invites Ella's preschool

> class to come visit the ranch. Thought you might get a kick out of seeing human babies hang with animal babies.
>
> BILLIE: Well shit
> BILLIE: You just made me cry into my keyboard
> BILLIE: I'm so in
> BILLIE: Taking a sick day
> RYDER: Kids will be here at ten
> BILLIE: I'll be there at nine because I'm an overachiever. I also hate my job so...
> RYDER: We need to work on that

I type something out. Delete it. Type it again.

> BILLIE: We?
> RYDER: Get your ass over here little lady
> BILLIE: Fine, twist my arm
> RYDER: But it's broken
> BILLIE: Wanna break my back too?
> RYDER: lol

Oh God.

Oh God, oh my *fucking* God.

I can only stare, jaw on the ground, as I watch Ryder squat beside a chestnut foal and grab a little boy's hand, gently guiding it to the foal's nose. Together, they pet her, a big old smile breaking out on the little boy's face.

"Aw, yeah, buddy," Ryder is saying. "Look how much she likes that. You're a natural. Should we give her a little treat?"

Ryder is wearing broken-in Levi's and a blue

bandana that matches his eyes. Barn boots. Stetson. His plaid button-up draws taut over his shoulder blades and back as he moves. When he turns his head, I glimpse his handsome profile.

Heaven above, the man is so gorgeous it *hurts*. It's the chiseled edge of his jawline. The perfect slope of his nose. The way the October sunlight turns his thick scruff red and gold.

My pulse hiccups, though, when I see the purple smudges underneath his eyes. Did he not sleep? I hope our conversation the other week didn't upset him. Surely he wouldn't have reached out if he were annoyed or angry with me, right?

Or does he somehow know I can't stop thinking about how much fun we're having together? How being with him feels like a breath of fresh air I didn't know I needed? I can just be myself when we're together. No pretending to be sweet or easy or uncomplicated. He laughs at my raunchy sense of humor. Doesn't balk at my honesty.

That kind of acceptance is rare.

The little boy laughs shyly. "Yeah, sure. Her nose is so soft."

I nearly jump at the nudge at my side. Ava stands there, holding out an apple slice. "Wanna get involved?"

"For as long as I've been alive," I murmur, taking the apple. I'm still wearing my sling, so the motion is a little awkward. "Hi."

"Hey." She carefully wraps me in a side hug. "Ryder said you might make an appearance."

"He randomly invited me."

"Is it random? Rumor has it y'all rode each other. I mean, rode *with* each other. In a tractor or something?"

RYDER

I laugh, lifting the shoulder of my good arm. The soreness in my bad elbow comes and goes. Today it's more sore than usual. "I was bored. I miss racing. So I decided to take a drive after dinner and bring Ryder some dessert."

"I know you miss racing. Are you scared?" Ava's eyes are kind. "To get back in the saddle?"

"No." I shake my head. "I can't wait. Honestly. The thrill, the flow of it all…There's nothing like it."

Ava nudges me again. "Makes life worth living, right?"

"Totally. But my parents really want me to, you know, quit putting life and limb at stake in competitions that are essentially meaningless, so I can build a respectable, God-fearing life."

Ava frowns. "Aw, sweetie, it's not meaningless. Not to you, and that's what counts."

Ryder's standing now, so I excuse myself and head his way, squatting beside the little guy on his right.

"I hear this sweetheart here might want a treat." I hold out the apple slice to the boy. "What's your name, little man?"

"George." He's blushing, and it's so damn cute I can't help but smile.

"Hello, George. I'm Billie. I'm glad you were able to come today. You're a natural with the animals."

"I like being around the horses," George replies, hooking his thumbs in his belt loops. "It makes me happy. Can you help me give her the treat please?"

I grin, handing over the apple. "Such good manners."

"That makes one of you who acts right." Ryder is wiping his hands as he looks down at me. His blue eyes are piercing in the morning light. "Hi, Billie."

My face flushes with heat. Looking away, I watch George feed the apple to the foal. "Hey, Ry."

"Is she your girlfriend?" George looks up at Ryder. "She's real pretty."

Ryder chuckles. "Everyone keeps asking me that. And she is pretty, isn't she?"

My heart gallops. I bite back a big, goofy grin.

"We're friends. Do you have friends?" I ask George.

He nods. "My best friend is my brother. But he has very big feelings and gets very afraid sometimes. He's over there with my mom." George points to a woman holding the hand of a boy in *Toy Story* cowboy boots. The boy smiles as he carefully pets a goat who is busy munching on some clover.

My chest pings. "He seems to like the animals too."

"They make him feel better. That's what my mom says. She was so happy she could bring him today."

There's a catch in my center as I meet eyes with Ryder. "That's pretty cool."

"Very cool," Ryder says. "I feel better when I'm around the horses too. It's very calming. Therapeutic, even."

George wrinkles his nose. "What does that mean?"

"It means…" I think on that for a minute before putting my hand on my chest. "You know where your heart is? Right here? It means your heart beats steady and strong. No part of you is afraid."

George puts a hand over his heart. "Mine feels pretty strong."

"That's great news, buddy." Now Ryder's feeling his heartbeat too. "Mine *was* calm. Then Billie got here…"

Extreme cuteness overload. "Sorry not sorry."

"I'd be upset if you *were* sorry."

"How about we take some deep breaths?" I ask. "That helps me calm down sometimes."

"Okay! I am very, very good at deep breaths." George takes one, then another, and Ryder and I follow him. The October air is deliciously crisp, and when it hits the bottom of my lungs, a sense of irrepressible joy blossoms inside me.

"Wow." I gently nudge George. "I feel so much better. Do you?"

"Yeah."

"And you?" I glance up at Ryder.

In reply, he pops into a squat beside us, his elbows on his knees. His scent fills my head, the woodsy pine and citrus, and I wonder how a cowboy who works in the dirt all day can smell so good.

Does he take multiple showers every day?

Would he like company for any and all of them?

"I feel better'n I have in an age." Ryder's eyes twinkle. "I mean that."

I roll my eyes, grinning like an idiot. "Such a cheeseball."

Ryder chuckles, a deep, happy sound. "I knew you'd call me out."

"How?"

"'Cause I know you. And now I'm starting to know myself a little better too."

Deep breaths. There are many things that make Ryder sexy. His confidence. His eyes. But this sudden burst of self-awareness just might be the sexiest thing about him.

"Ew, are you guys gonna kiss?" George is making a face. "Because my parents kiss after they talk, and it's gross."

My heart does a neat little backflip. "Kissing is totally gross."

"Totally." Ryder looks away. "How about we go see this baby's mama over there?"

The two hours I get to spend with the kids and the cowboys is truly the highlight of my week. Month. Year. Well, other than that tractor ride. And this morning when Ryder texted me out of the blue.

After the kids are loaded up into a caravan of waiting cars, Ryder touches my arm. "Can you stay a little longer?"

Please, for the love of God, ask me to stay forever. "Sure."

"I have a little surprise for you. A token of my thanks."

"Thanks?" I furrow my brow. "For what?"

But Ryder doesn't say anything as he leads me up the hill that connects the barn and corral to the New House's backyard.

Just when I start to worry that something is wrong, he says, "I went looking for my guitar last night."

I slow. Then I stop, grabbing his arm. My eyes feel like they're liable to pop right out of my head. "You found it."

His gaze slides to meet mine. The sun slants across his face, his hat casting a shadow over his eyes. "I played it too."

My heart throbs inside my ears. "And?"

"And what?"

"Well, why didn't you call me? Surely you remember what an excellent vocalist I am. Christ, Ry, we could've covered half of Taylor's catalogue if you'd invited me over."

His lips twitch. "Why do you think I invited you today?"

Who is this man? Why does it feel like he's drawing me closer, when for so long, he's pushed me away?

Hell, Ryder keeps *everyone* at arm's length. But today he's doing the opposite, and it doesn't compute.

"You're looking at me funny," he says.

"Yeah, 'cause you're acting funny. You're really gonna play your guitar for me today?"

"Actually." His Adam's apple bobs. "It was a lot. Playing. I only got through two songs."

The sun's warmth pours down my shoulders and back. I blink back the sudden sting in my eyes. "Yeah?"

"Felt like an excavator was demoing my insides. Like all my electrical wiring and insulation was exposed after being hidden away inside my walls."

My heart does another flip. "That's...a vivid image."

"It was excruciating. Made me miss my mom. It made me miss a lot of things."

"Aw, Ry." I curl my fingers around his arm and give his shockingly solid bicep a squeeze, my heart squeezing too at the way he's opening up. This is a *big* deal. "But today you feel better."

His eyes light up with surprise. "I do. I went to bed...not feeling great, but less weighed down, I guess."

"Less scared, maybe?"

The sun catches on his eyelashes as he looks at me. *Looks.*

Heat blooms in the space between us. Heat and tension. The kind that has the front of my thighs prickling with awareness. My eyes are drawn to his mouth.

"Scared of what?" His voice is like gravel.

"Your feelings. Your grief. Your past." I search his gaze. "Me."

I mean it as a joke—or maybe I don't—but either way, Ryder doesn't laugh. My stomach dives straight through my center and into the core of the Earth as he leans in instead.

Holy God, is Ryder going to kiss me? Right here, right now, for anyone and everyone to see? This is happening so fast.

So. Damn. Fast.

Then again, hasn't this moment been a lifetime in the making? I've only wanted Ryder to kiss me for, oh, over a decade now.

"How'd you know all that?" Now he's the one looking at *my* mouth.

It takes a lot to make me nervous. Before my race at the rodeo, all it took to get me in the right mindset was a pep talk from Xander and a healthy swig of tequila.

Now, though, my legs are literally shaking.

"I pay attention," I manage. "You were around a lot when I was growing up. You're still around a lot."

A muscle in his jaw tics. "That a problem?"

"I'm not complaining."

One side of his mouth kicks up, and he looks so cockily handsome, so *happy*, that everything inside me turns upside down. "You like me, huh?"

"I do. Which is why I'll let it slide—the fact that you're not gonna play for me…*yet*."

He puts his hand on his hip. He's so close his knuckles brush my side as he leans on one leg. "Who said I was gonna play for you at all?"

"I did." I slide my hand down to his forearm. "So why'd you *really* invite me over today, huh?"

I nearly pass out when he steps closer, our knees touching. "Thought you could use the excuse of helping us out with the kids to play hooky. Also, girl time."

"Girl time?" My pulse leaps.

"Girl time. I may have thrown in a pair of custom Bellamy Brooks boots to sweeten the deal. I know you've been looking for more girlfriends, so…"

My eyes are stinging all over again. "What deal? I don't follow."

"Mollie, Sally, Wheeler, and Ava—I think her girls are gonna be there too—they're waiting for you in the studio."

"The studio?" I feel like an idiot asking all these questions.

"Construction just wrapped on Bellamy Brooks's second headquarters here on the ranch. Wait 'til you see it. The views are unbelievable." He holds out an arm, and that's when I see his truck parked in the New House's driveway. "I'll give you a lift. Yes, Billie, the surprise is that I got you a pair of their boots."

I gasp. "You didn't!"

Living in Hartsville, of course I've heard about Bellamy Brooks. Mollie and Wheeler have gotten pretty damn famous for the gorgeous, fashion-forward boots they've made for several years now.

Like every Texas girl with a pulse, I'd love to own a pair. But they cost over a thousand bucks a pop. There's no way I could ever afford that.

"I did, to thank you for pushing my buttons." Ryder meets my eyes.

I can only stare at him. "Never thought I'd hear you say those words."

"Me neither. Life is funny, ain't it?"

It is funny. And terrifying.

But sometimes, like right now, life can be awful sweet too.

———

I'm shaking as I climb the steps to what might be the most beautiful studio in the world.

The building is made of pale limestone that matches the landscape perfectly. It has big steel windows and a dramatic sloping roofline that makes me think of an old-timey farmhouse. A brass sign beside the front door reads "Bellamy Brooks Headquarters No. 2."

I hear music coming from inside. And voices. Lots of them.

"This is too much, Ry."

"Least I can do, Billie." He reaches for the knob and opens the door for me. "The girls are excited to see you."

I feel like I'm in a dream as I step inside, Ryder right behind me.

If the studio's exterior was a dream, the studio's interior is pure girly heaven mixed with a hefty dose of Texas Hill Country charm. A wall of windows at the back overlooks the shimmering Colorado River, while the limestone walls are lined with shelves bearing the most beautiful—and most colorful—array of cowboy boots I've ever seen.

Reba plays over the speakers. The air smells like jasmine and orange blossom, a mix that's elegant but fun at the same time.

Mollie welcomes me with a hug. "Hey there, cowgirl!"

Ava presses a glass of champagne into my hand. "I'm so glad you were able to stay a little longer."

"This still seems excessive." I cast a panicked glance in Ryder's direction.

"You're excessive, so it works."

I nod. "Fair point. Y'all really don't have to—"

"But we want to. Welcome, Billie," Mollie continues. "We're thrilled to have an excuse to show off the new studio. Is your arm okay?" She glances at my sling.

"Arm is better. And this studio—it's fabulous." Sipping my champagne, I glance around. "Y'all are really living the dream."

Wheeler chuckles. "You missed the nightmare that was the first five years of running Bellamy Brooks."

"Dark days." Mollie crosses her arms. "But we survived."

"And now you're thriving." Ryder looks at me. "Gives you somethin' to think about, doesn't it?"

I take another sip of champagne in an effort to get a grip on my feelings because they're spinning out right now. The champagne is deliciously cold and just the right amount of sweet, the bubbles dancing over my tongue.

Another sip because I still feel wobbly. "Definitely."

"Welp." Ryder digs into his front pocket, the one with the telltale crease in the shape of a rectangle, and pulls out his pocketknife. "I best get gone. Got cowboy things to do."

I bite my lip. "I'll be bugging you later."

"If you can find me."

"I know my way around these parts."

He grins. "You do."

Then he turns and strides out the door.

Mollie grabs my arm and squeezes, her smile lighting up her whole face. "Who are you, and what have you done to Ryder? We need to know because we need you to do more of it. He never, *ever* has been so—"

"Happy," Sally says.

"Horny," Wheeler adds.

"I have…no idea what is happening." I watch through the window as Ryder lopes down the steps and climbs into his truck. "One minute, he actually agrees to ride in the ambulance with me, and the next, I'm, well, here."

Also. I'm kinda dying over the fact that I'm spending time with a girl gang after twenty-four years of hanging out almost exclusively with boys.

Mollie steers me toward the wall of cowboy boots. "When he called me to ask for a pair of boots for you, I about had a heart attack. He only said you 'did him a solid.' Care to elaborate?"

I put a hand on my face. "Honestly, your guess is as good as mine. The only thing I can think of is that I opened up to him about hating my job, and then he opened up to me about, well, a little of everything."

Ava exchanges a meaningful glance with Wheeler. "This is gonna be juicy."

"Aw, yeah." Wheeler rubs her hands together.

Ava wags her eyebrows. "I know I keep making riding puns when we're together—"

"You do," I say with a grin.

"C'mon, Billie. It's right there. Ryder, ride her…"

Mollie laughs. "So let's get you a pair of boots for that ride, okay? Maybe they'll be the only thing you're wearing when it happens."

I chuckle in an effort to distract everyone from the

furious rush of heat working its way up my chest and into my neck and face. "Y'all are jumping many, *many* steps ahead."

Wheeler nods. "It's called manifesting."

"I'm just going to come right out and ask." Mollie's eyes glimmer. "Do you like Ryder that way? Like, do you actually *want* to ride him? I think I know the answer, but…"

My face is on fire now, but I'm still able to laugh. I don't know this woman well, but I do know she's got a thing or two to teach me about that manifesting stuff.

So I just come right out with the truth. "Yes, Mollie, I really do like Ryder like that. I have for about as long as I can remember."

Ava's hand lands on her thigh. "I knew it!"

"So tell me, Billie—what's your favorite color?" Wheeler asks.

Twenty minutes later, I'm wearing a pair of midcalf metallic blue cowboy boots embroidered with hearts and horseshoes.

"Y'all should be so proud." I'm actually getting a little choked up as I look at my reflection in the mirror. The boots match my sling, which makes me smile. "These boots, the studio—it's all so, so beautiful. And I imagine it took a lot of elbow grease to make it happen."

Wheeler loops her arm through mine. "Like I said, it took us years to get here, honey."

"Years, lots of crying," Mollie says, "and a nearly constant negative balance in our bank accounts. But we stuck with it."

"How'd you know it was the right call? In terms of, you know, making a career out of it?"

"Great question. I think about that all the time. Like, were we brave to stick to our guns? Or were we stupid to try to keep a business alive that had been on life support for so long?" Mollie turns her head to look out the window and sighs. "I don't know what the right answer is. What I do know is that I'm really fucking happy in my life right now, and I don't think that would be the case if I had abandoned Bellamy Brooks. The struggle made the success that much sweeter, you know?"

I swallow hard. "Sounds like you always knew what you wanted to do, though."

"Yes and no." She tilts her head back and forth. "I was always a creative person, but I only got into fashion when I was in high school. Do you know what you want to do?"

I pick up my champagne flute. "I have no clue what I want to do with my life, other than not be an accountant on my family's ranch."

"Good thing there's plenty of other things to do on a ranch."

"Like what?"

Wheeler runs a hand over the swell of her belly and grins. "Hookup with hot cowboys, for starters."

"Really, y'all, my brother would kill me and Ryder if that happened."

"You really think Colt would get bent out of shape like that over two of his favorite people having some fun together?" Ava sips thoughtfully on a glass of champagne. "Your brother seems more civilized than that."

"Colt's got enough on his plate. I don't want to add to the pile, you know? And my brothers…they like to think of themselves as my protectors even though I can protect myself just fine, thank you very much."

"Tell Colt that, then," Mollie says, "and then go have your fun. Lord knows Ryder could use some of that."

I tug my bottom lip through my teeth. I like talking to these women. They seem to have good heads on their shoulders. They're also happy in their careers and relationships. Why not pick their brains a little? Maybe they'll have some good advice for me, because I feel like I'm spinning my wheels here.

"I'm not sure I even have a shot with Ryder." I keep my voice low as if the cowboy in question—or one of our brothers—is hiding behind a door. "He's a love 'em and leave 'em type, I know that much. I don't think he's interested in dating anyone."

"He might date you." Mollie takes a thoughtful sip of champagne. "You'll never know until you try."

Wheeler cuts me a look. "Honey, he organized this whole little ladies-who-lunch situation just for you."

"I don't get why, though," I reply, though I'm starting to think that I actually *do* know why he might've gone out of his way to put a smile on my face.

Holy shit, does Ryder like me?

Ava reads my mind and says, "Because he likes you. *Likes* you."

The idea makes my pulse skid. I look away, putting a hand on my face again. My skin is on fire now. *Could they be right?*

Does Ryder Rivers actually want me too, as more than just a hookup?

My thoughts whirl. How would it work? Would we tell Colt? How do I keep convincing Ryder to let me in the way he has today?

The sex would be hot.

So hot it'd burn and likely leave a scar. Am I ready for that?

Fuck yeah, I'm ready. But what if sex is all that's on offer? Ryder and I could very well want different things. And then what? I die of a broken heart watching him do what he's always done and pick up a different girl every time he's at the Rattler?

"You *like* him too, huh?" Sally is looking at me.

I really do. Even if we ultimately *do* want different things.

I also really don't want to lie to these girls. Maybe because I feel like they'd never lie to me.

It also feels good to have people to talk to about this stuff other than, well, the horse I used to race on.

"I've always liked Ryder," I say on an exhale, tucking my hair behind my ear. "He's just always seemed way, *way* out of my league. Or maybe just not interested, you know? I'm his friend's little sister. What's lamer than that?"

"Correction: What's *hotter* than that? Forbidden love?" Sally makes a folding motion with her hand. "Gimme."

"Even if my brother wouldn't murder us, Ryder's not exactly a Steady Eddie."

"He might be for you. There's only one way to find out." Wheeler rests her chin on my shoulder and meets my eyes in the mirror. "I think you wear these boots and the pair of jeans that makes your ass look the hottest, and you do what you do best."

"What's that?"

"Ride, honey."

CHAPTER 10
Tit for Tat
Billie

Heart drumming, I press the heel of my hand on the center of my steering wheel and honk.

Once. Twice.

I consider a third time, but then the front door of the tiny farmhouse is opening and Ryder emerges, looking like a snack in a pair of sweatpants and a broken-in T-shirt that clings to his torso in an alarmingly sexy way.

Relief floods my veins. *He's actually home.*

His hair is a little wet. It curls out at the ends in these adorable little tendrils that have my fingers itching to touch them.

He's clearly in his comfy clothes, which I hope means he doesn't have plans tonight. The soreness in my elbow has almost completely disappeared, so I decided it was time to venture out of the house without my sling.

Really, it was an excuse to venture over to *Ryder's* house.

Wiping his hands on a dish towel, he squints against

the dying light. "The Rattler's the other way, you know." He nods in the general direction of town.

"What makes you think I'm going to the Rattler?"

"Your hair is down. You're not wearing your sling." He lopes down the steps, tossing the towel over his shoulder. "And you have lipstick on."

He's noticing…everything. That means something, right?

I lift my chin. "So?"

"So." Leaning down, he rests his forearms on the passenger side windowsill so he can peer inside my SUV. "Why'd you get so dressed up if you're just coming to bother me?"

I cling to the steering wheel for dear life. "Don't say no."

"Color me intrigued." His grin is cocky. Cute.

How the hell do I survive this man's hotness? My body throbs with almost painful awareness of how close he is.

Is it stupid to think that one day he'll mosey over to my side of the car and kiss me?

I bet he's a *good* kisser. How could he not be? With that mouth and those lips and the intelligent, almost fierce way his eyes flicker when they move over my face, I bet he's an absolute rock star at it.

I don't like being this nervous around Ryder Rivers, but here we are. I've always had a crush on the guy. But for the first time in the history of our friendship, I think there's a possibility that he might be developing a crush on me too.

"But seriously, you might start saying no once you find out why I'm here," I manage.

"Oh yeah?" He hangs his hands inside the door.

RYDER

His very big, very calloused hands. The way that thick veins crisscross the tops of them—

I can't.

"You got me boots." I lift my knee, and his eye darts down my leg to the pair of Bellamy Brooks I'm wearing. Then I lift the picnic basket I borrowed from Aunt Lee, Mom's sister. "So I got you dinner. Get in, loser, we're gonna go make a bonfire. Bring your guitar."

He looks at me for half a beat, eyes locked on mine. My mind scrambles to decipher the emotion that glimmers there. Heat? Fear? Both?

I get it, man. We're playing with fire tonight, literally and figuratively. But give me a chance. Please.

I felt pretty damn cute leaving my place. I curled my hair, put on my favorite white T-shirt—the one that makes my tits look good—and yes, I absolutely did put a swipe or two of lipstick on my mouth just because I could.

But now, with Ryder looking at me like *this*, I wonder if it's all too much. I should've called first, or at the very least texted like he did the other morning. Should've ended this cute little game of tit for tat we've got happening while I was ahead. These boots are fabulous. The gesture? Even better.

Why'd I have to take it a step too far? I just can't help myself, especially when I feel so good when I'm with him—

"Nice night for a fire." He shifts, glancing up at the clear evening sky. "How's the arm?"

"It'll feel better if you say yes."

He scoffs. I can smell his soap, or maybe it's his shampoo. He must've just gotten out of the shower.

Perfect timing: He's clean, but he hasn't eaten dinner yet.

"Answer's yes, on one condition," he replies. "If I bring the guitar, I decide what to play. Got it?"

Yes.

He said yes.

Holy fucking shit, Ryder Rivers is going on a kinda-sorta date with me that's definitely not a date but also not not *a date?*

And *he's bringing his guitar?*

I've died and gone to heaven.

I spent all day at my desk, pretending to work while I was plotting tonight's picnic. Slash, I was fantasizing that it would go so perfectly, that we'd have such a memorable time confiding in each other, I'd end up naked. Totally blissed out in a postorgasmic haze and wrapped in a blanket while Ryder played me songs on his guitar without his shirt on.

Now I'm starting to think there really is a chance of something *good* happening tonight. A small chance, mind you. Maybe one or two percent. But something is changing between Ryder and me, and our relationship is moving in a direction I like. A lot.

It's a win I need right now. My job is more unbearable than ever, and Dad dropped another not-so-subtle hint today about me hanging up my rodeo dreams for good.

"You can play what you want." I shake the hair out of my eyes. "But I bet I can get you to play what I want too."

He pushes out his lips. "Them's fightin' words, little lady."

"I'm no lady. Get your shoes and let's go."

He's full-on smiling now, the kind that touches his eyes and makes me feel lightheaded. "But you are a good friend. Gimme five?"

I don't wanna be just friends. Never did.

I clear my throat and shake the nonexistent hair out of my eyes again. "You got it."

Exactly four minutes later—not like I've been staring impatiently at the clock on the dash or anything—Ryder emerges once more from his house.

There's a sudden, sharp drop in my middle, like the way my stomach dips when a plane hits a big bump in the air.

Ryder changed into jeans and boots. He's still wearing the same T-shirt, but he threw a suede jacket over it.

He's also wearing a cowboy hat.

Also *also*, he's carrying a guitar in one hand and a fifth of reposado tequila in the other. I can tell by the color of the liquid in the bottle. It's expensive stuff, a little sweeter and smoother than blanco tequila, and it's all Ryder drinks.

My nipples tingle, hardening to tight, aching points as I watch him approach the car with his unhurried, bowlegged stride. I frown when he rounds the front of my car, confused as to why he's heading for my side.

"Outta the driver's seat," he says, setting the tequila on the hood of the car so he can open my door.

"What?" I blink. "Why? I'm the one taking *you* on—"

"You're with me, you don't drive. You also need to rest that arm." He tilts his head. "I know it's your nature to fight me on everything—"

"Well, yeah. It's fun, isn't it?"

He gives me that lopsided smirk, the one where one corner of his mouth is curled upward, and I swear my heart stops beating for a full five seconds.

"Sometimes." The edges of his eyes crinkle. "But please don't fight me on this, yeah?"

I meet his eyes. "Fine. Just this once, though. And if you want me to drive home, just say the word."

"That won't be necessary. Now scoot your ass over."

I climb over the center console, plopping down into the passenger seat with about as much elegance as a newborn foal who hasn't learned to use its legs yet.

He hands me his guitar, which feels like a big moment. But I don't have time to process that because then *he's* in the car too. My SUV isn't huge, but it's not small either. You wouldn't know it, however, by how *enormous* Ryder looks in the front seat. His legs are so long that his knees almost touch the dashboard.

Chuckling, he adjusts the seat, sliding it all the way back. Then draping his left arm over the steering wheel, he reaches for the gear shift with his right hand and swings his head to look at me.

"Ready, darlin'?"

Even if Colt murders us after whatever goes down tonight, it will have been worth it just to experience this moment. "Born ready, baby."

He smiles, putting my car in drive. I carefully tuck the guitar into my lap, cradling it like I would a newborn. It's surprisingly light.

It also needs a strap. Maybe one with Ryder's name on it? I make a mental note to research where I might get something like that made.

RYDER

A cozy feeling settles over me. As wired—nervous—as I am, I'm also excited to spend a beautiful evening outside, in front of a fire, with my superhot crush who's also becoming a really close friend.

The weather is perfect, warmer than it was a few days ago, so I have the windows rolled down. My hair dances in the breeze as we head away from the cabin.

"So where ya takin' me?" he asks.

I try not to stare as he leans toward me, turning the wheel with the heel of his hand. Why is it *so* effing sexy when a guy drives your car?

"I thought we'd head toward Canyon Creek." It's a sweet little spot with some of the best views in all of Hart County.

It's also super close, maybe three or four miles from here. I don't want to waste time driving when we could be eating, playing music, or playing with each other.

Ryder nods. "I like this plan."

"I knew you would." I clear my throat for what feels like the hundredth time.

Assuming Ryder feels this weird, delicious tension between us, I wonder if he wouldn't be opposed to exploring ways to relieve it. But I know Colt will absolutely have a shit fit if he finds out I hooked up with his best friend.

Then again, *does* Colt have to find out? Maybe Ry and I only tell him if things get serious. He won't love the idea of us dating, but he'll hate it less than the idea of us having very hot, very casual sex. Because while I'm definitely interested in dating Ryder, I have no idea what *he's* looking for. It could very well be just a hookup. If that's the case, I feel like telling Colt would just cause a bunch of unnecessary drama.

I'm assuming a lot. But in the universe we live in, you have to think about these things. You don't survive as a rancher if you can't rely on your neighbors and friends to be honest and show up for you when you need them.

A betrayal like this might not seem like a big deal to the outside world. But to ours, it can literally be the difference between life and death. If Colt can't trust Ryder—if he can't trust me—I'm not sure where that would leave us.

Or maybe I'm just making a mountain out of a molehill. Ryder and I are two consenting adults. What we do behind closed doors is our business, no one else's.

I think it's worth the risk. I really do. Because not only is Ryder a good guy, a better friend, and a super *superhot* cowboy. He's also showing he can change. When his parents died, he shut parts of himself away. Like the part that played the guitar and sang along with me to pop songs. Before the accident, he was lighthearted. Thoughtful. He'd talk to me about everything and anything, never making me feel stupid or silly.

But after he lost his parents, he started responding to my questions with grunts. I'd try to start a conversation, but he would never reciprocate the effort. He just... vanished in a way.

Then I mention that guitar recently, and all of a sudden, he's playing again.

He's trying.

I wanna keep drawing out this side of him. What a waste it would be if he kept living half a life, one where he didn't feel pain, but where he didn't get to experience joy and love and connection either?

"You likin' the boots?" His eyes slide down my legs to my feet.

I bite the inside of my bottom lip. "I love them. Thank you again. You really didn't have to—"

"But I wanted to."

If he *doesn't* want me, he sure as hell is making it very confusing as to how he feels about me. Us. Whatever's happening here.

Do friends do this kind of thing for each other? Buy boots and set up picnics and risk the wrath of a particularly ornery mutual acquaintance just so we can hang out?

Somebody pinch me. I still can't believe Ryder and I are *hanging out* on a *Friday*, just the two of us.

Just because.

Really, just because I had the balls to show up at his place for a second time in a week. I am down bad, and I guess I don't care who knows it.

Only, I care very much. At least, I *should* care. And therein lies the rub.

We park beside a juniper tree and set up camp on top of a nearby ridge, where the Rivers boys and my brothers used to hang out back in the day. There's a moment when I'm holding one end of the Pendleton blanket I brought and Ryder's holding the other, and the blanket billows upward on a breeze as we try to set it down on the ground.

It flies out of my hand and blows in Ryder's direction. He lets out a yelp of surprise before the blanket knocks his hat clean off his head.

"Whoa whoa *whoa*." He pretends to flail backward as he's tangled up in the blanket, arms windmilling, eyes wide, lips pulled into a wide, white smile. "You tryin' to kill me, Billie Wallace?"

"Why do you think I brought the blanket?" Without thinking, I dart forward and grab his hand, yanking him upright.

I yank him *against* me. Well, almost. My arm—the good one—ends up trapped between his chest and forearm. We're suddenly close.

Very, very close.

When I look up, his mouth—his face—is two inches from mine. I can make out the flecks of indigo in his otherwise crystal clear cerulean irises.

"Why's that?" His chest rises. Falls. His hair sticks up every which way. It's adorable.

My lips throb. "I planned to use it to roll up your lifeless body. Obviously."

His eyes do that crinkling-at-the-edges thing again. "You're puttin' some kinda murder on me, that's for sure."

"Oh yeah?" *Is he joking? He can't be joking. But—*

"Yeah."

We hold eye contact for one heartbeat. Another. Another.

I'm not sure my pulse worked this hard during my one and only official rodeo race. There's a flutter between my legs too, the longing in my core unfurling so quickly it takes over my whole body in the blink of an eye.

But then Ryder is clearing his throat. He lets go of my hand and turns, setting the blanket down on the ground.

I'm disappointed he didn't kiss me. But I'm also… thrilled? Because I could tell he *wanted* to lean in.

I can tell the tension between us is eating him alive too.

Is this actually gonna happen? Is this cowboy actually going to let me lay him down on that blanket and do as I please?

Bending down, I help straighten the blanket, then I grab Ryder's hat. He holds out his hand, but I shake my head.

"You know what has to happen if *I* wear this hat."

"But then your DNA is gonna be all over me"—he grabs my wrist, and a bolt of lust cracks down my middle—"and you'll be the primary suspect in my suspicious death."

"I want to make a joke about little deaths—you know, the French word for—"

"I know, Billie." Do I detect a hint of pain in his voice? He releases my wrist. "Hat, please."

"Fine." With a sigh of exasperation, I go up on my tiptoes and drop the hat onto his head. "But we both know it would look better on me."

"Darlin', everything looks better on you."

Get over here, then.

"Let's take a shot," I blurt.

"Don't gotta ask me twice."

He grabs the picnic basket, and I grab the tequila. We sit on the blanket, keeping a respectable distance between his right arm and my left.

I'm the one who's going to end up dead, I think as I uncork the bottle and take a swig. The tequila is sweet on my tongue. I want to smack my lips at the deliciousness of the liquor's fiery slide down my throat.

"Sorry I forgot to bring cups." I hold out the bottle to Ryder.

He takes it from me, shaking his head as he brings the bottle to his lips. "Tastes better straight from the bottle anyway."

I watch, transfixed, as he tips back his head and his throat bobs on a swallow. I feel the slide of his Adam's apple between my legs.

I hold out my hand. He presses the bottle into my palm. Taking a longer pull of tequila, I imagine I can taste him on the glass.

Now that I'm a little buzzed, I ache *everywhere*. My hands shake as I help Ryder build a bonfire in the firepit he and the boys dug out here years ago. I can barely eat the supper I packed us even though it's really good stuff: Mom's fried chicken, succotash, and broccoli-and-cheese cornbread.

The sky darkens, and the stars put on a spectacular show. But they don't hold my attention the way Ryder's mouth does. Or his legs. He stretches them out toward the fire, and it hits me just how long they are.

The man is huge. And strong. And thick in all the right places.

My eyes stray to his crotch. *Is he huge and thick everywhere?*

He's got the tequila in his hand again, and he's looking intently into the fire. A pair of deep, thoughtful grooves are etched into the spot between his eyebrows. My stomach flips at his handsomeness. Heart throbs with the desire to know what he's thinking.

To *understand* him. Or maybe to know him in a way he's only now allowing me to, years into our relationship.

Let me in again, Ry. Please.

"What's on your mind?" I tug at my jeans as I casually stretch out my own legs, pretending like my pulse isn't going haywire inside my skin. "I can tell those wheels are turnin'."

He tips his chin downward and uses his palm to pop the cork back into the bottle. "I was thinking about what song I wanted to play for you."

I smile. "So you really are gonna play."

"You really want me to?" He sets the bottle aside.

"Of course I want you to." Reaching back, I grab the guitar that I carefully set behind me earlier. "Why the hell do you think I brought you out here?"

"I thought you wanted to thank me for the boots." He taps his toe against mine. "And for the excellent CPR."

I hand him the guitar. "I like you best when you're doing your cowboy-who-knows-music thing. So please, *please* play."

"Yeah?" Arching a brow, he folds up his legs and settles the guitar in his lap. "You forgot the hot part, by the way. *Hot* cowboy who knows music."

Laughing, I nudge his knee with mine. "I think you're *hottest* when you open up and lose yourself in the music and just…let go."

He scoffs, running his fingers over the guitar strings. "Of course you do."

My heart lurches as goose bumps rise on my arms at the sound. "What does that mean?"

"Nothing." He shakes his head, the light from the fire flickering over his features. "You're just…*you*. Like no one else. You cut to the quick, and you ask the hard questions, and you push my buttons, and…yeah, Billie." He turns and meets my eyes. "I know we joke a lot, but I appreciate how unbullshitty you are. It's a breath of fresh air."

I let out a nervous laugh. "Unbullshitty?"

"It's a compliment."

Oh Lord, I'm about to have a heart attack, aren't I? "Why does that appeal to you?"

"Because." He strums the guitar again, breaking eye contact to reach up and tune a string. "Makes me realize how full of shit I've been about some things in my life. Or numb to them, at the very least."

"What things?"

"I think we're done with twenty questions, darlin'."

"I like it." Swallowing, I tuck my hair behind my ear. "When you call me that. Since we're being honest and shit."

He smiles. A real, joyful smile, the kind that makes deep grooves appear around his mouth in the shape of half-moons.

"Honest and shit. You in a nutshell." When his eyes lock on mine, my heart heaves at the way they reflect the flames of the fire. "Please don't ever change."

Then he starts playing a song. It takes me all of three seconds to recognize the lilting notes.

"Landslide," by Fleetwood Mac.

CHAPTER 11
Walking Away
Ryder

Billie's eyes light up, making my chest turn over.

Does she remember how we do this? And then she answers my question by singing along, because *of course* she just goes for it. No self-consciousness. No hesitation.

Just a lot of heart.

I really am a dead man.

I blink back the burn in my eyes as I struggle a little to keep playing the notes. I haven't played since the other night. Too afraid. Too confused. So I haven't been able to practice, and it's been ages since I played *any* song.

But this was Mom's favorite tune—she was a huge Fleetwood Mac and Stevie Nicks fan—and I played it for her often enough that I know the notes by heart.

I went straight for the jugular, playing this damn song.

Felt wrong not to, though. Billie…she's got some kinda weird faith in me that makes me wanna have faith in myself.

Faith that I won't die if I revisit this stuff again.

Faith that I might keep feeling better if I put down my dukes and let myself remember it all. The good, the bad, the ugly. Even if falling apart makes me less of a man in the world's eyes.

Her voice is pretty. She laughs when she has trouble hitting the high notes, but it's just the hit of levity I needed to keep from drowning. Her green eyes glimmer in the light of the fire as she sings and I play, and the world seems to slow to a stop around us to listen.

She's leaning back, her legs stretched out in front of her, arms propped up behind her with her hands planted on the blanket. The posture pulls her shirt taut over her chest, making her tits look…fuck, like the most perfect handfuls that ever existed. I nearly swallow my tongue when her nipples suddenly make an appearance, like she's turned on by my staring.

I allow myself to *briefly* fantasize about leaning over and sucking on them through her shirt. I imagine her head falling back. Hair trailing down the length of her arms as she pants my name. She'd knock off my hat before yanking me in for a hard, hot kiss.

Billie is not the kind of girl to fuck around. She'd bite my bottom lip. Pull my hair.

A pulse of heat shoots up my dick and lands with a thudding heartbeat in my tip.

Fuck.

Fuck fuck *fuck*.

Cannot. Get hard. While thinking about Colt's sister's tits.

So I clear my throat, avert my eyes, and try my damndest to focus on the music.

RYDER

The logs crackle and pop, putting off a wave of heat that hits my legs and face. *Feel that.* My fingertips smart as they pull on the strings. *Focus on that, the music.* My callouses have long since disappeared.

Do I have the courage to build them back up?

The hot press of tears on the backs of my eyes returns with a vengeance. Now that I really am focused on the music, I'm facing down my emotions in a way that terrifies me.

I glance at Billie, pulse thumping. I'm scared she'll see me cry and be turned off. Disgusted, even.

But my pulse soars when I just see softness in her expression. Soft eyes. Soft smile.

A soft place to land, then?

Before the other night when I unearthed my guitar, I hadn't cried in front of anyone since before Mom and Dad's funeral. I shut off that spigot the day we put my parents in the ground, and I never turned it back on. I had to.

As the baby of our family, I always tried to be the "easy" kid—the one who didn't cause any trouble or put anyone out. Going with the flow felt like second nature with four older brothers in the house. Someone always needed something, and I could tell how overwhelmed my parents were by my brothers' constant demands. I didn't want to add more to the pile.

Makes sense that I wanted to keep being easy after the accident. Cash took over as head of the family, and I could tell he was overwhelmed too. What nineteen-year-old wouldn't be flattened by suddenly becoming the guardian of his rowdy younger siblings?

So I just kinda kept to myself. Didn't burden anyone

with my grief or my loneliness. I think that's why I got so close to Colt over the years; with him, I never felt the pressure to perform the easy role.

Now I see how playing that role has left me stunted. Unhappy. The kind of life I thought I'd live, the love I thought I'd find—I'm never gonna get those things, am I, if I don't let anyone in?

If I'm not allowed to be difficult and inconvenient and, well, a whole human being.

Billie sure as hell doesn't seem to mind when I'm being difficult.

A tear slips. My stomach lurches. But before I can wipe it away and erase all evidence of my grief, Billie is doing it for me.

She gently arcs the pad of her thumb over my cheek, sending a shock wave of something sharp and real and... strong through me.

I feel like I'm bleeding on the inside, but instead of panicking, I keep playing.

I'm *feeling*. Letting oxygen into spaces that have been airless for way too long.

And you know what? Billie doesn't run, so neither do I.

Another tear slips. Another swipe of her thumb. This time my body heats at her touch. She leans into me, leans her head lightly on my shoulder, and now I *am* drowning.

Not in grief, but in desire.

Interesting. Makes me wonder if being able to lean into my feelings, to let my guard down when it comes to my grief, is also allowing me to recognize what I actually feel for Billie. The other side of the coin thing?

The song ends. Quiet descends on us in a fire-scented rush, my body prickling with the awareness that Billie hasn't moved.

I'm practically choking on the need to set down this guitar and get Billie on her back and put my face between her legs.

She'd be so soft there too. I can taste her already, hot and sweet. She'd come on my mouth quick and hard, and then I'd come inside her.

"That was beautiful." Her voice is quiet. "You're beautiful."

I blink, drawing a deep breath through my nose. "I know. Cowboy plus guitar plus cowboy tears equals hotness—"

"You really need to stop calling yourself hot."

I nudge her with my elbow. "Somebody has to!"

"Let it be me, then."

"Fine."

"Fine!"

Her body shakes with laughter against my own, and it hits me that I've never cried and laughed at the same time.

It makes my chest feel sore in the best way. Like I've just finished a punishing day out in the cold, and now I get to come inside. Get warm. Maybe come inside *that* way too.

Would Billie let me? But what if that got us into trouble? Condoms are a way of life for me. My parents drilled into us that safe sex is good sex.

In this fantasy, though, Billie and I aren't safe at all. We're reckless. And the sex is really, *really* fucking good. How incredible would it feel to fuck this pretty girl bare?

Nothing between us? I got nothing to worry about on my end.

Because I'd keep her safe. Keep *us* safe, including any babies we'd make.

I wince when my dick goes full salute.

Jesus Christ, did I just get hard thinking about knocking up Billie Wallace?

Since when is that shit sexy? Thank God I still have the guitar on my lap to hide the tent in my jeans.

If I'm being honest, I did feel a pang when I found out Duke and Wheeler were pregnant. At the time, I chalked it up to feeling a little left out. Because now I had to share Duke with a girl *and* a baby when I'd had him to myself for so many years.

But now…I wonder if I was jealous. If I *am* jealous. And if that jealousy is pointing me in the direction of something I haven't allowed myself to want.

A woman like Billie. Maybe a baby too.

My heart races. So do my thoughts. How the hell did things get so deep so fast tonight? We've been together for all of an hour, maybe two, and here I am, thinking about doing life with Billie.

"Your mom." Billie still has her head tucked against my shoulder. "She loved Stevie Nicks. I remember that song playing in your kitchen when y'all had us all over for your tenth birthday. Remember?"

You're fucking killing me, honey. "I do, yeah."

"Tell me."

"What?"

"All the ways she loved you." A pause. "All the ways you loved her."

I'm laughing again, even as I raise my free arm to

wipe my eyes. "You really like seeing me cry, don't you?"

She looks up at me, brows pulled together. "I don't like seeing you in pain. But I do like seeing *you*. The real you."

How are you the only one who's picked up on the fact that I'm hiding?

Why are you the one who cares enough to call me out on it?

As I search her pretty eyes, an alarm goes off in the back of my head. I gotta call it a night. I'm worried that if I spend another minute with this girl pressed up against me, all honesty and fearlessness, I'm gonna do something real fucking stupid.

Colt's been betrayed before by someone he loves. I ain't gonna be the guy to repeat that.

Even if Billie weren't his sister, I know her well enough to recognize that she wants more from me than just a good fuck by the fire. I'm not sure I'm capable of giving her *more*, though. I've never wanted it with anybody else. Who's to say I won't end up hurting this woman? Breaking her heart? Yeah, I'm opening up now. But there's no guarantee that will keep happening.

I wouldn't forgive a friend who broke any of my brothers' hearts that way. I wouldn't expect Colt to forgive me either.

I can't live without his friendship.

Suddenly, though, I don't think I can live without Billie's either.

"Now that I'm thinking on it…" I let out a silent sigh of relief when I'm able to get a grip on the situation in my pants. "Mom loved me no matter what. Like I could cry in front of her too, and she would just, you know, give me a hug and ask me what was wrong."

Billie nods. "She was your safe space."

"Something like that, yeah." My voice is thick.

"You okay?"

"Nope. But also..." I think on the words. "This feels right."

Her eyes widen, and my stomach flips when I realize I just shoved my boot in my mouth.

"This, uh, meaning playing the guitar and letting out my emotions and...uh, that stuff." *Not "this" like you and me.* "It's the right move, yeah?"

She blinks. Is that disappointment I see in her face? "Yeah. Totally. Play another song? Pretty please?"

I hesitate. "You sure I shouldn't be gettin' you home? It's late—"

"You do know I live by myself and that I'm also twenty-four years old, right? My parents aren't, like, waiting up for me or anything."

Yeah, but how would they feel knowing you were out here alone with me while I was fantasizing about putting a baby in you?

Pretty sure Old Man Wallace would put a bullet in *me* if he knew that. Wouldn't blame him. Now if my intentions were good, that would be a different story.

I'm not sure they are, though.

Case in point: Before I know what I'm doing, I'm picking out a new song on the strings. Billie lets out a delighted trill of laughter.

"*Yes!*" She jumps to her feet. "Look, I love this song so much I'm gonna dance after only two shots of tequila."

"Yeah!" by Usher was always a hit with the girls

whenever I played it, even on an acoustic guitar. Guess some things never change.

I chuckle. "What a rebel."

"Don't stop." She throws her arms over her head and starts to sway her hips. "I really will murder you if you do."

"Noted."

To be fair, it's almost impossible *not* to dance to this song. But Billie—she's a notoriously terrible dancer, and now that she's got her bum arm, she's even worse. She shakes her ass but not to the beat. Her left leg goes one way and the right goes the other, making her look like a stork who's had too much to drink.

The best part? She knows she's terrible and she doubles down, dropping into a half squat to twerk. Only she loses her balance and falls over, thankfully on her right side this time, and then we're both laughing so hard we're crying.

Seriously, my sides ache from how hard and how long I laugh.

"Stop," I gasp. "I can't—air—I need to breathe—"

"Fuck you," she manages. "I'm the one who fell."

Setting aside my guitar, I get to my feet and grab her good hand. "No more of that, okay? You've given me enough scares to last a lifetime."

She lets me help her up. Because I'm a masochist, I pull her a little too close. The way *she* pulled *me* close earlier. I keep her hand in mine a little too long.

It just feels so fucking good to touch her. Be touched *by* her. The way she smells like fresh peaches, and how she only has eyes for me.

I can do no wrong in this moment, and that's liberating in a way I can't quite describe.

Now our joined hands are on my hip—who did that?—and her fingers tentatively explore the hem of my shirt. "Do I really do that? Scare people for no reason?"

I search her face while trying to clamp down a renewed wave of screaming need. "You're thinking about your parents, aren't you? And what they'd do if you quit tryin' to please them and did what made you happy instead."

She scoffs, looking away. "Not to put too fine a point on it." After a beat, her eyes flick back to mine. "But what would I do? I think they'd be proud of me no matter what, I just…"

"Don't want to disappoint anyone."

Her fingers tighten around my hipbone. "I've always been *that* kid in our family. The one always running her mouth and causing trouble."

"As the kid who never caused trouble, I'm telling you, trouble ain't always a bad thing."

Her eyes toggle between mine. "You think so?"

"Your family's gonna be just fine if you quit doing that bookkeeping shit, Billie. Will they be disappointed at first? Probably. But they'll find someone else. You know who's not gonna be fine if you stay?" I tap the knuckle of my first finger against the spot where her collarbones meet. "You. And that's who matters most. So make trouble, Billie. Hell, I'm trying to make more of it myself."

Grinning, she rolls her eyes. "*Such* a troublemaker, helping out your brother with his preschooler's field trip to the ranch. You're really good with kids."

"So are you." I tilt my head. "Maybe that's an angle to think about. You were definitely lit up hanging with those cuties."

Her eyelashes flutter. "Maybe. I hadn't considered that. I'd have to go back to school to teach—"

"No, no. I don't mean teach like in a classroom. Maybe you figure out a way to work with kids and horses and stuff. You gotta be outside, working with people. And animals."

What about the animal therapy? I loved it as a kid, and I vaguely remember my instructors being pretty gung ho about the whole thing.

I make a mental note to come back to the idea. Maybe I'll bring it up to Billie later, after I've had some time to flesh out the thought.

"You sound like you know me."

"Darlin', I do know you. And I know you're never gonna be satisfied sitting at a desk for the rest of your life."

She wrinkles her brow, nostrils flaring as her eyes flick to my mouth. "Remind me again why you care?"

'Cause you're something special, and it'd be a fucking tragedy to see you wither away trying to keep everyone happy.

"These days, caring about *anything* feels like giving this fucked up world the finger. And I'm learning from you the power of a little rebellion."

Her face splits into a smile so pretty it takes my breath away.

Literally. I can't breathe. I can only stare, wanting to lean in and kiss her so bad my chest hurts.

"Are you saying I'm a punk?" she asks.

"And a brat. Yes. But I'll take that any day over—"

"Someone who's full of shit."

"Yes."

Her throat works on a swallow. "Ry?"

"Yeah?"

Ask me to kiss you. Please. Anywhere you want.

"Are we… Is this how friends talk?" Billie's voice wobbles. "Because I don't really have friends, I only have brothers. And this feels different. Not—not in a bad way, but I… If I'm being honest…being more than friends… I'd be okay with that."

Her words send an arrow through my heart. She's feeling this tension, this desire, same as me. I wanna give her a high five for having the balls to acknowledge it.

But that means I gotta decide, right now, what my next move's gonna be. No more of this wishy-washy, I-wanna-eat-her-out-but-I-can't crap. Either I jump in with both feet, or I don't jump at all.

Could I be good to Billie? Treat her the way she deserves to be treated? I've hooked up casually in the past, but I was never anyone's boyfriend. I don't know how dating is done or if I'm even capable of things like monogamy and truthfulness.

Because Billie is telling the truth, and I owe it to her to do the same.

Truth is…

I don't know. And there's too much at stake to fuck around without having a solid game plan in place.

A shadow descends inside me, cloaking my good mood in a blanket of doubt.

My voice sounds like gravel when I say, "You have friends, Billie. I'm one of 'em."

Her gaze flickers. Aw *shit*, I hurt her feelings. That was not the answer she wanted to hear.

I get it, darlin'. I want you. But this is a loaded gun we're playing with here, and I'm scared someone is gonna get hurt.

"I know what you're asking." I carefully tuck her hair behind her ear, resisting the urge to trace the outline of her lips with my thumb. "And no, friends don't usually talk like this. But you and me—this friendship is important. It's special. We can't risk that, yeah, by letting things get messy?"

She nods, blinking before looking away. "Yeah."

It's all I can do not to grimace. "Please don't do that."

"Don't do what?"

"Retreat. Pull away." *I'm sorry I pulled away over all those years. I'm sorry I'm doing it again now.* "Tonight—it's meant a lot to me, and I—"

"You can't. My brother, our families…" She offers me a tight smile. "I understand."

"It's always the right call, you know. To put yourself out there."

"Why aren't you doing it, then?"

The question haunts me all the way home, Billie and me riding in her car in tense, heavy silence.

CHAPTER 12
Rent Free
Billie

Run. Faster.

You gotta speed up or you're gonna be burned alive.

Glancing over my shoulder, I see the flames licking my heels. I pump my legs harder, the burn in my thighs mirrored by the one in my lungs.

I'm running so fast I can't catch my breath. I open my mouth to take in more air, but suddenly there is no air. There's only the fire, the heat, and the horrible cramping in my chest as my need for oxygen becomes acute.

I can't keep running.

I also can't stop.

My knees buckle. I fall, my stomach pitching as the burning pavement rises up to meet me. I brace for impact—

I'm yanked from the dream—nightmare—by the sound of rain pummeling the tin roof of my apartment.

No fire, then. Just a storm.

I'm soaked in sweat. My heart is racing.

These fucking nightmares just won't quit. Like I'm

not having enough trouble sleeping after Ryder unceremoniously said he didn't feel the same after I bared my heart to him. Now I have horrible dreams about being trapped in a postapocalyptic hellscape.

Fun times.

I lie awake, body aching, until the thin gray light of dawn peeks through the shutters above my bed.

Then I get up and go to work, feeling more dead than alive.

My cell phone pings on the desk beside my computer.

My stomach drops the way it does every time I've gotten a text over the past seven days. It's been exactly one week since Ryder turned me down that night by the bonfire, but like the lovesick idiot I am, I still hold out hope that he'll text me—call me—and confess that he was lying, that he was scared of hurting me or my brother or whoever, and ask me out on a proper date.

Because that's not pathetic or anything, continuing to pine after a guy who unequivocally shot you down.

Glancing at the screen, my heart falls when I see that the text isn't from Ryder.

Instead, it's from Xander. He's going to be in town tonight, and he wants to know if I'd like to hang out with him and some of his friends at the Rattler.

The guy's a piece of shit. I haven't heard boo from him since my accident. He hasn't so much as sent a "Hey, you ok?" text. He definitely hasn't gotten me out of the office and treated me to a pair of custom-made cowboy boots like Ryder did.

But Ryder said point-blank he only wanted to be friends, and a girl has needs. Especially after being turned down. I'd very much like to move past the humiliation I felt, and still feel, despite Ryder's obvious attempts to let me down easy.

Nothing like a little fun between the sheets to clear the proverbial slate, right? Xander is a good lay.

At the very least, he's a sure thing.

I won't need a wingwoman to come to the bar with me to help pick him up. But suddenly I'm into the idea of having some moral support there, just in case Ryder happens to show up.

I shoot off texts to Sally and Ava, and then I hit up Mollie and Wheeler too. Yes, Mollie has a newborn and Wheeler is pregnant, so in all likelihood, they're not going to want to hang out at a dive bar that smells like cigarettes and stale beer. But I enjoyed hanging out with them, and maybe they'd like a little Friday night break from being at the ranch.

Immediately my phone pings with responses.

MOLLIE: Yes! I was just saying how I miss dancing. Haven't been out since baby came!
MOLLIE: I'm in. Here, I'm going to loop us all in on a text thread because I just saw you pinged Wheeler too. She's sitting right next to me ☺

LONG LIVE COWGIRLS TEXT THREAD

I grin. I like these ladies.

MOLLIE: Y'all, how cute is the name of our group?

> *You're welcome. So our gal Billie needs some wingwomen tonight at the Rattler. Y'all in?*
>
> *WHEELER: How do you think Tallulah is going to feel about having this pregnant ~lady~ at her bar?*
>
> *SALLY: You are the cutest pregnant lady on earth. I think Tallulah will be delighted to pour you some fake ranch waters*
>
> *MOLLIE: Otherwise known as just Topo Chico, which I'll also be drinking because I'm still nursing this nugget. Womp womp*
>
> *AVA: And the lime! Don't forget that! Makes it almost as delicious as the tequila does. Almost.*
>
> *AVA: Sawyer and I have date night, but we will join y'all afterward! Or I can kick his ass to the curb if we want it to be strictly girls only?*

My stomach dips. If Sawyer comes out to the Rattler, does that mean the rest of the Rivers boys will too? They don't always move as a pack, but they do often enough for it to be a thing.

Squaring my shoulders, I tell myself I don't care if Ryder shows up or not. As his *friend*, I feel neutral about his presence.

Still gonna wear something hot, though. Maybe put on a little eyeliner too. This *is* my first time on the rebound. I've dated some in the past, but I wouldn't say anyone's broken my heart.

Not like Ryder actually broke my heart or anything. But his rejection still hurt in a way I don't think anyone else's ever would.

WHEELER: *Sawyer is always welcome. I'm in! Gotta confirm—is the cowboy you're after named Ryder Rivers? Just so I can fulfill my wingwoman duties to the best of my ability...*

I could pretend his rejection didn't happen.

But then I think about Mollie's warmth and Wheeler's generosity and Sally and Ava showing up for me in the middle of the day even though they definitely didn't have to.

And it's not like they won't find out eventually about Ryder and me. Really, I have much more to gain than lose here. Just because I got burned putting myself out there with Ryder doesn't mean the same will happen with these women.

I could use their advice. And their help.

BILLIE: *(Not so) funny story...I told Ryder I had feelings for him the other night, but he said he wanted to be just friends* ☹

SALLY: *Aw, honey, I'm so sorry!*

WHEELER: *That truly and deeply sucks. But kudos to you for being honest. That takes guts.*

MOLLIE: *Proud of you. But TBH...that doesn't make sense to me. I'm not sure Ryder was telling the truth. The way that man looks at you...*

BILLIE: *Who knows? I get why he turned me down, though. He and my brother are so close, and it'd get messy*

AVA: *Not if you played it right. How could the guy NOT be obsessed with you? I am* 😊

> BILLIE: *Y'all are making me blush. Thank you for making me feel better*
>
> BILLIE: *Whatever the case, I gotta move on. This bull rider I know is going to be in town, so I'm setting my sights on him I think?*
>
> MOLLIE: *Sounds like a plan*
>
> WHEELER: *10–4*
>
> AVA: *Wear your new boots. We'll take care of the rest.*

My phone hasn't stopped pinging. Dad's chair creaks as he spins it around to face me. "Sounds like something's happening. What kinda trouble you gettin' up to now?"

See? Always causing trouble. But didn't Ryder say I should keep doing that? Do more of it, even?

Part of me still thinks I should scrap the whole idea. I *am* stirring the pot by hanging out with Xander again. But if I can't have the guy I want…well, what the hell am I supposed to do? Sit at home and wait for Ryder to change his mind? I have to do *something*, or I'm going to die of sexual frustration.

"You know me," I deadpan. "Can't help myself. It's nothing, I'm just getting together with some girls at the Rattler tonight."

Dad's brow wings upward. "Elizabeth May, are you pulling my chain? What girls?"

As if summoned by the use of my full name, Mom appears, throwing open the door. "Well, howdy, y'all."

"Hi, Mom," I reply, pasting on a smile.

Dad turns to Mom. "She says she's getting together with some friends tonight."

"Oh, honey, which friends are you talking about? Do I know them?"

I remember Pawpaw, my mom's dad, telling me my eyes would get stuck if I kept rolling them so much.

Considering I've rolled them as much as I have, it's a miracle they *haven't* gotten stuck. I try very hard not to roll them again right now.

"Of course y'all know them. It's just gonna be me, Ava, Sally, Mollie Luck, and Wheeler Rankin. You know, the gal who owns Bellamy Brooks with Mollie."

Mom and Dad stare at me for a full beat.

"What?" I roll my thumb over my phone screen in a failed effort to keep my face from flushing. "You can call them and check if you'd like."

Mom sets down the plate on my desk and claps her hands. "I love this for you, Billie. It's one of my biggest regrets that we couldn't give you a sister."

"Had to call it quits at some point." Dad runs a hand over his face. "Man's gotta retire, and that wasn't ever gonna happen if we kept having babies."

Mom tucks my hair behind my ear. "Y'all go have fun. Holler if you need me to pick you up, all right? No drinking and driving."

I glance at my phone. "Actually, Wheeler is pregnant, so she just offered to be our designated driver."

"Excellent." Dad nods. "Good for you, Billie."

I'm smiling for the first time all week, and it feels good.

Dad notices. "That right there is what I like to see. I know you've been in a funk this week. Whatever y'all are doing, I hope you have fun. You deserve to blow off a little steam."

I close my eyes and try to breathe through my nose. Sometimes, I think my parents don't really understand me. But other times, they seem to understand me better than I understand myself.

At the very least, they love me unconditionally, and they always look out for me. And that's why I'm terrified of letting them down.

"Thanks, Dad."

"You sure you don't wanna talk about it?" He ducks his head, brow furrowed.

I swallow hard. "I'm fine, really. Or I'll be fine."

"You sure?"

"Yeah."

"I love you, sweetie."

"Love you too."

Forty-seven years later, the day ends, thank the Lord. It was a long day in a long-ass week, and I am running on fumes.

I could flop on my couch and rot there for the rest of the night, easy. But as tired as I am, I'm more *frustrated*. If Xander is offering, I'm going to take him up on it.

So I force some pep into my step and head for my car after I leave the office. Only I'm intercepted two minutes later by Colt, who's heading to Mom and Dad's house to pick up Dean. I can smell the earthy scent of tobacco that rises off him. He said he's cutting back on the cigars, but today must've been an exception.

"Heading out to the Rattler tonight, I hear." He puts his hands on his hips. My stomach clenches with envy when I see how deeply tanned his face and hands are from a day spent outside.

You lucky bastard.

"Yup. Meeting some friends."

"The girls from Lucky River Ranch, right?"

Seriously, how many times am I going to roll my eyes today? "Can y'all mind your own damn business for a single second of your lives?"

He smiles. "I'm glad you're hangin' with those gals. Should be a good time—wish I could make it, but Dean's got a sleepover at our house."

Wrong that I feel relieved Colt will be at home tonight? He hasn't mentioned Ryder at all over the past week, which makes me think Ryder didn't tell my brother about what went down between us. Not like there's anything particularly juicy to tell. But for a hot minute there, I was worried Ryder might tell Colt that I confessed to having feelings for him.

Colt would likely rip me a new one if he knew. *What the hell is wrong with you? Out of all the dudes on this planet, you gotta fall for the guy who's never put his head on the same pillow twice? He's only gonna hurt you.*

My brother wouldn't be wrong. Ryder takes girls home, but as far as I know, he's never dated anyone. Who am I to think he'd break his rules for me?

I think we're also all walking on eggshells around Colt when it comes to things like loyalty and honesty. His wife, God rest her soul, was unfaithful, and that betrayal cut Colt deep. I'd hate for him to think that I betrayed him too.

I was just trying not to betray *myself*, so I told a really great guy how I felt about him.

"You'll be missed," I say.

"Nah, you won't miss me. But thanks for saying that

anyway. Be safe." He pecks me on the cheek, and my stomach clenches for an entirely different reason. "And be good."

See? My family can be great when they wanna be. Seriously, what's wrong with me that I can't seem to remember that fact when I'm at work or when I'm around Ryder Rivers?

"You know I'm not gonna be good," I reply, my throat tightening up again.

Colt laughs. "Yeah, I know that, Billie. Can't hurt to say it, though. We've all noticed how you're feeling blue. Hope this gets you back to bein' your old self again. I miss you."

"Aw. That's actually very kind of you to say."

"You surprised I'm kind? 'Cause *that* ain't very kind at all."

My turn to laugh. "Just…Sometimes I feel like I don't deserve you. And other times, I wonder what crime I committed in a past life *to* deserve you and your pain-in-the-assness."

"Guilty. Since I am such a pain in the ass, can I ask what's been goin' on with you?" He squints against the ardent late afternoon sun. "Mom and Dad are worried."

Now I *really* feel like an asshole.

"I won't say anything to them," Colt continues. "But I'm worried too."

I choose my words carefully. "The bookkeeping—I'm not sure I'm cut out for it."

"You tell them that?"

"No."

"Why not?"

"You know why."

Colt sighs and runs a hand down his face. He looks so much like Dad when he does it that my pulse skips a beat.

"I can tell you aren't cut out for it either," he finally replies.

That makes my pulse skip another beat. "Thank you. Hearing that makes me feel like I'm not losing my mind or just, you know, being lazy."

"You're not lazy. But you gotta advocate for yourself, Billie. If your vision for the future doesn't align with Mom and Dad's, speak up now before it's too late."

I scoff. "How the hell do I tell them?"

"You have a plan, that's how. Don't just go in there and quit. Come up with something else you could be doing for the ranch—a concrete idea they can't say no to."

Looking away, I wonder how the hell I'm going to make it to seven o'clock, when I'm supposed to meet all the girls (save Ava) downtown. I'm *tired*.

I wonder how the hell I'm going to survive my twenties. Why does no one tell you how hard this shit is?

"That's just it. I have no clue what else I'd do. All the positions I can think of are filled."

"That's on you to figure out. You're a big girl now." His eyes meet mine, and his expression softens. "I believe in you, Billie. We all do. You were so ballsy out there in the arena, so be ballsy everywhere else too. Except the Rattler. Please don't be ballsy there."

"That's a lot of balls for one sentence."

He chuckles. "Part and parcel of being a Wallace."

"Bad joke."

"Why you laughin', then?"

I reach out and give him a shove. "I'll think on it."

"You should. And if you need help, just holler, all right?"

"I will."

CHAPTER 13
Older and Wiser
Ryder

No she didn't.

Oh Lord, but Billie *did* wear a short-ass skirt and a teeny-tiny crop top to the Rattler tonight.

It's the kind of look that has everyone, including me, making eyes at her.

And goddamn her, she knows it.

Striding into the bar, she tosses her long, dark hair over her shoulder and smiles. Her legs look a mile long in her Bellamy Brooks boots, and her pouty mouth is emphasized by the bright red lipstick she's wearing.

She sways her ass to the beat of the song the band plays. Frisky Whiskey is on fire tonight, although they're missing Sally because apparently she wanted to hang out with Billie.

Anger—longing—it wraps around my torso like a steel band, tightening with every step she takes. Heads turn in Billie's direction. One guy even has the gall to let out a low whistle.

That band tightens to a painful degree when I see a line of familiar faces trail into the bar after Billie. There's Mollie, Wheeler, and, yep, Sally too. Apparently Ava and Sawyer will join later, after they have dinner at the restaurant next door.

Cash is the one who tipped me off that the girls were getting together tonight. I told myself I was coming to the Rattler anyway to cut loose after the longest week ever.

Go figure, having a days-long case of blue balls will make your life a living hell.

If I'm being honest with myself, though, I need to see Billie. I wasn't expecting to miss her. But I do. A lot.

I miss her so much that it keeps me up at night. I tried playing guitar by myself, but it was an exercise in self-flagellation. I couldn't play a song if you paid me without Billie there.

Why, I have no clue. But I've been feeling suffocated without her around. And I don't know what the fuck to do about that.

It's not fair of me to be here right now. She told me how she felt, and I told her we should just be friends. I get why she'd be on the prowl tonight. Hell, technically I'm on the prowl too.

I couldn't stay away. Shitty of me? Yes. But I feel more lost than ever, and I didn't know what else to do.

Billie's whole face lights up when she spots a guy in a black cowboy hat and matching shirt. Going up on her tiptoes, she flings her arms around the asshole's neck. He has the audacity to loop an arm around her back—her *low* back—and pull her against him.

I grit my teeth, ignoring the zap of pain in my breastbone.

That asshole looks familiar.

Shit, it's that bull rider from the rodeo, isn't it? Zach or Zoolander or whatever. What the hell is *he* doing here? Did she ask him to meet her? Are they hooking up again?

Christ, I can't breathe.

"You all right there, buddy?"

I feel Duke's eyes on me, but it's only when he taps the neck of his beer against mine that I realize I'm holding the bottle in a death grip.

"Shots. We need them. Tallulah!" I tear my gaze from Billie to glance at the bartender, who pins me with a knowing glare.

"You got a ride home tonight?" she asks.

Duke sighs. "We got him, yeah."

"Somethin' you wanna get off your chest?" Tallulah doesn't look up from pouring us each a double shot of reposado tequila.

One of the perks of living in a one-stoplight, one-honky-tonk town is that the bartender always knows what you're drinking.

I grab the glass and knock back the tequila in a single gulp. It burns its way through my chest.

It does nothing to relieve the pressure there.

It does absolutely *nothing* to relieve heaviness between my legs. Billie and I haven't so much as met eyes, but I already want her. Bad.

A week away from her did jack shit to cure me of this inconvenient fucking need to have her. In fact, the separation's only made it worse.

Great.

"I'm an idiot." I set down the shot glass with a thud.

Duke keeps sighing, holding his full shot in his hand. "That about sums it up, yeah."

My twin is the only person I told about what went down with Billie. I even went so far as to tell him how I genuinely feel about her.

He clearly doesn't agree with my reasons for keeping my distance.

"Do I want to know?" Tallulah arches a brow.

I shake my head. "You don't."

"All right, then. I'm here if you need an ear to bend."

"Bend mine instead, would you?" Duke says after we've turned back around. "Tell me why Colt wouldn't adore two of the people he loves most in the world, er, falling in love?"

I frown. "Weren't you just telling me to keep my distance from Billie?"

"I've changed my tune since Wheeler and I got together. Being with the right person…that trumps everything, even if it's inconvenient for everybody else."

I wait for the tequila to soften the edges of all the terrible shit I'm feeling. Billie's looking up at Zink like he hung the fucking moon.

Meanwhile, the hand he has on her back creeps lower. I swear to God, if he starts groping her ass—

"Cash already punched someone in the mouth over a girl here," Tallulah is saying. "Can we not have a repeat tonight, pretty please?"

Duke nods, raising his beer over his head. "You got it, Tallulah." Then, lowering his voice, he says to me, "Dude, you're gonna give yourself away if you keep staring at her like that."

"I'm not ready." I drain my beer. "For her, I mean.

With her, it would be real, and I can't—I'm just not ready for that."

I can tell Duke is trying very hard not to roll his eyes. "You would be if you got your head out of your ass."

"Great advice. Thanks."

"Either get your girl, or get gone. You know I'm right, Ryder. Otherwise, you're gonna cause a whole world of trouble for dumbass reasons."

I cut him the nastiest glare I can manage. "You think protecting a friend who's like another brother to me is a dumbass reason?"

"Colt doesn't need you to protect him. He needs you to be honest. With him and with yourself. And you want Billie. So do the right thing, man: Tell Colt, then stake your claim before somebody else does." He nods in Zayne's direction.

I motion for another beer. "What if I can't, though? Be good to her?"

"You won't know until you try."

Yeah, but what if I fuck it up and I end up losing her and Colt *and the respect of my family?*

What if I can't open up the way she needs me to? No one can fall in love with half a person. And that's what I've been for over a decade now, a human being who shut down his pain and, without knowing it, his joy too.

Joy I only felt with Billie, singing stupid songs like the stupid idiots we are.

Fuck, she was cute doing that awkward little dance of hers. And the way she laughed *with* me, felt shit *with* me—that was everything.

My dick is sore from tugging one out too many times this week thinking about her. The sounds she'd make, the way she'd taste, how hot her mouth would feel as my length slid home down the back of her throat.

Bet she'd give *good* head.

Bet I give better.

Even so, I'd only end up letting her down. That, more than anything, is why I gotta stay away.

"You and Wheeler end up hanging those new curtains today?" I tip back the fresh Shiner Tallulah hands me. Why the hell can't I seem to catch a buzz tonight?

When Wheeler moved in with Duke, I helped hang some curtains in their guest room. The two of them had some sweet trim added to the curtains now that the guest room has become their future nursery.

Duke looks at me for a long, hard beat. "We did. They look fucking great. Why are you changing the subject?"

"You know why. Nursery is turning out awful cute. Still can't believe y'all are having twins."

"I can't either. We're all going through it, you know. The grief. It doesn't end. But if you let yourself feel it, share it, it does get…less intense. Less heavy." He puts a hand on my shoulder. "You're gonna be all right, Ryder. But that's only if you do shit like go after the girl you really want."

"I don't… Billie's always been off limits. You know that about—" My voice catches. It hits me that I'm the one being a punk now, antagonizing my brother like this. He's just trying to give me good advice, and here I am, egging him on. Arguing just for the sake of pissing him off because *I'm* pissed off.

Really fucking pissed off that I can't seem to figure

out a workaround for this deep-seated fear that I'm never gonna be enough for someone.

Being safe is better than risking destruction.

I'm so fucked up I don't even know where to begin to fix it. Me. Whatever.

"I'm fine," I say at last. "Go dance with *your* girl. I give her credit for coming out. I know she's tired."

Duke sighs, giving me one last hard look. "This is gonna sound harsh, but it's my job as your older brother—"

"By four minutes!"

"Doesn't matter what the time span is. I'm older, so I'm wiser too. That's just how it works. What I was gonna say is, Mom would be real disappointed in you right now. She didn't raise you to be this guy. The one drinking himself into oblivion at the bar while watching everyone else live their lives. You're better than that. You know it. Mom knew it. I know it. And so does Billie."

All my vital organs seize at the same time. I'm unable to so much as blink or swallow for a full beat. I wonder if I'm having a stroke. The pain that gathers in my middle is unreal, like I've been kicked square in the chest by an ornery horse.

Apparently animal therapy worked wonders on me. Would psychological therapy—whatever the term is for the kind you do on a couch—work too?

"You're right," I wheeze, putting a hand over my heart. "That hurts."

Duke's eyes are sad. "It should. I'm rooting for you. We all are. But you gotta make some changes, Ryder, if you're ever gonna get what you want. What you *really* want, deep down there." He taps my chest. "Mama didn't raise no chickenshit, yeah?"

I laugh, even as my eyes burn.

Before I can fight him on the shit he just said, though, Duke turns and heads for the dance floor.

I watch, a horrible weight in my center, as he takes Wheeler's hand and leads her toward the band. They make a handsome couple two-stepping cheek to cheek, the way Mom and Dad used to do in the kitchen after supper.

Aw, hell, now Billie is leading that bull rider to the dance floor. The band is playing a slow song, so she and the asshole start to sway together. They turn, allowing me a glimpse of his hands at her tailbone, his fingertips inching down her ass.

I see red.

I see myself launching over the bar and grabbing his shirt and telling him to stop pawing at my girl.

I see her crying.

I see Colt coming for me with his fists. Or a gun.

And still, I can't look away. *Damn it, I should be the one dancing with her.*

The girls join them on the dance floor. It's Mollie's first night out since the baby was born, so she's ready to party. Wheeler looks adorable dancing with her not-so-little bump alongside Sally.

Ava and Sawyer show up. They stop by the bar to say hello. My brother gives me a weird look, but then Ava is yanking him toward the band. I wave him away, a silent affirmation that I'm okay.

Only I'm definitely not okay when Billie's eyes lock on mine from the dance floor, making my stomach nosedive. Her eyes bulge and those red lips part, and I wonder what she's thinking.

If I were her, I'd be mad as a hornet that the guy who turned her down is still ogling her from across the room like a creeper.

I have no fucking right.

But I *can't look away.*

I also can't seem to move. Every time I convince myself that I need to either walk out or walk over there and cut in, my legs won't budge.

I can tell it pisses off Billie, because after a song or two, she really starts to go for it with Z guy. He holds her hips as she grinds against him when Frisky Whiskey plays its signature cover of "Wobble." I nearly black out when she wraps her hand around his nape, pulling him closer.

He's a dead man if he kisses her.

He doesn't. But she looks like she sure as hell wouldn't mind if he did.

I have enough sense to quit drinking. I don't wanna be *that* guy, the one who needs to be carried out of here after he pukes his guts out. I ask Tallulah for a water.

What if he takes advantage of her?

What if she gets too drunk?

I stand there, and I glower at him with all my might, indulging in the fantasy that I'm sticking around to save her. Even though Billie Wallace has never needed saving and likely never will.

Every so often she looks my way. And every time she does, she seems to double her efforts to make me wanna die. She plays with his hair. She slides her hand inside his shirt. She leans in and whispers in his ear.

RYDER

I stand there for hours. Or maybe minutes, I don't know.

I nearly jump when Mollie appears at my elbow.

"Earth to Ryder. Are you ill?"

Leave it to her to get straight to the point.

"Don't worry." I shove my hands in my pockets. "I'm going home."

"You could go home." Mollie glances out at the dance floor. "Or you could go ask Billie to dance with *you* instead of that rando."

"What's the deal with girls always liking bull riders?"

Mollie shrugs. "They're bad for us, and therefore we like them. Simple girl math. But you...I don't think you'd be all that bad for Billie."

"I'm not—she's not—I ain't getting in her way."

"Whatever you say," Mollie says with a sigh, rolling her eyes. "Could you stop staring at her, then? It's making everyone uncomfortable."

You got no idea how uncomfortable I've been all damn week with a dick that won't stay down and sleep that won't come.

"I'm just looking out for her. Like you said: Can't trust a bull rider."

Mollie rolls her eyes again, then orders another round and heads back out to dance.

Only when the bull rider whispers in Billie's ear and they exit the dance floor several songs later do I blink, the awful fucking spell broken.

He leads her by the hand in the direction of the Rattler's front entrance. Wait, where are they going? Is he taking her home?

I've officially lost my ever-loving mind.

Our gazes meet one last time as she lets him lead

her out of the bar. I can't tell if the look on her face is a pleading one—*please, please, come get me*—or one that's defiant. *Fuck you, loser.*

Either way, I can't just stand here and do nothing. Even though that's *exactly* what I've been doing for God knows how long.

Go. The fuck. Home.

I actually do go home. I ignore the persistent feeling in my gut that I should follow Billie. Instead, I dig the keys to my truck out of my pocket and drive it all the way home.

I'm in my bed, naked and sweating and restless, when the text comes through.

Billie.

Goddamn it.

But I slide my thumb over the screen anyway. My stomach immediately bottoms out when I see what she sent me.

CHAPTER 14
Come Again
Billie

BILLIE: *Are u ok?*

I debated for the whole ride to the field party whether or not I should send Ryder a text. We're just friends. And friends don't check in with each other on Fridays at midnight.

Then again, friends don't stare you down with daggers in their eyes while you dance with other guys.

Ryder *stared*. All night. At one point, Mollie even went over to talk to him about it, but he just told her he was "looking out for me."

I'm not sure what to think. All I know is, I'm not buying it.

RYDER: ...
RYDER: *I'm fine. Are you okay? I saw you leaving with that sleazebag*
BILLIE: *And I saw you staring at us the whole*

> *time, looking like you wanted to commit a crime. What's your deal?*
> RYDER: *Just looking out for you is all*
> BILLIE: *I know that's just a line you gave Mollie. I can look out for myself, thank you very much*

Another pause, three dots appearing, disappearing. Appearing again.

> RYDER: *Think what you want. It's not a crime to want you to get home safe*

My pulse skips several beats. I'm angry. I'm confused.

Ryder's being kind of an ass tonight. That should turn me off, right? Jealousy's not a good look on anyone. But if I'm being honest…

It's hot. In a really fucked up way. Then again, this whole thing—me falling even harder for a guy who turned me down, and who's also known for one-night stands and one-night stands only—is pretty fucked up. So, yeah. Not really sure what to do with that.

I'm not really sure what to do with *myself* right now.

> RYDER: *Where are you*

I don't know why he's asking that question, but I do know it makes my stomach do somersaults.

> BILLIE: *That feels like a dangerous question. Go to bed, buddy*
> RYDER: *I'm not your buddy*
> BILLIE: *What are you then*

> RYDER: Just tell me you're okay and that you're not gonna let that dipshit get in your pants?
> BILLIE: As my *friend*, it's none of your business who gets into my pants.
> RYDER: Where are you
> BILLIE: GO TO BED
> RYDER: Not until I know you're safe at home. ALONE. Also you're the one who texted me. Don't pretend you don't enjoy stirring the pot

Ugh, he's right.

He's right because he knows me in a way that Xander never will.

Ryder cares. Why, then, did he turn me down? I'm not sure that I buy the idea that someone would turn you down because he cares too much. In my experience, people don't have that level of self-control.

Or maybe that's just me.

> BILLIE: No comment.
> RYDER: Ha. But really, you shouldn't rub shit in my face like you did tonight
> BILLIE: You have to be kidding. You know what? Screw this. Screw you. Maybe I did rub it in your face. You did turn me down, and yeah, maybe I need someone to help lick my wounds. He makes me feel better, even if just for tonight

My heart is pounding when I hit send. I wait, barely breathing, for Ryder to respond. But he doesn't.

"Hey, sweetheart. Whatcha doin' over here all by your lonesome?"

Glancing up from my phone, I see Xander holding out a Solo cup. He's wearing his signature smirk, the one that he uses when he wants to get laid.

Then again, Xander wants to get laid all the time, so I'm not sure why he feels the need to add a smirk to the mix. Feels a little overkill.

Whatever. You need relief, and he's offering it to you. Beggars can't be choosers in a small town like Hartsville.

This field party is Exhibit A. There's maybe twenty people here, all of them hanging out around a huge bonfire. I've known all of them for most of my life, with the notable exception of Xander and the handful of friends he brought with him. They competed in a rodeo outside of Austin last night, so they decided to make a pit stop here in Hartsville. They're staying in the bunkhouse at a ranch down the road from here.

I thought for sure Xander would want to head to my place after the Rattler. But his friends insisted we come to this field party, and I was a little surprised when Xander agreed.

"Don't worry," he'd said in my ear. "We'll sneak out right after we get there."

Only that hasn't happened, which is why I ended up texting Ryder. Xander's been too busy shooting the shit with everyone to pay much mind to me.

I almost wish I'd taken up the girls on their offer to come with me. But I could tell Mollie and Wheeler were beat, and Sally and Ava were just as horny as I was—am—so they went home to their cowboys.

I paste on a smile as I take the Solo cup. "I'm just waitin' on you to make good on your promise."

"Aw, sweetheart, I ain't good at keepin' promises."

His eyes meet mine over the rim of his cup as he sips. "But for you, I'll try."

He's so full of shit it's almost painful. Really, what did I ever see in this guy? I don't remember him giving me the *ick* when we first hung out.

Now that I've been hanging out with Ryder, however…Xander isn't nearly as attractive as I thought he was.

I try to choke down the lukewarm pilsner in the hope it will give me a much-needed pair of beer goggles. If I go one more day without getting laid, I may have a legit nervous breakdown. A vibrator can only get you so far when you've been sharing romantic tractor rides and bonfires with handsome cowboys.

"Who are your friends again?" I ask.

Xander shrugs. "Wouldn't call 'em friends. Just some guys I met on the circuit, really. I'd keep your distance if I were you. They don't exactly keep their noses clean, if you know what I'm sayin'." Xander runs his finger down the side of my neck.

I wait for the familiar shiver of anticipation to dart down my spine.

It doesn't. Instead, it takes everything in me not to recoil.

Yup, my vibrator will have to do yet again tonight. I'm not staying here another minute. But I know Xander will do everything in his power to convince me to stay, so I think it's best if I pull a Houdini and sneak out.

"Hey, Xander I…gotta. You know." I tilt my head toward the stand of juniper trees to our left. "I'll be right back?"

"You need some help takin' off that skirt? Looks

fuckin' sexy on you, but I think you'd look even better without it."

Great. Now I'm going to vomit in my mouth.

"Thanks, but I got it."

Before Xander can reply, I turn on my heel and make a beeline for the trees, praying I don't encounter any snakes or foxes.

Glancing at my phone, I see that it's almost half past twelve. Not late by normal standards, but when you live on a ranch, that's practically morning.

I didn't think I'd need an escape plan tonight. But I also didn't think I'd be turned off by a guy who, up until very recently, turned me *on* in a big way.

I race through my options. Anyone I call at this hour will be dead asleep. Mom offered to pick me up, but I don't want her judgment when she sees me at this dumbass party with all these dumbass people. I need her to trust me to make good decisions, and she sure as hell isn't going to trust her daughter who chased an idiot bull rider to a field in the middle of nowhere at midnight.

I could call one of my brothers. Tate is the night owl of the family, but even for him this is late. Beck, Nash, and Mack would come, but they'd be pissed about it. I'd also owe them big time.

Colt—

Well, he's got a kid. He'd also put two and two together and somehow find out that Ryder was at the Rattler too, and that he was giving me looks to kill. The less Colt knows about what's gone down between me and his best friend, the better.

I don't want to bother any of the girls again. They've already done so much for me.

RYDER

Guess I go for my least worst option.

Sighing, I start to type out a text to Tate when headlights slice through the trees.

My heart plunges at the throaty throb of a diesel engine.

Looking up, I see Ryder's vintage Dodge Ram pickup stop just outside the circle of light put off by the bonfire.

I blink. Blink again, wondering if Xander laced this beer. Am I seeing things now?

But then Ryder's getting out of the truck and slamming the door. I can tell it's him by the backward baseball hat he's wearing, the same one he had on at the Rattler. A couple people look up. Xander, I notice, immediately ducks his head and disappears into the shadows. He was good at ignoring Ryder at the Rattler, telling me to ignore him too. But now all of a sudden, Xander is running scared.

What a spineless douche.

Part of me thinks I should run too. Ryder and Duke would occasionally show up to field parties in their early twenties, but once they got serious about cowboying, they stopped coming. Now that they're partners in the highly lucrative Lucky River Ranch, they wouldn't be caught dead here. Their lives are much, much cooler than mine.

Makes me think Ryder came for one reason and one reason only.

Me.

He glances around, a muscle in his jaw twitching.

Anger and disbelief and arousal unfurl inside me, elbowing for space. I hurtle his way, nearly falling on my face after tripping on a root.

That's when he sees me. Our eyes meet, and everything inside me heaves.

Holy God, he's really here.

How'd he find me? Why come all this way?

Even in the dark, he looks good. The backward baseball hat, a barn jacket, broad shoulders. Jeans and boots and eyes that pierce the inky blackness around us like two bright blue beacons.

A throb ignites between my legs. It's the kind of deep, *deep* desire that immediately catches fire and consumes my entire body in the space of a single heartbeat.

I'm burning up, and it's all for him. The man who wants to be *just friends*.

I'm moving toward him before I know what I'm doing. I'm shaking and sweating despite the cool night air.

Did he somehow get bigger since I saw him last? Because he towers over me when we come to a stop barely a foot from each other.

Without a word he grabs my cup, tosses its contents onto the ground, and drops it into the nearby trash bag that hangs from a tree branch.

I want to speak. To cuss him out or beg him to kiss me or *something*. But my mouth isn't working.

People watch as he grabs my hand—*what in the world is happening, oh my God, what in the world*—and gives me a none-too-gentle tug toward the night that surrounds us.

"Ryder?" I feel stupid. His grip on my hand is firm, unyielding. "What—why are you here? Where are we going? How did you find me?"

No answer.

He leads me back toward his truck, just out of everyone's earshot.

"You're a fucking brat, you know that?" His voice is low. Gravelly.

I decide *not* to rise to the occasion.

"Thank you. But also: Excuse me?" I stop, tugging on his hand to make him face me. He does, his boots catching with a small sigh in the dirt.

"*He* makes you feel better?" Ryder continues. "Are you serious?"

Anger bubbles up at the back of my throat, along with a hefty dose of *what the actual fuck*?

Maybe that's why I say something stupid. "Yes, really."

"A brat *and* a liar."

"Hey. Call me anything you want except a liar."

Only, he's right.

He's right to call me out. He doesn't put up with my bullshit, and I like that. I respect that.

I love that about him.

"Aim higher." Ryder is back to grunting at me.

My heartbeat trips to a sudden, painful stop. "I tried. With you."

Dead silence. The lack of noise is unnerving. It becomes a throbbing, living thing that fills my ears and chokes off my air supply as Ryder's head falls back and he closes his eyes.

"I'm no better," he says at last. "You know that."

"But you are better. *So* much better." The words burst from my mouth. "You're generous, and brave, and funny and…Look, I know you think we rib on each other like old friends, or brother and sister, but I think there's so much more there—"

"*Stop.*"

The pained sound of the word has everything inside me doing backflips.

In all the years I've known him, Ryder has only ever let his emotions get the better of him twice: a week ago during our picnic, and tonight. Right now.

Three times, actually, if you count our time in the ER together.

And all three times, he's been with me.

Holy shit.

He opens his eyes, and they move to me, glittering in the darkness.

Yep. Those eyes are swimming with emotion. I see it. I *feel* it.

My heart starts working again, taking off at a thousand frantic beats per minute.

The tension in the air is thick enough to cut with a knife.

"I am *not* your brother." Ryder's Adam's apple bobs on a swallow. "And yeah, Billie, there is so much more between us. You drive me *batshit* crazy. The way you move and how your eyes light up when you laugh and"—he runs a hand down his face—"Christ, that fucking shirt."

I can't move. "What about my shirt?"

"You know what that shirt does to a man. That's why you wore it."

My body goes up in flames. I *am* the bonfire now. I can almost feel the smoke rising off my skin.

Is Ryder actually admitting that he's into me? That he *was the one who lied?*

Holy fucking *shit*, is he actually going to let something

happen between us? Because he's talking about my shirt, which means he's thinking about my tits.

He might as well be touching them for the way my nipples immediately pebble. I'm wearing my flimsiest bra and a tissue-thin crop top, which means Ryder can see everything.

But he also talked about my smile and my laugh and—

His eyes flick to my chest. His mouth flattens to a tight line. But his eyes—

The emotion in them is suddenly edged with *hunger*.

I have been dying to reach for this man for years now. As long as I can remember. He's giving me an opening, one I never in a million years thought I'd get. He's right about one thing: I know better than to let this chance slip through my fingers.

"What if I did wear it on purpose?" My voice sounds strange. Breathy, quiet. "What if I wore it for you?"

His expression is stark now. Strained. "You happy now? Saying out loud how you're putting me through hell?"

"Hell?" A let out a bark of disbelieving laughter. "You have no idea the hell I've been through wanting you the way I have. But then you tell me you just want to be friends even though you're always *here*—"

"Because you asked me to be! *You* texted *me*, remember?" he explodes. "You're the one who's always showing up on my doorstep."

"You're the one who showed up just now without any prompting at all on my part! And you knew I was gonna be out at the Rattler tonight, didn't you? That's why you were out too, right? *Right*?"

His throat bobs again. "I'm not gonna lie to you, Billie."

I scoff. "So do you wanna be *just friends,* Ry? Or do you wanna be more than that? Because I'm real fuckin' confused, buddy."

He puts his hands on his hips. That muscle in his jaw jumps again. After a beat, he rounds the truck and opens the passenger side door. "I told you not to call me that. Now get in the truck. That's why I came: to make sure you got home safe."

"I call bullshit."

"Get. In. The *fucking* truck, Billie, or so help me—"

"What?" I step forward. "What're you gonna do?"

He leans in, his face an inch from mine. "*You* know and *I* know that you don't wanna stay here with Zephyr. If you did, you'd be with him right now. So get in the truck, and I'll drive you home. Otherwise, you're gonna be spending the night at some shitty bunkhouse with a bunch of assholes leering at you while that dickhead, Z whatever-his-name-is, tries to cop a feel."

God, why does this man have to always be right about everything? It's infuriating.

"His name isn't Zephyr. It's Xander." Sighing, I climb into the truck. "I hate you."

"No you don't." Ryder shuts the door.

A beat later he's climbing into the driver's seat and starting the engine. I can feel its rumble through the vinyl seat. It stokes the growing throb between my legs in a way that makes me want to squirm.

"Hey!" Xander shouts as we pass him. Guess he's done hiding now that he's safe? "Where are y'all goin'?"

Ryder doesn't answer, and neither do I.

Instead, I roll down my window and gather my hair

in my hand at the top of my head. The breeze feels good on my overheated skin.

"But really, how'd you know where I was?" It's the only thing I can think to say.

Well, other than, *Can we please fuck already, for the love of Christ?*

Truth is, though, I don't think I could withstand the humiliation of being turned down a second time. If someone's gonna make a move, it's gotta be Ryder. I already put myself out there. It's his turn to show his cards.

"Took a guess." Ryder guides the truck onto the smooth blacktop of the recently repaved County Highway Number 5. "Sawyer heard those toolbags talking about a field party, which left me with a few options. Figured the Horton's was my best bet—those boys are always havin' bonfires this time of year." He glances at me. "Still waitin' on a thank-you."

"You're not gonna get it because I didn't ask you to come."

"You're glad I did, though."

"C'mon, Ry." I turn my head to look at him. "You know I like trouble. I've learned by now how to get myself out of it."

He jams on the brakes. I jolt forward with a gasp, the seat belt biting through my shirt as Ryder pulls far enough off the road to offer us plenty of privacy beneath a starry, wide-open sky. The tires pop over the uneven dirt, and then we stop, Ryder shoving the truck into park.

I put a hand over my heart. "What the hell?"

"You want trouble?" His jaw tics.

His voice sounds different. Scraped bare, like he can barely breathe.

I'm aware of just how hard my nipples are now. The throb between my legs is unbearable.

"Always." I swallow.

Panicked elation rips through me when Ryder reaches over to unbuckle my seat belt. I watch, feeling lightheaded, as he hooks a finger in my belt loop.

"Then get the fuck over here."

CHAPTER 15
Pushing Buttons Pays Off
Billie

I don't hesitate even though my mind races.

Why now? What's changed? Will Colt ever forgive us? How is this already so effing good, and I haven't even touched Ryder yet?

My hand trembles as I put it on Ryder's shoulder. He helps me climb onto his lap so that my bad arm doesn't get caught between us, my legs straddling his hips. His big hands find my waist, and then we're face-to-face, the low rumble of the engine the only sound between us.

"Since when do *you* like trouble?" I'm panting. I *love* the feel of him between my legs like this.

His hands knead my sides, thumbs moving north toward my breasts, and a bolt of need cracks through my center. "Since I started hanging out with you. Such. A. fucking. *Brat*."

And then he tilts his head and leans in and slants his mouth over mine.

The heat of him—his lips, his breath, his body—is shocking in the best, most arousing way. I moan, overwhelmed, when he brushes his nose against mine and notches his bottom lip between my own.

He drags his tongue over the seam of my mouth, opening me to him, and my clit screams when I let him in and he drinks deeply, his tongue gliding into my mouth with an ease—a confidence—that has me moaning again.

"A brat you like."

"A brat I can't stay away from. So yeah."

The kiss is his—*I'm* his—and I let him take the lead. He tastes clean, like toothpaste, and I imagine he was getting ready for bed when I shamelessly sent him that text. The kiss guides us in a rhythm that quickly becomes frantic, needy. His thumbs brush lightly over my nipples, and I bite down on his bottom lip hard, spreading my knees so I can press my center more firmly against his.

He grunts. His hands find my hips, and he presses me down even more. At the same time, he rocks his hips upward, and my eyes roll to the back of my head when I feel his erection nudge me where I want him most.

This already feels so, so good.

Ordinarily, I'd let a guy stay in the lead at this point. As a woman, you never want to come across as too eager, too bossy in these situations. Guys like to think they're in control.

Fuck that. I've wanted this man for practically my whole life. I'm done playing it safe. Done playing games.

I've never liked doing what I was supposed to do anyway.

Grabbing the hem of my shirt, I break the kiss to yank it over my head and toss it aside.

Ryder makes a sound, half pleasure, half pain, as he looks down at my tits. My flimsy bra is red lace with little rosettes dotting the top of the cups. It's sheer enough that you can see my nipples in the light of the dash.

"Jesus *Christ*." Pressing a quick kiss to my throat, Ryder ducks his head to kiss the tops of my breasts, working his way down to my nipples. "You're so fuckin' beautiful, Billie. You got no idea how much I've been dyin' to do this. Since the rodeo...I been *dyin'*."

My heart hiccups. I don't want to think too much about what that means, but...

Yeah, the idea that he's wanted me since that night makes me feel all warm and fuzzy inside. He doesn't want to be *just friends*. Which makes me think he turned me down because he's trying not to hurt anyone, not because he doesn't want me.

When he sucks my left nipple into his mouth, I nearly howl at the painful twist of lust that reverberates through my center. I knock off his hat and jam my fingers into his hair, giving it a tug that's not at all gentle.

"Aw, darlin'. You ain't afraid to tell me what you like. Keep doing that, yeah? Tell me everything. I wanna know everything." Ryder takes my nipple between his teeth. At the same time, he reaches around and unhooks my bra. His fingers guide the straps down my arms, goose bumps breaking out on my skin when the crisp October air hits my bare breasts.

I feel exposed.

I feel *sexy*.

He wants to know me. Everything about me.

I take his hand and put it on my breast. "Lemme teach you, then."

His throat works on a swallow. His eyes are hazy, unfocused. I guide our thumbs over my nipple, my head falling back at the pure ecstasy of how good his calloused hands feel on me.

"Aw, baby." He pushes my hair over my shoulder before reaching around to gather it in his fingers, wrapping the strands around his fist. He pulls, tilting my head back so that my neck is bared and my tits are thrust practically into his face. "I want to see all of you. You're so—fuck, darlin'. Just…fuck."

"Exactly the reaction I was going for."

"So you finally admit it." He leans in and sinks his teeth into my neck. "You been fuckin' with me."

"That's"—I hiss when he pinches my nipple—"kind of my MO tonight. Fucking with men I apparently can't have."

He trails his mouth over my collarbone before sucking my other nipple into his mouth. "But you have me."

Only for tonight, though, right? Because this can't happen.

I don't say the words out loud. I don't think I need to. Sure, Ryder wants me. But like I said, he also doesn't want to fuck up his friendship with Colt or cause any stupid drama between us or our families.

I get it, even if I want more than just a single night with him. I'll take what I can get. Maybe hooking up with him will finally get him out of my system.

Ha. You're delusional.

I guide his hand down my stomach. "I do. You're all mine, cowboy."

He gives my hair another pull. This one isn't as gentle, and I feel it everywhere—the tips of my breasts, my clit, the fronts of my thighs.

Yum.

"All yours." Our tangled fingers find the button of my skirt. But instead of working it through its hole, he reaches down and shoves up the denim. He puts his hand on my thigh and arcs his thumb closer, closer, *closer* to where I want him most.

He bites down on my nipple hard, and I cry out. At the same time, he presses his thumb against my panties. "Show me how much you like havin' me. Get on your knees, darlin'."

When guys call me *darlin'*, it usually makes me cringe. There's something cheesy about the endearment. Maybe because men use it so damn much around here that it doesn't sound endearing at all? It just comes off as a lazy attempt at getting laid.

When Ryder says it, though, my toes literally curl. I *love* it.

I've never, ever heard him use it with another woman.

Pushing into the hand I have on his shoulder, I do as he tells me and rise onto my knees. He uses both hands to push up my skirt even more.

Then he's looking me in the eye. Leaning in for a bruising kiss before curling his first finger through my thong. He begins to trail his finger back and forth, back and forth, his knuckle tracing a line of fire through my slit.

His turn to bite *my* bottom lip. "Soft. Don't tell me you—"

"Shaved for Xander? Nah." I roll my hips into his touch. "I shaved for you. On the off chance—"

"I ended up fucking you in the front seat of my truck?" He tugs my thong aside.

"You really gonna fuck me for the first time in the front seat of your car?"

His thumb grazes my clit as he lets out a dark chuckle. "Where else you want me to do it?"

Lust, liquid, white-hot, bolts through my center. "On the hood. In the bed. In the backseat too."

The side of his mouth quirks up. "But we gotta be gentle. You're hurt."

"You be gentle, I'm gonna scream."

"That's kind of the idea, makin' you scream. But only because you feel so good." He parts me with his fingers, then glides one through my slickness. "Aw, darlin'. I like this. So fucking much."

"Show me." I'm practically riding his hand at this point. "Show me how much you like it."

He gathers my arousal on his fingertips and uses it to coat my clit. He goes slowly, savoring me, circling my clit again and again. I press against his fingers, begging for more. In reply, he slips those fingers lower and notches them at my entrance.

Pressure. Already.

More.

Leaning in, I kiss his mouth. His tongue glides to meet mine, and he mimics the motion with his finger. Its wide, blunt tip nudges my cunt before slipping inside.

We both shudder. There's an unexpected catch in my chest.

He's into this. Into me. And that makes me think...
What?

That we have a chance in hell of being together?

I don't know what this means, what *he* means when he says he can't stay away, but I do know I couldn't ask him to stop if you paid me.

I do know I feel safe, accepted in a way I never have before with a guy. The stakes are so, so high. But weirdly enough, I also feel like I have nothing to lose.

We're both adults. If this really is a onetime thing we never talk about again, so be it. I can let loose without worrying about whether or not he'll come back for seconds.

Might as well enjoy myself, then.

Might as well make the most of this marvelously unexpected moment, the one where I'm in Ryder's truck, in his arms, his hands all over me.

I am in *heaven* as he fills me with his finger. He presses the heel of his hand to my clit the deeper he sinks inside me. My cunt flutters around him, my legs beginning to shake, and his other hand moves to my breast and plays with my nipple.

Just like I taught him. The thought that he's paying attention, that he's trying to learn my body, my likes, makes my heart swell.

"Ry," I whisper into his mouth, rocking my hips. "More. Give me...*everything*."

He kisses me, his scruff catching on my chin, my cheeks. "You're so little here, Billie. If you really want to—"

"I want to."

"I'm gonna get you a little more relaxed, yeah?" I feel his second fingertip nudging against me. "It'll feel like a lot at first, but I promise I'll make it feel good. Trust me to make you feel good? Please?"

I cup the back of his neck and pull him in for a deeper kiss. "Always. You always make me feel good."

His hand falls from my hair and finds my hip. He holds me steady as he smoothly thrusts his first finger in, then out. He grunts when I try to rock my hips again.

"I know it's in your nature to ride, but you gotta be patient, yeah? I don't want you hurtin' something else. The arm is enough."

I nod my head, closing my eyes at the sudden rush of emotion that shoots up the back of my throat.

If you don't care, Ry, then why are you so careful with me?

He slowly—*slowly*—works his second finger inside me. I moan at the sudden increase in pressure. It's a pinch that's painful but wildly arousing too.

The need for release is overwhelming.

He pushes his fingers inside me at the same time he presses my hips down. I gasp at the feeling of fullness. My legs are shaking hard now—*I'm* shaking hard—but Ryder doesn't let up.

"You tell me, yeah, if it's too much?"

I nod, keeping my eyes closed. "I like it when it's too much."

Another dark, velvety chuckle. "I had a feeling you might. You're perfect here, darlin'. You're gonna feel like heaven. Can you come for me first, though? Let me know you're feelin' good?"

I keep nodding, unable to formulate words when his thumb finds my clit. Then he's using his other hand to thumb my nipple too. He's kissing my neck, my face, my mouth.

I feel worshipped. Adored.

I feel overwhelmed in the best, most terrifying way.

Together, we chase my orgasm. Or really, I hold onto Ryder for dear life while his fingers bring me closer and closer to release. He's got both fingers fully inside me now, and when he begins to thrust, I shudder so hard that he husks out a groan.

"Aw, darlin', let go already. I'm right here. Let go, Billie, and I promise I'll catch you."

The need for release spikes, coiling inside me, and then bright light bursts through me as the orgasm hits. My cunt tightens around Ryder's fingers.

"*Oh my God!*" I'm shouting. "Oh my fucking *God.*"

I collapse against him. He kisses my neck, murmurs my name in my ear while I ride out the shock waves.

He keeps playing with my clit, stoking the orgasm to continuous life. It's wrenching.

It's the best, most epic release of my life.

In the back of my mind, the realization dawns that I may very well never recover from this orgasm. At the very least, I'll never forget it; I know in my bones that this will be the sexual experience I measure all others against.

What if it's never this good with anyone else?

What if I'm about to have the best sex of my life for the first, and last, time?

I feel hollowed out by the time the orgasm subsides. Legit can't breathe when Ryder carefully pulls his fingers out of me and moves them to my breast, where he coats my nipple in my arousal before leaning in to lick it off with his tongue.

"You taste just right, darlin'. Just fuckin' right."

An ache takes root low in my belly. *My God, what I'd give to make you mine, cowboy.*

I'm so beyond fucked at this point it's not even funny. These are deep waters, and I'm in way, *way* over my head. Part of me knew that'd happen when I let Ryder put his hands on me. I was half in love with this man already.

Now?

Now, I realize it's not just my body on the altar tonight. It's my heart too. And that's a sacrifice I'd willingly make a hundred times over to be the sole object of Ryder's attention for a single night, hour, minute.

I dig my fingers into his hair again, more tenderly this time. Because that's how I feel inside—tender, even sore. Already.

"Can I taste you?" I ask softly.

His pupils are blown out, enormous. He absently draws his thumb across my mouth. "Much as I wanna come in your mouth and watch you swallow—"

"Who says I swallow?" I smile.

"I do. You'd drink every last bit, wouldn't you?" His thumb moves to the corner of my mouth, wiping away an imaginary smear of cum. The muscle in his jaw jumps. "Much as I'd love to see that, I wanna fuck you more."

"Okay. Yes. Please."

"Since when are you polite?"

"Since your dick was on offer." Reaching between us, I stroke the bulge in his jeans. "You wanna put it inside me, or am I gonna have to do that?"

He growls. A literal growl, a deep, guttural, animal sound that makes my nipples tingle. "Quit playin'. You want my dick, you do the work."

I'm smiling now, even as my heart spasms. "Rude."

"C'mon, Billie. You know I can't keep my hands off you. What do you think the best way to do this is? So we don't hurt your arm?"

"My arm is barely sore anymore, but it's probably better to be safe than sorry." I ponder this for a minute. "I could do a little reverse cowgirl in your lap?"

"I wanna see your face." His hand wanders to my side and gently squeezes me there. The fact that Ryder's so openly affectionate with me—that's no small thing.

The ache inside me pulses. "Why do you have to be so difficult?"

"Ha. Pot, meet kettle. Could you ride me just like this?" His hands are on my thighs now, moving up, up. "Or are your legs too tired?"

"Stop pretending like I'm made of glass. Let's do this."

His lips twitch. "Impatient much?"

"You have no idea, Ry." I somehow manage to unbutton his jeans and pull down his fly with one hand. I reach inside and immediately find his cock.

My stomach flips. "Do you always go commando?"

"I sleep naked, and I was in bed when you texted. Didn't have time to get fully dressed."

Curling my fingers around his girth, I feel my stomach flip again.

He's *big*. I thumb his head and marvel at how substantial he is. No wonder he wanted to warm me up.

"You were in that much of a rush to get *me* naked, huh?" I ask. His dick fills my hand as I give him a slow, tight tug.

Ryder's mouth forms a neat little O. "I needed—I had to know you were okay. Had a feeling…"

"That I shaved?" I thumb his head again.

His chest barrels out on a laugh, even as his nostrils flare. "Something like that. Here, lemme grab—"

"Condoms? In the glove box? Got it." I smear a bead of precum over his tip before climbing off his lap and opening the glove compartment.

It's my turn to laugh when I see what's inside it. "Since when do you smoke cigarettes? And drinking and driving?" I hold up the bottle of tequila. "Tsk-tsk."

"I may have confiscated Wyatt's cigarettes after he and Sally got together. Didn't want him revisiting any vices. And the tequila…I don't got an excuse for that other than life is hard."

I grin, putting away the tequila before grabbing a foil packet and shutting the box. "So are you."

He takes himself in his hand. "You're up."

"How am I, like, almost completely naked," I ask as I open the condom, "while you're still fully dressed?"

"That's how I like it. Put the condom on, Billie, and then put me inside you."

"You best be patient, sir."

"Or what?"

Leaning over—there's no center console, just the bench—I tuck my hair behind my ear. "Or I'll do this."

I lick his head, lapping up another bit of precum that appears as he pumps his hand. Ryder's stomach caves, and he draws a pained breath through his teeth.

"I thought you weren't doing that," he bites out.

Looking up, I meet his eyes. "But I am doing it. And you're gonna like it."

Then I duck my head and take him into my mouth. An inch. Maybe less. His tip is velvety and tastes of salt.

"Aw, fuck." Now he's taking my hair in his hands and holding it away from my face so he can watch. "You look good with my dick in your mouth, darlin'. Real good. You gotta be careful because I wanna come inside that sweet little cu—*fuck*. Fuck, you're good at this."

Say you want another round.

Ask me if I want to do this again tomorrow. And the day after that too.

I'm gently sucking on him now, bobbing my head to take him deeper with every up-down motion I make. I gag a little when his hips jerk and he hits the back of my throat.

His hand forms a fist in my hair. "Billie. Quit. I'm too close. Put the condom on."

I want to keep torturing him—I want to keep making him feel as good as he makes *me* feel—but I also want him inside me.

So I give his head one last suck, swirling my tongue over his tip, and then I sit up. "Hold yourself."

He does as I tell him, fisting his cock in his hand, and I'm able to roll on the condom with one hand.

Then he's practically lifting me back onto his lap. Taking one nipple in his mouth, then the other, he shapes my waist with his hands. I reach down and find him, lining him up at my entrance.

I look up, and our gazes lock.

It's suddenly very, very quiet inside the cab. Just our breaths between us.

"Don't tell him. Colt. About this." I have no idea why I choose this moment to say that. I guess I'm afraid. And yeah, I like the idea of having something that's just between us, me and Ryder.

Our own secret.

A story that only we know.

Ryder's hands knead my sides. His blue eyes are thoughtful. "You think that's the right call?"

"Yes. No. Is it wrong to say that I don't care?"

Biting his lip, he lifts his hips so that he sinks the tiniest bit inside me. "Everything about this is wrong."

I nearly choke at the feel of his thick head entering my cunt. "Maybe that's why it's so good."

"Maybe."

Putting my hand on his shoulder, I lower myself another inch. Wince at the hard pinch between my legs, even as I feel a renewed flutter of desire in my core.

"You okay?" Ryder's voice is soft.

I nod. "It's just…very full this way."

"Don't try to be a hero." He cups my breast. Thumbs my nipple. "Go slow. We don't got anywhere to be."

Closing my eyes, I focus on breathing. "Are you really gonna fit?"

"I'mma fit just fine." He chuckles. "Now relax and *go slow*. You feel fuckin' amazing. You're doing so good, Billie."

I sink a little lower. Gasp. Ryder's playing with my cunt now, stroking my clit.

"Can you come again?"

"I don't—not usually." Lower. I'm split open, coming apart the more I sink onto his girth. "But—with you—maybe. Probably."

I hear the smile in his voice when he says, "Definitely. Just get all the way down and I'll take care of the rest, yeah?"

"This is my life." I'm barely able to speak. The

penetration *hurts*, but I keep going. "I'm not allowed to have anything apart from my family—anything for myself. But this, I'm keeping. I wanna keep it just for us. Just for now."

He grunts. His hand finds mine on his shoulder, and he twines our fingers. "I hear you. I won't say a word. This—it's just for us. Promise me one thing, though?"

My legs are shaking. I can't hold myself up anymore.

Rocking my hips, I take him the rest of the way inside me so that he's sunk to the hilt.

A burning stretch has me crying out.

Ryder kisses my shoulder. "Aw, Billie."

"The promise." I'm panting. "What is it?"

He kisses my mouth. "Promise you won't fall in love with me."

He's laughing, and now so am I. The hit of levity feels good, even as my heart squeezes.

Too late. I'm falling, Ryder. Plummeting to my death. And I wouldn't have it any other way.

"Fuck you, you presumptuous asshole," I reply.

"Would you? Fuck me? Please?"

I bite the corner of his mouth. "Yes, baby."

I don't know why I keep putting myself out there with Ryder after he turned me down. He clearly has some major hesitations, and I feel like I should have some sense of self-preservation. I should hold back a *little* bit.

Here I am, though, calling him *baby*. What's more vulnerable than that, using an endearment with someone for the first time?

But judging by the way the look in Ryder's eyes

shifts—it softens, but it's sharp too, and *oh God*—he likes that, doesn't he?

He impales me on a vicious thrust, capturing my cry in a deep, messy kiss.

Holy shit, Ryder Rivers likes it when I call him baby.

CHAPTER 16
The Opposite of Safe Sex
Ryder

While I like calling Billie darlin', I'm not a fan of being called nicknames myself.

They're cheesy. Overdone. In most cases, they're downright cringe-worthy.

But when Billie Wallace calls me baby?

Lord above. My balls contract and my pulse gallops and it hits me like a fucking train that I *love* nicknames. With an important caveat: Only when *she* uses them.

She sits on my cock like she means it, rolling her hips so she takes me deeper. My dick is in agony inside her perfect little pussy. She's fucking *tight*, her grip on me warm and fierce and somehow soft too.

Billie in a nutshell.

"Wait." I grab her hips to still them. Close my eyes. Breathe through my nose. "A minute. I need a minute."

"Ry? Are *you* okay?" She cups my face in her hand.

I last longer than this.

Much fucking longer. Ain't like me to come five seconds after I'm inside a girl.

Here I am, though, about to do exactly that. It's embarrassing. And scary.

The tips of Billie's bare breasts brush against my chest. Even through my shirt, the feel of her sweet little nipples makes goose bumps break out on my arms.

I have to stay in control. This could get out of hand real fast if I don't keep my wits about me.

How can I do that, though, when she's so fun to fuck?

When she's so real, so generous, so playful?

"Naw, darlin', I ain't okay. You…" I smile tightly and shake my head. "It's never felt this good."

Her thumb arcs over my cheekbone. "That a bad thing?"

"I don't—" I suck in a breath through my nose. Billie's been fearlessly honest tonight. I owe it to her to return the favor. "I hate the idea of disappointing you. If I don't last as long as I should."

"Ry."

"Yeah?"

"Look at me."

I open my eyes. Hers are soft. Kind. Hair everywhere. She's the kind of pretty that makes it hard to breathe. "That's the problem, Billie. I can't stop looking."

"I like that." She takes my hand and guides it back to her breast. "I like *you*. No such thing as 'should' tonight, okay? Just be who you are, and take what you need." She grins. "I sure as hell am."

Aw, hell, because I wasn't feeling some kind of way about this girl before *I got her naked in my truck.*

I squeeze her tit. "Brat."

"You wanna fuck that outta me?" She reaches down and slips her good hand inside my shirt. My abs immediately contract at the feel of her palm gliding over my bare skin.

Shit, now I'm laughing again, even as my cock surges inside her slick heat. When was the last time sex was this fun?

When was the last time I felt so much that I struggled to stay in control?

What if I don't need to be in control at all?

"Yeah." I gently wrap my fingers around her neck. I put my other hand on her hip. "Yeah, I do wanna fuck that outta you. I said I'll handle the rest, so now I'm gonna handle it, yeah?"

"I'm waiting."

The only word I can think to describe her expression is *feral*. Her eyes are wet with curiosity. Lips swollen. Tits bouncing as I guide her up. Down.

Back up.

Her pussy flutters. I see stars.

And just like that, I'm lost.

She's lost.

In losing myself like this—allowing myself to surrender to all these feelings—I feel *connected*. To the universe. To whom I am and what I want.

I feel connected to Billie.

We're moving together, rising on a wave of shared breaths. Sweat breaks out along my scalp and on my neck as I piston my hips upward on a hard, punishing thrust. She presses down at the same time, our bodies making a lewd slapping noise. She won't stay still—she can't—even as I tighten my grip on her throat. She rides my cock like she means it, and I fuck her like I don't have everything to lose.

We chase the release we were never meant to share. But now that we're here, I wonder why the fuck we waited so long.

She yells.

I yell.

Her hand fists in my shirt. Her fingernails dig into my skin. I roll my thumb over her clit just how she likes it. The tightness of our fit, the way her pussy swallows my length again and again—

"You close?" I bite the inside of my cheek to keep from coming myself.

In reply, her pussy clamps down on my length.

"*Ry*." A shout. A plea. An exuberant declaration of relief.

She comes again, and my chest puffs out a little. I may not last as long as I'd like, but at least I made Billie come twice tonight.

Am I really only gonna make Billie Wallace come twice in my life?

That thought is depressing.

"Do I gotta—you want me to pull out—?"

"*Don't*." Her eyes fly open on a gasp. "Please. I love—the feel of you inside me—"

"Good." Carefully wrapping my arms around her, I pull her against me and thrust one last time and come. Hard.

I bury my face in her neck and pray like hell I don't die. Because this, coming inside her—it's obliterating.

Her trust. The way she lets me hold her.

The way she holds *me*.

How the fuck am I gonna let this girl go?

I feel the hot seep of my cum fill the condom. There's a lot of it.

Is it wrong that I'm turned on by the idea of my cum dripping down Billie's thighs? Because tonight, she's *mine*. I want her to know that.

Jesus Christ, what is wrong with me?

If Colt knew—

Yeah, not going there. Not tonight.

We both know we shouldn't be doing this, which means it's gotta be a one-time-only thing. Are Billie and I assholes not to tell Colt about it? Maybe.

Or maybe we're doing the right thing. People hook up all the time. As long as Billie and I are honest with each other, no one's going to get hurt.

You sure about that?

She's curled up on my chest, breathing hard. I run a hand down her naked back, marveling at how soft her skin is.

My truck smells like sex.

Sex and sweet peaches.

She shifts, lifting her head to kiss the underside of my jaw. "Hi."

"How're you feeling?" I murmur into her hair. "Any pain?"

"No pain. I feel…" She sighs, a happy sound. "Like there's definitely no brat left in me."

I burst out laughing. "My job here is done."

"Where the hell do you get the energy? I'm honestly asking because I feel like you work so hard all day long…"

My chest tightens. "I get by. And I like knowing my people are safe."

"Safe sex *is* good sex."

"This was good sex."

"Excellent."

She's quiet as she traces her fingertips over my shirt. I'm smoothing her hair down her back now.

I wanna take her home so bad my teeth ache.

But we can't do this again. One time only, remember? The danger of blurred lines and all that shit. But God, the thought of letting her go, putting her clothes on, taking her home—it feels wrong.

I don't want my job to be done.

Which makes absolutely no sense. Neither does fucking your best friend's baby sister, though, so I guess I wasn't an arbiter of good sense to begin with.

"Darlin'."

"Yeah?" Her voice is sleepy.

Aw, Billie, you got no idea how bad I want to take you home. Fuck you again and again. Then, when we're too tired to keep going, I'd watch you fall asleep in my bed.

I never invite women to sleep at my place. Told myself it's because I wouldn't be able to sleep next to someone else. People snore. They toss and turn.

The magic dissipates real fast when you wake up drooling next to someone else who's drooling too.

Now I'm wondering if I'd sleep *better* with someone next to me. Sure as hell not sleeping great alone, am I? And I weirdly like the idea of Billie drooling on my pillow. Means she'd feel totally at ease at my place. Comfortable.

At home.

RYDER

What the fuck is happening to me right now?

"Much as I want to hold you like this all night, I don't want you getting a UTI. Can I clean us up real quick?"

She moans, turning her head. "Yes. But please don't make it quick."

"Too late." I chuckle. "Sorry, bad joke."

"You weren't too quick, and you didn't disappoint me, you know." She sits up and looks at me. "Really, I think you just made every other man seem disappointing in comparison."

My heart has wings. That image alone should send me running for the hills. I don't do mushy.

Here I am, though, feeling real fucking mushy. I don't hate it.

"I'm not satisfied unless it's a job well done."

She smiles, digging her teeth into her bottom lip. "It was very well done."

Colt would hate that we're sneaking behind his back like this, though, wouldn't he?

Only if I didn't treat Billie right. I think about what Duke said back at the Rattler—that I wouldn't know if I could treat her the way she deserves to be treated until I tried.

Now is my chance to try. But is treating her right giving in to the mushiness? Or is it keeping boundaries clear?

I find some napkins in my glove compartment—Colt and Sawyer have trained me to always keep some handy in the car—and after I take care of the condom, I put Billie on her back on the front seat.

Peeling off her ridiculously tiny underwear, I part

her knees and hiss when I see her pussy. In the red and green lights of the dashboard, she looks slick, swollen. Pink.

I gently run my fingers over the birthmark on her thigh. "This is cute."

"You're cute."

My dick perks right the fuck back up. That's a new record for recovery.

"Really, Billie, you're so pretty here." I gently wipe her down. The condom took care of most of the mess, but it can't hurt to pay attention to detail.

Her breath catches. "Thank you."

"You know I wanna go for round two, right?"

She nods, doing that thing where she bites her lip. "I want that too."

"Best if we call it a night, though. It's late. And I don't want you hurtin' too bad tomorrow."

Her eyes glimmer with disappointment. "The hurt feels good, Ry."

I hang my head. "You *gotta* listen when I ask you to stop right now."

"I'll stop." She reaches up and digs her fingers into my hair. "I know we're friends. Only friends. And friends don't…"

I laugh. "Do anything we just did?"

Her face creases into a smile. "Exactly."

It kills me to push her knees back together and offer her my hand. Kills me to pull her up to sit. Help her back into her shirt. Watch her buckle in.

My thoughts, feelings—they're a jumble of, *This is so right*, and, *I'm doing something wrong*. I can't tell up from down.

RYDER

My hand shakes as I tuck her panties into my other front pocket—the one without Dad's pocketknife in it.

"Those belong to me, you know." Billie cuts me a hot look.

I start the truck. "They're mine now."

It's wrong that I'm stealing her panties. It also doesn't feel right not to have some token of the best sex of my life, especially considering I'll never have sex with this woman again.

You wouldn't know I had Billie yelling my name minutes ago by the way she sits quietly and looks out the window on the drive back to her place. Legs crossed, the hand of her good arm tucked between her thighs.

Thankfully her apartment is on the opposite side of the ranch from Colt's house, so there's very little risk of him catching us. Just the fact that I'm worried about that makes me feel a stab of guilt, though.

Sneaking around sucks. It's for teenagers and cowards.

Last time. This won't happen again. Everyone makes mistakes.

Only making Billie come doesn't feel like a mistake.

Instead, it feels like a revelation. Allowing myself to plug into my feelings, my body, my thoughts like she always does—like I just did when I was inside her—it didn't kill me.

It didn't change how Billie felt about me. She wasn't grossed out or turned off. In fact, she seemed pretty damn turned on by my vulnerability. I *love* being able to talk to her about how weird and wild and awesome tonight has been.

I *love* not having to tell myself to *numb, ignore, deflect.*

Makes me realize how exhausted I am by my attempts to outrun my feelings. My desires.

I put the truck in park outside her house and cut the ignition.

"I'll walk you up." I unbuckle my seat belt.

Billie just laughs as she opens her door. "Please don't. I can only handle so many mixed signals in one night."

"You're not walking alone in the dark."

"The door is right there." She gestures to the windshield. "It's, like, five steps away."

I grab the door handle. "Don't care."

When I hustle around the truck and open her door, I don't miss the way she flashes me a glimpse of her pussy as she takes my hand and climbs down.

"Do me a favor." I don't let go of her hand.

She doesn't let go of mine either. "Yeah?"

"Don't ever wear that skirt in public again."

Her laugh is high and light, and I have the insane thought that it'd be the best job in the world making her laugh like that over and over again for the rest of our lives.

Quit while you're ahead.

"I'll consider it if you give me my underwear back. That's my cutest pair."

We stop at her door.

We're still holding hands. The only girls I've ever held hands with have been Ella and June. And Mom, of course.

"No deal."

She squeezes my hand, digging her teeth into her bottom lip. "We'll have to agree to disagree, then."

I can't look away from her eyes. They glimmer in the light of the moon.

"You're gonna be sore. Take it easy tomorrow, yeah?"

She scoffs, finally dropping my hand to grab the doorknob. "You're wild."

"What does that mean?" I curl one hand around my nape and shove the other in my front pocket in an attempt not to reach for her.

"You claim you don't wanna blur any lines, but then you go and say sweet shit like that."

See? It's so easy to talk about hard shit with Billie. I don't have a solution, but she's also not asking for one. We're swimming in this weirdness together, and neither of us is pretending like we know what happens next.

You know what has *to happen.*

I scoff. "Just because I'm a mess don't mean I can't be sweet too."

"Stop using the whole 'oh, poor me, I'm such a mess' excuse. You're better than that." She opens the door.

"Just like you're better than Xylophone."

She's laughing again. "That's not his name."

"Don't care."

Her eyes flick to my mouth. The urge to grab her and toss her over my shoulder—gently, of course—and bring her back to my place is so strong it makes me sick to my stomach.

If we start up again, we'll never *stop.*

"This was fucked up," she says. "Thanks."

Now I'm the one laughing. "Just doing the Lord's work. I got you home safe, didn't I?"

"Yeah."

"And we're not telling Colt."

"No."

"Not sure if that's the right call, but if it's what you want…"

She looks at me. Her eyes are full. Wet. *I want you.*

At least that's what I imagine she'd say if she opened her mouth.

Instead, she nods. "Yeah. It's better this way."

"Right."

"Yup." She sucks in a breath. "Welp, goodnight, I guess."

"Night, Billie."

CHAPTER 17
Supper
Ryder

"Do y'all think I'm a mess?" *I wipe my mouth on my* napkin. "If so, how annoying is my messiness on a scale of one to five?"

You could hear a pin drop for how quiet it suddenly gets inside the New House's kitchen.

Sawyer drops his fork.

Mollie's eyes dance.

I didn't necessarily plan to create a shock-and-awe situation at Sunday night supper. But I've been turning over so many thoughts and ideas in my head all weekend, and I guess I just...decided I would stop keeping it all in.

I'm learning the more I open up, the more the world opens up to me. And the more that happens, the less suffocated I feel.

The better I sleep.

I thought for sure I'd toss and turn all night, tortured by guilt, after having the most obscene sex ever with my best friend's sister. While I still don't feel great about keeping a secret from Colt, I sure as hell passed the fuck out when I got home. Slept twelve hours straight, only waking up when Duke came over to check if I had a pulse.

I slept well *again* last night too.

Cash gives me a long, hard look. "Blink twice if you're being held against your will."

"By who?" Wyatt chuckles. "A random-ass alien that's possessed him and is finally getting him to talk about things?"

Junie shoves a forkful of mashed sweet potatoes into her mouth. "I believe in aliens. Mom, can I be an alien for Halloween?"

"Sorry, June Bug. Remember we already bought your unicorn costume?" Ava asks.

"Fine. But you have to put money in the swear jar, Uncle Wy."

My older brother has the grace to look sheepish. "Sorry, honey. I'll put a five in."

"Yes, it's annoying." Duke's lips twitch as he sets his napkin beside his plate. "I'd give it a six."

"Seven," Cash corrects.

I push back my chair. "So much for tryin' to keep it real—"

"Aw, c'mon." Sally puts a hand over mine. "You know they're just busting your chops."

Ella frowns. "What's a chop, and why does it bust?"

"Does it *burst*, just like I do when I have to tee-tee?" Junie taps a thoughtful finger to her little chin.

I don't wanna smile, but I do. They're so damn cute.

"Are you bursting now?" Patsy scoops some of our ridiculously delicious brussels sprouts gratin onto her fork. "I can take you to the potty if you need to go."

Junie grins. "No thank you."

Before Sally and Wyatt got together, Patsy and John B would only be at the ranch Monday through Friday. Patsy would stock the fridge for the weekend with plenty of leftovers and stuff to make sandwiches, and we'd be on our own Saturdays and Sundays.

Now that the Powells are officially family, we all decided we'd make a big deal out of Sunday supper. It's a really nice way to start the week. We gather in the New House's kitchen at around three, and together we make a whole bunch of delicious food.

We rotate who gets to choose the recipes every week. This week, it was Duke and Wheeler's turn. They chose to roast some chickens, with sides of sweet potatoes and brussels sprouts gratin. I was in the kitchen early to assist.

Molly sips her wine. "I think people who acknowledge the truth—who try to *live* their truth—they're always going to be messy because life is messy."

Ava nods. "I agree. I think being messy is a good thing."

"Why?" Duke's eyes are kind. "Are you finally ready to come off your BS?"

"Hey. That BS was my coping mechanism of choice." I give him a look. "We all have 'em. Coping mechanisms. Different ones, maybe. But losing Mom and Dad the way we did, that's not something you come out of without some wounds you gotta cover up with armor."

Cash is still staring at me. "You ready? Finally? To talk about it?"

"Talk about what?" Sawyer scratches underneath his chin. "I'm not giving you a tough time, I'm just genuinely confused about what we're talking about here."

Ava gently elbows him. "I think Ryder is ready to talk about your past. Your parents too. As long as I've been around, he's never done that."

"Thank you, Ava. And seriously, Cash, 'finally'?" I scoff. "Cut a guy some slack."

Wheeler leans her head against my shoulder. "He *is* the baby."

"And the favorite." Wyatt helps himself to a third helping of chicken. "Makes sense why he'd be the most tenderhearted."

"Can I also get some credit for being the easiest kid in the family?"

Wyatt chuckles. "There's a dirty joke in there—"

"That you're not gonna make because there's children present." Duke rests his forearms on the table. "But really, Ry, you are the easiest out of all of us. And that's saying something."

"Watch your mouth." I'm grinning as I reach for my wine.

Wheeler keeps her head on my shoulder. "But really, I have an appreciation for the roles we all take on in our families. I tried to be the easy one too, Ryder. Forgive the terrible pun, but it's certainly not easy to manage everyone's comfort every second of every day by pretending like you don't feel or need anything."

Shit, I'm gonna cry.

The impulse to swallow my feelings like I always do is strong. I'm not sure if that knee-jerk reaction will ever go away.

But now I can walk myself through other options. Like just letting myself simply…sit with my feelings because I know they're not gonna kill me. It'll be uncomfortable, sure. Possibly unbearable. But the more I do it, the more time passes, the less it seems to hurt.

I feel sad. Seen. Relieved that I shared my thoughts so I could be seen at all.

None of this would be happening if I kept trying to be *easy*. Not this conversation. Not all the conversations I've had with Billie. Not the epic sex or playing guitar by the bonfire or connecting with my family in a way I never have before.

Holy fuck, this really is happening.

My face burns—this is a *lot*—but I still let the tears fall.

"Dang." I tug my forefinger and thumb over my eyes. "You hit the nail on the head there, Wheeler."

"Aww, Ryder." She runs a hand over my back. "I didn't mean to make you emotional—"

"I'm glad you did."

"Should we get a priest?" Sawyer pretend-whispers. "Some holy water at the very least?"

"Not funny," I say, even as I scoff.

"Just to add a little fuel to your fire," Wheeler says, "it was only when I stopped pretending that everything was 'just fine' that I was able to be who I really was and do what I really wanted. My parents still don't love that I chose to be entrepreneur instead of a lawyer, but I had to let that go. Embrace my messiness."

Mollie raises her glass. "You had to live your truth."

"I'll cheers to that." Wyatt raises his glass, eyes on mine. "So what's your truth, brother?"

I suck in a breath through my nose. "Truth is, I miss Mom and Dad, and I'm sad—angry—fucking gutted, really, that they're gone."

I've never said those words out loud.

I've never admitted to having those feelings. How could I when I didn't even allow myself to feel them in the first place?

I wait a beat, then another, for the freight train of grief to hit. For the shame and the regret to bowl me over.

It's all there, right in my chest and belly and blood. But surrounded by the people I love, that awful shit doesn't feel near as, well, awful.

Cash sniffles. "They couldn't get over your cheeks. How chubby they were. When Mom was getting an ultrasound when she was pregnant with y'all, apparently all they could see were how fat y'all's cheeks were." He glances at Duke.

"Cheekies!" Junie shrieks. "I love them."

Sawyer leans over to kiss *her* cheek. "Yours are scrumptious."

"Your scruffies are not." She recoils, making the table burst out in laughter.

"I remember Dad pretending to eat your cheeks before every meal," Wyatt adds. "We thought it was hilarious, the way he'd use this *Sesame Street* voice while nibbling on y'all."

Cash laughs. "I would ask him to stop because I was worried you wouldn't have any faces left when you got older."

"Aw, baby, you may be the handsomest, but you were never the smartest, were you?" Mollie wags her brows.

"I was." Wyatt gives us the side-eye.

More laughter. *Damn, Billie would fit right in here, wouldn't she?*

She'd join in on the ribbing. The jokes and the innuendo.

"If gambling like a degenerate was a marker of intelligence, then for sure you'd be the Einstein of the family," Sawyer says.

Wyatt holds up his hands. "Never said I was an angel."

"Definitely no angel." Sally's got stars in her eyes as she beams at her husband. "Thank goodness for that."

"Mom never put you down." Cash nods at me. "I remember Aunt Lolly coming to visit and asking Mom why you were always on her hip. Mom told Lolly to stick it where the sun don't shine. You were her last baby, and she knew very well that babies don't keep."

Duke pulls his brows together. "Why didn't she hold me that much?"

"Because I was cuter," I say matter-of-factly.

"We literally have the same exact face."

"That's true." Wyatt points a finger at Duke. "None of us could tell y'all apart for the first, oh, five or so years of your lives."

Sawyer nods. "Quite frankly, we didn't care who you were, as long as we could beat you up."

"No wonder I never wanted to leave Mom's hip." I'm still crying, but I'm able to breathe now.

"You had that speech delay." Cash brings his water to his lips. "Pawpaw said it was because Mom was always talkin' for you. Duke was yammering away in complete sentences by the time he was three, but you were fine to let her keep speaking for you even then."

"I remember. Animal therapy was awesome."

What I don't say? That I reached out to the therapist my primary doc recommended last week. I'm still waiting to make an appointment, but it felt like a step in the right direction.

Wyatt looks at me meaningfully. "Probably why you're so good with animals now."

"He can moo with the best of them," Cash replies with a grin.

Ella's eyes go wide. "Can you really speak with the cows?"

"I sure can." I put my hands on the table. "They don't say much back, though."

"You're funny," Sally says.

"No, I'm not. But I appreciate you saying that."

Speaking of animal therapy—I still need to do some digging before I bring up the idea to Billie.

I'm thinking about her again.

I can't quit. I'm not sure if I want to anymore.

I sip my wine and glance around the table. There are some glassy eyes, even some tears. But everyone looks happy. Even Junie and Ella are smiling, kicking their little legs underneath the table as John B passes a fresh bottle of wine around.

"Kinda crazy to think that this time last year, there were half as many people around the table." I trace its edge with my finger.

Cash glances at Mollie. "It all started with this troublemaker."

My chest twists. I have my own troublemaker now, don't I? Only, Billie's not mine. Not yet anyway.

How the hell would I make that happen without losing Colt or losing the trust of her parents?

How do I proceed with caution while also allowing myself to go all in? Because that's what she deserves. A guy who jumps in with both feet. Not because he has to, but because he has no choice.

He's so obsessed with her he wants nothing more.

"Your lives were turned upside down in the blink of an eye when you lost your parents." John B sits back in his chair. "Maybe fate is finally delivering on the other side of that—the good to the bad. Life happens fast, no matter which way it moves. I'm happy for y'all that it's moving in the right direction."

Sally dabs at her eye with her napkin. "That's sweet, Dad. Thank you."

"It's a bummer, though." My voice is thick. "That Mom and Dad aren't at the table too. They'd—Jesus." I'm breaking down.

Cash gets up from his chair and pulls me up too.

Pulls me into a hug.

"They're here," he murmurs. "In their own way, they see all the good shit that's happening. Time for your good shit to happen, yeah?"

I hear Wheeler sniffling. "God, what is it about bro hugs that gets me every time?"

"Hoes love their bros," Wyatt says.

"Swear jar," Mollie says. "Wheeler is definitely a ho, though."

"I am. How do you think I got pregnant?"

We're all laughing again. Laughing and crying and holding up our glasses to toast to Mom and Dad, and all the moms and dads at the table too.

Ella asks why we're talking about Santa. It takes us a minute, but then we figure out the *ho ho ho* thing. Then we're talking about our Christmases growing up and how, without fail, some kind of stomach bug or flu would hit our house Christmas Day.

Wheeler has to make a mad dash for the bathroom

when she laughs too hard at the story of Duke puking eggnog all over Dad. Wyatt asks if anyone knows the recipes Mom used to make all her holiday cookies, and Duke says he'll look through her cookbooks, which he keeps in his cabin.

Funny, but by opening up about my folks, I've helped our whole family honor Mom and Dad in new ways while carrying on new versions of family traditions too.

Ella and June tell us what they want for Christmas this year—two unicorns and fake nails with gemstones on them, naturally—and then we devour the strawberry pie Sawyer and Mollie made earlier.

Patsy adds a healthy scoop of hand-churned vanilla bean ice cream to each of our plates.

"Just because I can," she says with a smile.

By the time I'm heading out the door, I feel wrung out and so full that I feel like I'm the one bursting.

Duke intercepts me as I'm walking to my truck in the driveway. Wheeler went home a little earlier to put up her feet, so he's alone.

"So." He slips his hands inside the pockets of his jacket and falls into step beside me. "How long you been sleepin' with Billie?"

My heart ricochets off my ribcage like a pinball. "What?"

"You forget I know you better'n anyone. And I know you've changed in large part because of Billie Wallace. I also know you wouldn't be able to spend so much time with her without, well, spending some time between the sheets with her too."

Sheets weren't involved.

I'd like them to be, though.

"Because she's excellent, and you're excellent, and y'all bring out the best in each other," Duke continues. "She's had the hots for you forever. I knew it was only a matter of time before you fell too."

"I didn't—Christ, Duke. I cry *once*, and all of a sudden, you feel like you can just say whatever the hell you want to me?"

The bastard grins. "Yup. So how was it?"

"The sex? I'm not talking to you about—"

"The conversation. The connection. Obviously that's what I'm talking about."

I grunt.

"So you did have sex." He lets out a holler. "I was right! Don't worry, I won't tell a soul. But talk about shit getting *messy*."

My boots catch on the gravel as I come to a stop. Closing my eyes, I tip back my head. "I'm serious, Duke. No one can know."

"How do you think Colt will react when you ask him if you can date her?"

"We're not dating."

"Bullshit."

I scoff, something unpleasant rising up inside my chest. "I told you—"

"Bet Billie would have some thoughts on whether or not you treat her right." He nods at the phone in my hand. "Hell, I bet she's texted you about them often this weekend, hasn't she? Thoughts like, *Wow, that was great*, and, *You're great,* and, *I really like you and think you should be my boyfriend*—"

"That's not what she texted."

"But she *has* been texting."

Heat crawls up my neck.

As a matter of fact, Billie and I have been texting a little all weekend. Not a lot. But more than we typically would.

I'm trying to keep boundaries in place. But it was the polite thing to do, right, to check in on her? And that text turned into a dozen, and then a dozen more today, and I only ended the conversation an hour later when I had to head to the kitchen.

We didn't talk about anything, really. She said she was fine, that her arm was okay, and that she was tired but not hungover. She asked me how I was.

I didn't get into too much detail. But not gonna lie, felt nice knowing that she was thinking of me.

And now I'm thinking of her. *Again*. I've thought a lot about just showing up at her place. I've thought even more about asking her to come over to mine.

Would that be the right move? The wrong one? I don't know.

All I know is, she's helped me change how I'm living my life so I can thrive. How great would life be if we could thrive together? I really have to float that animal therapy idea—bet she'd be into it. At the very least, it might be a jumping-off point. She can't be chained to that desk for the rest of her life, or she's gonna shrivel up and die.

Not on my watch.

"You know, tonight was the first time you've talked openly about Mom and Dad in a while. Really, ever." Duke's voice is quiet. Kind. "I feel like I'm finally getting my brother back."

I blink. "What? I didn't go anywhere."

"But you did. The real you disappeared for a while. I knew it was part of your process, so I never wanted to push you. We all gotta grieve in our own way." He takes a breath. Lets it out. "Billie, though—she pushed you just when you needed it, huh?"

Goddamn you.

"She don't take no for an answer, that's for sure," I manage around the tightness in my throat.

He puts a hand on my shoulder. "I don't need to tell you that you'd be an idiot to let a girl like that slip through your fingers, right? Because only idiots and bull riders would make that mistake."

"Bull riders *are* idiots."

Duke meets my eyes. "Don't be like them, then."

"Not all of us move fast, you know." I swallow hard. "I think I need a little time."

"Perfect! Because you know what takes time? Dating someone. Getting to know them. Figuring out how y'all are going to fit into each other's lives."

I roll my eyes. "We get it. You're obsessed with Wheeler, and you want her to have your babies. Which is why she *is* having your babies."

"Pretty sweet, ain't it?" His eyes crinkle as he smiles. "You could be next."

"I don't know if I even want kids."

Duke shrugs. "Then go figure it out. Life's out here, waitin' for you to stop playing it safe."

I know.

God, do I know.

Just wish my heart would get the memo.

CHAPTER 18
New Faces
Billie

Wheeler is Having a Baby!
Please Join Us for a Shower on
Saturday, October 29, at 11 a.m.
Brunch, Margaritas, and Baby Surprises Will Be Served
Hosted by Mollie, Sally, and Ava
Please RSVP by October 22

"Aw."

Mom looks up from the laundry she's folding. "What's that?"

"Wheeler Rankin invited me to her baby shower. You know, Duke's—"

"Girlfriend. Yes! Oh, how wonderful. I'm so happy for them." Mom tilts her head. "And I'm happy for you that you're making new friends. I like those girls."

"I do too." I slip the invitation back into its envelope.

Even though I moved into my place years ago, my mail still gets delivered to Mom and Dad's house. Everybody's does. It would take the postman literally all day to deliver mail across the ranch, so my parents simplified things and have everyone's stuff get delivered here. I usually stop by after work to pick up my mail, which these days is mostly bills and, randomly enough, fliers for cheap land in Tennessee of all places.

"How's Ryder?" Mom shakes out one of Dad's shirts. "I still think about the way that man leapt for you when you fell off that horse. I thought *he* was gonna break a dang arm too!"

My stomach flips for the hundred thousandth time this week. It happens anytime I so much as *think* his name.

I glance at my phone, which I set beside me on the kitchen table.

No texts or calls since I checked it last, a minute ago.

Nevertheless, a flash of heat low in my belly lets me know I am definitely not over the sex Ryder and I had last weekend. It's only been four days since we hooked up, but you'd think I'd spent forty days and forty nights in the desert for how much I miss him.

How much I wanna call him and have phone sex with him, and then invite him over for actual, physical sex.

I got you, baby, I'd tell him.

He'd call me darlin', and then he'd kiss the shit out of me while tearing off all my clothes.

I know thinking about Ryder is an exercise in self-flagellation. Yeah, we had life-altering sex after having several life-altering conversations. Sure, he was the first to get to me after I fell off my horse and literally saved my life. Yes, I'm the only one he'll play his guitar for.

But none of that means a damn thing if he doesn't ask me out. Which he hasn't even though we did text a lot over the weekend. I haven't heard from him since Sunday.

I've learned that guys are funny like that. You can have the best time ever with them—you can get deep, talk about intimate shit—and think your connection is real and special. But then they ghost you for no discernible reason other than *they can*.

I'm intense. I own that. I just wonder, how many times do I need to learn that other people don't read as much into things as I do? That they don't take things as seriously?

Because I took my hookup with Ryder pretty fucking seriously. And now here I am, checking my phone every five seconds just to make sure I didn't miss his text.

Honestly, Mom, I have no idea how Ryder is. I just know I wanna see him again. Preferably naked.

"Ryder is good." I choose my words carefully, not wanting to give myself away. "Busy. But otherwise good. He's excited for the babies."

"That man is so good with kids. Dean is obsessed with him. I'll never forget the way he showed up for Colt after Abby passed. I'm not sure what we would've done without him."

Knife to the chest.

That's how Mom's seemingly innocuous comment feels right now.

Trust me, existing without Ryder in my life right now is killing me, just like the things you're saying.

I stick my hand inside the laundry basket in an effort to distract myself from the vortex of shame and need and confusion swirling inside my gut.

Of course the item of clothing I pluck from the pile is some of Dad's underwear.

Dropping it, I grab some socks instead. "Why are you still doing Dad's laundry? I know he has time now." My brothers are the ones working long hours these days. Dad's not retired, but he's keeping a regular seven-to-four schedule along with me.

"Because, honey, I like taking care of him. That's how marriage works."

"Has he ever done your laundry?"

Mom nods. "He did. Who do you think took care of *me* when I had six babies?"

"Grandma."

"She helped too, of course," Mom says with a chuckle. "But your dad stepped up in a big way. You'll see when you get married."

Ugh, Mom and the zingers today.

Maybe I'm just extra sensitive to it right now because I'm PMSing. Or maybe I just need to accept the fact that Ryder wasn't joking when he said, *Don't fall in love with me.*

"You all right, honey?"

I realize Mom is looking at me, her face etched with concern. "Yeah. Sorry. Spacing out here. I'm pooped."

"Dad says the office has been quiet." Her frown stays put. "I know you're still probably shaken up from your injury, but the sooner you get your head back into work, the easier it'll be."

"Did you like your job?"

"What? Being a mom to y'all?" Mom smiles, smoothing her hands over the shirt she just folded. "It wasn't easy. But it was right for our family, and right for me too. I loved raising you kids. Some of our happiest times were when y'all were little. Life was chaos, and we were just surviving a lot of the time. But there was a clarity of purpose that I miss, because that job—it does end. Not being a parent, but having kids at home."

My chest twists. Leave it to Mom to unexpectedly relate to my occupational angst.

"Knock knock!"

Glancing over my shoulder, I see Dad stride into the kitchen. I do a double take when a woman walks in behind him.

She's cute, probably around my age, with brown hair and a big smile.

"Y'all, I'd like to introduce you to Lainey Brown." Dad nods at our visitor. "She's the daughter of a friend, and she's in town from Austin, where she just graduated business school."

Lainey smiles and crosses the kitchen, holding out her hand. "Nice to meet y'all. Dale told me so much about his family that I already feel like I know you. He's so proud of y'all."

I shake her hand. "He should be. We're awesome."

"You must be Billie." Lainey smiles. "You're a barrel racer, right?"

"She *was* a barrel racer," Mom corrects. "But she's always been our A-plus accountant. She even got her degree in math."

"Oh?" Lainey tilts her head. "Where'd you go to school?"

"I got my associate's degree online so I wouldn't have to leave the ranch."

"Girl, I get it. I wouldn't want to leave this slice of heaven either. Your family's property is stunning. It's truly an honor to help y'all with some updates. I already have so many ideas!"

RYDER

I raise my brows and look at Dad. "Updates?"

"I had lunch with Lainey's father in Fort Worth earlier this year." Dad rocks back on his heels as he slips his hands in the front pockets of his jeans. "You know, when I was there for the rodeo? Anyway, we got to talking, and he mentioned Lainey was a branding whiz."

Mom frowns. "Not branding as in—"

"I don't work with cattle, if that's what you're asking," Lainey replies with a laugh. "I help businesses brand themselves so they're more recognizable to the public. I'm here to give y'all a whole new look—new logo, new website, new tagline. The whole shebang."

"I had no idea that job existed. How cool." I mean that. I love living in Hartsville, but there's not a lot of variety around here when it comes to professions. Sometimes it feels like everyone on earth is either a rancher, a cowboy, or a cook.

"It took me a long time to land on this as a profession," Lainey continues. "But I love it. The creativity aspect is really what drew me to the field, and I started taking on projects while I was still in business school."

My heart thumps. "I'm amazed. Welcome to the ranch, Lainey. I look forward to working with you."

"I don't want to count our chickens before they're hatched, but I think giving your ranch a few key updates in terms of your marketing and the look you're going for will really push your numbers in the right direction. Sky's the limit."

"I'm *so* on board." I glance at my father. "I'm kinda surprised you signed up for this, though."

He shrugs. "I'm not gonna be around forever, Billie. I wanna make sure I leave y'all an operation that's in tip-top shape. I know y'all work hard to make our little world go round, and I have every intention of honoring that."

Mom and I chat with Lainey for a while. Apparently Dad offered her housing on the ranch while she's working here. She'll be starting sooner rather than later, although she and Dad are still ironing out the details.

Later, I head out to the barn, where I know I'll find Tate. He's brushing down a gorgeous Andalusian that we named Dwayne after The Rock, AKA Dwayne Johnson, because the horse is fifteen hands high and an absolute giant.

"If I tell you something juicy, will you tack up a horse and come for a ride with me?" I ask Tate.

My brother cuts me a look. "You know it'd be just our luck that you'd fall off again, and this time, you'll mangle your arm so badly they're going to have to amputate it. I know you *can* take on the world with just one arm, but do you *want* to?"

I laugh. "I'm not gonna fall again. Law of averages."

"Explain that law to me."

"The average chance of falling off a horse is, like, two percent, and since I just fell off on my last ride, I have ninety-eight thousand more rides until I fall again."

He shakes his head, a big old smile on his face. "That makes zero sense."

"Please, Tate. I'm losing my mind, and I really need a friend to talk to right now. And I'm not even wearing the sling anymore. I promise, my arm is fine."

His smile fades. "Everything okay?"

Yes. No. I don't know.

I look at him. He looks back.

At last he sighs. "Fine. But if anyone finds out, I'm saying this was your idea."

A rush of relief leaves me feeling woozy. "Thank you."

I need to use a mounting block to get up on my horse. It's humbling, to say the least. But the second I'm in the saddle, the worn leather creaking in a familiar way, I immediately feel better.

The tightness in my shoulders and chest dissipates. Guiding my horse into the October afternoon, I suck in lungful after lungful of crisp autumn air.

"So what's goin' on?" Tate guides his horse into a trot beside mine.

"Dad wants to rebrand the ranch. He's thinking a whole new look, logo, website. Everything."

Tate scoffs. "Okay. That's not what you need to tell me, though."

"It's not." I give him a rueful smile. "But I do think it's interesting. He's bringing a woman in, Lainey, to give us some ideas. She's a branding expert."

"Didn't know there was such a thing."

"Me neither. She just got her MBA at UT Austin. She's so confident and…" I carefully lean forward to pat my horse's neck. "Interesting. She got into a line of work I didn't even know existed. Apparently she loves it."

Tate looks at me from under the brim of his cowboy hat. "And you know all this how?"

"By talking to her for ten minutes with Mom. Obviously."

"Obviously."

"I'm a fast learner."

"I like that she's giving you some ideas to chew on.

You've been stuck for a while now, so it's good to have someone like that shake things up a bit."

Closing my eyes, I tilt up my face to the sun. My pulse thumps. Tate and I have always been close, and I've confided in him plenty over the course of our lives. But this secret is a big one.

And yeah, maybe part of me is scared to say out loud how I really feel about Ryder. Because if—when—Ryder turns me down again, Tate will know about that rejection too.

I don't want to be the type of girl who pines after guys who don't return her feelings. That's just embarrassing for everybody. Tate would mean well by showing sympathy, but I'm pretty sure I'd process that as pity.

I don't need his pity or anybody else's.

Only, I can't keep this inside anymore.

Talk about shaking things up.

"Tate, I slept with Ryder."

To my brother's credit, he doesn't so much as blink. He just continues to ride beside me in thoughtful silence, squinting against the sun. It's gotten warm—downright hot, actually—despite the fact that we're nearly halfway through October.

The stuff inside my torso swells. Tate sure as hell ain't perfect, but he's a good brother. He's never judged me. He may be the baby of the family, but he's the wisest of all my brothers.

"I also think I'm falling in love with him."

"Okay."

I laugh nervously. "Oh, sweet Tate, we both know it's not okay."

"Why?"

"He's not in love with me. Obviously."

Tate looks at me. "Now that doesn't seem quite so obvious to me. Didn't we just spend a good chunk of dinner the other night talking about how he was the first to reach you in the arena after you fell?"

"Well, yeah—"

"He was always kind to you when we were kids. We used to tease him about having a soft spot for you."

Aw, now I'm feeling all soft inside.

I also feel like I'm going to cry.

"I don't think he will. You know, consider a relationship."

"Because you were brave and told him how you felt. Aw, Billie. I'm proud of you."

Sniffling, I wipe my nose on my sleeve. "How'd you know that's what happened?"

"Because I know you."

"And you don't hate me for crushing on Colt's BFF?"

Tate chuckles. "Why would I hate you for that?"

"Do you think Colt will hate me? Hate us?" I swallow. "I told Ryder I didn't want to tell him."

"Now *that* I'm not sure I agree with."

"Why? Pretty sure this was just a onetime thing. Ryder and I haven't hung out since—"

"But you should." Tate tugs on his reins, and his horse slows. "You should hang out with Ryder. Which means you should tell Colt. You're afraid of betraying him, I get it. But that's exactly what you're doing by sneaking around behind his back like this."

My stomach knots with guilt. "It wasn't intentional. It just…happened. I think I needed a minute to process it."

"Well, take your minute, but don't let it go on much longer than that."

"But what if Ryder decides he is open to dating me, but then it doesn't work out? I don't want to put Colt in a weird position—"

"You're putting us all in a weird position by not coming clean. Just tell him. You hooked up with his friend. So what?"

I give Tate the most withering stare I can muster. "It's not that simple. I don't want to be the reason they stop being friends. And yeah, maybe I don't want Colt interfering when things are so...new. Fragile. You know how domineering he can be."

"I do. I also know he'd be happy for two of his favorite people finding happiness with each other."

"That's jumping, like, thirty steps ahead."

"Don't you like to race? If you could, I think you'd literally move fast for a living."

I smile. "Awful wise for one so young."

Tate shrugs. "I'm a textbook Capricorn. I came into the world knowing shit. And I know Ryder likes you just as much as you like him. He's afraid. Lucky for y'all, though, *you're* awful good at the long game. Persistence is your superpower, which you'll use to keep breaking down those walls of his."

"I don't know. Seems like a lame superpower to have."

"Are you kidding? It's the best superpower ever. Grit is everything in this world. Because you're persistent, I know you'll eventually find a job you love. You'll be the next Lainey whatever-her-name-is, mark my words. You'll have work that you love and a man you love too, and y'all will live happily ever after."

I laugh at that because it's so absurd.

Because the idea of any of that being possible is so beautiful I can't stand it. I feel like I'm being tickled from the inside out, giddy and breathless and *hopeful*.

"If Colt doesn't kill us first." I guide my horse around a sinkhole. "Feels like a long shot, Tate, that this doesn't blow up in my face."

Tate holds up a hand. "I won't say a word to Colt. But you need to tell him if you and Ryder keep doing what y'all are doing. That's the only way things work out in your favor, yeah?"

He's right, of course. Thinking about telling Colt fills me with dread. But I also feel this weird little shiver of excitement. Maybe because telling Colt about Ryder and me would mean we're a real *thing*—that there's actually a chance we could work out.

Thunder rumbles overhead. I glance up at the sky, surprised to see clouds rolling in.

"Is it supposed to rain?"

Tate chuckles. "We really need to get you back out in the field, Billie. Since when do you not check the weather?"

"Why'd you tack up our horses if you knew it was gonna rain?"

"'Cause I knew you needed some time in the saddle. C'mon, let's head back." Tate pulls his horse in a half circle, turning around.

More thunder. I can smell the rain now, taste the minerality of water meeting dry earth in the air.

I need more time to think.

I need more time in the saddle. Who cares if I get a little wet? It's toasty out here. My phone is tucked safely inside the saddle bag. And maybe the rain will finally help cool off my raging hormones.

Maybe it will help clear my mind so I can make some good decisions. I'm playing with fire here, and I need to be smart about what my next moves are.

"You go ahead. I'll catch up."

Tate glances over his shoulder. "Be careful, all right?"

"I'm always careful."

I hear him chuckle. "No, you're not. Love you, sis."

"Love you more."

CHAPTER 19
Kiss the Rain
Billie

I ride for a long time, my pace slow but steady.

There's a meditative quality to the sound of my horse's hooves clomping in the pale earth. My pulse beats in time to her steady cadence, my body rolling with her movements in a way that makes me feel capable. Strong.

I know I've only known Lainey for all of five minutes, but she seems to have no problem at all trusting herself. I should take a page from her book and trust *myself* to do the right thing here.

I don't love my job, so I should start exploring other options.

I'm falling in love with Ryder, so I should tenderly—*patiently*—explore the connection we have.

I respect my brother and want the best for him, so I should come clean about the feelings I have for his friend.

I don't know what I'll do if Colt tells me point-blank to stay away from Ryder. I'm not sure he would do that, but I understand *why* he would. The Rivers boys have their, ahem, reputation for a reason. Especially Duke and Ryder—they're known to chase women but never keep them. Duke dated around a little, but as far as I know, Ryder's never had a girlfriend. Picking up girls at the rodeo is more his style.

Then again, isn't Duke settling down with Wheeler proof that the boys will change for the right person? What if I'm the right person for Ryder?

I know Colt just wants to keep me safe. He doesn't want to see my heart get broken. But at some point, he has to trust me to make the right decision. I'm not anyone's baby girl or kid sister anymore.

I need space to figure myself out. Make mistakes.

Maybe make some magic while I'm at it.

More thunder. Goose bumps break out on my arms and legs as I watch the storm roll in, the warm breeze picking up. The old oaks creak overhead, their leaves sighing as the first raindrops begin to fall.

I like the gentle sound they make when they hit the ground. Somehow the sun is still shining, creating this gorgeous rainbowlike effect where the bright yellow light glints off the rain, transforming it into sparks of silver and gold.

My being aches at the beauty of it. The hills, the rain. It's coming down in sheets now. The way my horse doesn't break her stride, clearly content to get soaked along with me in the hot weather.

"What are we gonna do, sweet girl?" I whisper.

I know what my next move *should* be. But am I really ready to burn life as I know it to the ground? Because it's a good life. Perfect? No.

It's good, though. Decent. Safe.

Am I an asshole to want more than that? How much happiness and fulfillment and joy can I expect out of life?

I don't expect things to be perfect, though. I don't *need* them to be perfect. I just want my life to feel more like *me*.

I'm not safe or decent. I'm also not sweet. It's kind of a crime when you think about it, that we expect girls to be docile and kind, *sugary sweet*, when boys can be as untamed and ill-behaved as they please.

"I don't know why I just called you sweet." I'm patting my horse again. "I'm sorry about that. You don't need to be sweet for me. Be as wild as you like, sister. Maybe that'll give me permission to be wild too."

Like you ever needed it.

I urge her into a trot. My elbow bangs against my side, lighting up with pain, so I have her slow down again.

That's when I spot it. Movement in a nearby valley. A cow? A car?

I start to shake, and I don't know why. I have no reason to be afraid right now. If I ride fast, Nash's cabin is twenty minutes away. Probably less.

Not like I'd need his help. I can outride anything, a bear or a bobcat or a deranged lunatic in a truck.

Well, I couldn't outrun the truck. But I could duck inside those trees over there and make a run for it before he even made the turn.

Shit, it is a truck. I can just hear the throb of its engine over the sound of the rain and the thunder.

That engine—it's diesel—

How the fuck does this guy keep tracking me down?

Is it really him?

Oh God, it's definitely him, and he's definitely heading this way.

Ryder crests a nearby hill and cuts the engine. I take that as a sign that I should stop, so I do.

Everything inside me takes a swan dive into the dirt as I watch him climb out of the truck and stalk toward me.

He keeps his head down, rivulets of rain pouring off his Stetson and soaking his dark T-shirt. It sticks to his arms and torso like a second skin.

My nipples immediately harden to tight, tender points. I shiver even though the air is warm. My heartbeat throbs in my throat. The roll of his massive shoulders, his huge, steady stride, the way he glances up and locks eyes with me, unabashed—he looks like some kind of apex predator about to go in for the kill.

Me.

My pulse thunders when I realize I'm the one up for slaughter.

Or maybe I've already died and gone to heaven, because holy *shit*, the vision of this man approaching me, clearly on some kind of serious mission, might be the most glorious sight I've ever witnessed.

I'm aware of the way the rain gathers on my eyelashes and drips over my lips.

I shiver again, but there's a burning awareness left in its wake that spreads from my bones outward. It singes my skin, flushes my face.

I'm on *fire*.

"Ryder Rivers," I manage.

"Billie Wallace." He looks up and our eyes meet.

"What are you doing here?"

He puts his hand on my calf, wrapping his fingers possessively around the muscle there. He gives it a squeeze that has my cunt spasming.

"Can't stop thinking about you."

My heart's in my throat now. "Oh yeah?"

"Yeah. I tried to stay away, Billie. It's not my intention to mess with your head or give you mixed signals." He tips back his head and our eyes meet. "But I can't, darlin'."

I lick my overly sensitive lips. "Can't what?"

"Pretend like I don't wanna be with you every second of every fuckin' day."

The rain has soaked through both our shirts now. I wanna take mine off.

I wanna take everything off.

"I've been thinking about you too." The words come out thickly. "Why do you think I'm out in this rain?" I hold up my good arm. "I'm risking life and limb to get you out of my head."

He gives my calf another squeeze, his hand moving north to my knee. "We gotta talk. And then we gotta talk to Colt."

"Yeah." I roll my hips, pressing my clit against the seam of my jeans as his hand moves to my thigh. "But first, can I ask how you found me?"

"Had to see you. Went to your place but you weren't there. So I called Tate."

My heart flips. "You called my brother?"

"Why're you so surprised?" Ryder blinks when a raindrop lands in his eye. "I know y'all are close. Figured I had nothing to lose. Other than, well, everything. He said my timing was impeccable and that you were out here on horseback. Now, I gave him a piece of my mind for letting you ride—"

"You let me ride you."

His lips twitch, and my chest lights up. "That was supervised. This isn't."

"Care to supervise me again?"

His hand is on my hip now. His thumb moves between my legs and presses against my clit. "I wouldn't mind that."

I nearly come from the contact alone. "Help me down?"

He nods, and now his hands are on my waist. "Can I tell you why I came before we—"

"That's not why you came?" I put my good hand on his shoulder, but that's completely unnecessary, because all of a sudden, he's lifting me out of the saddle—God, this man is tall—and he's scooping me into his arms, damsel-in-distress style.

"Well, I came for that." He shifts so that he has one arm under my back and the other under my knees. I'm able to slip my good arm underneath his so that it's hooked around the ball of his shoulder. "I'll *come* for that."

"From that?"

He chuckles, and I reach down to slip my hand inside the back of his shirt. Marvel at the way his thick muscles bunch and release beneath my fingertips as he begins to walk us toward his truck.

His skin is hot to the touch.

"Will your horse stay put?" Ryder asks.

I glance over his shoulder at my mare, who's happily

munching on some grass. "She's good. She likes the rain when it's this warm out."

"Good." He groans when I run my fingertips down the furrow of his spine. "I came to tell you about an idea I had. A possible career pivot for you."

Something hot and fierce slashes through my middle. *He really has been thinking about me. Me, the person who's struggling with her life path. Not just me, the body he likes to touch.*

He's been paying attention.

He's letting me *know* he's been paying attention.

He's showing that he cares, which is Ryder's way of putting himself out there.

Tears prick my eyes. "Tell me more."

"I talked about my parents at supper for the first time in…well, a really long-ass time." He carefully sets me down in front of the hood of his truck, chuckling again when he sees my shocked expression. "Yeah, yeah, that's exactly how my family looked at me too. Anyway, we were talking about Mom and Dad, and we talked about the speech delay I had as a kid. Animal therapy really helped me with that."

I blink. "Like when you hang out with animals and it helps with anxiety and stuff?"

"Bingo. Animals apparently made me feel comfortable and safe enough to open up. Kinda like *you* made me feel safe enough to pick up my guitar again." Grinning, he puts his hands on my hips again and uses the bulk of his body to crowd me against the hood, my backside meeting with the grill. It's still warm. "Anyways, I've done some research over the past few days, and it seemed like something right up your alley. Animals. Kids. The outdoors. Doing something that requires creativity. Something you could build from the ground up with the help of your family."

I can only stare at him. My heart has apparently grown wings because it's soaring through the wide-open space inside my ribcage.

He searches my eyes, then pulls his brows together. "If you don't like the idea, no biggie. It'd be a massive undertaking—"

"I love it."

I think I'm in love with you too.

His brows curve upward, eyes sparking. "Really?"

I go up on my toes so I can take off his hat, which I place on the hood. Crown-side down, of course.

"Really. Just thinking about it—Ry, my heart." I take his hand and place it on my chest. "It's pounding. You did research? For me?"

He grins. "I did."

"But I have no idea how I'd pull it off—"

"We'd help you, of course." His hand moves to my breast.

"There you go again, saying 'we.'" I grab the hem of his soaked shirt and start to work it upward, baring his chest.

He kneads my breast before giving my nipple a soft pinch through my shirt. "At the end of the day, that's all we got, ain't it?" He leans in and hovers his mouth over mine. "Each other."

Then his lips are on mine, and I'm lost.

CHAPTER 20
Tired of Running
Ryder

Fuck, I'm hard.

The taste of her mouth. That's all it takes.

That, and the way her heart pounded strong and healthy against my hand after I floated my idea.

I debated for hours—days—whether I actually should share the whole animal therapy thing. If I should even come here. What right do I have to see her again? I was operating under the assumption that our hookup was a one-time-only thing.

But that good sleep I was enjoying? It dissipated the longer I was away from Billie. Last night, I tossed and turned, barely getting a wink. Then I spent the day either pacing in my tiny living room, my knees aching, pulse popping inside my skin, or googling shit like, "animal therapy start-up costs," "how to build an animal therapy program," and "working with your significant other good or bad."

Fuck it.

That's the conclusion I finally came to after all of *four days* of denying myself her company.

I can't do this anymore. I have to see her.

So I ditched my chores and hopped in my truck and drove to the Wallace Ranch.

Before, I would've been proud of my ability to deny myself. The longer I could stay away from a girl like Billie, the stronger I was.

I was safe. And that's what mattered more than anything.

Now I'm coming to grips with how much I'm missing out on by playing it safe. Self-restraint hasn't made me any happier.

It's cut me off from the pleasures, both small and profound, of being alive.

Anyone could've seen me on my drive over here.

Anyone can still see me even though I was careful to park my truck far from the road. This is the Wallace's property. Colt lives here, and so do his parents.

And calling Tate? Big gamble. He's a stand-up guy, but he could easily tell his brothers I was looking for Billie.

I'm risking everything to make these moves. But I'm too wound up—too sick of being alone—to care.

I don't know how Billie and I will make this work. *If* it will work. I'm not sure I could forgive a friend for falling for one of my siblings without saying a damn word to me about it.

I just gotta hope that Billie and I can figure out a way to make things right.

In the meantime, I'm gonna lay this girl down. Give her what she wants, then take what I need.

She rises into the kiss, her fingertips trailing ribbons of need up the naked slope of my stomach and chest as I play with her nipple.

She's so *soft* everywhere. Soft and hot and eager.

I pull back. Tug her bottom lip between my teeth. Then I'm leaning in again and slipping my tongue inside her mouth.

At the same time, I give her nipple a hard pinch. She gasps.

"I hate you." She breaks the kiss to try to yank my shirt over my head.

It gets stuck, so I help her take it off. "Tell me more."

"You're a fucking tease, making me wait." Both her hands are on my chest now, her fingers catching on my own nipple. A bolt of lust lands in the tip of my dick. "Being so hot."

The rain hits my skin and rolls down my back. The contrast between the cool water and the heat that throbs inside my skin sends a shiver of pleasure down my spine.

"I think I need some evidence of how hot you think I am." Curling my hands around her waist, I toss her up onto the hood of the truck. Then I part her knees and step between them, reaching for the fly of her jeans. "How wet you gonna be for me, darlin'?"

Her hand finds my nape. She digs her fingers into my hair, and I bite back a groan at how *good* it feels.

"Quit playin' around and find out."

I duck my head and sink my teeth into her neck, making her yelp. "I'mma have to fuck the brat out of you again, aren't I?"

"Uh-huh," she pants.

Her jeans are soaked to the point that they're like a

second skin. Total pain in the ass to take off, but I gotta see her. All of her.

So I pry off her boots. The jeans. I cuss when I see the cute pink panties she's wearing.

"Didn't think they could get any tinier than the ones you wore the other night." Taking them off, I hold them up and marvel at the little strings and delicate lace they're made of. "Why even wear them?"

Billie is naked from the waist down now. Propped up on the hood of my truck with her nipples poking through her shirt, her dark hair plastered to her forehead and neck, she looks like the wet T-shirt contestant from heaven.

Lord, thank you for the bounty I'm about to eat. Receive. Whatever.

"Because I like them, and they make me feel sexy. No, you can't keep—"

"Too late." I tuck them into my back pocket. "If you don't want me stealin' 'em, you shouldn't be wearing 'em."

Her hazel eyes ignite. "You really should give me a heads-up, then, when you're gonna show."

I slide my hands up her legs. Resting them on her inner thighs, I push so that she's spread nice and wide. "I think the surprise turns you on."

Her nostrils flare. "I think you're a jackass."

"Let's see who's right." Reaching up, I part her pussy with my thumb.

We both hiss at the slickness I find there. She's swollen and hot, and when I dip my thumb inside her entrance, she contracts around me.

All the while, the rain pelts the hood of the truck.

"Aw, darlin'," I say with a low, dark chuckle. "I think I win this one."

Her eyes go hazy. "Don't think I won't put up a fight."

"Nuh-huh." I use my thumb to draw the moisture out of her entrance, then coat her clit with it. "You're gonna watch me eat this pretty little pussy, and then you're gonna let me fuck it however I want. Yeah?"

Her breath catches. "Since when did you get creative?"

"You've been rubbin' off on me."

"I like it."

"I know." Rolling my thumb over her clit, I use my other hand to bend her leg and push it to the side, spreading her even more. "You know how I like to see you. All of you."

She nods, her tits rising and falling as she struggles to catch her breath. "Perv."

"For you? Yup." I shove her shirt up over her tits. Then I pull down her bra so that her breasts are propped up, bare nipples aching to be sucked.

So I suck them. Gently at first. My baby arches against me, digging her hand into my hair.

"Oh, Ry. I'm so happy. So damn happy you came." She gives my hair a hard tug, urging me to meet her eyes. "I want you to know that. How happy you make me."

Emotion radiates from my center outward. I'm one big ball of feeling: the heavy throb of need in my dick, the lightness in my chest, the burn in my hamstrings, the carbonated feeling of joy in my throat. The craving to know her and possess her and show her there's no one else.

She's not gonna want anyone else after she has me.

"Why you think I can't stay away?" I nuzzle my nose into her neck. "I'm addicted to the way you make me feel."

I kiss my way down her belly. The scent of her arousal fills my head as I put my hands on the creases between her legs and pelvis. Her hand is still in my hair, her eyes still locked on my eyes when I kiss her.

Her flavor hits me in a mouthwatering rush. She's salt. Heat. Earth.

She's watching me kiss her, eat her, moving my head so that I can suck on her clit. Stroke her with my tongue.

I go all in, using my thumbs to hold her open so I can lick inside her entrance. She moans, her brows curved up like she's in pain.

"Ry. Baby. The way you do this—how well you—"

Love me.

I silently beg her to say it. Because even though it's way too soon to be saying shit like that, my heart doesn't balk at the idea.

For the first time, neither does my head.

"You need me to stretch you out a little?" I press my lips to her clit. "So you're ready for me?"

She nods, making a sound that has me thinking she's on the verge of tears. Her hips rock against my face.

"I like you sore, so you think of me when you move." I sink a finger inside her pussy. "But I don't want you hurtin'."

"I like it when you make me sore too," she pants. "Whatever you wanna give me, I can take it."

I'm not sure my heart's in my body anymore. I can't locate it. I feel its beat in my cock. Hear it in my ears.

But my chest feels simultaneously hollowed out and overly full.

Oblivious to my ongoing cardiac event, Billie starts to play with her tits. I watch, dick screaming, as she circles her nipple with her thumb, her hips rolling as her head falls back.

"Watch," I growl.

Her head pops back up, a smirk on her lips. "It feels too good, Ry."

"I don't fucking care. *Watch*."

I thrust my finger in and out, in and out, her pussy fluttering around me. Her grip on me is tight and soft, and it makes me want to howl.

The rain keeps coming down. It drips off the peaks of Billie's nipples.

Her legs start to tremble. I use my free hand to hold one down.

At the same time, I work my second finger inside her. This time, I know I don't need to go slowly. Billie is quick to adjust to me, rocking her hips to push my fingers deeper. I continue to lick her clit, slow, steady strokes.

Her pussy clamps down on me. Once. Hard.

"Ry." She's sobbing. "Please. Please. Please, baby."

She's wound so tight she doesn't know what she needs.

Good thing I do. I use my teeth to nick her clit. At the same time, I slip my fingers out of her pussy and paint her slit with her slickness. Wind her even tighter when I shove them back inside her.

"Fuck." The word comes out as a cry. "Fuck you, Ry."

Her neck is bent and so are her knees. She's watching me bring her to the brink just like I told her to, and I want to fuck this flash of obedience right out of her.

Billie's not a good girl. Thank God for that.

Her hips jerk against my mouth. Her pussy tightens around my fingers.

Just when she's about to come, I pull out my fingers and lean up to kiss her mouth.

"*What?*" she yells. "No no no! I'm—"

"So close you wanna die?" I kiss her mouth so that she can taste herself. "I know. But I told you that I'm gonna fuck you how I like. And right now, I'd like you to come when I'm inside you."

I dig into my back pocket for the condoms I shoved in there before I left my house. Wanted to bring extra in case the supply in my glove box didn't last us.

Her eyes are wild, unsteady, as they toggle between mine. "Cruel."

"Yes." I rip open the packet with my teeth. "I know cruelty well."

"You do?" She grabs the condom from me.

I unzip my jeans, but before I can pull out my dick, she does it for me. I can't formulate a sentence, a thought, when she thumbs my head just the way that I like. I just blindly grope at her tits, squeezing them in my hands while she squeezes me.

"No one's been crueler to me than I have been to myself," I reply, groaning when she gives me a long, torturous tug. "Jesus, baby, that is—"

"Everything?" She bites her lip. "I know. Lemme be good to you, then, so you can learn how to be good to yourself."

I grit my teeth, barely able to withstand the lust that whips through me like a hurricane-force gale as she rolls the condom onto my length. "I've already learned. From you."

She notches me at her entrance. Then she thinks better of it, though, and guides my tip up and down her slit.

Even through the latex, she's burning up. So soft and small I could scream.

I lean my forehead against hers. "This isn't normal."

"How good it is? I know."

"And you're okay with that?"

She scoffs, a sound that catches when she presses my head to her clit. "I'm scared shitless, Ry. Of course I'm not okay. I've never been fucking better."

Now I'm laughing. She's kissing my jaw, and she's laughing too, and the tender motion of her putting me back at her entrance and nudging her hips so I'm inside her again wrenches my chest right the fuck open.

The feeling of fullness inside me spills over as I push, hard, sinking to the hilt in a single stroke.

She curses.

She bites my shoulder.

I thumb her clit, and she comes.

Right there on the hood of my truck, Billie shouts as she comes, her orgasm milking my dick in a way that has me incoherent.

The rain.

The pressure.

I can't fucking *handle* it.

Next thing I know, I'm pulling out of her and I'm turning her around. Always careful not to get her bad elbow caught, I put a hand between her shoulder blades and gently press her front onto the hood. Arms splayed wide.

"This—"

"It's okay, Ry. I'm okay. Now get the fuck back inside me, or I really will kill you."

I laugh, stepping forward. I nudge open her legs with my knees. Suck in a breath when I peek the dark pucker of her asshole.

Patience.

"Talk to me." I use my thumb to pull aside her ass cheek, opening her to me again. "Anything hurts, you let me know right away."

She nods, reaching back to pull me against her. "Don't stop, Ry."

She looks just as pretty from this angle. Sinking inside her pussy, I groan. She feels better from behind. Tighter. Not sure how that's possible, but it's real.

I grab her hips and angle her ass upward. I begin to thrust. I smile when she moans, her pussy still spasming with the echoes of her orgasm.

My balls tighten. I thrust harder. Faster. Billie goes up on her toes to meet me, pressing back against me so that our bodies meet with a rude slap.

The rain gets in my eyes and blurs my vision.

"You on birth control?"

The question must take us both by surprise, because Billie looks at me over her shoulder. "I have an IUD, yeah."

"Anything else I need to know about?"

Her eyes flicker. "No. All good here."

"All good here too. You mind if I take off the condom and try something different?"

RYDER

I wait with bated breath for her to turn me down. Blow me off. Hell, she could even be disgusted by my request.

Instead, she smiles. A bright, happy thing, teeth and all.

"I love trying new things." As if to hammer the point home, her pussy clenches around me.

I let my head fall back. Close my eyes. Pray to my Lord and savior that I'll be able to survive this moment, because my heart's not working. My pulse is at a standstill.

It strikes me that I *have* to keep going if I want to survive this.

I have to keep feeling. Doing. Trusting.

Because Billie is trusting me, and I'd be an idiot not to return the favor. Hell, if someone as smart and capable and self-aware as Billie has faith in me, I probably should have a little faith in myself too.

Sex is better if I open up. Connect to what I really want.

So is life.

Curling my body around hers, I lift her torso so that I can cup her breasts. I fuck her while I play with her nipples, marveling at the way her tits fill my hands.

I trail my lips over her neck. "You gotta talk to me. If you don't like it, I need to know."

"You really think I wouldn't tell you if I didn't like something?"

"Fair point."

"I'm not going anywhere, Ry. Trust me. Your dick is too nice."

"Nice?" I say with a laugh.

"Perfect. Big. Just the right size. Tastes good too."

I have to grit my teeth to keep from coming.

Only by the grace of God am I able to pull out without blowing my load and yank off the condom.

I hold open her cheek again with my left hand. I pump myself with my right.

"Never." My brain flatlines. "This. Not with anyone else. Ever. You hear me?"

"Yes, baby, I hear you."

A blinding flash of light arcs through me.

Then I'm coming on Billie's asshole, agonizingly hot spurts that coat her and coat me and empty my body of any thought, any feeling, except one.

Her.

She's it. The one.

She's saying my name, saying how good it feels, saying how she loves my pervy mind, my daring.

She's saying she likes how I feel dripping down her legs.

I'm trembling when I pull her up and turn her around and pull her against me.

My pulse throbs in time to my thoughts.

We're in trouble.

We're never coming back from this. But maybe that's a good thing.

The best thing that ever happened.

CHAPTER 21
Where the Buffalo Roam
Billie

"Your place is—"

"Shitty?" Ryder pops a cracker slathered with blue cheese and honey into his mouth and grins. "I know. I'm sorry, baby. Exhibit A why being the 'easy' one sucks sometimes." He chews thoughtfully for a moment. "A lot of the time."

I reach for another cracker, but Ryder beats me to it. He smears it with a good bit of the decadently delicious cheese and a dollop of the local honey the hostess at the Homestead Hen insisted we needed.

Ryder told me I was coming home with him after the epic sex we had in the rain. He didn't ask. Didn't hesitate. Just said, "I'm taking you home with me," and that was that.

He rode my horse back to the barn while I drove his truck, the two of us exchanging sexually tinged obscenities through the truck's open window as thunder rumbled in the distance.

Luckily the barn was deserted, so we were able to dry off somewhat and untack my horse without anyone being the wiser. Ryder called in a to-go order from the Homestead Hen, and I hid out in the truck while he ran inside to get the food. No one spotted us there either.

At least I *hope* no one spotted us. My phone's been dead silent since we left a couple hours ago, which I take as a good sign.

Now we're at his place, a rundown farmhouse—more of a shack, actually—on the far edge of Lucky River Ranch.

"Open your mouth," Ryder says.

Now I'm the one grinning. "I thought we said dinner first, *then* blow jobs."

"Can you not provoke me for once?" His jaw tics. "I'm trying to be a gentleman here. You know, feed and water you and shit *before* I defile you."

I lick my lips, glancing at the tequila soda he made me. "I was hoping defilement would be on the menu tonight."

"Always. Now open your goddamn mouth, Billie."

I let him feed me the cracker. The combination of salty and sweet, the creaminess of the cheese and the crunch of the cracker, has me moaning.

Ryder's eyes darken. "Exactly the sound you make when I'm the one in your mouth."

"You're delicious too. I told you that." I swipe my thumb over the corner of my mouth. "Giving you head is a pleasure, truly."

Ryder's hand comes down on the table with a *thwack*. "Billie."

"Ryder." I'm smiling so hard my face hurts.

"You gotta give me a chance to catch my breath here, baby."

"I like it when you call me baby."

His expression softens. "I like calling you baby." He picks up another cracker and begins to load it up with cheesy goodness. "I meant what I said earlier. That I don't want you bein' with anybody else."

A ferocious roar of happiness rips through my middle. "Good thing I don't wanna be with anybody else."

"We're doing this."

"Are you asking me to be your girlfriend, Ryder Rivers?"

"Listen, Billie Wallace, I ain't askin'. I'm telling you this is what we're doing—yeah, you're my girlfriend. Which means I'm your boyfriend."

I bite my lip. "So bossy. My answer's yes, by the way."

Grinning, Ryder leans in and presses a scruffy kiss to my mouth. "Now that that's settled, you ready for dinner?"

Thunder rumbles overhead, and I glance up at the ceiling. Like the rest of the farmhouse, it's made of slotted wood, and it looks to be about a hundred years old.

I knew Ryder moved out of Lucky River Ranch's bunkhouse after Garrett died. That's when he and his brothers shuffled housing among the property's various available structures in an attempt to start living less like heathens and more like adults. Ryder apparently drew the short straw, because this place is…rustic to say the least.

"Everyone else got a cushy renovated place." Ryder reads my thoughts as he piles a pair of plates with filet mignon, roasted butternut squash, and truffled mac 'n' cheese. "I took this spot because, well, no one else would touch it with a ten-foot pole. I didn't want to cause a fight."

I sip my cocktail, chest twisting. "Meaning you wanted your brothers to love their new homes because when they're happy, you're happy."

"Something like that." Ryder's gaze twinkles as he sets my plate in front of me and holds out a napkin and silverware. "The house keeps getting pushed down on the list of renovations, but you'll be happy to hear that I sent Cash a text while I was waiting for the food and told him to send a crew here first thing tomorrow."

"Look at you, being a pain in the ass." I hold up my glass, the smell of the food making my mouth water. "Cheers to that, Ry."

He chuckles as he taps his glass against mine. "Don't get too excited, because Cash hasn't responded yet. But now that I got my girl, I need a nice place to bring her home to."

"Damn, Ry. You're good."

He sits across from me and puts his napkin on his lap. Our eyes meet over the table. He looks, and I look. Several heartbeats pass, and I wonder what I'm supposed to *do* with all this happiness.

Feel it, probably. Trust it.

Hasn't that been my message to Ryder all along? To feel his feelings instead of running away from them?

"You're real fuckin' beautiful, Billie." He holds my gaze. "I should've told you that sooner, and I'm sorry."

I swallow hard, not daring to breathe. "This is a big change, Ry. A sudden change. I want to trust you—"

"I want that too. I know it's gonna take time to earn

your trust after everything I've said—everything I've done—but if you're willing to give me that time, I'm gonna rise to the occasion. I promise you."

I've never heard Ryder make a promise before. But he's a Rivers. A cowboy too. And in our world, your word is all you have. You're either trustworthy or not. People know whether or not you keep your promises.

Ryder is the kind of man who keeps his promises. The fact that he's making one to me—

My eyes sting. "Of course I'll give you time."

He lets out a breath. "Good. Thank fuck. I was worried—"

"That I'd turn you down after all that?" I laugh, using the flat of my palm to wipe my eyes. "Stop."

"I'd also like to talk to Colt and your daddy about this. Us."

I turned over that idea in my head on the drive here. And while I get that Ryder wants to have a conversation man-to-man, I also think I should be the one to broach the subject with my brother first.

"Okay, let me try to explain this." I grab my fork and knife and cut into my steak. It's medium rare, just how I like it. "I want Colt to think of me as an adult. I'll always be his baby sister, but I'm also a grown-ass adult. I think he'll appreciate it if I'm the one to talk to him first. It'll show him I'm more mature than he thinks, and maybe that I actually have my shit together. Or I'm trying to, at the very least. I need him to respect the choices I make."

Ryder nods as he goes to town on his butternut squash. "That's fair. Long as I can talk to him right after, I'm all right with that."

"What's our plan if he blows up?"

Ryder lets out a breath and leans back in his chair. "I love your brother. Have for as long as I can remember. I'd like to think I know him well enough by now to say he'll…" A long pause. "Well, I think he'll be happy for us eventually."

"Oh Lord."

"We just gotta tread lightly. You know, with everything that happened in the past."

I furrow my brow. "I was young when all that happened. How did he survive it? Honestly? Her cheating on him like that?"

We all know the broad brush strokes of what went down: Abby, a teacher at Hart County High School where I was a senior, had an affair with the football coach. Because we live in a small town and secrets don't stay secret for long, people found out about it pretty quickly. But I guess my brother was the last to know; he doesn't like to leave the ranch now and didn't then either, so it was only when his wife and the football coach were fired that he found out.

A month later, Abby was diagnosed with cancer. Six months after that, she was gone.

"He was not okay for a long time," Ryder replies. "To be honest, I don't know how he survived. I mean, I think he just had to. Simple as that. Dean was a baby."

"We were all babies back then."

"But we're not anymore." Ryder picks up his cocktail. "Whatever happens, we can handle it, okay?"

I push the mac 'n' cheese around my plate and manage a tight smile. "Timing couldn't be worse. With me, you know, wanting to quit my job to do something totally off the wall too. I'm worried… If I'm being honest, I'm pretty scared that my family will think I'm an idiot."

"Why? Because trying to date a guy who doesn't date is a poor decision?" His mouth twitches as he brings his cocktail to his lips. "The nerve of them to assume we got nothin' but air between our ears."

I don't want to laugh, but I do. "Exactly. I need them to see you how I see you, Ry."

"You mean you want me to play guitar for them?"

"Yes." More laughter.

I *love* how this man goes out of his way to make me laugh. How much easier is life once you stop taking everything so damn seriously?

"You need me to put on a show, I'll put on a show, darlin'."

"Really?"

"Really." There's a steadiness to the way he meets my eyes now that has my stomach doing several backflips. "You need me, I'm there."

"Wow," I breathe. "Wow, Ry, you're a really great boyfriend for someone who's never dated before."

He lifts a massive shoulder. "Maybe I've been wantin' to date for a while, just been too chickenshit to do it. I got a lotta pent-up love to go around."

My mind catches on the word.

Love.

Oh God, oh *God*, that's gotta mean something, doesn't it?

"Eat your food, Billie." Ryder nods at my plate. "I'm serious. You're with me, you don't go hungry."

"I'm always hungry when I'm with you. Not for food, but for your gorgeous—"

"*Billie.*"

"Your gorgeous *spirit*, Ry. I love your gorgeous spirit."

His shoulders shake. "Goddamn it, if I choke—"

"I'll give you mouth-to-mouth."

"You'll be doin' something with that mouth." His eyes glimmer. "But that's up to me. Now eat."

The food is delicious, but the steak is the standout. Although I probably only think that because the Homestead Hen sources their beef from Lucky River Ranch, and I know how hard Ryder and his brothers work to care for their cattle.

"So, this animal therapy program." I reach across the table to steal a piece of Ryder's steak because I ate all of mine. "Talk to me about it."

He pushes his plate toward me, offering me more. "I think it'd be a natural extension of the Wallace Ranch's equine programs. I know your parents would love the community outreach angle."

A shiver of excitement darts up my spine as I eat my boyfriend's steak.

My boyfriend.

"They'd definitely love it, hopefully more than they'd hate losing an accountant."

"Your Dad can, and will, find another accountant, Billie."

"I know. I just start to feel stressed thinking about him having to find someone, and then train them, and then hope that the person is trustworthy and isn't going to, you know, steal our money or anything."

Ryder lets his head fall to the side as he gives me a look. "The chances of that happening—"

"Aren't zero."

"They're pretty close to it, though. You ever let the fear of getting hit by lightning keep you from fucking in the rain?"

My pulse flutters. Cunt floods with heat. "You're funny."

"It's why you like me so much."

"I told you, I like you because you have a great dick."

He chuckles. "Hearing that never gets old. Look, if you're not into the idea—"

"I'm into the idea, Ry."

"Then let's come up with a plan to make it happen."

My pulse is going absolutely haywire now.

Ryder, if you don't want me falling head over heels in love with you tonight, speak now, or forever hold your peace.

"You're serious about helping me." It's a question even though I don't say it that way.

Ryder chews his food, totally oblivious to the earthquake happening inside me. "Wouldn't have mentioned the whole thing if I didn't want to be involved. I've heard of therapy programs existing on ranches in other parts of Texas, but according to my research, there aren't any programs in Hartsville. Mom had to take me all the way to Austin for my therapy. That's what Wyatt remembers, anyway. Apparently he'd beg to go with us."

"He was always obsessed with your mom too."

Ryder's gaze softens. "I have yet to meet someone who *wasn't* obsessed with my mom."

"Maybe we name our program after her, then."

"That's—" He blinks. Swallows. "That'd be a kind move on your part, baby."

"*Our* part. Because this would be our program."

Ryder nods. "We do make a great fucking team."
"Do you mean that literally? Because hard agree."
"Ha. Now who's the perv?"
"I am because you're rubbing off on me."
"And rubbin' *up* on you."
"Care to do that right now?"

Wiping his hands on his napkin, he tosses it onto the table. "Ask and you shall receive. Lemme show you the bedroom."

CHAPTER 22
Wake-Up Call
Billie

I'm yanked from sleep by the sound of an unfamiliar alarm.

Seriously? It can't be time to get up already.

Because that would mean it's time for me to leave Ryder's surprisingly comfortable—if somewhat small—bed.

That would mean it's time to go home. Face the music.

Face the choices I've made. The changes I need to make. Although I didn't have any nightmares last night. That seems noteworthy, considering I've had them more often than not these past few weeks.

The deep rumble of a masculine growl draws my nipples to tight, aching points.

"Fuck." The deep, scraped-bare sound of Ryder's voice in the morning—it's *everything*.

"I know."

"Too early."

"I know."

"Didn't we just fall asleep?"

"Yes. I think so. We—so many times I—"

"Lost count?"

"Yes."

I only remember I'm naked when Ryder's hand moves lazily down my bare belly. I'm a back sleeper, and he's on his side.

His stubble scrapes my shoulder as he kisses me there.

"Mornin', beautiful."

I bite my lip. *This is so good so soon. It's scary.*

"Morning, handsome."

His hand moves lower. I moan when his fingers part me, slipping gently inside my slickness. Who knew you could wake up soaking wet?

He growls again. "Fuck."

"*I know.*"

"You sore?"

"Yes."

"Good."

"Again. Can we? Please?"

It's pitch dark in the room, which means it's pitch dark outside. No surprise there. Ryder set his alarm for three a.m.

"I don't want you hurtin'." He runs the pads of his fingers over my clit. "How about I make you come like this? Will that suffice?"

"No."

He chuckles. "I'll be gentle, then."

Ryder rolls on top of me, using his knee to nudge my legs apart. He kisses my collarbone. My neck. He carefully bends my leg and presses my knee to my chest.

His leaking head meets with my leg as he ducks to kiss my nipples. They tingle, and I gasp.

Beard burn. I bet if I looked, my skin would be red. Chapped.

Sensation bolts through my center to land in my clit.

Ryder goes still. "Too much?"

I run my hands down his back, wrapping my leg around his hip. "No. More."

"Yes, ma'am."

I feel tender and raw and achy everywhere.

More, please.

We both moan when he pushes inside me. I'm sore to the point of pain. I've never had sex that many times in one night. Not even close.

To be honest, I didn't think it was possible. But no joke, Ryder and I fucked *five times* since we got into bed after dinner.

Five.

Now we're going for round six. Even though I'm exhausted and scared and in pain, I couldn't stop if you paid me.

Ryder sinks into me slowly. All the while drawing lazy circles on my clit with his fingers. His mouth is on my tits. My neck.

I make an embarrassingly high-pitched sound when he starts to thrust. At the same time, my cunt spasms around his length.

"Already close, huh?" He's chuckling again.

I nod, lost in the mindfuck of being filled by this man in every sense of the word but not being able to see any part of him.

He rests his forehead on mine. It's damp with sweat,

and now it's my heart that spasms. It's taking real effort on his part to hold back. Go slow. Be gentle. He fucked me hard and fast last night, over and over again, his strokes punishing, his body taut with tension and the need to rut.

But this? This is something else entirely. It's not fucking. Not even sex.

This is being *loved*. Tended to.

He patiently brings me to orgasm, his thrusts luxuriously slow, his fingers gentle. I surrender to the release, unable to do anything except whisper his name as I hang onto his neck for dear life.

"You're perfect," he whispers back, lowering his weight onto mine so I'm pinned to the mattress. "You're everything. I wanna make you mine like this every morning, yeah?"

Coming down from the high of my orgasm, I feel like I'm floating in a warm, calm ocean. He comes inside me with a grunt, going still. The first time he did it, he asked before it happened. *Baby, I really wanna come inside you, but you gotta tell me it's okay, yeah?*

I said okay that time, and the time after that too. He got the picture then.

Is it wrong that I like the sensation of being filled by him this way? I already feel his cum leaking out between our bodies. There's always so much of it.

Jesus, am I really fantasizing about Ryder getting me pregnant? The idea makes my cunt flutter.

He stays on top of me for a minute, breathing hard.

"I don't wanna take you home." His lips brush mine. "Can I just keep you in my bed all day?"

I laugh, running my fingertips over his back the way he likes. "We're only two days away from the weekend."

"I can't wait that long. Can you?"

"No."

A ripping sensation in my chest has me closing my eyes. "We have to talk to Colt."

"I know. You still think your mama and daddy are gonna let you spend the night, even if they know my intentions are good? I know they're...uh, let's call it 'traditionally minded.'"

"I've lived on my own for years now, Ry. Where I sleep is my business."

It's his turn to laugh. "If you say so. All right, baby. Much as I hate to say it, I gotta get moving."

He kisses my forehead, and I swear to God my internal organs—the important ones, anyway—melt.

Could this be the way I start the morning...every morning?

On the drive back to my place, I allow myself to picture what my life could look like in a year if I'm brave and make good choices and encounter a little luck.

I could be living with Ryder. Or he could be living with me. Honestly I don't care as long as he makes love to me every morning.

Instead of dreading a day spent doing taxes, I could be looking forward to a day spent working with horses, kids, therapists, the community. I'd be making a real impact.

I'd be outside in this glorious fall weather. I wonder what role I'd have in the therapy program. Coordinator? Community outreach...person? Liaison, maybe?

I'm exhausted after a night of interrupted sleep and intense athletic activity, but you wouldn't know it from the way my skeleton vibrates with energy.

This idea is lighting me up, and that means something. It's not the giant neon sign I was hoping would appear to point me in the right direction. But it's a definite nudge.

Maybe the rest is not up to the universe but up to me.

Dad always says that action is the best medicine.

Once we're on my family's property, I have Ryder take the back way to my house. It's a dirt road that barely merits the name, and we bounce around hard enough that my head hurts by the time we pull up to my front door.

Grabbing the door handle, I lean over the seat to peck Ryder on the mouth. "I'll talk to Colt earliest chance I get."

"Fill me in when you do?" Ryder's eyes are full in the semidarkness. "I'm not opposed to us talking to him together. I think the sooner we rip off the Band-Aid, the better."

I nod. "I don't disagree. Let's see where the wind takes us, okay?"

"Okay." He's kissing me again, groaning when he moves to my neck. "You taste so fuckin' good, baby. Tonight—"

"Yeah." I'm trying not to pant. If we get worked up again, there's no telling what will happen. "We'll figure something out."

"Good. And unless you want me to put a baby in you, don't forget to take your birth control."

A burst of...something moves through me. *Wait, is Ryder thinking about making some babies too?*

"I have an IUD, remember?" I reply carefully.

"Ah." He nips at the hollow underneath my jaw. "Right."

"But...do you want to put a baby in me?"

What a totally inappropriate question to ask. I flush with embarrassment, even as my body pounds with yearning.

I want—need—to know his answer.

He pulls away, nostrils flaring as he locks eyes with me. "All we been through, and you're still pushin' my goddamn buttons, huh?"

"You'd better get used to it." I tuck a stray strand of hair behind his ear.

His eyes are still on mine when he says, "Yeah, Billie. One day I'd love to make some babies with you. I got work to do—a lot of work—in the meantime. We have the work we're gonna do together now too."

I smile, a cloudless sky opening up inside my chest. "We do."

"But does the idea of you havin' our baby get me goin'? Yeah, darlin', it does."

Whew.

"That's...a lot." My hand shakes as I continue to curl the hair around his ear.

Laughter rumbles inside his chest. "You asked."

"You answered. Thank you."

"Thank *you*. For last night. For everything else too."

My lips twitch. "You're welcome."

"Such a brat," he says with a shake of his head.

"Have a good day?"

His eyes search mine. "I'll try. You'd best answer when I call you, you hear me?"

I smile as I press one last kiss to his lips. "I promise."

I've been to exactly one baby shower in my life: It was the shower my mom threw for Abby when she was having Dean. I remember it being...tame at best.

If I'm being completely honest, it was boring as hell.

Mom didn't let me partake in the mimosa bar Abby's friends set up at my parents' house, where the shower was hosted. So basically I just sat there stone-cold sober and watched Abby open a bunch of presents I didn't find particularly exciting. I remember having to try *very* hard not to roll my eyes when she opened a car seat and everyone *oohed* and *aaahed* over the fact that it matched the stroller she'd opened a few gifts prior.

Needless to say, while I'm always excited to hang out with the Lucky River Ranch girls, I'm not sure what to expect when it comes to the baby shower part.

Turns out I shouldn't have worried. The second I step into the New House's beautifully decorated living room, I already know the vibe is *totally* different from the saccharine sweetness of my sister-in-law's gathering.

Could these *girls be my new sisters-in-law one day?* Abby and I were never close, so it's a refreshing change of pace to be welcomed with genuine enthusiasm by Sally, who pulls me in for a tight hug while her mom, Patsy, offers me a frosty margarita, complete with Tajin rim.

"Y'all are my people," I say with a laugh.

Patsy smiles. "Cheers, honey."

Mollie hollers when she sees me. "Billie! We're so glad you could make it!"

"*So* glad." Wheeler grabs my hand and gives it a squeeze. "How are things?"

"Things are good! But really, I wanna hear about you." I nod at her belly, which has gotten noticeably bigger since I saw her last even though it's only been a couple of weeks. "Those babies making any moves?"

"Not yet. How great is this, though? Duke and I were at my doctor's appointment yesterday, and Dr.

Hernandez looked him right in the eye and asked, 'Twice in one night, huh'?"

Mollie chuckles. "Joke's on her, because it definitely happened more than twice that night."

Wheeler gets a dreamy look on her face. "It did, and I have no regrets."

My heart squeezes when I think about the conversation I had with Ryder the other morning—the one where we talked openly about making babies together. I understand Wheeler's joy. I can only imagine how overwhelming the happiness of growing a family with the man you love would be.

I hope to experience it one day myself.

Ava comes over to give me a hug, Junie and Ella hot on her heels. They look adorable in their matching dresses and cowboy boots.

"We're going to get two baby cousins," Junie tells me proudly. "Isn't that the coolest news you ever heard?"

Ella smiles up at me shyly. "We're going to babysit them."

"Y'all are going to be the best babysitters ever." I lean down to meet Ella's eyes. "Can I come over to help?"

"Yes," Ella replies.

Ava pats her on the back. "So many exciting things to look forward to, right, honey?"

"Like the cake we brought," Junie replies. "When can we eat it, Mom?"

Ava laughs. "We have to wait until after Wheeler opens all her presents." She nods at the enormous pile of gifts by the fireplace. "I bet she'll let y'all help her open them if you ask nicely."

Junie lets out a literal scream of delight as she makes

a beeline for Wheeler, who's chatting with a younger guy whose hair is the same shade of copper as hers. Her brother, if I had to guess.

Patsy ushers us into the dining room, where we sit down for a delicious lunch of enchiladas verdes. She serves them with a corn and black bean salad and a spicy rice pilaf that's out-of-this-world delicious.

"Can we have a baby shower every weekend?" Ella asks. "This rice is so good, Miss Patsy."

Patsy grins. "I'll make it for you anytime, honey. Glad you like it."

When it's time to open gifts, Sally loops her arm through mine and pulls me down onto a sofa beside her. Mollie jots down who each gift is from as Junie and Ella help Wheeler unwrap the presents.

It's actually fun seeing her reactions to each gift, probably because her joy is palpable and her gratitude is genuine. She gasps, holding up matching onesies dotted with cowboy boots and horseshoes. Her eyes mist over when she opens the gift from her mom: a yellow gingham blanket Wheeler's grandmother made for her when she was born.

We all cry when she opens two pairs of teeny-tiny, custom-made Bellamy Brooks baby cowboy boots, one blue pair, one pink.

"Mollie! How the heck did you get these made without me knowing?" Wheeler covers her mouth. "They are perfect."

Mollie sniffles. "Love you, friend."

"Love you too."

I watch, throat tight, as they embrace.

"I know I keep saying this," Mollie murmurs into

Wheeler's shoulder, "but I'm so happy we get to have our babies together."

What if I get to have my babies with them too?

"Your girlfriends are more important than ever when you're a mom," Ava replies. "Y'all will be each other's lifeline. I hope I can be that for you too."

Wheeler crosses the room to wrap Ava in a hug. "You already are. Thank you, Ava. Sincerely."

Wheeler claps her hands when Junie hands her my present. Mom and I had a blast putting together a "bath time goodies" gift, grabbing some items off Wheeler's registry—a baby bathtub shaped like a whale, washcloths, bath books—plus some things we picked out just because they were so cute we couldn't resist: a pair of hooded towels embroidered with fish and a set of rubber duckies dressed up as cowboys.

"Bath time is going to be my favorite part of the day, I can already tell," Wheeler says before pulling me in for the day's five hundredth hug.

After Wheeler finishes opening all the presents, it's time for the Texas sheet cake Junie and Ella helped Ava make. They decorated it with rainbow sprinkles and glittery candles shaped like unicorns, which of course we all *ooh* and *ahh* over.

"It's not Miss Wheeler's birthday, but it will be her babies' birthday soon," Ella proudly explains. "That's why we put those candles on there."

"What a smart idea," I say with a smile.

Junie nods. "We are the smartest. At least that's what Mommy says."

I end up hanging with some of the girls in a corner of the room as we polish off our cake.

"So, Billie," Mollie says, keeping her voice low. "How are things with you and Ryder? Any updates?"

My pulse leaps. Truth be told, I've been dying to talk to the girls about what's been going down. I feel like they'll have some good insight, maybe some advice too.

I've spent every night at Ryder's place since that day in the rain. Exactly zero nightmares to speak of. Things are *good*.

So good that sometimes I have to pinch myself to make sure it's not a dream. Last night Ryder built a fire, and we sat in his tiny den for hours, sipping tequila while he played his guitar and I sang along, warmed by the liquor and the crackling logs. I can still smell the woodsmoke in my hair.

Still feel his hands on me, the way they peeled off my clothes and adored every inch of my bare skin right there on the floor.

Only problem? I haven't been able to talk to Colt yet. He was out of town for part of the week at a livestock auction in Houston, and then he was tied up with some stuff at Dean's school the past few days. Colt, being the overachiever he is, volunteered to be room parent, and he ran a drive to raise money for improvements to the school's cafeteria and art studio.

As much fun as Ryder and I are having together, the fact that we're having that fun behind Colt's back hangs over us like a dark cloud. The longer we sneak around, the more anxious I feel.

The more convinced I am that he's going to be *pissed*.

"Funny you should mention that." I clear my throat.

Sally's eyebrows pop up. "This sounds promising."

I take a fortifying bite of cake. Then I blurt out everything.

The bonfire. The middle-of-the-night rescue from Xander. How Ryder came looking for me in the rain. Our first dinner date at his place.

"I had a feeling something went down!" Mollie exclaims, grabbing my forearm. "I knew when Ryder called Cash and demanded that his cabin be next on the list to be fixed up that y'all were doing the dirty."

Sally shimmies her shoulders. "Aw, he's creating a little love nest for y'all."

"So freaking adorable." Wheeler is literally squealing. "I was hoping this would happen! The two of you are excellent for each other."

"You think?"

Sally nods. "We know. Ryder brought up his parents at dinner the other night for the first time in, sheesh, forever. He's never talked about anything remotely that deep or painful since their accident."

"He's never brought them up around me either," Ava adds. "Now all of the sudden, he's talking about real stuff even though I can tell it's not easy for him. You're helping him become a whole man again, Billie." There are tears in her eyes. "It's really beautiful when you think about it."

Shit, now I'm the one who's crying. "He's helping me too. My job at the ranch—I'm good at it, but it's never really felt like *me*, you know?"

Wheeler scoffs. "I totally get it. My parents always wanted me to be a lawyer, but I couldn't make myself do it. Just didn't feel right."

"You'd make a great lawyer," Ava says. "But you're

a better boot maker. And entrepreneur. And fashion icon."

"Not so sure about the icon thing, but thank you." Wheeler smiles. "So wait, is Ryder helping you figure out what your next step is going to be careerwise?"

I nod, setting down my plate on a nearby table. "He is. We've been kicking around the idea of creating an animal therapy program on my family's ranch."

Ava gasps.

Sally grins.

Mollie and Wheeler look at me with huge smiles on their faces.

"What?" I ask sheepishly.

"I love it," Wheeler says.

Ava nods. "It's so *you*."

"How do we get started?" Leave it to Mollie to literally roll up the sleeves of her adorable gingham dress. "Also, when do we get to see you race again?"

CHAPTER 23
Dead End
Ryder

My boots crunch on the gravel driveway. "So the girls open the presents at the shower—"

"They play games too." Cash glances up at the afternoon sky. "Mollie had me printing these little game cards with pictures on them. You have to guess if the pictures are boobs or baby butts."

"That's…weird." Colt turns his head. "Hey, Dean, this way, buddy! Junie and Ella are gonna be so psyched to see you."

Wyatt shrugs. "The whole concept of showers is weird."

"Not when you're showering with someone else." Duke is grinning like the Cheshire cat.

"Dude." Cash shoots him a look.

"Sorry. Just excited to see my girl is all." He glances through the nearby window. "Looks like we got some good loot."

I climb the wide front steps that lead to the New

House's front door. "Like I was saying, the girls open the presents, and we—"

"Load them up and get 'em to my place?" Duke nods. "Yup."

I run a hand over my face. "Y'all really gotta work on letting me finish my thought."

"Surely they'll let us have some cake, though?" Cash grabs the doorknob. "A fee for our services?"

Dean sticks out his lower lip. "Daddy said there'd definitely be cake. What if there isn't any left?"

"Buddy, we'll cross that bridge when we get there." Colt grabs his hand.

"I'm gonna be really mad, Dad," Dean whines. "If the girls get cake and I don't—"

"I'll make it right." Colt closes his eyes, clearly taking a second to gather himself. "Let's cut it out with the whining in the meantime, okay?"

"I'm *not* whining."

Colt sucks a breath through his nose. "Sure you're not."

"Here." Sawyer takes Dean's hand. "Can you keep a secret?"

That gives Dean pause. "Yeah."

"I have a stash of popsicles in the freezer inside"—Sawyer nods at the house—"for emergencies like this. I promise I'll get you one if there's no cake left, all right?"

Dean is still pouting, but at least he's climbing the steps now. "Fine."

"What do you say, Dean?" Colt asks.

"Thank you, Mister Sawyer."

"Anytime! And look at those manners. Let's go see everyone, yeah?"

"Thanks, Sawyer," Colt murmurs.

My brother waves him away. "They listen better when it's not you telling them what to do. Trust me, I get it."

My chest cramps. From what I've gathered, parenthood is hard. Single parenthood? Even harder. Before Ava showed up, stole his heart, and became his co-parent, Sawyer tried to hide the fact that he was drowning, but we all knew he struggled.

"No good deed." Colt shakes his head. "I bring him all the way out here thinking he'll get a kick out of seeing his friends, but instead, he's being a serious pain in my behind."

I put a hand on his shoulder, feeling like I'm going to be sick. "Hang in there, man. It'll get better."

But not before it gets worse after you find out I've been sleeping with your sister.

Neither of us, me nor Billie, have been able to pin down Colt since we decided to tell him. I want to give her the opportunity to have the discussion with him first, but it's killing me not to say something.

Wheeler's baby shower is not the time nor the place, though. Duke has been on cloud nine all damn week in anticipation of it. We watched football at Cash's place and hung with his baby girl Daisy while the girls showered Wheeler with all the love.

My twin got a little emotional after knocking back a couple Shiners. I did too. I'm just so dang happy that *he's* happy. Mom and Dad would be proud of the man he's become and the father he'll be, and we had to hug it out for a long while after I told him as much.

You're next, he'd whispered in my ear.

I could only nod. Part of me wanted to tell him to shut the hell up. What if Colt heard that? But another part—a bigger part—wanted to turn to Colt and spill the beans right there and then.

Pretty sure Duke invited Colt for exactly that reason, using the excuse that the girls told Sawyer they miss seeing Dean at preschool. Much as I love my brother for trying to give me a nudge in the right direction, I also don't want to risk ruining a special day.

But no matter what Colt's reaction would be, I can only imagine the relief of unburdening myself. Not only because I hate feeling like I'm sneaking around behind my friend's back, but also because I'm bursting with all this good news that I want to share but can't.

Y'all, I'm falling in love.

I'm playing guitar again. Also, I started therapy.

I'm waking up for the first time since Mom and Dad died, and it's a beautiful day.

Who knew acknowledging your feelings turned you into a ginormous cheeseball?

Cash opens the door, and we follow him inside the New House. My chest lifts when I see Billie standing in the corner with Wheeler and Ava and Sally, Mollie gesticulating wildly while she tells them an apparently hysterical story.

Ella and June make a noisy beeline for Dean, yelling his name at the top of their lungs because they're *that* excited to see him.

I get it, girls.

Because I wanna yell too when Billie glances across the room and our gazes collide. Happiness expands like a bubble inside my center as she smiles, and I smile too.

She looks real fucking pretty in her skirt and boots, her long hair hanging in loose waves over her shoulders. She's wearing makeup today, this glittery eyeshadow that makes the green in her hazel eyes really pop.

Her eyes—her face—her whole *being* is lit up. She's got a margarita in one hand, and Wheeler holds Billie's other hand to her pregnant belly.

"You feel that?" Wheeler asks.

Billie laughs. "Amazing! They're pretty active, huh?"

"*Very*," Wheeler replies with a rueful smile. "I'm not sleeping a ton these days, but I like feeling them move around in there. It's like the world's best little tickle. Well, it's actually not so little anymore, especially when they're kicking me in the ribcage."

"Or they're kicking your bladder," Mollie adds.

Wheeler groans. "Not my favorite bit about being pregnant, that's for sure." Glancing up, she smiles when she sees Duke. "Hey!"

"Hey, Blue." He strides across the room to plant a hugely noisy, totally inappropriate kiss on her mouth. "Y'all having fun?"

"It's been magic," Wheeler replies. "The girls truly pulled out all the stops."

Ava leans her head on Mollie's shoulder. "It was our pleasure. We can't wait to meet these little angels."

"Doc still saying we should expect their arrival around Christmas?" Colt asks.

I don't miss the way Billie's expression flickers when she sees her brother.

"Yup. Although with twins, you never really know. My goal is just to make it past thirty-five weeks," Wheeler says, oblivious to the tension that's suddenly filled the room.

Or maybe that's just me imagining the weird energy between me and Billie and her brother.

Speaking of brothers—I'm jealous Duke gets to just kiss his girl like that. In front of everyone. No shame and no drama.

Yeah, this sneaking around shit has gotta end.

It's all I can do not to grab Billie's hand. Slip an arm around her waist and bury my nose in her hair. I know she'll smell like peaches.

I imagine I'd be able to smell my aftershave on her too. Just a hint. I had my mouth all over her at five a.m. this morning—we slept in a little on account of it being the weekend—and she went so far as to accuse me of intentionally giving her beard burn on her thighs.

Guilty.

The pull between us is impossible to ignore. Shoving my hands in my pockets, I curl my fingers around my dad's knife and head across the room.

"Hey, ladies." I nod. "Billie."

Is she blushing? "Hey, Ry. How's it going?"

"Going all right. Looks like y'all had quite the party."

Mollie gives me a knowing look. "We're so glad Billie could make it. Ever since you sent her our way to get fitted for those boots, we've developed a bit of a girl crush on her."

"Hard not to fall for a fellow free spirit," Ava adds, a glimmer in her eyes.

They know.

Aw, hell, Billie definitely told them about us, didn't she?

The thought makes me smile. Billie can't keep it

inside either. Why would she? What we have—what we've found—should be shared. Celebrated.

I'm gripped by the thought that one day our families will gather to celebrate *our* milestones. The engagement and the wedding. The promotions and the babies.

The room is filled with familiar voices and the smell of something good—Patsy's Tex-Mex, if I had to guess—and I fantasize that all those gifts by the fireplace are ours. Mine and Billie's. Our baby is in her belly, and I'm taking her to our home.

Fucked up? Maybe.

But not as fucked up as keeping this from her brother.

I help the boys load up all the gifts in the back of Duke's pickup truck. We give him and Wheeler a little sendoff, hollers and whistles filling the chill autumn air.

Everyone starts leaving in pairs. Mollie and Cash are going to relieve her mom, who left the shower early so she could stay with the baby while Cash helped us. Sally and Wyatt were last seen sneaking away on an ATV, passing a thermos between them of what I can only assume is her famous cider.

Junie and Ella insist on taking Dean back to their house for a playdate, which Colt agrees to only after the idea gets the stamp of approval from Ava and Sawyer.

John B comes to pick up Patsy, who tells us there's leftover enchiladas in the fridge if we get hungry later before they head out too.

Then it's just me and Billie and Colt standing in the driveway. My heart thumps. I look at Billie, who looks at me.

Now?

She nods. *Now.*

I get that seasick feeling again when I clear my throat.

"So, Colt. You got a minute?" Billie squints against the ardent late afternoon sunshine.

"Sure." He puts his hands inside his front pockets. "What's up?"

The sun catches on her eyes when she looks at me, turning them to pools of gold. My stomach dips hard.

She's so fucking pretty.

We're in so much fucking trouble.

Billie clears her throat too. "I'm not sure how else to say this, so I'm just going to, well, come out and say it." Her eyes dart to her brother. "Colt, Ry and I—we're together."

Silence, ice-cold, settles between the three of us.

CHAPTER 24
Mistakes Were Made
Ryder

"Together." Colt spits out the word. "As in—"

"We're dating." Billie grabs my hand, and my heart turns over. "I wanted—*we* wanted to tell you sooner, but you've been kinda hard to track down these days." Her voice shakes. "I'm sorry we didn't have this conversation before, but we wanted you to know because we're happy, Colton. Really happy. And we've having a good time together—"

"A great time." It takes every ounce of self-control I have not to look away when Colt glares at me. "Billie—she's brought out a side of me I thought died when my parents did. Neither of us were expecting this to happen, Colt. But it did, and we hope you can be happy for us."

I've practiced my speech about a hundred thousand times over the past couple weeks. Now that the moment is here, however, I can't seem to find the right words.

The air vibrates with emotion as Colt's eyes dart between Billie and me.

"How long?" The words come out as a grunt.

Billie glances at me. "I don't think it's any secret that I've had a crush on Ryder for a while—"

"But you never talked to me about it. Not openly." Colt's expression contracts, and it hits me that he's more hurt than angry.

My heart sinks. Anger, I can deal with. But hurt? Disappointment? Knowing that I let my friend down this way is like a knife to the chest.

Billie's face is red. "I was embarrassed, Colt. What do you think you would've said if I told you?"

"I don't know! But I would've appreciated the fact that you were honest with me. After everything that happened with Abby…"

"I know." She blinks, fighting tears, and I give her hand a squeeze. "And I'm sorry. But I'm not Abby. This is different."

"Is it?"

"Yes, Colt, it is," she replies thickly. "I'm sorry I didn't say anything earlier. But you have to understand where I was coming from. I didn't think I had a chance in hell of ever getting Ry's attention." She glances at me. "Seemed silly to confess a crush when the person you're crushing on is so far out of your league it's laughable."

Colt chuckles, the sound mirthless. "You ask me, you're the one who's out of his league."

"Agreed," I say.

"Doesn't matter now, does it?" Billie asks. "We're together, and we make each other happy. That's all I've ever wanted for you and our brothers, Colt—for y'all to be happy. I hope you want the same for me."

"Forgive me, but I was under the impression that

Ryder was out to make *himself* happy. Which is fine, so long as he's not hurtin' anyone." Colt's eyes are hard when they flick to my face. "I think we can all agree, Ry, that you've never taken someone else's happiness and well-being into consideration."

I feel the bite of anger, sudden and unexpected. "Are you kidding? I've spent my whole life thinking about everyone else's well-being. My family is everything to me, same as yours is to you. Christ, for years now I've put my own needs aside so everyone could have the space *they* needed. And don't get me started on how much I've done to help you and Dean."

"I'm talking about women," Colt replies steadily. "You can't tell me you ever cared about a girl like that."

More anger. Probably because Colt is right.

"I know I don't have experience being someone's boyfriend, and I have no idea what kind of partner I'm going to turn out to be, but—"

"Exactly." Colt steps forward. "That's exactly why I don't like this. The two of you bein' together. Because Billie, you deserve—"

"The kind of man standing right in front of you," she answers, and my pulse skips at her ability to think this quickly on her feet. "Of course Ryder's a good man. No way you'd be such good friends with him if he wasn't. You and I both know he's going to be a great boyfriend."

Colt's chest barrels out on an inhale. "He can be a good man, but that don't mean he's gonna be good to you."

"He's been better to me than anyone else I've ever been with." She glances at me from the corner of her eye. "He's always been a good friend to me. Now we're more than friends, and it's... Colt, I'm happy. Happier than I've been in a long, long time. I won't speak for Ryder—"

"But you can, Billie," I say. "You know and I know that I'm happier than I've ever been too. And that's because...well, Colt, your sister cracked open something inside me that I'd locked away. Didn't realize I was living half a life until she nearly lost *her* life. Her beautiful, brave life that she's always lived with this...this *integrity* that I admire. Now I wanna live like that too. No more bullshit. No more distractions. Surviving...it ain't enough anymore. This is what I want, Colt. Your sister is who I want."

Billie is blinking back tears now. She gives me a watery smile. "You know you don't have to convince me, right? I already said I'd be your girlfriend."

"So y'all had that conversation already." Colt appears unfazed by my brazen honesty. "Which means this has been goin' on for a while."

Billie frowns. "We've actually only been together for a couple of weeks now. Yeah, we started flirting after my accident, but nothing happened until very recently, and that's because I've been the one pursuing him. I basically forced Ryder to stay with me at the hospital because I was so scared. We kind of connected that night, and then I was the one who pushed for more."

"With Billie, it was different from the start," I say. "Trust me when I say we both fought it like hell because we didn't want this to happen. But it did, and while I'm real fuckin' sorry we didn't tell you sooner, I'm not sorry we ended up together."

She manages a tight smile as she looks at me. "You

really fought me. Like, hard. Man made me work for it, that's for damn sure."

A flicker of uncertainty moves across Colt's eyes. "That true?"

"It is, yeah." I run a hand over my face, the weight of my exhaustion suddenly too much to bear. "Dude, look at me. I'm about to fall the fuck over. I've lost so much sleep over this I can't even tell you. I hate the idea of losin' you, or at least losin' your trust. This wouldn't be happening if I wasn't one hundred percent sure that being with Billie is worth the risk."

Her throat works on a swallow. "That means a lot."

"*You* mean a lot to me." I turn to Colt. "You need me to prove that I'm good enough for your sister? Fine. But you gotta give me the time, then. If I don't treat her right, you can put a bullet through my chest. Right here." I tap my fingers to the center of my breastbone. "I'll take it because I'll deserve it."

I hear Billie's sharp intake of breath. "Ry—"

"We don't tolerate that shit in our family," Colt replies steadily. "Anyone breakin' hearts just because they can."

"I'm not that guy anymore," I say steadily.

Now Billie's rolling her eyes. "Jesus, Colt, that's why I've always had to sneak around! You and Nash and Mack and just—all y'all wouldn't let any guys near me growing up. It was suffocating, and that wasn't fair."

A deep groove appears in Colt's forehead. "Our hearts were in the right place, Billie. We were just protecting you—"

"That's bullshit and you know it." Billie's fire is back. Thank fuck. "Y'all were making my decisions for me, just like you're doing now. You assume you know better than me—you assume you know *what's* best for me—without a care for what *I* want. Who *I* am."

Colt has the grace to back down. "That was never my intention, Billie. I see what you're saying, but—"

"But what? 'That's just how things are done around here'? I don't accept that excuse anymore, Colt. I believed that shit for years, and look where it's led me. I live alone. I have a job I hate. I'm so terrified of disappointing everyone else that I've just…ugh, left myself behind, and no one seems to give a shit."

"You think I don't give a shit?" The pain in Colt's voice rips a hole through my center. "I love you, Billie. That's all this is. I love you too much to let you end up heartbroken. Because I've been there before, and it's… Billie, it'll wreck you."

Her voice is trembling again when she says, "I love you too. I'm sorry you were betrayed before, and I'm sorry I betrayed you again. That wasn't right. But I need you to see how different these two scenarios are. This one could have a happy ending, Colt." She pauses. "Please don't take that away from me."

Colt closes his eyes and takes a deep breath, just like he did when Dean was giving him a hard time earlier.

My chest twists. The guy hasn't had it easy. But he still gets up every damn day and works his ass off for the people he loves. Me included.

"We're all just trying to do the right thing here, Colt." My voice is hoarse. "Show us some grace, yeah? I get that this is hard for you, but it doesn't have to end badly. You haven't exactly been available lately either—you gotta trust us when we say we would've told you sooner if you'd been around."

Colt opens his eyes. He blinks, then shakes his head with a rueful scoff. "This fuckin' month just won't quit. First Dad brings some random-ass sorority girl to the ranch for a 'rebrand,' whatever the fuck that means. Then I find out my best friend's been sneaking around behind my back with my sister." He scoffs again. "If that's not one kick to the nuts after another…"

Billie stares at him. "You've got to be kidding. Are you really making this all about you right now?"

"It's never just about me, same as it's never just about you," he shoots back. "I have a kid to raise. A legacy to protect. Y'all sure as hell don't make that easy."

"I think about our legacy all the time!" Billie shouts. "But what does that legacy matter if we're all miserable trying to keep it alive? Why can't our legacy be, I don't know, unconditional love and acceptance? How radical would *that* be?"

Colt wipes his eyes on his sleeve. "Y'all are adults. You can do whatever the hell you want. But I don't—" He hesitates. "Y'all hurt me today. Whether or not you meant to, I still feel betrayed, and both of you know that's a sore spot. Billie, you don't accept the fact that I wanna keep you safe? Then I don't accept the fact that you wanna date a guy whose track record leaves a lot to be desired. Don't let me see y'all together, and definitely don't come running to me, Billie, when he does what he always does and leaves."

Watching him turn and walk away, I feel like dying.

I feel weak with relief. Regret. Complete and utter exhaustion.

Billie looks up at me, tears leaking out of her eyes left and right.

"Aw, baby, come here." I fold her in my arms and bury my face in her neck. "That sucked. It was also the right thing to do."

"I just… I'm so *angry*, Ry."

I chuckle. "You and Colt are definitely related, and you're definitely more alike than you think."

"You mean he's awesome and open-minded and one hell of a barrel racer? Because that's not the Colt I know."

"Hey. I'm the one who's supposed to be using humor as a deflection."

Billie pulls back, shaking the hair out of her face. "Aw, baby, you were so good at that for a while there. Glad that phase is over."

"*Mostly* over."

"I'll take it." She puts a hand on my cheek. "Thank you. Everything you said was perfect."

"You're perfect," I reply. "I don't get how I can be more obsessed with you than ever, while simultaneously feeling like I've been drawn and quartered with an especially sharp cattle hook."

That makes her laugh, and the ache in my chest lifts. "This shit hurts, huh?"

"We knew he wasn't gonna love the idea right off the bat." I lean in to kiss the corner of her mouth, tasting the salt from her margarita. "We asked for time. Now we just gotta show him that we mean business."

Billie nods. "Yeah. Yeah, you're right."

Still, her eyes brim with sadness when they meet mine.

"C'mon. How about I play some guitar? You wanna sing for me, darlin'?"

"Yeah." She smiles, but it doesn't touch her eyes. "Yeah, I'd love that."

CHAPTER 25
Evil Plan
Billie

***"I didn't know brainstorming sessions came with** reposado."*

Watching Mollie sip her paloma, I grin. "Since y'all won't let me pay you for your expertise—"

"Why would we?" Ava takes a seat at my kitchen table. "We're family. This is delicious, by the way."

I made a batch of palomas earlier, figuring it'd be a fun twist on the margaritas we had at the shower. To make a paloma, you mix tequila with some grapefruit juice and a squeeze or two of lime. Then I top it all off with Topo Chico, a sparkling water staple here in Texas, and serve it with a salted rim.

The resulting cocktail is boozy, not too sweet, and deliciously refreshing.

"And this is what family does. We help make each other's dreams come true." Sally turns from the sink, where she's been squeezing an extra lime into her cocktail. "Did you really prepare a sales deck and everything?"

She motions to the thick packet of paper in the middle of the table.

Taking a deep breath, I square my shoulders and nod. "If I'm gonna do this, I'm gonna do it right. Full transparency, I didn't know what the hell a deck was until Beck told me I needed one."

Bless him, my brother patiently walked me through the process of creating a presentation deck in PowerPoint. Lucky for me, my brother got tons of experience making decks thanks to his entrepreneurial endeavors in the hospitality space. It took me two weeks and more tears than I care to admit to draft my own, but I finally had thirty slides outlining my concept: an on-site animal therapy program at the ranch that caters to children and adults of all ages. The program would employ handlers, social workers, and therapists, plus an administrative professional and a community liaison.

Beck holds up his glass. "You need real ammo if you're gonna convince Dale Wallace to let you quit your job. Just helping you cover your bases, B."

"I appreciate that. Really, I appreciate all y'all lending a hand." Shit, now I'm getting emotional. "I mean, look. There's so many of us we can't even fit at my table."

Ryder gives me a soft smile. "You're really surprised by that?"

"We love you, honey," Wheeler says. "They say it takes a village to raise a kid. I say it takes a village to create a *life*. I'm honored to be part of your story."

Eight people showed up tonight.

Eight.

The girls—Mollie, Wheeler, Sally, and Ava—plus

Ryder, Beck, Tate, and Duke. Mack and Nash are out of town, so they couldn't make it.

Colt is notably absent. He never replied to my texts inviting him over. He never called me back either.

We've seen each other in passing on the ranch. Ryder came over for Sunday supper, and we shared with my family that we were 'an item,' as Mom adorably put it.

She was thrilled. Dad couldn't stop smiling.

Really, *everyone* was thrilled. With the exception of Colt, who didn't even show up. He didn't show up to Sunday supper the week before that either. I swear he found out Ryder was coming and faked sick the first time, saying he and Dean were hit by a nasty virus.

The second time, he didn't even bother to give an excuse.

I was hoping to make some headway with my older brother during Ryder's visit. But Colt apparently refuses to acknowledge that we exist, much less that we're dating.

Ryder keeps reminding me that we need to be patient. I know he's right, but I still feel like I'm banging my head against a wall. Colt's always been a pretty even-keeled guy. It takes a lot to ruffle his feathers, but when they're ruffled—Lord, watch out.

"So, let's do some prep work here before you talk to your folks." Duke picks up the deck and opens it, turning to the first page. "Tell me your vision for the program. Where'd you come up with the idea? Why does it appeal to you? And where do you see yourself fitting into all of it?"

My lips twitch. "Tell me you're an entrepreneur without telling me you're an entrepreneur."

Duke likes the compliment, grinning as he wags

his brows. "Only wanted to do something different my whole life. It's a ride, Billie. One I think you're gonna love."

"Agreed," Mollie says. "The road to success can be a lot longer and lonelier than you thought possible. But the satisfaction of finding success, knowing you deserve every minute of it because you persevered? Because no matter how hard it got, you never quit, never stopped believing that you were doing the right thing?" Her eyes shine in the light hanging over the table. "It's pure fucking magic, Billie."

A swell of joy fills me. Joy and determination.

I meet eyes with Ryder again. He gives me a tiny nod. *Go on with your bad self, darlin'.*

Taking another deep breath, I begin.

"The people who know me best joke that I was born with a fifth of tequila in one hand and reins in the other. Ranching is literally in my blood—I don't need to tell y'all our property has been in my family for generations. Six, to be exact. Growing up, I always dreamed about what my role in our family's legacy would be. Would I be foreman like my dad? A trainer like Mom's cousin Randy? Or would I develop different parts of the land the way y'all have done at Lucky River Ranch?"

Duke nods. "Lots of possibilities."

"Right. So I pictured myself in this very integral, physical, management-type role. I thought it'd be a natural fit because I could ride like nobody's business, I did well in school, and I was relatively outgoing."

"'Relatively outgoing,'" Ryder says with a scoff. "That's one way of putting it."

Beck laughs. "I believe the term her teachers used

was 'spirited.' Or 'giant pain in the ass,' depending on the day."

"Yup." I smile proudly. "Point being, I saw my older brothers launching these exciting careers on the ranch, and I thought I was next in line. Only when it was my turn, Dad brought me inside his office and offered me a job as the ranch's new bookkeeper."

"A natural fit," Mollie says with a roll of her eyes.

"The idea came from a good place. But—and this is a theme that's come up a lot recently—it was a misguided choice. My parents have old-fashioned ideas about right and wrong and what a woman's place should be in our world. Anyway." I hold up my hands. "Long story short, my role as accountant has not been a great fit for me. I miss being outdoors. Being with the animals and kids and around other people. I've been stuck inside for years now, and it's made me realize how much happier I was when I was on horseback training to race. It calmed me. Helped clear my head."

Wheeler snaps her fingers. "Bingo. I see where this is going. I think you really home in on this point—that you've experienced firsthand the benefits of time spent outdoors with animals."

"*Yes.* Exactly. And while our family's very much involved in the community here in Hartsville, I think we're not nearly involved enough with the younger population. My family has all these animals—literally, we have multiple stables of horses alone—but we're not doing a great job of sharing that bounty with people who don't have access to that kind of thing. An animal therapy program fills that gap."

"I have chills." Mollie holds up her arm, which is

covered in goose bumps. "I think that's brilliant. Playing devil's advocate, though—how much is this gonna cost? Won't having all these random people on the ranch interrupt operations?"

Grabbing the deck from Duke, I flip to the page printed with a map of my family's property. "We'd designate one of the barns as our therapy headquarters. I had a great call with the guidance counselor at Dean's elementary school earlier this week—"

"Yeah you did." Sally holds up her hand.

I give her the high five she's looking for. "She actually worked at a program like this back in Wyoming, where she's from, so she had some really solid ideas in terms of how we can set things up. I'll create an LLC, which we can then turn into a nonprofit. That allows us to focus on the community impact piece of the puzzle. The program wouldn't be a huge money maker, but it would allow the Wallace family to put their name on a program that directly impacts people's lives."

Ava shakes her head and smiles. "That's beautiful. Can Junie, Ella, and I volunteer once or twice a week?"

"Only if I get to volunteer too," Sally replies. "I'd gladly offer my veterinary services for free in exchange for hanging out with some kiddos. What kind of training would we need?"

I answer as many questions as I can. I'm pleasantly surprised to discover my confidence grows the deeper I dive into the program's details. I don't know everything—for instance, when Beck wonders aloud if we should hire someone who deals exclusively with medical insurance companies, I tell him I like the idea but that I don't know where we'd find someone with that particular skill set—but I do end the presentation feeling energized and affirmed.

Is this really happening?

Am I really about to burn down my life as I know it and take this giant leap into the unknown?

I wouldn't say I'm without a safety net. My family is awesome, and I know there'll always be a place for me somewhere on the ranch. But if I fail, I could very well end up back where I started. I could also cost my family—my parents—a shit ton of money. The program I'm proposing would be an investment in the future. *Our* future, and the future of the community.

But it'd be exactly that: an *investment*. Meaning the payoff wouldn't be immediate.

It might not come at all.

"I know it feels like a huge, *huge* step," Mollie says, reading my thoughts. "But if you don't take that step, you're always going to wonder 'what if?' Like, what if this is what you were meant to do all along? What if the whole accounting job fail was part of that? Maybe it was the universe's way of forcing you to pivot."

"Forcing you to choose yourself over everybody else," Ava says, and the table nods in agreement.

Sally slides over in her chair a little and motions for me to sit beside her. I rest a single butt cheek on the chair and sigh. "I hear what you're saying. And I think—I have a feeling my parents will be open to the idea of the program. But the thought of telling my dad that he has to find another accountant makes me want to vomit."

"Do you feel guilty about quitting?" Duke asks.

I tilt my head back and forth. "Yes and no. I know it's the right move for me."

Ava looks me in the eye. "You have to be selfish about these things, Billie. I know that might sound bad, but it's true. If you're not putting yourself first in your career—heck, in your life—then you're never going to be happy."

"Totally agree," Wheeler says. "Opinions are like assholes: everyone has them."

"Always such a lady, Blue," Ryder replies with a grin.

"And by always, you mean never. But as I was saying, everyone's going to have an opinion about what you *should* do. The only opinion that matters, though, is yours. You're the one who has to decide what you *want* to do, and then you have to go out and do that. You owe it to yourself. To the people you love. Think about it this way: You being happy is going to help your family and your ranch thrive. Sure, your parents might have to go through the hassle of hiring a new accountant. But that's much less of an imposition than having to watch their daughter be absolutely miserable."

Ava nods. "I think all the time about what my choices teach my girls. I can tell them until I'm blue in the face that being a people pleaser is gonna lead you down a road to nowhere. But if I'm not actually, actively choosing myself on a daily basis, then they're not going to choose themselves either."

I catch Ryder looking at me, his blue eyes soft and full.

He's thinking about *our* kids. Because we're out of our minds and we've already talked about that shit, and now I'm thinking about our kids too.

Specifically any daughters we have. I don't want them to ever feel trapped or suffocated the way I have in my life. I want to show them that getting in the dirt and loving animals with your whole heart, that daring to be different, is where it's at.

It's okay to get your dress wrinkled.

Hell, it's okay if you ditch the dress altogether.

"I love that idea," I reply. "And I certainly agree with it. At the same time, I think part of the issue I'm having is also how hard it is *for me* to let go of the image of the perfect daughter and sister and woman I always thought I'd be. Like, it's hard to accept that I'm not that perfect person. I'm way messier, and while there's something really freeing about that, it's also super uncomfortable at the same time."

"Ooopf." Sally puts a hand over her heart. "I feel that in my soul. I always wanted to be the perfect daughter too. I tried so hard to make myself fit inside that box."

My heart palpitates. "*Yes*. But turns out, that's a very small box."

"At the end of the day, I think we all just want our parents to be happy," Mollie adds. "And as kids without fully developed prefrontal cortexes—cortexi? Not sure what the plural there would be. Whatever the case, as kids, we tend to think that if *we're* perfect, if we never annoy our parents and only make them proud, then we can *make* them happy. But now that I'm a parent myself, I'm realizing that my parents' happiness was never about me. It's on *them* to figure that out. Just like it's on me to figure out my own version of peace, whatever that looks like."

I nod, letting the words sink in. "So we have to throw that perfect daughter shit out the window and love who we actually are instead."

I haven't had nightmares in over a week now. I wonder if that's because I'm formulating a new plan—a viable, thrilling one—for my future. First, I acted on my feelings for Ryder. And now I'm acting on making big changes in my career.

There's finally air in the proverbial room. I'm not suffocating anymore, and it feels glorious.

"Yes!" Ava beams. "There's our girl."

But I'm not ready to let my parents down.

Maybe I'll never be ready. Maybe I just have to decide I'm ready and…go for it.

At this point, I have no choice, do I? Everything inside me is screaming, telling me to be the hero of my own damn story.

CHAPTER 26
Under Arrest
Ryder

Saturday.

Bless the broken road that led me to the weekend. 'Cause *damn* is life good today.

I can tell it's past seven by the light that burns through my closed eyelids. Slipping a hand behind my head on the pillow, I stretch out my legs. My calves and hamstrings sing pleasantly, just the tiniest bit tight from last night.

The sheets are warm, soft.

Best of all, they smell like peaches. And sex.

My dick is hard, and I wince when my overly sensitive tip catches on the top sheet. I always wake up hard when I'm in bed with her. You'd think after a month of dating that my hunger for my girlfriend would be slightly less ferocious, especially with the holidays approaching. We've had a lot on our plates: making plans for Thanksgiving, making meals for an impromptu Friendsgiving we hosted with my brothers and their significant others, and just making merry in general as my girl and I enjoy our time together.

I'm hungover far too often. But I'm also happy as hell.

Now that my place is basically a construction zone, we've been shacking up at Billie's cute little apartment. Yeah, I gotta wake up an extra hour early to make it to work on time—there's the twenty or so minutes I spend making love to Billie every morning, and then the twenty-minute drive back to Lucky River Ranch—but I don't mind.

Who needs sleep when you're living in a dream?

Fucking cheeseball. Like I fucking care.

Colt is still not talking to either of us. Won't even show his face at family dinners or at the Rattler on Friday nights. I only know he's alive because I've been bugging Beck every few days, asking if Colt's said anything about, well, everything.

Colt and Beck work together at their ranch, so of course Beck sees a lot of his brother. But Beck told me Colt hasn't mentioned Billie or me. It's like we no longer exist to him.

My chest feels heavy thinking about it. I miss my friend. I'm falling hard and fast for his sister, and I want to tell him about it. Get his opinion on shit. Celebrate this major win with one of my favorite people on the planet.

I want him to be part of our story, damn it. The fact that my brothers are happy for me and Billie makes everything that much sweeter. They're participating in our shared life, and that means the world to me.

Colt is missing out. And I'm missing out on his life too. So is Billie. I know she is dying to see Dean more.

As things stand right now, she only sees him in passing or if she happens to run into him at her parents' house.

I also know there's nothing to do but wait it out and hope for the best, but…

Yeah, the whole thing sucks.

Not gonna let that ruin a perfectly good Saturday morning. I smile when I hear the whirr of Billie's electric toothbrush. Opening my eyes, I see that the door to the bathroom is closed.

She'd best still be naked. I told her in no uncertain terms that jammies are not allowed at our sleepovers.

Tossing off the covers, I stand and stretch again, this time with my arms over my head. I have a headache from the tequila we sipped last night by the fire, but otherwise, I feel good.

Horny as hell, but good.

I reach down and give myself a lazy, indulgent tug. Thinking about how pretty Billie looked last night on her knees, her eyes watering as she took me deeper, deeper still in her mouth, I grip myself tighter.

Yep, this is a dream.

Turning, I head for the bathroom. I catch a glimpse of myself in the full-length mirror beside the closet and stop, moving back a step. Do I look different?

Peering at my face in the mirror, it hits me that yeah, I *do* look different. I'm just not sure how.

I touch my scruff, overgrown and in need of a good trim. Billie likes it a little longer, though, so I'm letting it grow out.

I think it's my eyes that have changed. They're not bloodshot anymore. Or is it those laugh lines on either side of my mouth that weren't there a month ago?

I like 'em. I also like the way the crow's-feet at the edges of my eyes have deepened.

Fuck me, I look happy, don't I?

"Admirin' the fine work God did before he sent you to walk among us mere mortals?"

Turning my head, I see Billie standing in the open door of the bathroom. She's leaning a hip against the jamb, the John Deere shirt she's wearing hanging off her shoulder.

"That's my shirt, you brat."

She bites her lip. "You'd better come take it off me, then."

Her hair is gathered in a messy knot at the top of her head. Strands hang down the sides of her face and brush her neck.

She looks so pretty, so relaxed and content, that for a second I can't breathe.

"You all right there, Ry?"

It's the way she smirks. How she casually strides toward me, the tips of her breasts poking through my shirt, those whiskey eyes never leaving mine.

"No, I'm not all right."

Her brows pinch together. "Talk to me."

Really, it's her fearlessness in the face of how clearly emotional I am right now. She tucks a hand onto my cheek, her fingertips brushing my ear, and looks up at me. All earnestness.

All willingness and heat and vulnerability.

"Promise me." I have to clear my throat to keep going. "Whatever I say next, you ain't gonna run."

She slowly blinks, running her thumb over my lips. "I promise."

"You're a girl who keeps her promises."

"Learned that from you. And my parents. And my brothers."

I laugh, even as I know I'm about to cry. "And basically everyone else in Hart County."

"Dad used to always tell us that 'our word was our bond,' and I'd be like, 'Okay, but what the fuck does that actually mean?'" She's smiling now too. "Now I get it. So talk to me, damn it."

I put my hands on her hips and glide them inside my shirt. My pulse jumps when I discover she's not wearing panties.

"I wanna be around to see you pull off your plans for the animal therapy program, because you're gonna make it happen." I search her eyes. "I wanna go for tractor rides with you every night of the week. And I wanna be that guy at your next race, the one who makes an ass of himself cheering so loud that people clear the area because they're annoyed."

"Can't promise I won't fall," she says, lips twitching.

"I can promise I'll be there to catch you. Or give you CPR. One of the two."

Her eyes fill, and she blinks. "Are you about to tell me that you're in love with me?"

"Jesus Christ, Billie." I chuckle. "Fuck. Fine. Yes. Yes, baby, I'm in love with you. Let me be part of your story. Shit sure as hell ain't perfect right now, but I'm starting to think—" I sniffle. "As long as we got each other, we can get through anything. If being with you has taught me one thing, it's that life's too damn hard to do on your own. It's also too damn short to live it only half alive. So live it with me, darlin'. Pretty please."

"With a cherry on top?"

"There's a dirty joke in there about cherries that I'm not gonna make—"

"Ryder Rivers, don't you *dare* hold back on me. Because maybe I'm a tiny bit in love with you too."

My chest explodes. A full-on blast that has me glancing around the room, looking for blood and pieces of bone.

"'A tiny bit'?" It's all I can manage to say. "Are you *still* waiting on me to grow on you?"

Billie grins, her eyes flicking to my crotch. "Oh, you've grown on me, all right."

I'm profoundly shaken. In all the best ways.

"It was the mouth-to-mouth, wasn't it?" I ask.

"You're not supposed to deflect with humor anymore."

"Told you, I ain't perfect."

"Thank God for that, because I'm not perfect either." She pecks my lips. "I'd like to think that gives us permission to be our perfectly imperfect selves with each other."

Smiling, I lean in and kiss her. Slip my tongue inside her mouth. "My therapist said something along those lines too."

She pauses, eyes toggling between mine. "You're in therapy?"

"Started recently, yeah. I wanna keep thriving the way you taught me to. Figured it wouldn't hurt to have some help staying on track. You know, so I don't fall back into old patterns."

"Wow. Wow, that's… I'm so proud of you, Ry. That might be the sexiest thing to ever come out of a man's mouth."

I grin. "You're welcome."

"I love you." She loops her arms around my neck. "Lemme show you how much."

I slowly suck on her bottom lip, and she digs her hands into the hair at the nape of my neck, pressing her tits against my chest.

I start to guide her shirt up the soft slopes of her belly. She holds up her arms, and I break the kiss to tug the shirt over her head. I catch a glimpse of her cute little ass in the mirror, and my dick surges.

More of that.

Dragging my lips over Billie's neck, I gently spin her around so that her back is to my front. We meet eyes in the mirror.

"This okay?" I cup her breasts, then flatten my hands so I can circle my palms over her nipples.

She moans. Her pupils blow out, making her eyes look bottomless. Deep, dark depths for days.

I press my dick to her ass. *Can't. Come. Before she does.*

She nods. "This is—it's more than okay. I like this, Ry." Reaching behind her, she pushes her tits into my hands again as she plays with my hair.

"You see how pretty you are?" I kiss her neck and knead her breast. I slide my other hand down her stomach and use my fingers to part her pussy.

Her leg gives out when I press my first two fingertips to her clit. She's not wet enough for my liking, so I pinch her nipple and bite her neck and push those fingertips a little deeper.

I find her entrance. Slip a finger inside and find the moisture I'm looking for.

Glancing in the mirror, I see Billie biting her lip as she watches me finger her. I like how *into* this she is. Now she's rolling her hips, and I'm thrusting my finger, and she's playing with her tits too.

Eyes on herself the whole time.

"See?" I smirk, nipping at her shoulder. "You turn on everyone, yourself included."

She nods, her stomach caving when I spread her moisture over her clit. She's wet enough now that my fingers glide easily through her slickness.

I play with her clit. Her head falls back onto my shoulder.

"Would you—can you—is there a way we could watch?" she pants. "Once you're inside me, I mean."

Still smirking, I give her clit a soft pinch before moving my hands to her tits again. "Yeah, baby, I can figure out a way to fuck you so you can watch in the mirror. Can you put your hands on the wall? Bend over a little?"

She nods. Her hair falls over her shoulders and into her face as she does as I tell her. Rotating the mirror so it reflects our sides, I move to stand behind her. Then I put my hands between her shoulder blades and press down so that she's bent at the waist.

"Now turn your head." I gather her hair in my hand. "Can you see us?"

She meets my eyes in the mirror again. "Oh, this is good, Ry. Really fucking good."

Reaching back, she grabs my dick and pumps her hand.

At the same time, I do that thing we both like and use *my* hand to pull aside her ass cheek and open her to me.

I sink my fingers inside her pussy again. She feels tighter at this angle. More narrow.

"You're gonna feel some pressure, yeah?" I unwrap her hand from my dick and take myself in my hand.

Thrusting my fingers one last time, I tap my dick against her ass.

"You're obscene," she moans.

"Such a brat. You want me to put this dick in your mouth instead?"

She grins. "I want you inside me. Now."

I pull out my fingers. Gather her hair in my hand again. "You'd best be ready, then."

Pressing my head to her entrance, I push inside her in a quick, hard thrust. No gentleness. No warning.

I just *go*, burying myself to the hilt. I also give her hair a pull.

She makes a strangled sound. "*Ry.*"

"Watch me fuck you." Holding onto her hip with my free hand, I begin to hammer into her from behind. "That's what you wanted, right? *Right?*"

She turns her head a little so she can watch us in the mirror. Her mouth forms a neat little *o* when I slip my hand between her legs to play with her clit again.

I *love* seeing the way her ass cheeks rock in time to my movements. Her tits bounce. Her back arches when I pull on her hair, and she yells.

"*More.* Hot. This is—the hottest thing, Ry."

I start to sweat. Need rockets up my dick with every stroke, a tightening that has me gritting my teeth.

"Come," I grunt. "You gotta come before me, baby."

And she does, locking eyes with me in the mirror, her pussy clamping down on me. Then I'm lost too.

I'm coming too, howling like the animal I am.

It takes several heartbeats to come back to Earth. Then, before I can think better of it, I put my hands on her hips and pivot us a little so that her ass is fully facing the mirror.

"Watch," I say, starting to pull out of her. "You're gonna like this."

I step aside. Billie has to strain a little to see, but she looks over her shoulder, and her eyes go wide when she catches a glimpse of my cum leaking out of her pussy.

"Obscene," she repeats. "Can we do that again?"

Monday.

It starts off pretty damn great. All my days do right now because I'm waking up next to Billie. Both of us naked.

I'm only able to tear myself away from her at the very last minute. That means I'm late for work, a fact which Wyatt, who became foreman of Lucky River Ranch after Cash took over as chairman and principal, does not appreciate.

"Dude, I get you're enjoying your little love nest situation." He grunts as he tosses a saddle onto a nearby horse. "But we gotta prep this herd for winter, and I need every spare pair of hands. You bein' late every damn day throws off our whole operation. I'll whoop some ass if I need to whether you're my brother or not."

I do feel guilty. Despite the hot summer and warm autumn we've had here in Texas, they're calling for record cold this winter. More than that, the cold is supposed to last well through March and April. Which means it's more important than ever that we have our ducks in a row on the ranch, because when those low temps hit, being prepared is the only way we'll keep our fifteen thousand head of cattle alive.

If only my focus hadn't been entirely somewhere else lately. "Sorry. Once my place is ready—"

"Could be months. Be here by four tomorrow, or don't come at all."

"Got it."

We turn out the horses and muck stalls until the sun rises. Then I head out to the corral, where branding the calves we missed in the spring is already underway. Duke is at the gate, glancing over his shoulder as I approach.

Now that he splits his time between cowboying and being partner in Bellamy Brooks's growing boot empire, he's with Wheeler and Mollie more often than not in the studio. But winter is almost here, he's put his literal and proverbial cowboy hat back on and working on the ranch twenty-four seven.

He smiles. "You finally came up for air, huh?"

"Don't be gross." But I'm smiling too as I slap his back. "How's it going?"

Shrugging, he squints against the bright morning light. "Wyatt's pissed."

"I know. I feel like a jerk, but—"

"You're in love. I get it."

I blink. Blink again. "How did you—"

"Know? Same reason I can finish your sentences. I'm your twin, remember? We have the same brain."

Laughing, I shake my head, even as my heart pops around inside my chest. "We have the same genes, idiot.

And yeah." I can't help but smile. "I said it first this weekend, and she said it right back. Pretty cool."

"Aw, man, I'm thrilled for you. We've all been waitin' for it to happen. Now that you're opening up and shit, figured you'd be spilling your guts sooner rather than later." He looks me in the eye. "I'm proud of you, Ry."

I nod. "I'm proud of me too."

"So when are you gonna ask her to marry you?"

"That's a bold assumption," I reply, cutting him a look. "Also, why does every story gotta end with a wedding? There's a million different ways to ride off into the sunset with someone."

"I know. I'm Exhibit A of the alternative happy ending. No ring, no wedding, but we are having two babies, so." He gives me a wide, white smile. "Still counts as a win."

"Any updates on that front? How's Wheeler feeling?"

Sawyer has arrived, and he's calling us over to help rope a calf.

Duke opens the gate and holds it for me. "She's uncomfortable, and sleep is hard to come by. But we're getting really excited. Starting to feel real, you know?"

I give his shoulder a squeeze. "You're gonna be a great daddy."

"Appreciate you saying that. *You're* gonna be toast if you don't help out around here while I'm gone."

"Just because I'm being nice doesn't give you permission to be a dick."

His smile is back. "Love ya, brother. You make any headway with Colt?"

"Nope. Not for lack of trying, though. We're both reaching out all the time—me and Billie. He always was a stubborn motherfucker, but this..." I let out a low whistle. "It's a whole new level."

"He'll come around."

"Yeah. Maybe."

Duke grabs my arm. "He *will* come around, Ry. He isn't gonna stay mad at y'all forever. He can't. You mean too much to him. I can't imagine cutting someone out of my life because they fell in love with my sister. That's some bullshit right there."

"It's more complicated than that."

"Is it, though?" Sighing, he looks away. "If he don't come around soon, I'll be having some words with him."

"Please don't. I know you're just trying to help—"

"The longer he's pissed, the more he's gonna regret it down the road. Think about everything he's missin' out on—his best friend and his sister just found their soulmates in each other. Is there anything better than that? Makes me wonder if he's jealous of y'all." Duke closes the gate behind us. "Now quit messin' and let's get this done."

Prepping for winter is...not my favorite. It's nice having pretty much everyone we know on hand to help, but that means the days are total chaos. The new ranch hands need a lot of guidance. Despite the fact that we're well into autumn, the sun is hot, and I'm soaked through with sweat by the time the lunch bell rings.

Everyone is exhausted, and tempers fray. John B and Cash get into it when John B takes a hoof to the face while wrangling a calf into submission.

I get kicked square in the stomach by an especially ornery Friesian horse. The surprise of it is the worst part, but it still knocks the wind out of me.

I get shit on. Lose my grip on a rope, and it ends up giving me a good burn on my wrist. Sweat rolls down my face and drips into my eyes.

I can tell by the way the skin on my nape and forearms smarts that I'm sunburnt even though I'm wearing 70 SPF.

Never mind the fact that Wyatt keeps an eye on me all day, like he *knows* I'm gonna bolt the second I'm able to sneak away.

Makes keeping an eye on my phone pretty damn difficult. Billie is supposed to present her idea for the animal therapy program to her parents today, and I'm dying to know how it went.

I love my job. Always have. But some days, the physical misery of this work makes you question all your life decisions. Your sanity too.

By the time I climb into my car at quarter to four that afternoon, my back is shot, and I'm caked in mud, sweat, and God knows what else. I stink to high heaven, so I roll down the windows on the drive over to Billie's place.

No word from her yet. I can't tell if that's a good sign or a bad one.

She's not home when I get there, so I grab a shower. Shiver at the sheer pleasure of putting on clean, comfy clothes. Mrs. Wallace stopped making supper every night once her brood moved out, so the family doesn't eat together seven days a week the way we do.

Honestly, it's kind of a relief. I very much look forward to staying in tonight with Billie. I'll make something easy and quick for dinner—breakfast tacos with that leftover chorizo we made for brunch yesterday?—and we can eat on the couch while zooming through some episodes of our current obsession, *The Great British Bake Off*.

Paul Hollywood's gruffness reminds me so much of Cash that it kinda freaks me out.

My hamstrings *scream* as I bend down to pull a pan out of a drawer in the kitchen. I turn on some Nirvana and make dinner.

Only when I glance at my phone do I realize how late it is. After six, which for us might as well be ten p.m.

Billie is home without fail by four thirty every day.

My stomach drops. *Something's wrong.*

No idea how I know this, but I just do.

I try calling her. Texting her too.

No response.

I'm probably overreacting—definitely overreacting—but better to be safe than sorry. Covering dinner with tinfoil, I grab my keys and head out to my car.

I drive way too fast to the ranch's offices. Wondering all the while what the hell is going down to keep Billie there so long. She did mention waiting until the end of the day to make her proposal. Apparently her mom's mood improves the closer it gets to dinnertime.

I really, really hope everything's okay.

I pull up to the limestone building, my headlights slicing across the steel windows.

My heart trips to a stop when I see Billie in the window.

She's crying, holding her face in her hands.

Shit.

CHAPTER 27
Lessons Learned the Hard Way
Billie

"Just so I understand." Dad furrows his brow, pressing his fingertips into the pristine surface of his desk. "Are you going to build this program in your spare time? Because I'm not sure how you'll be director *there* and bookkeeper *here*."

Mom is frowning as she stands beside Dad, who sits in his chair. "That sounds like an awful lot to put on your plate right now, Billie."

Closing my eyes, I take a deep, steadying breath. I thought that presenting my idea at the end of the workday, when Mom and Dad are usually their jolliest because their favorite time—dinner together—is imminent, I'd have a better chance of winning them over.

Judging by their confused, skeptical expressions, that is not the case.

Fuck.

"I don't think it's any secret I've been unhappy in my position for a while." I choose my words carefully. "It's time for a change. I'm resigning as bookkeeper so I can be director of the therapy program."

Dad's eyebrows pop up. He glances at Mom, whose frown deepens.

I feel seasick all of a sudden.

"I can't say that I'm surprised to hear this," Dad says after an excruciating pause. "Of course I know you've been in a funk. But I thought that was solved now that you and Ryder are together."

"My love life and my career are two separate things. I don't love being an accountant, Dad. In fact, I kind of hate it."

"But you're so good at it, honey!" Mom clasps her hands. The knuckles are white. "It'd be a waste to let you quit now. The experience you've gained—"

"We need a bookkeeper, Billie. The idea of a therapy program is neat, but that's not an immediate concern of ours. Paying our taxes is. Running payroll for our employees is."

My eyes prick. Damn it, I didn't want to get emotional, but I can already tell I'm fighting a losing battle.

Or more succinctly: My parents don't understand what I'm trying to say.

They don't understand *me*. And that hurts.

"I'll help y'all find another accountant," I manage around the tightness in my throat. "Just because I'm good at something doesn't mean I *should* do it. I miss being outside. I miss—God, I miss everything about being with the horses. I'm meant to work with people and animals. Not numbers. I'm dying a slow death being trapped inside this office all day."

Mom's frown deepens. "Well, honey, sometimes that's just life."

I shake my head. "Y'all aren't hearing me. If I stay in this job—stay in this office—I'm gonna wither away. I refuse to let that happen. I'm resigning, Mom, whether y'all approve or not. Now can we please talk about the therapy program? I spent weeks putting together that deck." I nod at the stapled packet in Mom's lap.

My parents exchange another glance. My stomach clenches. They're worried, which doesn't help my own anxiety over whether I can pull off this crazy idea.

"I can tell you've put a lot of thought into this." Dad glances at the presentation. "And I love the community outreach angle. I really do. It's something I'd hoped to focus on one day. But that's down the road a ways, honey. It's something your mother and I could think about in our retirement."

"So retire already, and help me make this dream a reality. The boys practically run the ranch themselves anyway, Dad. Doing something like this—something that's creative, that has a real impact—it really is a dream of mine. Y'all know I'm a hard worker. Whatever I put my mind to, I make happen. I'm asking you to trust me to make this happen too."

Judging by the way Mom sighs and Dad blinks, I'm not making great headway in that respect.

"We'll have the help of experts in every field," I add. "Everyone's offered advice and help. I know y'all respect the hell out of Mollie and Cash for turning things around at Lucky River Ranch. They think big, and I wanna think big too. That's why you're getting us rebranded, right, Dad? It's time to think outside the box."

His smile doesn't touch his eyes. "You're so young, Billie. Too young to be making this kind of leap. It's important to work hard at your age. Save your money, so you can—"

"Quit once I start a family?" I stare at him. "That's not my plan. I like working."

Mom crosses her arms. "You might feel differently one day."

Now I'm really gonna cry. Not just because I'm hurt—and I am really hurt—but also because I'm hugely frustrated.

"Do y'all know me at all?" My voice is thin. I curl my fingers into my chest, tears leaking out of my eyes. "That's not who I am. That's not who I ever was. I'm sorry I'm not the perfect daughter y'all always wanted, but I can't pretend to be happy trying to be her anymore. I am who I am."

Mom gets up, her eyes watery, and wraps me in a hug. "You're breaking my heart here, Elizabeth May. I've always loved you just as you are. You don't have to be anybody else for us to love you, okay? Let's get that one thing straight."

I nod, inhaling the familiar jasmine scent of the lotion she uses on her chapped hands. "Okay."

"If I ever put pressure on you to be someone you weren't, I apologize. Sincerely. I was just doing what I thought was right. That's how I was raised."

I keep nodding, unable to speak.

"We've always wanted to set you and your brothers up for success," Dad says gently. "I told you before that I never got much guidance when I was young. I felt like I could've really benefitted from someone helping me out the way I'm trying to help you. Accounting is a very noble profession. It can be lucrative too."

"We were helping you make good decisions so you wouldn't have regrets later. Or so we thought." Mom leans back, her hands on my shoulders. "Why didn't you say something sooner?"

"Because I didn't want to rock the boat, Mom. I wanted so badly to *want* to be an accountant. I knew how proud y'all were, and I felt like I was making a real contribution to the ranch. But I can't…" I shake my head, eyes closed. "I can't do it anymore. I should've said something. I'm realizing…"

I take a deep breath.

"What, honey?" Dad asks.

"For someone so outspoken, I've never really talked about important things with y'all. Colt asked me why I never told him I had a crush on Ryder—"

"Did you really need to tell us?" Mom grins. "We all knew, honey."

"Exactly! But wouldn't have hurt to say it out loud. Maybe then Colt wouldn't hate me so much right now. It wouldn't have been such a shock, you know?"

Dad gently runs a hand up my arm. "I've had some words with your brother. I understand where he's coming from, but I don't agree with him holding a grudge like this. That's not how things work in our family."

I wave Dad away. "Thank you for speaking up on my behalf. But I just… I own that I'm to blame here. So even though it feels like my relationship with Ryder and this idea of starting an animal therapy program are coming out of nowhere, I've actually been thinking about them for a long time. I've thought about Ryder for years, and

I've wanted to do something other than bookkeeping pretty much from the second I started doing it."

Dad's chest rises on a deep, thoughtful inhale. "If you're really that unhappy, Billie, we need to make some changes. I'm sorry I didn't pay better attention—I should've known you needed something different."

"Thank you for saying that." I manage a tight smile when Mom wipes away my tears. "We both have some work to do, yeah?"

Mom grins. "You're even starting to talk like Ryder."

"Oh God." I put my face in my hands. "I'm turning into that girl, aren't I?"

"Love makes you do wild things," Dad singsongs.

Mom's eyebrows pop up. "Love, huh?"

"Love," Dad confirms, eyes on mine.

"Y'all need to mind your own business," I tease, then I look up as the headlights arc across the room.

I'd know the sound of that diesel engine anywhere.

Everything inside me drops a hundred stories as I watch Ryder climb out of the car and slam the door.

He runs—*why is he running?*—into the office, his footfalls loud.

I'm reaching for the door just as he knocks.

"Billie? Billie, baby, you okay?"

I yank open the door to see him standing there. His face is sunburnt, and his eyes are full of concern, brows curved upward.

He's breathing hard. Stepping forward, he takes my face in his hands.

He smells like my soap.

"Aw, Billie, why're you—"

"They're happy tears. Well, kind of." I glance at my

parents, who are watching us with a funny gleam in their eyes.

"Mr. and Mrs. Wallace." Ryder nods.

Dad puts his arm around Mom's shoulders. "How many times I gotta ask you to call me Dale?"

"At least one more."

Ryder's eyes move between my parents and me. "Can I ask how things are, uh, going?"

I sigh, trying to swallow the tightness in my throat that won't quit. "They're going all right. We just agreed we all have work to do about opening up to each other, even when it's painful or inconvenient."

"How ironic." Ryder's lips twitch. "That's only what you've been teaching *me* to do. With great success, might I add."

"I'm good at everything I do." I'm teasing again.

Ryder, though, takes me seriously. "You really are. You made the pitch?" He glances at the deck, which Mom put on Dad's desk.

"I did."

"And? Please tell me we're starting an animal therapy program."

I look at Dad, who looks at Mom. While they do their silent communication thing, I'm hit by the idea that maybe my parents' marriage isn't as traditional as I'd always assumed. I thought Dad took his role as head of our household seriously, meaning he was in charge—he made all the decisions.

Now I see that Mom might actually be the one in charge. Have I been so blinded by my own assumptions that I couldn't see how my parents' relationship *actually* worked?

"I'm hoping that's what we're about to do," I reply.

Ryder's eyes are full as they toggle between mine. "And *I* hope *you* are ready to change a lot of lives, Billie. Because that's exactly what you're gonna do when you build this program and bring people into the fold here on your family's ranch." He glances at my parents. "Y'all have something so, so special, and what a brilliant idea to share it so others can heal and maybe see that life is infinitely richer if you know nature and know how to show it respect too.

"Billie's got a pretty amazing vision for how it would work," Ryder continues. "She's been working on her plans nonstop. Her phone literally died yesterday because she was on the phone so long with Mollie Luck. She was picking Mollie's brain about a little bit of everything—payroll, hiring practices, mission statements."

Mom cocks an eyebrow. "So what's your mission statement, Billie? In a single sentence."

I meet Ryder's eyes. Think for a beat. Another.

"My mission is to share my love of a life lived alongside animals—a love of the outdoors—with others, while helping to find a respect for the awesome healing power of nature and community. I speak from experience because I've been healed by y'all literally"—I lift my arm—"and figuratively. I think it's also worth mentioning that my nightmares have completely stopped, since I started working on this plan."

Now, Mom's the one who is blinking back tears. "Seriously?"

"Seriously."

"Oh, honey, I'm so—" She swallows hard and covers her mouth with her hand. "So relieved. They were awful."

My voice wobbles. "Thank you." I look at Mom and Dad, heart thundering. "We're kind of a dream team, if I say so myself."

Dad smiles. "I love how y'all support each other. That's important."

"It's important to support each other," Mom replies. "We'll have to talk about this a little more—a lot more—but Billie, I think you've hit on something real interesting here."

"I imagine there's a need for this kind of program in Hartsville too." Dad is nodding. "I haven't heard of any other animal therapy programs in the area."

"Believe it or not, ours would be the only program in a hundred-mile radius."

Ryder nods. "My mom had to drive me to Austin."

"You had therapy with animals?" Dad asks.

"I did. I had a speech delay when I was little. The therapy really helped."

Dad looks at Mom again, and I know with a certainty that's nonsensical they're going to say yes.

Holy fucking shit.

Holy shit, this is happening.

The life I've dreamed of but never thought would happen is, well, happening. Right now.

"We're interested," Dad says at last.

"Very interested," Mom says.

"Interested in what?"

I turn, pulse halting to a sudden, painful stop when I see Colt standing in the doorway.

CHAPTER 28
Good News, Bad News
Ryder

"More importantly," Colt continues, *giving his sister a* look I can't decipher, *"what're the tears about?"*

I can tell by the way Billie clenches her jaw that she wants to roll her eyes, but she's trying to play nice.

"They're not there because of Ryder, if that's what you're implying." Turning, she curls an arm around my waist so that we're standing side by side.

I return the favor and wrap my arm around her shoulders. "Hey, Colt."

He looks...not great. Bags under his eyes. His face his scruffier than usual, and his hair curls out from underneath his hat in a tangle of curls that are several inches too long.

I feel that stab of guilt again. *Am I wholly responsible for the way he looks?* I know the new consultant Mr. Wallace brought on, Lainey, has been busting his chops. Beck told me as much when I called him again to ask how Colt was doing. And being a single parent is always an exhausting endeavor.

Still, I hate to see my friend suffering this way.

"Hey."

It's a single word. But it's the only word Colt has spoken to me in weeks. Fucked up as it sounds, that feels like progress. Wonder if he heard me just now? Did he see how I'm wholeheartedly supporting his sister? How I'm trying my damndest to make her dreams come true?

Because the friend I know would respect the hell out of that.

Then again, Colt is hurting. He's not exactly in the right frame of mind. Who knows what he's thinking.

"Billie and Ryder here were just making a very convincing argument that we should set up an animal therapy program here on the ranch," Dad says.

Colt's eyes flicker. I can't read them.

"Ryder helped me come up with the idea," Billie says. "He's been with me every step of the way. My accident—it made me realize that I needed to make some changes."

Mrs. Wallace grabs the presentation deck and holds it up. "Look at this pitch they put together. Thirty pages!"

Colt's shoulders rise on a deep, aggrieved sigh. "Seems kinda out of left field, no?"

"Read the deck, and you'll see a program like the one I'm proposing is beautifully aligned with our values as a family," Billie replies. "I'd be happy to make the full pitch to you if you'd like."

"And I'd be happy to chime in if you need help," I add.

Billie looks up at me. "You're the best. Thank you."

"Anytime. This is exciting stuff. Just grateful to be a part of it."

I glance up to see Colt looking at us. There's a tug in my center when it hits me that the look in his eyes is sadness.

Of course. He misses Abby.

Despite the shit they went through, he loved her with his whole heart. There were times when I thought losing her might destroy him if her infidelity didn't.

Deep down, Colt's a romantic. He may swear off marriage—relationships in general—but I know he misses being in love.

I get it now, because loving someone and being loved by them in return is pretty much the best thing ever. Duke was on to something when he said Colt might be jealous of Billie and me. I know he doesn't wish us ill. I also know he'd like to have a partner in life again, even if he does come off as surly and standoffish.

"Maybe later," he says at last. "I gotta get home to Dean."

Mr. Wallace pins him with a look. "You really should stay and hear what your sister has to say."

"Dad, I was with Lainey all damn day. I'm tapped out, all right?"

Mrs. Wallace frowns. "Did it not go well with Lainey?"

"It never goes well with that woman. I'll… Yeah, I'll see y'all later."

Then he disappears out the door.

That weekend, I'm pulling the biggest lasagna I've ever seen out of the oven in the Wallace's kitchen when Lainey strides in.

"Well, hey there, honey!" Mrs. Wallace smiles warmly as she drops a handful of freshly grated parmesan cheese into the salad she's making. "I'm thrilled you'll be joining us for supper tonight."

I met Lainey not long after Billie and I told everyone we were in a relationship. She's young, but she knows her shit, and I'm well aware of how a rebrand can take an operation to the next level.

I'll never forget when Mollie made her pitch to combine Lucky and Rivers Ranches. There wasn't a dry eye in the room. I think we all fell in love with her that day, just like we fell in love with the idea of Lucky River Ranch.

Mr. Wallace is a smart guy. I think he's seen the progress we've made on our property since the rebrand, and now he wants a piece of the action. I also know he's eager to honor his family's legacy by having his ranch in tip-top shape before he hands it over to his children.

The Wallace kids pretty much run the place already. But Old Man Wallace still pulls the reins—or pulls the strings, if we're being grammatically correct—and I know he's itching to retire.

That's why he hired Lainey. I think she's great. I also see a lot of the hatred Mollie and Cash had for each other in the dynamic between Lainey and Colt. They're always arguing about something, but I don't miss the way she'll check him out when she thinks no one is looking, or how he refills her water bottle for her, grumbling all the while.

Kinda cute when you think about it.

"Thank you for the invite. The bartender at the Homestead Hen joked the other day that I should just sleep in one of the booths because I practically live there these days."

Mrs. Wallace pulls her brows together. "You gotta come eat with us more often, then! It goes without saying the door is always open."

Lainey smiles. "Thank you, Paige, that means a lot. Honestly, I end up getting a lot of work done while I eat at the restaurant, so it's no biggie. Also, I think Colton might literally kill me if I bug him all day and show up to his family supper at night too."

"Colt's been in a grumpy mood lately. He'll come around." Mrs. Wallace crosses the kitchen to inspect the lasagna. "Looks done. Thank you for your help, Ryder."

I take off the oven mitts and slip them in the drawer beside the stove. "No problem. And sorry about Colt's grumpy mood, Lainey. That's my fault."

"How dare you treat his little sister with respect and adoration." Mrs. Wallace clucks her tongue, a smile tugging at the edges of her mouth. "What a crime."

Lainey leans her elbows on the counter. "He's super protective of the people he loves, huh?"

"You have no idea." Mrs. Wallace rolls her eyes as she heads for the freezer, pulling out a loaf of garlic bread.

"I got that." Taking the loaf from her, I read the instructions on the package before opening it. "You made the lasagna and the salad. Go sit."

But Mrs. Wallace just keeps on smiling. "Now you know that's not gonna happen. You're sweet to help."

"Is he, though?" Tate walks into the kitchen with wet hair, wearing clean clothes. As the youngest of the Wallace clan, he's stuck being on weekend duty caring for the horses, so he's worked in the barns all day.

Billie is hot on his heels. "Wouldn't you like to know?"

I came over to the house early to help Mrs. Wallace with dinner, so Billie could continue to work on the business plan for her program. It's now a fifty-page document that includes more spreadsheets than I think I've ever seen in my life. In true Billie fashion, she's leaving no stone unturned.

"Sweet as pie, in my opinion," Lainey replies. "You got a good one, Billie. They're few and far between."

Billie grins, going up on her toes to peck my cheek. "That's why I've been chasing this guy down for years. I knew he was a keeper."

Tate glances at the lasagna. "You made Italian, Mom? Hell yes."

"Smells good in here." Mr. Wallace wipes his feet after walking in the back door. "Whatever that is, I'm about to put a hurtin' on it. Lainey! Ryder! To what do we owe the pleasure?"

"Lainey needed a home-cooked meal," Mrs. Wallace replies. "And the Lucky River Ranch crew was kind enough to let us borrow Ryder for the evening."

"Give my regards to your people." Mr. Wallace taps the brim of his Stetson before he takes it off, hanging it on the hat rack beside the door.

"Will do, sir."

"It's Dale."

"Right. What can I get you to drink, Dale?"

A big old smile breaks out on his face. "Finally. I got a sixer in the fridge outside. Lemme grab it."

Billie is the last to join us at the table in the dining room. Well, other than Colt and Dean, who haven't attended Sunday supper since I started coming. Mrs. Wallace still sets a place for them at the table, but they never show.

We're just toasting to Billie's business plan, which she says is coming along swimmingly, when the front door opens.

"Mimi! Pawpaw! Are you here?"

My chest squeezes at the sound of Dean's cute little voice. A second later he's running into the dining room, his gap-toothed smile of pure delight making all of us laugh.

"We're here! Oh, sweet boy, I'm so glad you were able to come." Mrs. Wallace wraps her grandson in a tight hug. "I've missed you."

"I miss you too. Miss Lainey, you're here for dinner?"

Lainey wipes her mouth with her napkin and grins. "Your grandmama invited me. Isn't that so kind?"

"Can we play UNO after we're done?"

"As long as you eat your vegetables and mind your manners."

"That a deal?" Dean asks, holding out his hand.

Lainey takes it. "That's a deal. Such a good handshake."

"Thanks. My dad taught me."

"I'm sure he did," Lainey says, looking up wearily as Colt walks into the room. "Hello, Colton."

My stomach bottoms out. Billie and I meet eyes, and I can tell she's wondering the same thing I am. *This a good thing or a bad thing?*

"Lainey." He nods, then looks around the table. "Why y'all so quiet?"

"Because you've been giving us all the silent treatment for, like, a year now, and suddenly you decide to show up to supper like it's no big thing." Mack cocks a brow. "Care to explain yourself?"

Colt leans down to kiss his mama before he takes his seat. "Me and Dean were hungry."

"Right," Beck says slowly.

Colt helps Dean put his napkin on his lap. "This looks amazing, Mom."

"Ryder helped too, you know," Mrs. Wallace replies. "He's an excellent kitchen assistant."

"That so?" Colt cuts me a look.

I reach for my beer and take a gulp. "My mom always used to say many hands make light work."

"You're kind of a living embodiment of that, Ry," Billie says.

Lainey chews thoughtfully on a piece of garlic bread. "All y'all are. Watching you work together day in and day out is really something else."

"That's 'cause we're doin' real work." Colt gives her a tight smile. "The kind you do with your hands."

Lainey, bless her, isn't having it. "You really gonna start with this right now?"

"Daddy, Miss Lainey does real work too. Matter of fact, we worked together today."

Colt's brows pop up, a piece of garlic bread poised over his open mouth. "I thought you were showing Miss Lainey how to ride a horse."

"We were riding horses, Daddy. We were also talking strategy."

Mack is laughing into his napkin. "I like the sound of this."

"Can we tell them?" Dean begs Lainey. "Please please please? Your ideas are the neatest."

That has us all laughing again.

Lainey nods. "Sure. Why don't you tell everyone the idea we were kicking around today while you were being such an excellent teacher?"

"Double U Ranch!" Dean proudly exclaims. "Get it, Mimi? Instead of The Wallace Ranch, our new name would be—wait, what did you call it, Miss Lainey?"

Lainey laughs, reaching over to ruffle Dean's hair. "A play on words. Wallace starts with the letter *w*, so we just spell that letter out in a different way. *D-o-u-b-l-e...*"

"*U!*" Dean claps his hands. "Remember you wrote it out for me and I got it because I know how to read now?"

"You are so smart it's amazing," Lainey replies. "Of course I remember. Just like I remember how much you're learning in kindergarten."

"Kindergarten is the best." Dean is beaming now. "I'm so good at it."

I lean over to whisper in Beck's ear. "Is it just me, or does Dean have a serious crush on Lainey?"

Beck's lips twitch. "I think Dean *and* Colt have a serious crush on Lainey. Lucky for her, she don't gotta choose between 'em."

Mr. Wallace's eyes go wide. "I think that's mighty clever. What do you think, Mama?"

"I think I love it," Mrs. Wallace replies simply. "It's just different enough to stand out, but still classic and very tongue-in-cheek. Just like my sense of humor."

"Dean informed me he saw the letters in the color yellow."

Dean nods. "It's my favorite color."

"Well then, our new logo has to be yellow, then."

Billie glances around the table. "I don't know how y'all feel, but I am really digging this."

"Thank you, Billie. Appreciate the vote of support." Lainey looks at Colt. "Although I don't think the new branding will pass by unanimous vote tonight."

Colt picks up his water glass. "What makes you say that, Lainey?"

"You and your stubborn behind," she replies steadily. "You were gonna shoot us down even before we shared our idea."

I bite back a smile. "For what it's worth, I like it too."

"Of course you do." Colt shakes his head. "Am I the only one who thinks this whole rebranding business is a waste of time and money?"

"Yes," the table replies in unison.

Colt scoffs. "Great."

"How about we shelve that conversation for later?" Mr. Wallace interjects diplomatically. "Tonight, I wanna enjoy this delicious lasagna and the company of all my *well-behaved* children. Plus their significant others." He nods at me. "We've been waiting an age to add some more places at the table. Thank you for coming, Ryder."

Heat works its way up my face. "Thank y'all for giving me a chance to prove that I'm worthy of your daughter. She's somethin' special, and I can't wait to watch her soar."

Billie's eyes get that soft look in them that I'm learning can mean a lot of things.

She's happy.

She's tired but in a good way.

She's turned on.

I'll take any of the above tonight, please and thank you.

"Amen to that." Tate raises his glass. "To Billie and Ryder. May the mouth-to-mouth resuscitation he gave her that night at the rodeo be the start of a beautiful love story."

"Cheers!" Dean raises his own glass with such enthusiasm he spills water everywhere.

The rest of the table toasts us too.

I don't think any of us misses the fact that Colt raises his glass. He doesn't say a word. Doesn't meet my eyes. But he does participate in the toast, and that small but significant gesture means everything to me.

It means shit just might really work out—for the better.

CHAPTER 29
One-Eighty
Billie

We get the call at noon on the Tuesday after Thanksgiving that Wheeler is in labor. She's not due for a few weeks, but apparently it's super common for twins to be born early.

Ryder and I ended up attending multiple Thanksgiving meals on the actual holiday. We kicked around the idea of combining our family celebrations, but Patsy had already ordered the food for Lucky River Ranch's meal, and Mom had already invited a dozen extra guests to *their* house. The logistics of trying to combine all that were obviously a nightmare. So Ry and I had lunch at Mom and Dad's house with my family, and then we did dinner at the New House with his crew.

All in all, it was a lovely holiday. Mostly because I got to spend the whole day with Ryder.

Wheeler and Duke asked that we wait to visit them until they're home with the babies, so it's no surprise that everyone starts sending a zillion texts in the Long Live Cowgirls Thread trying to get the scoop on what's going down.

> MOLLIE: My bestie is having HER BABIES TODAY OMG OMG OMG
>
> AVA: YAY! Thinking of you Wheeler! Sending all the good vibes. Love you!
>
> WHEELER: Aw, thank y'all. We're at the hospital and I just got the epidural. Feeling pretty good so far!
>
> AVA: The epidural is everything
>
> MOLLIE: Agreed!
>
> SALLY: I could not be more excited for y'all. GOOD LUCK!
>
> BILLIE: Ryder and I are over here freaking out in the best way. I hope everything goes well friend! You got this
>
> MOLLIE: Can we be the first to bring you sushi and tequila pretty please?
>
> WHEELER: I wouldn't expect anything less. Love y'all
>
> BILLIE: I'm going to be the favorite aunt
>
> SALLY: Back off, bitch, that title is MINE
>
> AVA: Not if I get it first. Y'all forget how good I am with babies.
>
> MOLLIE: I think it's fair to say that I'm the one with the most recent experience in that department. Babies love me!
>
> MOLLIE: Actually they love my husband more, but that's neither here nor there
>
> SALLY: Y'all, Wyatt just burst into tears when I saw

> him. It's the cutest thing ever. He is so excited and happy
>
> BILLIE: I'm bursting into tears reading that. How the heck am I supposed to work with all this excitement happening?!
>
> MOLLIE: Ditch work and come drink with me
>
> AVA: Am I invited?
>
> MOLLIE: Always. Meet at the studio in half an hour? We can break in my new mah-jongg set
>
> WHEELER: Have one or five margaritas for me pretty please!
>
> BILLIE: Consider it done

Margaret Rose and Robert Haines are born later that day. Duke assures Ryder on a quick call that everyone is happy and healthy, and that they can't wait to see us when they're home from the hospital.

Ryder takes it upon himself to be the very first to visit that weekend. I stay home in an attempt to give Wheeler and Duke the space they need to adjust to life as a family of four. As much as it kills me to stay away from those sweet babies, I know I'll have the opportunity to meet them when the time is right.

While Ryder is gone, I tack up my horse for an easy ride to clear my head. I *may* have just interviewed a gal who could very well be Double U Ranch's very first hire for our animal therapy program, and I'm buzzing with excitement. Carmen has a background in physical therapy and a master's degree in social work. Not only that, she's one of the brightest lights I've ever encountered. Charismatic and caring, she's got energy and enthusiasm for days.

I honestly can't believe I lucked out finding her. I plan to make an official offer on Monday, but in the meantime, I want to ride the wave of goodness that's just come our way.

I'm back at the barn just as it starts pouring, a cold winter rain that has me shivering as I duck inside. Once my horse is in the crossties, I brush her, the motions meditative and familiar in a comforting way.

I smile. I'm gonna get to do this a lot more often once our program is off the ground. Which is actually gonna happen sooner rather than later because we struck gold and found my replacement for the accounting job after interviewing a mere *two* people.

I think Benton is going to be a much better fit for the role. A recent grad of Texas Tech, he's smart as a whip. More importantly, he actually enjoys bookkeeping.

"Hey."

I whip around, my heart leaping into my throat at the voice behind me. I blink when I see Colt standing beside my horse's stall, his hand in the front pocket of his jeans.

"Jesus fucking Christ, Colt. You scared the shit out me."

One side of his mouth kicks up. "That sailor's mouth of yours. Nice to know some things will never change."

"Well, yeah. Cussin' has always been part of my personality."

"Now where'd you learn to cuss like that?"

"My five foul-mouthed brothers might have something to do with it."

"Guilty." Colt steps forward to stand beside me, running a hand over my horse's flank. "You got a minute?"

"Depends." I cross my arms, careful to avoid knocking my arms or torso with the dandy brush and currycomb I'm holding. "You gonna be nice?"

His eyes bore into mine in the dim light of the barn. "I'm sorry I've been such a jackass."

I don't know what to say. Am I hearing things? Is this a dream?

"I heard Ryder sticking up for you," Colt continues. "That day you were making your pitch to Mom and Dad. I heard the whole thing because I was passing through the hall—heading home to grab Dean—but then I heard you talking about the animal therapy program stuff, and *then* I heard Ryder chiming in. I know it was wrong to eavesdrop, but I couldn't help it. Y'all sounded…certain. Excited."

I stare at my older brother, trying my damndest to formulate a coherent response. Part of me is still pissed he's given us the cold shoulder for so long. Another part wants to just give the guy a hug and beg him to put all this shit behind us, because I'm tired.

So tired of feeling like I did something wrong by falling in love.

Tired of doing life without my older brother.

"I'm glad you were able to listen in," I say at last. "Ryder…Colt, he's been so instrumental in helping me formulate this whole escape plan. The one where I don't have to work a job I hate anymore."

Colt's throat works on a swallow. "*I'm* glad he gave you the push you needed. I hated seeing you so unhappy, Billie. We all did."

"But I had to be the one to make the move. I know that now. And being with Ryder—I think it gave me the confidence I needed to do that." I search my brother's eyes. "I love him, Colt. With all my heart. I love you too, and I miss you like crazy."

He swallows again, blinking hard. "I've missed you too. Both of y'all."

I wait for him to finish that thought. Wait some more. He's running his hand down my horse's side again, and I can tell it takes effort to try and gather himself.

I knew Colt would have a lot to say about me dating his best friend. But I hadn't realized that he might have a lot to say about other things too.

Things we haven't talked about yet.

The space between us swims with emotion. I do my best to keep my head above the water, reminding myself to keep breathing.

"Y'all getting together—it wasn't just the betrayal that cut deep." Colt's voice is husky. "I'm ashamed to admit this, but it also made me sad. Like I almost couldn't be happy for y'all because I felt too sorry for myself. Yes, I know how shitty that is. But I had…" He puts both hands on the horse and takes a breath. "I wanted you to know why I've been avoiding y'all like I have. It's because I want to be happy for you, and I can't, and that makes me feel like the world's smallest, most selfish person."

The hot press of tears has me closing my eyes. "You've been through so much, Colt. None of it was fair. None of it was right. I still can't make sense of it all this many years later. You're a good man who always tries to do the right thing, even when it's hard. And still all that shit happened to you."

"I'm in therapy," Colt replies. "It's helping. But the

way I reacted to you and Ryder—it's made me realize how much work I still have left to do. While I'm definitely not healed, I can say I genuinely regret how I've treated y'all, and I'd love it if you'd—" He hangs his head. "I'd love it if we could start over. You, me, and Ry. Because y'all *do* deserve each other. You're both bighearted and creative and just all-around excellent human beings. If I'm being honest, I always pictured you with a guy like that. Someone who'd never try to tame your wild, who loved you for who you are. Because I love you like that. Or at least I've tried to."

Good Lord, since when is Colton Victor Wallace good at giving speeches?

Because *dang*, that one got me right in my feels.

"You've loved me exactly how I needed to be loved, Colt. You've got a big heart too. I know you were being protective because you *care*. A lot. You've just been through some shit, and that's gonna leave a scar."

He looks up. "I'm sorry. Really sorry, Billie. You deserve better, and so does Ryder."

"Have you talked to him yet?"

Colt shakes his head. "Wanted to come to you first. If you tell me to fuck off, I'll fuck off and leave y'all alone. But if you're willing to give me another chance, which I definitely don't deserve—"

"Everybody deserves a second chance, Colt." I manage a watery smile. "Even you."

He sniffs, his bloodshot eyes wet. "You mean that?"

"Of course I mean that." I drop the brushes on the floor, making my horse jump, and pull Colt in for a hug.

He tugs me tighter against him. "Thank you," he whispers.

"I'm glad we talked about this. I understand how you feel. But that doesn't excuse the awful things you said and did."

"I know. I'm sorry." Another sniffle. "At first, I thought I *was* just really, really pissed. But then I dug a little deeper and realized—"

"That your anger was really sadness. Mollie talked about that because she went through the same thing when Garrett died." I rest my cheek against Colt's chest. "I'm sorry I didn't make it a bigger priority to tell you about me and Ry. We've all been so busy. And to be fair, I had no idea where our relationship was gonna go. I also had a feeling you'd react the way you did, so…"

My older brother has the grace to scoff. "So you had some very good reasons why you wanted to keep your relationship on the down-low."

"Imagine that," I reply with a smile, letting him go so I can take a step back. "I'm proud of you for being in therapy."

Colt nods, spearing a hand through his hair. "Ain't easy, but I'm trying. For Dean. And for myself too."

"Can you do me another favor, pretty please? Since I got you where I want you."

Colt chuckles. "You ain't afraid to push your luck, huh?"

"Nope. Give Lainey a chance, okay? The ranch is gonna benefit from a little refresh, and believe it or not, all these young social media girlies are incredibly savvy when it comes to that stuff."

"That's a big ask."

"Not if you're willing to be the bigger person."

"You're barking up the wrong tree, sister. Clearly I'm petty and small-hearted."

"Only with me. With Lainey, you can do better."

He grins, and my heart lifts. "Maybe."

"Definitely." I nod at my horse. "Wanna help me put her up, and then grab a beer? Because we have to come up with a game plan for what you're gonna say to Ryder. I think we need some kind of grand gesture, don't you?"

"No?"

"Glad we're on the same page. I think…Hell, I almost think you fuck with him a little bit. Make him laugh hard so he'll be more likely to forgive you for your terrible fucking behavior."

Colt runs a hand down his face, shaking his head. "You're outta your goddamn mind. But I really did show my ass, so…I dunno, maybe I give your plan a try."

"Perfect." I gasp. "You know, he did leave his pocket-knife on my beside table."

Colt gives me a look. "Really?"

It's all I can do not to rub my hands together. "Yes, really."

CHAPTER 30
What the Actual?
Ryder

"Why did no one tell me they smelled so good?"

"Everyone knows that." Duke blinks at me. "Kinda like we all know the sky is blue, and how there's always a more handsome identical twin."

I sniff one of the little bald heads curled up against my chest, then the other. "They need to bottle this shit up. Sorry, *stuff*. They need to bottle this *stuff* up."

Wheeler laughs from her perch on the nearby couch. "Pretty sure we have some time before we need to start watching what we say around them. Although being with kids makes you realize just how bad your language can be."

"Right?" I smile when the baby dressed in a blue onesie yawns. "Aw, Robbie, you tired? God, that's the cutest sound ever."

Duke gets a little misty-eyed. "Honestly, sometimes I can't stand the cuteness."

Yep, now I'm crying too. "They're beautiful, y'all. Well done."

"Aw, thank you, Ry. Hard to believe this all started with the road trip from hell." Wheeler grins at my brother.

Duke grins right back. "You mean the best road trip ever. Minus the U-Haul. *That* thing was…not safe."

"Neither was the sex we had," Wheeler replies with another laugh.

I shake my head. "Really, y'all. You had so much of it you had to make not one, but two babies."

"People love making that joke." Duke groans. "Although it is kinda true. That weekend—"

"Was amazing." Wheeler gets this starry look in her eyes.

Maggie, *my brother's perfect daughter*, opens her eyes. They're unfocused, but very blue. Just like Duke's. Her full, wide mouth, though, is all Wheeler, and so is the smooth shape of her little chin.

Everything inside my chest swells to the point of pain. I keep falling in love with all these beautiful babies. Wonder when it will be *my* baby I fall in love with?

I'm in no rush. But would I marry Billie tomorrow if I had the chance? Fuck yeah. I'd have a baby with her the day after too.

First, though, we gotta get this therapy program off the ground. Then we gotta decide where we're living— her place or mine. I love the Wallaces and wouldn't mind starting a new life on their property. It'd be weird not living on Lucky River Ranch, though, especially now that I'm getting a bunch of renovations done at my place.

At the end of the day, home is wherever my girl is. Don't matter what the house itself looks like or where it's located. As long as Billie lives there with me, I'll be a happy man.

It's time for Wheeler to nurse the babies, so Duke helps her get situated on the couch while I grab the gifts I brought from my truck.

My brother meets me on his wide front porch. He yawns, blinking hard.

"One thing you're not prepared for is the sleep deprivation." He tucks his hands in the pockets of his sweats. "I thought a decade as a cowboy would make me immune to exhaustion, but Lordy, was I wrong."

I hold out a big brown paper and a cardboard drink holder containing two lattes from the Caffeinated Cowgirl. "Sorry I didn't wrap this. And if y'all ever need me to hang with the kids so you can catch some shut-eye, just gimme a ring, yeah? I'm everyone's favorite uncle for a reason."

"Because you let them do whatever the hell they want?"

"That, and I'm around the most."

"Might not be the case for long. You and your lady got some big projects coming down the pipeline."

I'm grinning from ear to ear. "We do. Wrong that I don't miss my free time?"

"Why would you? You spent it working. Of course you're gonna love spending that time with Billie Wallace instead."

"Fair point."

Duke takes the bag, and together we head back inside and fall heavily into some chairs in his tiny kitchen. He opens the pair of kids' cowboy hats I got them and chuckles, his eyes shining with tears.

"These are fuckin' cute, man. Thank you. The kids'll love 'em."

My eyes are wet too. "For later, obviously. When they get older and follow in our family's footsteps. We're always looking for more cowgirls and cowboys."

Duke's throat bobs on a swallow. Next thing I know, he's giving me a bear hug, the kind that almost hurts it's so ardent.

"Can't breathe," I gasp.

Duke just holds me tighter. "I love you."

He only lets me go when we hear the pop of tires on gravel outside. A beat later, someone slams the car door. My pulse jumps.

I don't know why, but a bad feeling settles in my gut.

That feeling intensifies when I glance through the screen door and see Colt's black pickup parked out front.

Duke looks at me, brow furrowed. "Colt Wallace? Did you—"

"Invite him? I didn't. No clue why he's here."

Maybe to give Duke a baby gift? Or maybe he's here to kill me.

Either way, shit's about to get real interesting.

Heart throbbing in my ears, I push open the door and head outside, Duke right behind me.

Colt waits for us just beyond the front steps. My knees turn to Jell-O when I see him holding something up.

Immediately my hand goes to my front pocket.

My *empty* front pocket.

I never, ever forget Dad's pocketknife. But I forgot to slip it in my jeans today because I was too busy worshipping Billie in bed this morning. Nothing like an orgasm first thing to make your brain flatline.

Fuck, I left it on the bedside table, didn't I?

Colt has to know I'm shacking up at his sister's place. I know he's seen my truck on his family's property. I know he's seen *me* around, even if he pretends not to.

He has to know that Billie and I are…er, intimate.

But to have that fact shoved in his face this way? That ain't good. I don't know why he'd be at Billie's place. Did he go over there to confront us? Or did he know I was gone, and so he went over there to confront Billie? Maybe try to talk her out of dating me?

My best friend is not that guy. Then again, I don't recognize the man he's been over the past several weeks, so who the hell knows what he's thinking? He's obviously not in his right mind.

"What are you doing here?" I cross my arms over my chest.

Looking up at me, he squints against the morning sun. I don't miss how puffy his eyes are. "Care to tell me why I found your pocketknife on my sister's nightstand this mornin'?"

I hear Duke's defeated exhale behind me.

"You do know we're dating, right?" I gotta keep this conversation on an even keel even though I really wanna call Colt out right now for being a total and complete lunatic. "Have been for a while now. So yeah, I was at her place earlier. Forgot my knife. What's the big deal?"

Colt's expression wavers, making my chest cramp. He looks at the knife, then tosses it up, catching it in his hand before he holds it out to me.

"Aw, shit." He chuckles. "This was a bad idea. Billie—she and I thought it might be funny if I messed with you—"

"Is this a joke?" I stare at him, pulse hammering. "If so, that's really fucked up."

Colt blinks. "I'm sorry, Ry. I just—I needed an excuse to come talk to you. I just had a good conversation with Billie, and if you'd let me, I'd like to have one with you too." He holds up his hands. "You tell me to eat shit, I get it. But I'd like to explain myself if I can have a few minutes of your time."

I glance over my shoulder at Duke. *Are you hearing this right now?*

His eyes, the same shade of blue as his daughter's, are wide. *Hell yeah I'm hearing it. You gotta talk to him.*

Duke feels our weird twin connection more than I do—he claims he gets this tingly feeling at the base of his skull if something's up with me.

Right now, though, I'm aware of how easily he and I communicate without needing to say a damn word. Kinda cool, actually.

"Hey, Colt." Duke raises a hand. "I'll leave y'all to it."

A pink flush crawls up Colt's neck. "I'm sorry to just barge in like this on y'all's visit. I can wait—"

"You kiddin'? I got two newborns inside. We're not going anywhere anytime soon. Y'all take all the time you need. Holler if you need someone to count paces."

I screw up my face. "No one's dueling."

"Another bad joke." Duke runs a hand up the back of his head. "Sorry, y'all. I'll just…see myself out. Or in. Or whatever."

My brother disappears inside the house, leaving Colt and me alone with the elephant in the room.

"I'm sorry," he repeats.

Running a hand over my scruff, I eye him. "I love

Billie, Colt. Simple as that. I'm tryin' my best to be the man she deserves—"

"You are. You already are the man she deserves."

Then he lets it all out in a torrent: how he overhead me supporting Billie during her pitch to their parents. How that made him realize that he was holding a grudge not because we betrayed him, but because he's lonely and heartbroken. Try as he might, he couldn't be happy for us before.

"You are now, though? What's changed?"

Colt sniffs and lifts his shoulder. "I miss y'all too fuckin' much. My grief is my problem, not yours. I'm working on it. And I think…My therapist said something interesting the other day about life not being a zero-sum game. Just because you found your person doesn't mean I won't find mine again. In fact, by supporting y'all— being happy for y'all—I'm putting out good vibes to the universe. I'm letting it know that I want what you have. She said jealousy isn't necessarily a bad thing. It's just pointing us in the direction of something we really, really wish we had. Something we should be working toward."

My eyeballs nearly pop out of my head. "Are you talking about manifesting shit and…shit?"

"Sure am," Colt says with a scoff. "Trust me, I can't believe it either. But the way I'm doing things ain't exactly working out how I wanted it to, so why not believe in some of this woo-woo stuff? Can't hurt."

Climbing down the steps, I take the knife from Colt. "So you didn't come to stab me with this thing?"

"Not this time, no."

"Ha."

"So many bad jokes today." Looking down, he kicks

the gravel at his feet aside. "Y'all hurt me, so I did the childish thing and hurt you too. I'll always regret that, Ryder. That's not the man I wanna be. Not the man I wanna raise either. Dean won't quit askin' when he gets to see Uncle Ry again."

I grin. "I was just sayin' inside how I'm everyone's favorite uncle."

"You gonna make me an uncle one day?" He looks up, still squinting. "Dean's only been waiting on a cousin for, oh, six years now. Bless my brothers, but they don't seem to be anywhere close to that finish line. You and Billie, though? Y'all are the real deal."

The fact that Colt can talk about this so casually—

That he wants me and Billie to have babies—

That he can't wait for that to happen—

Now *I'm* the one who's giving a bear hug. I'm squeezing Colt so hard he's wheezing, begging for mercy, but I give him none.

Instead, I thank him over and over again for letting me in.

For opening up to me. Because I finally have an appreciation for how difficult—and how rewarding—that can be.

"So we gettin' the families together or what?" he asks when I finally let him go. "We gotta make this shit official."

I'm smiling so hard it hurts. "How does tomorrow sound?"

CHAPTER 31
Rose and Thorn, Part Two
Billie

"Y'all didn't."

I stare, eyes welling, at the second farm table that's magically appeared in the New House's kitchen. Like the table beside it, it's beautifully set with blue and pink china that matches the block print tablecloth. Huge floral arrangements occupy the center of each table, along with candles that wink from mercury glass votives.

Patsy takes the basket of blondies out of my hand and sets it on the nearby counter. "You know how Mollie loves a party."

"I couldn't help myself." Mollie's eyes twinkle as she holds out her arms. "You're here! This is happening! Can you believe it?"

Ryder chuckles. "Hell yeah, I can believe it. You know how hard this woman made me work for it?"

"Slash, I didn't make him work for it at all." I give Molly a hug, feeling like my heart's liable to burst right out of my chest.

Colt groans as he takes off Mom's jacket. "I'd say to watch your mouth in polite company, but we're not very polite company at all, are we, Mom?"

Mom meets eyes with Patsy and shakes her head. "And here I thought I raised them right."

"You did, honey. It's so good to see you. How lucky are we that we're able to finally gather like this? I'm sorry Thanksgiving didn't work out. But now we've got all these people together!" Patsy grabs Mom's hand, and for a second, I think they're both about to burst into tears. "I love the little family that's forming here."

Sawyer hikes Ella onto his hip before giving me a peck on the cheek. "It's not so little anymore, Patsy. Listen to this racket."

He's right: Now that my family and I have arrived, the house is a scene of barely controlled chaos. Duke and Wheeler are here with the twins, one of whom is currently wailing while Duke sniffs her tiny little diaper butt. Dean and Junie are chasing each other down the front hall, their giggles echoing off the tall ceilings while Ella counts to ten somewhere nearby. The kids love playing hide-and-seek in this house because it's huge and there's tons of good hiding spots.

Cash and Colt are shaking hands, while Ava chats up Nash and Tate as they help her set out trays of delectable-looking appetizers: fried jalapeños, beef skewers, deviled eggs topped with diced pickles and bacon. We eat and chat, catching up on everything and anything.

Now John B is getting roped into a game of UNO by Junie and Dean, while Mack and Wyatt pop tops off Shiner Bock longnecks so Sally can hand them out.

The kitchen is loud and a little too warm. It smells

divine—Ryder let slip that Patsy's been smoking turkeys nonstop since she agreed to have us over for dinner—and it feels like home.

Not because the New House is particularly familiar, because it isn't. But because the people that now fill it immediately fall into an easy, happy cacophony of conversation and toasts and laughter.

Dad and Beck are doubled over as Mollie tells them a joke. Cash says it's time to feed Daisy, and literally eight people jump at the chance to offer their services. Mom and Tate take turns feeding the baby, while I tuck little Maggie inside the crook of my arm and rock her as I sip my beer.

Patsy announces it's time to open the wine, but I can tell Mom is already drunk by how loudly she laughs and the way her face is flushed.

Mom tries to open a bottle of Napa Valley cabernet but remembers halfway through the process that she doesn't actually know how to use a wine corkscrew. Wyatt takes over, patiently showing my tipsy mother how to do it properly.

Sawyer catches Ella sneaking sips of Sally's wine. I catch Junie sneaking a chocolate chip cookie from the basket I brought with me.

"Please don't tell my mom," she begs, mouth smeared with chocolate.

Laughing, I grab a napkin and make quick work of cleaning her up. "Why don't you grab an extra cookie, just in case you get hungry later?"

"I like you, Miss Bobby."

"It's Billie, but thank you."

She wrinkles her nose. "Isn't Billie a boy name?"

"I have five brothers. I think my parents just kind of gave up and started using a boy name for me too."

We all help Patsy set out the food once it's done. Then Cash has us gather around the kitchen's island. It's massive, but there's barely enough room for all of us. I grab Dean and have him stand in front of me, keeping my hands on his shoulders.

It could have something to do with the tiny baby tucked against his enormous chest, but Cash looks handsomer than ever as he clears his throat. "A little more than a year ago, life around here looked a heck of a lot different. There was so much grief happening. My brothers and me, we didn't know how we were gonna hold onto Rivers Ranch through another season. Then a city girl with a big mouth and bigger attitude shows up." He grins at Mollie. "And just like that, everything was turned upside down."

"You were awful," Mollie replies with a dreamy smile.

"The worst," Cash agrees. "*You* were exactly what we didn't know we needed. A swift kick in the—ahem, behind."

Patsy holds up her glass. "Amen."

"Mollie's arrival brought life back to our little corner of paradise."

"Ha," Sawyer says.

"Well, it wasn't paradise during branding season, but that's neither here nor there. Point being, Mollie shows up and changes *my* life. Then all of a sudden, Sally and Wy are finally acting on the crush they've had on each other forever, and then they're in love."

Wyatt lets out a holler. "Almost got shot in the process, but worth it."

"Sorry about that," John B replies with a chuckle.

Sally rolls her eyes. "Glad we can laugh about it now."

"In the meantime," Cash continues, rocking side to side when the baby starts to make noise, "the guys take me on a little bachelor party weekend to Austin, and Sawyer ends up meeting Ava at a honky-tonk."

Ella claps her hands. "That's where you kissed, right?"

"That's exactly what we did." Ava bites back a smile. "We kissed."

"So much kissing," Sawyer replies.

Dean sticks out his tongue. "No thank you."

"Little did we know that Mollie Luck was a package deal." Cash glances at Wheeler. "Her friend Wheeler starts showing up, and my brother Duke starts acting like a lovesick fool."

Duke holds up his hand. "Guilty. Was love at first sight for me."

"But me, I took some convincing," Wheeler replies. "Duke is nothing if not persistent."

"Grit *is* important," Dad says.

Patsy nods. "Ain't that the truth."

"Next thing we know, they're going on road trips together. Lord knows what went down on those trips—well, we actually have a very good idea of what went down, but I won't go into detail." Cash grins. "Now we have not one, but two sets of twins in the family."

Mom raises her glass. "Congrats, y'all. Cheers to all these beautiful babies."

"Cheers," the room replies in unison, the sound of clinking glasses and a sniffle or two filling the room.

"So all of a sudden," Cash looks at Ryder, "everyone had paired off except the baby of the family. It wasn't a secret that Ryder was always the favorite. I remember people saying that Mom didn't put him down for the first two years of his life."

Ryder shrugs. "So what? I was cute."

"We literally looked the exact same," Duke shoots back. "Still do. And Mom didn't hold me like that."

Now Ryder's smiling. "Mom and I just had that special connection."

"Whatever the case"—Cash holds up his hand—"I think we can all agree that Ryder has always been the most tenderhearted out of all of us. He took our parents' passing really hard, and I worried for a long time that he wouldn't ever come back from that."

"You? Worry?" Ryder tilts his head. "Never."

"You're funny." Cash gives him a tight smile. "But losing Mom and Dad—it changed you, Ry. And then falling in love with Billie Wallace changed you again. Changed you back into the tender, brave, ballsy soul you were before."

"What does ballsy mean?" Ella asks Ava.

Cash covers his mouth. "Sorry."

"It's another word for brave," I say quickly. "It means you have the courage to go after the things you want."

June smiles. "I'm ballsy."

The room erupts in laughter.

"That, you are," Sawyer says with a sigh.

"So I'd like to give a toast to Billie, for bringing our brother back." Cash raises his beer. "Thank you, from the bottom of my heart, for being *you*. And for loving my brother so dang well. Welcome to the family, Billie."

I would raise my glass, but I can't because I'm bursting into ugly, heaving sobs.

"Aw, honey." Mom comes over to give me a hug, and I see that she's crying too.

Everyone is crying. Ryder and Cash and Mollie and baby Maggie, who lets out a wail. Ava is passing tissues around, and Sawyer is hugging two of my brothers at once.

Ryder presses a kiss to my lips. "You really are family now."

"Aren't we *all* family now?" Colt wipes his eyes. "All fifty of us? Or however many people are in this kitchen right now?"

Dad nods. "I like that idea."

"I could get on board with that," Nash adds. "But do we need a significant other to be included? Because I haven't found mine yet."

I lean my head on his shoulder. "Your membership is pending your pairing off."

"Dang."

Beck sighs. "I'm out, then."

"Oh, please, y'all are in," Cash says. "Ain't no rushing these things. Your time will come."

Mom holds up her crossed fingers. "That's the hope."

When we sit down to eat, Colt makes a point of sitting next to me so that I'm wedged between him and Ryder.

"You're smothering me," I say as I sip my wine.

Colt unfolds his napkin and sets it on his lap. "It's how I show my love. You're welcome."

Ryder grabs Robbie from Duke so he can eat. The food is out-of-this-world delicious. I've never been the biggest fan of turkey, but I've never had it smoked before. The flavor is unreal, juicy and salty and just all-around perfect. Paired with Mom's corn pudding, Patsy's collards with bacon, and a big scoop of the most perfect dressing ever known to man, this food just might be my favorite meal that I've ever had.

"We have a little tradition in our family that y'all might like to hear about," Dad says. "Something we call—"

"Rose and thorn!" Dean wiggles in his chair. "Can we do it, Pawpaw? Please? I can start."

Colt chuckles. "Dude, you always start."

"But this is our new family." Dean glances around the tables. "So I wasn't sure if I could still be first."

Wyatt nudges him with his elbow. "Spotlight is all yours, buddy. Go for it."

"Okay." Dean straightens. "So this is how it works. You tell everyone what your least favorite part of your day was, and that's your thorn. And then after that, you tell everyone the best part of your day. That's the rose. Because roses have thorns. Get it?"

Sally nods. "I love this game already. Show us how it's done."

"Cool. So today, my thorn was having to leave school, because I love my teacher."

Colt grins. "You think you have a little crush on Ms. Loo?"

"Of course I have a crush on Ms. Loo." Dean grabs his water and takes a gulp. "She's the most beautiful girl alive. Well, after Lainey. And my rose was today being dessert day in the cafeteria."

"What'd you get?" Cash asks.

Dean's grin is a mirror image of his father's. "Chocolate cake!"

Sawyer's grabbing Ella and putting her on his lap. "I like this game. You wanna go next, Ella?"

It takes a while to go around both tables. Ryder puts

a hand on my thigh as we listen to our families sharing the randomest, funniest shit about their days.

Like who knew that Sally snuck out of work early to get her second tattoo? And how did Tate end up covered in dog vomit before six a.m.?

I laugh so hard my sides hurt. When it's my turn, I share that my thorn was my computer crashing earlier.

"My rose?" I smile hard. "I've been cleared by my doctor to race again."

Hoots and hollers. Even Mom and Dad congratulate me and say they'll be sitting front row for my next rodeo.

"Because it won't be your first rodeo, hopefully you'll stay on the horse," Tate says with a wink, and I have to resist the very strong urge not to reach across the table and smack him.

We clean up dinner while the kids inhale their dessert. Then the boys go build a fire in the living room's massive fireplace, and Ryder invites everyone to sit on the sofas in front of it.

Then he pulls out his guitar.

"Oh God." Cash makes a face. "Please tell me you're not going to serenade us with Dave Matthews songs."

Ryder ducks under the guitar strap I got him—it's embroidered with his name—and grins, taking a seat on the hearth. "No. I'm going to serenade y'all with *your* favorite songs. Billie, do you mind accompanying me?"

"Not one bit."

He plays Brooks & Dunn for Mollie and Cash.

Shania Twain for Sally and Wyatt.

Johnny Cash for Ava and Sawyer.

Salt-N-Pepa for Duke and Wheeler.

Finally, he plays Taylor Swift for him and me.

The kids dance the whole time, giggling and twirling and falling on the rug in front of the fire.

"Dang." Cash's eyes are wide. "Y'all are good."

Ryder scoffs. "Don't sound so surprised."

"You're welcome to come up on stage anytime with Frisky Whiskey," Patsy says.

Wyatt and Sally start to shamelessly make out. Ava falls asleep on Sawyer's shoulder. My brothers bug us with a zillion song requests.

It's late by the time we pack it up to head home.

I wrap Patsy, John B, Cash, and Mollie in tight hugs.

"Thank y'all for having us. This was a dream."

Mollie holds my hands. "This *is* the dream. We get to keep living it."

"We do, don't we?" I glance up at Ryder.

"Yeah, baby, we do." He leans in and lowers his voice. "Speaking of dreams—since ours started with a little mouth-to-mouth, can we keep living that dream too?"

Laughing, I nod. "Need to keep those lifesaving skills sharp since I'm gonna be racing again."

"Just doing the Lord's work."

"Wonderful. But would you do me now, pretty please?"

Ryder chuckles. "Only if you promise me you'll never change."

"As long as you promise to never change me."

"I promise."

Going up on my tiptoes, I kiss him. "Then so do I. Let's go home, baby."

THE END

EPILOGUE
Paper Rings
Ryder

"Yeehaw!" Sticking my fingers in my mouth, I let out the loudest whistle I can muster. "Get it, girl!"

Beside me, Duke chuckles as he covers his ears. "Since when can you whistle that loud?"

"Since now. That's her!" I elbow him and point to the gorgeous brunette making quick work of the cloverleaf in the arena. "That's my cowgirl. Look! Look! She's turning a damn fine barrel. Wow."

Ava, who's standing on my other side, leans her head on my shoulder and grins. "Of course she is. She's incredible."

"She's also getting laid on a regular basis," Mollie adds with a sly grin. "Helps keep the hips open, you know?"

I'm smiling so hard my face hurts. "She been bragging about me again?"

"Apparently there's lots to brag about," Sally replies.

I hold my breath as Billie rounds the second barrel. Her hair is flying everywhere. Her body moves gracefully in time to the horse's movements, the two of them working together in coordinated, athletic rhythm.

Billie rounds the barrel with expert precision, and I realize a beat later that the joyful yell that fills the arena is hers.

Turning her head, she flashes me a smile as she dashes toward the third and final barrel, her horse kicking up sprays of bright brown earth.

Her smile. The happiness I see there, and the relief. The pride too.

The love.

She fucking did it.

Joy cracks open my chest. I holler like an idiot, my eyes stinging and my heart thundering. I give myself over to the thrill of the moment as Billie rounds the third barrel and finishes the race.

Not only did she finish. Her official time puts her in the top three.

Ava is sobbing. Duke curls an arm around my shoulders and pulls me in for a hug. Junie and Ella and Dean are somehow piling on too, and we're all screaming, the arena breaking out in thunderous applause.

I feel a strong clap on my arm, and I glance over my shoulder to see Colt smiling down at me. He has tears in his eyes.

"She did good." His words are barely audible over all the noise. "Congrats, brother."

Before—when I came to see Billie race for the first time months ago—I would've put up a dam against the rush of emotion that courses through me.

I remember doing exactly that as I watched Billie ride that night like her life depended on it. Totally free. Totally fearless. She experienced it all, the exhilaration and the disappointment and the pain, but she didn't let that stop her from doing what she needed—wanted—to do.

Turns out, *my* life depended on accessing that kind of courage. I was stuck in survival mode after my parents died, and while there was safety in living that way, there was none of this.

Joy.

Pride.

Disbelief that I took a chance, stopped numbing myself, and didn't fall on my fucking face.

Billie didn't fall this time either.

Instead, she's on foot now, and she's running around the curve of the arena. My heart hammers as I wonder if she's coming for me.

Aw, yeah, she's definitely coming for me.

"That's not allowed," Dean says as he watches her.

Wyatt chuckles. "Your aunt's never really cared about what's allowed and what's not, huh?"

Dean shakes his head. "Nope. It's pretty cool."

"Very cool," Cash adds. He's got Daisy strapped to his chest again, although she's bigger now, chunking up in a really fucking cute way. And again, she's wearing those little pink headphones to protect her ears.

She smiles at me, all gums, and when she giggles, I just about die from cuteness overload.

I can't imagine missing out on this kind of happiness.

Actually, I can, because I missed out on a lot of things before Billie and I got together. Now I can smile with this sweet baby and not hear warning bells going off in my head. I'm not trying to bottle anything up or hold myself back.

Instead, I give in.

I look around me. All happy couples. Sally and Wyatt are full-on making out. Duke and Wheeler are looking at her phone, giggling over a picture of Robert and Maggie. Her mom is babysitting tonight, and even though Billie and I assured my brother and his fiancée that they didn't have to spend their first date night as parents at the rodeo, they insisted on joining us.

Cash and Mollie are kissing their baby's cheeks.

Sawyer and Ava are knocking back their beers while the girls giggle with Dean over a bucket of popcorn.

I'm still not over the fact that I'm one half of a happy couple now too. Never let myself even consider the idea until, well, Billie bulldozed her way through my walls.

I am happy to report that life is a hell of a lot better when you get to spend it with your best friend. Bonus points if you get to fuck her on the regular too.

When Billie launches herself over the railings and into my arms, I plant a messy kiss on her mouth and yell for everyone to hear, "Goddamn, girl, I'm so proud of you. So fucking proud."

"Swear jar!" one of the kids shouts back. "Five bucks for that one."

Billie laughs, biting the edge of my lips. "You really are one lucky son of a bitch. I looked great out there, yeah?"

I laugh, a buzzy warmth filling my veins. Billie will always be Billie. Thank God for that.

"Better'n that. You looked amazing."

"Can I give *you* mouth-to-mouth because you've gone into cardiac arrest from witnessing the perfection of my performance?"

"That's not funny," Mrs. Wallace says, but she's smiling as she dabs at her eyes with a tissue. "I am so impressed, honey. Congratulations. You really do have so much to be proud of."

"We're proud of you, Billie." That's Mr. Wallace, who's got his arm around his wife's shoulders. "Always have been. We're proud of what you've accomplished, and we're proud of who you are. I hope you know that."

Billie's crying and laughing and hugging everyone now, and it's only when we're in my truck a little later that I get to catch up with her.

"So." I hit the gas. "Tell me everything."

She's beaming as she turns to face me. "Ry, it was fucking incredible. I can't even describe how it felt to just *go* for it. I was nervous as hell, but once we made it around that second barrel, I knew we were gonna finish the race. And when we did…" She giggles, covering her face with her hands. "I thought I might explode with happiness."

Putting my hand on her thigh, I give her a squeeze. "I know the feeling."

"You really do, don't you?" She reaches over to play with the hair on the nape of my neck. "Thanks for being my most obnoxious cheerleader. I didn't see anyone clearing the area, but I did hear you, and that meant a lot."

"Are you saying I'm the world's best boyfriend?"

Her lips twitch. "For someone with zero experience, you truly are crushing it."

"Night's not over yet, darlin'."

"Oh?" Her hand slips inside the V of my button-up.

I chuckle. "That's gonna have to wait. I'm taking you out to celebrate."

We grab a quick bite at the Homestead Hen. Then we head next door to the Rattler.

Her mouth falls open when she walks in and sees the place is lit up with pink lights. Bunches of pink balloons float over the bar, while Frisky Whiskey warms up with "Shake It Off."

All of our family and friends—save the kids, of course—are here. They erupt into shouts and applause, making Billie burst into tears.

"Ry!" Her eyes are wide when they meet mine. "What the hell did you do?"

"I turned the Rattler into the Taylor Swift-themed bar of your dreams, obviously."

She laughs, tears rolling down her cheeks. I wipe them away with my thumbs. I'm dizzy with joy.

Joy and pride.

"Why?" she asks.

I lift a shoulder. "Why not?"

In reply, she curls her arms around my neck and pulls me in for a hot, hard kiss. More whistles. The band is playing "Bejeweled" now.

"If you're asking me to marry you," she murmurs in my ear, "my answer's yes."

My heart pops around my chest as I dig into my front pocket. There, looped carefully around my dad's pocketknife, I feel the paper ring I made.

Falling onto one knee, I hold out it to her. "Usually, I'd say assuming makes an ass out of you and me—"

"But you know me so well that rule no longer applies." She takes my face in her hands and leans down to kiss me. "Yes! Yes, Ry, I'll marry you with a paper ring."

"Oh, phew. You got the Taylor reference—"

But before I can finish the thought, she's kissing me again, and our people are shouting for us, and I'm slipping the ring onto the fourth finger of her left hand.

"Figure this way, you can come with me to the jeweler to pick out what you actually want," I say to her.

She admires the ring on her hand. "I kinda like this."

"I kinda wanna buy you a diamond."

"Fine." Her face splits into a smile. "'Cause you wanna make me yours forever?"

"Forever."

She's leaning in for another kiss. "Sounds like heaven. I'm in."

The pole barn is old, a far departure from the Wallace's newer, state-of-the-art facilities that they've built over the past few years. But you wouldn't know it from the way Billie takes in a lungful of musty air and smiles.

Looking at me, she says, "Welcome to the Anne and Robbie Rivers Therapy and Rehabilitation Center."

"Has a nice to ring to it." I grab Billie's hand. "Proud of you for making this happen."

She starts to walk through the barn. "Don't give me too much credit, because not much has actually happened yet." Kicking at a busted floorboard, she sighs. "We have our work cut out for us."

"Good thing your fiancé is handy."

"Handy? Or handsy?"

I shamelessly reach up to cop a feel through her fleece jacket. "Both."

But before we can follow that train of thought—or not—we both go still at a rustling sound.

It's followed by a moan.

My stomach flips. Billie freezes, her eyes darting to meet mine.

Another moan. Then—

Thump thump thump.

It's coming from overhead.

"The loft," Billie whispers, her smile returning. "Somebody's getting frisky up there."

I chuckle. "We should probably—"

"Look at you," a familiar voice grunts. "The perfect little princess, letting me fuck her in the hay and the dirt. You like it, don't you, Dallas?"

"Fuck you," a female voice replies. "I told you, don't call me that."

"You don't like it? Why're you about to come, then?"

Billie's eyes go wide.

That's definitely Colt. And he's definitely upstairs, having sex with none other than his nemesis, Lainey Pearlman.

Dear God.

I meet Billie's gaze. We both smile.

Interesting. And not at all surprising.

BONUS EPILOGUE
You Are In Love
Billie

The Lumineers.

I know this song.

Smiling, I open my eyes to look out the floor-to-ceiling sliding glass doors on the opposite side of the room. The curtains are pulled back to reveal a shaded patio that overlooks a stunning stretch of Caribbean Sea.

Ryder sits in one of the lounge chairs beside our private plunge pool. He's wearing a backward baseball hat. No shirt. His guitar is in his lap, its custom strap draped over his shoulder.

I smile harder. He doesn't need to use the strap when he's sitting, but he always insists on wearing it.

"Reminds me of you," he says. "I like keeping it close."

He's strumming yet another love song. It's all he plays since we landed in Mexico for our honeymoon three days ago, and I don't hate it.

I also don't hate the wedding ring he's wearing that glints from his left hand.

The sun slants through the pergola that serves as the porch's roof. There's not a cloud in the sky, and the nearby palm trees sway in a gentle breeze.

Gonna be another glorious day in what's turning out to be a glorious trip. It was no small feat to convince Mr. Scaredy Pants to get on a plane for our honeymoon, but I'm glad I stuck to my guns. It was totally the right call to have some R&R after the manic weeks leading up to the wedding.

Ry wasted no time buying me that diamond. And I wasted no time setting a date. I'd only been waiting basically my whole life to start my happily-ever-after with this man. So we had a big old party underneath the ancient oaks on my family's property on a clear spring day.

It was perfect. But not gonna lie, I kinda dig the honeymoon part even more.

Stretching, I throw off the covers and turn to put my feet on the floor. The diamond solitaire Ryder and I picked out winks at me from my own left hand. I press my thumb to the back of the ring, admiring how pretty it looks beside my new wedding band. It's simple, yellow gold dotted with a few teeny-tiny diamonds, but I absolutely love it.

The suite smells like luxe hotel mixed with a hefty dose of sex. It's been a nonstop fuck fest since we got here, and it's been as awesome as it sounds.

In fact, I'm kinda turned on already. Leave it to Ryder and his guitar to get me going before I'm even fully awake.

I'm naked, because honeymoon. But our villa is

tucked away in a private corner of the five-star resort Ryder insisted we book, so I'm free to pad to the bathroom without worrying about anyone seeing me. Come to think of it, the only time I've put on clothes is to go to the beach or a restaurant.

Otherwise, Ry likes me in the nude. And I'd hate to disappoint my *husband*.

Brushing my teeth, I spill toothpaste everywhere because I'm still smiling like a lunatic. I can't believe I get to call Ryder Rivers that. I married him. He married me. We're husband and wife.

We're gonna make babies together. Grow our businesses together. Sink our roots deep and stretch our wings *together*.

I'm so happy I want to cry.

Instead, I clip my hair in a bun and head outside.

Ryder glances over his shoulder at the sound of the sliding door opening. Seeing me, his deeply tanned face splits into a smile.

His fingers fall from the guitar's strings. "Mornin', wife."

I don't miss the way his blue eyes flash with hunger as they sweep over my bare breasts and belly.

Leaning down, I kiss his mouth. "Morning, husband. I love the morning serenade."

"I love you." He slips his tongue inside my mouth, making the awareness in my cunt bloom to sudden, vibrant life. "Sleep okay?"

"Slept great. You?"

"Darlin', you rode me so good last night I didn't have a choice. Passed out hard and only woke up when the sun rose."

I chuckle, recalling the very athletic sex we had after a couple post-dinner margaritas. At one point, I thought for sure I threw out my back, but I'm happy to report I'm feeling just fine this morning.

"You're welcome." I curl my fingers into the hair at the nape of his neck.

He groans, cupping my breast. "Care for a repeat?"

"But someone might see," I tease.

"Let's do something worth seeing, then."

My pulse flutters, light filling my torso. At the same time, Ryder thumbs my nipple. I make a sound somewhere between a moan and a sigh.

"Gimme the guitar," I say, but he's already ducking underneath the strap and setting the instrument aside.

Putting my hands on his shoulders, I climb onto his lap, straddling his thighs. He runs a hand up my back and clasps my nape.

His eyes are tender and hot. Achingly blue in the warm morning sunshine, which pours over my naked shoulders.

"You wake up wet for me?" His hands glide up my thighs.

I cup his erection through his shorts. "Always."

"Good. 'Cause I been hard since six."

My chest contracts. "Aw, baby, why didn't you wake me up?"

"Because you need your rest if you're gonna fuck me all day." He grins, leaning in to bite the corner of my mouth. His thumbs open my cunt. He slips two fingers inside.

He grunts at the slickness he finds there. I'm on fire as he circles my clit. I roll my hips into his touch, panting when he leans in to suck on my nipple.

"Lemme"—I bite my lip as he moves to the other nipple—"oh, get to work then."

I unzip his shorts. He's going commando. Really, why bring underwear at all to your honeymoon? It's a waste of space in your suitcase.

I bend my wrist to curl my palm over Ryder's leaking head. He grunts again, his fingers circling my clit faster. Harder.

When he pinches it between his knuckles, my legs nearly buckle. But I wanna wait to come. I love edging myself almost as much as I love it when Ryder edges me.

I kiss my way down his chest. Scooting back, I pull his shorts down his legs and meet his eyes.

"Hi," I say with a sly grin.

He folds his arms behind his head. He's all cockiness when he says, "Hey, darlin'. You gonna give me some good head?"

I laugh. *Like you even need to ask.*

I pump his shaft with my hand while I take his crown into my mouth. My kiss is wet, a little sloppy as I bob my head up and down, taking him deeper.

His stomach caves. "Fuck, you're gorgeous with my dick in your mouth. Open wider, darlin'. That's it. Make it messy." He's talking through clenched teeth now. "*Christ.*"

His hand finds my tits again. Kneading and toying and plucking at my nipples. My cunt floods with need.

I suck him to the point of agony. He's cursing, pushing my head down while simultaneously telling me to sit up so he can fuck me properly.

Swirling my tongue over his head, I do as he says and

straighten. Only I turn around so my back is to his front and let him pull me against him.

He grabs my waist and holds me there. "I like this," he breathes. "On your knees, Billie, so I can put myself inside you. Good girl. You let me fuck you now."

He lines himself up at my entrance. He has both hands on my waist now, and he pushes me down onto his cock.

"*Oh*," I cry out at the feeling of fullness as he fills me, tip to root.

He holds me there, allowing me to stretch to accommodate him. I look down and see myself splayed open around him.

My cunt flutters. Ryder chuckles, reaching around to play with my clit.

"Don't forget," he bites out. "We're putting on a show. Play with your tits. They're so beautiful."

Cupping my breasts in my hands, I close my eyes and lose myself to sensation. I thumb my own nipples while Ryder circles my clit. I pinch. So does he.

My legs shake. I rock my hips, seeking more friction, and next thing I know I'm *coming*. The orgasm detonates deep inside me, sending spasm after spasm through my center as I struggle to breathe, to hang on.

"Aw, baby, you feel so good." Ryder sounds like he's in agony too. "So tight. So fucking tight. I gotta fuck you. I gotta…"

Hands on my waist again, he guides me up and then back down on his dick. Up and down. I'm putty in his hands, boneless and sobbing, but he keeps going.

So does my orgasm. He stokes it to renewed life with every thrust, making me cry out.

"Look at you." His teeth are gritted again. "Coming on my cock like you were made for me. Feel how hard you squeeze me? You were made for this."

He comes with a shout, filling me with a warm rush. He leans his forehead against my back, his breath hot on my skin.

His cum drips out of me, even though he's still inside me.

I reach back to run a hand up his arm. "Now that we got our workout in," I say, breathless, "wanna grab some coffee?"

He chuckles, a deep, masculine sound. He presses a scruffy kiss to my left shoulder blade. "Between the sex and the caffeine and all this happiness, I think my heart might legit explode."

"I still owe you some mouth-to-mouth." Now I'm laughing too.

"You and that mouth." He uses his fingers to turn my head. Then he kisses me. "Don't ever change."

"I promise."

"Good. I'll make the coffee. Don't you dare get dressed."

"Wouldn't dream of it."

He bites my bottom lip. "You're the dream."

"I am." I'm grinning ear to ear. "Lucky you."

"Lucky me indeed."

Can't get enough of Ryder Rivers? Meet his brothers and the sexiest cowboys around in the rest of the *Lucky River Ranch* series . . .

Steamy and wildly sexy, *Lucky River Ranch* is a series of interconnected cowboy romance standalones, featuring a cast of five brothers fighting to protect both their family's ranch and their hearts from the women who turn their lives upside down.

READ ON FOR A PEEK AT THE
FIRST BOOK IN THE SERIES, *CASH*

CHAPTER 1
Kiss My Ass, Cowboy
Mollie

SEPTEMBER

I'm deep in cowboy country, but I still jam on the brakes when I see an actual cowboy park his actual horse outside an actual saloon.

Have I gone back in time? Or is the whole scene a mirage? My dashboard does say it's 109 degrees outside.

The cloud of dust that's followed me since Belton billows around my SUV, temporarily obscuring the view of a building marked *The Rattler*.

The Hill Country dust clears. Yep, that's definitely a horse. And that's definitely a guy in slim-cut jeans and a cowboy hat sliding off the saddle with an ease that makes my breath catch.

Mom's words echo inside my head: *Hartsville is a one-horse town*. I didn't know she meant that literally.

I feel a whisper of recognition as I take in the building's facade behind the cowboy and his horse. It's two stories, brick, with windows whose uneven panes glint in the hazy afternoon light. A faded green-and-black-striped awning bears the image of a white rattlesnake, its forked tongue protruding from between its fangs.

I was six years old the last time I was in this tiny town, smack-dab in the middle of nowhere. Why would I remember a bar of all places?

"Mollie? Did I lose you?"

My stomach seizes, the sound of Wheeler's voice on the phone yanking me back inside the Range Rover. Without looking, I immediately hit the gas, then send up a silent prayer of thanks that Main Street is deserted. No one to hit, thank God.

Well, except for the cowboy and his horse, who I glimpse in my rearview mirror. I'm less than two hundred miles southwest of Dallas, but I might as well be on another planet for how different this place feels.

I reach for the vent beside the steering wheel and aim a blast of AC at my face. "Sorry, I'm here. I just got to Hartsville and…I think I may have just had an *Outlander* moment? But a Western-themed one, with a saloon and a cowboy."

My best friend and business partner's raspy laugh pours through the speakers. "Bring cowboy Jamie back to Dallas. Tell him city life is better."

"No shit." I peer out my windshield as my GPS tells me I'm approaching my destination. "Mom wasn't joking when she said there was nothing out here."

"Get your money and get the hell out of Dodge. Call me when you're done, okay? I'm thinking of you."

I smile, even as my stomach seizes again. "Thanks, friend. I can't wait for the pop-up."

"Same. I'm so curious to see how it goes."

One of Dallas's better-known boutiques is hosting a pop-up shop for our cowboy boot company this week. The boutique's clientele is fashion-forward and well-heeled, so we'll hopefully make a decent number of sales. Lord knows we could use the revenue.

Hanging up, I slow down in front of the last building on the left before Main Street continues down a desolate stretch of nothingness ahead. The chalk-colored dirt, dotted sparsely with trees, cacti, and brush, wavers in the midafternoon heat.

A brass placard beside the building's door reads *Goody Gershwin, Attorney at Law, Est. 1993*.

"You have arrived at your destination," my GPS informs me.

I pull into an angled parking spot beside an enormous candy-apple-red pickup truck. It also appears to be from 1993, its windows rolled down to reveal a front bench seat upholstered in faded gray fabric. A box set of Brooks & Dunn's greatest hits sits on the passenger side of the bench.

It's a box set of *cassette tapes*.

Maybe I really have gone back in time.

The heat hits me like a slap to the face the second I hop out of my car. It radiates off the blacktop and singes my bare legs.

At the same time, the sun bears down on my head and shoulders from above. It's like being pressed inside a griddle.

Looping my bag over my shoulder, I wonder why the hell anyone would live out here. What did Dad see in this place?

I can't believe I'm actually here. I can't believe he's actually gone.

Most of all, I can't believe I lost the chance to ever make things right between us.

Grief, mixed with a hefty dose of anger, sits on my chest like an elephant.

A literal bell jangles above the door as I enter the building. It's blessedly cool inside the office. The familiar scent of brewing coffee makes me feel slightly less discombobulated.

A young man with round glasses smiles up at me from a nearby desk. "You must be Mollie Luck. Welcome! I'm Zach, Goody's paralegal." He rounds the desk and holds out his hand. "Can I get you anything? Water? Coffee? I hope the drive wasn't too bad."

I take his hand. "Three hours. Not terrible. Nice to meet you, Zach. And I'm fine, thanks."

He eyes my metallic-pink boots. "Those are *spectacular*."

"Aw, thank you. They're part of my boot company's most recent collection."

"You own a boot company?" A woman with short, dark hair in a light-colored linen suit emerges from a door to my left. She appears to be wearing a bolo—black, silver buckle—without a trace of irony. "How amazing!"

"They're manufactured right here in Texas."

The woman's eyes crinkle as she smiles at me. "Even better. I'm Goody Gershwin. Nice to finally meet you, Mollie. Your dad talked about you often. He was so proud of you."

My eyes burn, and my heart twists. Was Dad proud of me? He never showed it. Definitely never said it. But I'd like to think he'd be a little proud of how I turned out at least.

I paste on a smile. "Nice to meet you too."

"I'm so sorry for your loss. The community here has taken Garrett's death hard, but I can only imagine how tough it's been for y'all."

A piercing ache shoots through my heart and settles in the back of my throat. "The community" must've been a lot closer to Dad than I was. Then again, no one except Mom, Mom's parents, Wheeler, and I showed up to his funeral in Dallas three months ago, so who knows?

"I appreciate that."

"Well, we're glad you're here." Goody drops my hand. "Today should be relatively straightforward. As the executor of your father's will, I'll walk you through his estate and the distribution of his assets, along with his wishes for—"

Goody looks up at the jingle of the bell behind me. The creases at the edges of her eyes deepen.

"Hello, Cash! Always a pleasure seeing you."

Cash. Why is that name familiar?

"Ma'am. Good afternoon."

Something about the deep voice—its scraped-bare sound maybe, or the thick-as-molasses accent—has me glancing over my shoulder.

My heart takes a tumble at the *very* handsome man standing just inside the door. He looks to be in his late twenties, maybe early thirties. Tall—six three, I'd guess—with the kind of build you see on quarterbacks: broad shoulders, thick arms, long legs with thighs that strain against his fitted jeans. Wranglers, if I had to guess.

He's holding a cowboy hat to his chest, like he just swept it off his mass of messy brown hair, which curls out at the ends. Veins crisscross the back of his hand. He's sporting a scruffy beard that's longer along his top lip—I don't normally find mustaches attractive, but somehow, it's downright hot on this guy—and a white-and-blue-striped button-up that complements his cobalt eyes.

Eyes that are so blue, in fact, they seem to glow against his deeply tanned face.

Those eyes lock on mine. My pulse blares inside my ears. One beat. Two.

The intensity of the extended eye contact, the ballsiness of it, makes my stomach drop. His gaze flickers. Why do I get the feeling he's annoyed? Angry even?

The memory hits me: a pair of gangly blue-eyed boys in the bed of a pickup truck. One of them was punching another in the head, the blows increasing in frequency until a voice shouted at them from the cab to quit it.

The Rivers boys.

Despite the obvious prevalence of bodily injury in their family, I was so jealous of those kids. As an only child, all I wanted was a house full of siblings, and here were the Riverses with oodles of them. I distinctly remember seeing Mrs. Rivers in the passenger seat, her hand on her pregnant belly.

Their family owns the ranch next to Dad's property. I remember seeing the boys at the tractor supply store here in town and at the rodeo out in Lubbock once. Not often enough to be friends—their mom homeschooled them on their ranch, so they weren't around a lot—but often enough to know who they were.

Unable to withstand Cash's gaze another second, I look down at his boots. They're square-toed, dark brown. The leather is creased with age but obviously well cared for, the color gleaming from a recent coat of conditioner.

The whisper of vague recognition I felt earlier returns.

Thanks to my job, I know cowboy boots better than anyone. This is a pair of Lucchese: expertly made, expensive, and classic. They're the kind of cowboy boots you pass down from generation to generation.

Dad wore Lucchese. I don't know how I remember this, but the certainty of it sits in my gut like a brick.

"Mollie, allow me to introduce Cash Rivers." Goody extends her arm. "He's been the foreman at your family's ranch for, goodness, has it been—"

"Twelve years."

Cash's clipped reply makes me think he really is annoyed. With me? But why? And he's working on our property now? What happened to his family's ranch? I'm confused.

That does explain why he'd be at the reading of Dad's will, though. As the foreman, maybe he'll be giving me the literal lay of the land?

Not like it matters. The second Lucky Ranch is in my name, I'm putting it up for sale. I have absolutely no interest in running a Hill Country cattle ranch. I've always been more of an indoor girl, and my whole life is in Dallas anyway—my friends, my family. Bellamy Brooks, the cowboy boot company I started with Wheeler, is also based in the area. Business is finally taking off, and the inheritance I'm about to get will definitely bring us to the next level.

Acknowledgments

Y'all. Y'ALL. We did it! We pulled off a five-book series about cowboys and cowboy feelings and cowboy sex. What a RIDE IT HAS BEEN. Cash and his brothers changed my life, and I'll always be grateful to you, my readers, fellow writers, and friends, for making that happen. Thank you from the bottom of my pervy heart!

Cash Rivers came to me in a dream. Dream meaning, my awesome agent Nina floated the idea of me writing a small town cowboy romance set in Texas about a dude named Cash. And so Lucky River Ranch was born. I remember feeling totally out of my element as I began writing his book. What *is* a cattle ranch, exactly? What's this beef life cycle that keeps popping up on my random-ass Google searches? How do saddles work? Are "reading of the will" events things that actually happen?

Needless to say, it was not an easy book to write. It was also a very slow burn, which felt dicey considering I'm known for my spice. I fell in love with the characters, but I truly had no idea what to expect when we released *Cash* in the summer of 2024.

Little did I know it was the beginning of the year that some of my biggest dreams would come true. I'm legit choking up as I write this, because for a long time—over a decade!—I felt like those dreams might not come true. I think *Cash* is somewhere close to the thirtieth book I've written. I wanted to give up many, many times. The disappointing releases, the negative checking account balances, the scathing reviews—I felt like I was spinning my wheels.

Now I know the universe was telling me to wait for a tall, mustachioed cowboy with blue eyes and an attitude problem.

Four more blue-eyed cowboys later, I've officially wrapped up my most favorite series of books I've ever written. I am so, *so* proud of these stories. More than that, though, I'm proud of my perseverance. Good things come to those who wait (and bust their asses learning how to write very explicit sex scenes)! My heart is full to bursting. I so appreciate y'all being along for the journey!

Thanks to my own crew of incredible cowgirls, Meagan, Jodi, Nina, Chasity, Mandy, Kenysha, Tara, Rachel, Najla, Christa, Madison, Diana, Saida, Logan squared, Catherine, MK, Rachel, Reagan, and Charlotte. Y'all rocked this series, and I am forever grateful for the love you've shown my cowboys.

Thanks to my main squeeze, Ben. It's been a long road, but I am honored to walk it with you. Let's go live our best lives together. Love you!

To all the booksellers who put the Rivers boys in the

hands of readers everywhere. You guys are truly doing the Lord's work. Thank you!

To the teams at Fred & June's and Trope Bookshop here in Charlotte—I cannot thank you enough for hosting all the lovely events to celebrate Cash and his brothers. Katie, Mandy, Stephen, and Morgan, I adore you!

Thanks to the team at Bloom Books for taking a chance on a new-ish name. Y'all have been a dream to work with, and I can't wait to see what we cook up in the future.

Huge, HUGE thanks to everyone who took care of the kids and the house and the dog and everything else so I could write my smexy stories. Balancing art and motherhood—and business!—is some tough shit, and I wouldn't be able to do it without the small army of people who help me every day. Thank you!

Thanks to my accountants, Nadia and Marlene, for keeping me on track, and for not shaming me for not knowing jack about how my business actually works. I've learned so much from y'all.

Thanks to all my social media girlies who shouted about Cash and his brothers from the rooftops. None of this would have happened without you, and I so appreciate y'all taking a chance on someone new. Thank you! Special shout out to Caro Chambers for showing my OG Harbour Village series all the love. You are a gem!

I've had the best time hanging with the Rivers boys and their lady loves, and I sincerely hope you did too. Remember, cowgirls can't be tamed. Neither can readers of spicy cowboy romance. Let's ride, y'all!

Bringing a book from manuscript to what you are reading is a team effort.

Renegade Books would like to thank everyone who helped to publish *Ryder* in the UK.

Editorial
Saida Azizova

Contracts
Stephanie Evans
Sasha Duszynska Lewis
Isabel Camara

Sales
Megan Schaffer
Kyla Dean
Dominic Smith
Sinead White
Georgina Cutler-Ross
Ellie Walker
Jess Harvey
Natasha Weninger-Kong

Rights
Ben Fowler
Emma Thawley
Catherine de Mello
Alexis Alderton

Design
Chris Callard
Sara Mahon
Andrew Smith
Sasha Egonu

Production
Kelly Llewellyn

Publicity
Corinna Zifko

Marketing
Laura Hunt

Operations
Jairiza Rivera

Inventory
Victoria Stephenson
Dan Jones

Finance
Chris Vale
Jonathan Gant

RAISING READERS
Books Build Bright Futures

Dear Reader,

We'd love your attention for one more page to tell you about the crisis in children's reading, and what we can all do.

Studies have shown that reading for fun is the **single biggest predictor of a child's future life chances** – more than family circumstance, parents' educational background or income. It improves academic results, mental health, wealth, communication skills, ambition and happiness.[1]

The number of children reading for fun is in rapid decline. Young people have a lot of competition for their time. In 2024, 1 in 10 children and young people in the UK aged 5 to 18 did not own a single book at home.[2]

Hachette works extensively with schools, libraries and literacy charities, but here are some ways we can all raise more readers:

- Reading to children for just 10 minutes a day makes a difference
- Don't give up if children aren't regular readers – there will be books for them!
- Visit bookshops and libraries to get recommendations
- Encourage them to listen to audiobooks
- Support school libraries
- Give books as gifts

There's a lot more information about how to encourage children to read on our website: **www.RaisingReaders.co.uk**

Thank you for reading.

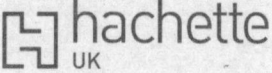

---

[1] OECD, '21st-Century Readers: Developing Literacy Skills in a Digital World', 2021, https://www.oecd.org/en/publications/21st-century-readers_a83d84cb-en.html

[2] National Literacy Trust, 'Book Ownership in 2024', November 2024, https://literacytrust.org.uk/research-services/research-reports/book-ownership-in-2024